STARGATE
ATLANTIS ™

UNASCENDED
Book seven of the LEGACY series

JO GRAHAM & AMY GRISWOLD

FANDEMONIUM BOOKS

An original publication of Fandemonium Ltd, produced under license from MGM Consumer Products.

Fandemonium Books
United Kingdom
Visit our website: www.stargatenovels.com

STARGATE
ATLANTIS

™ ™

METRO-GOLDWYN-MAYER Presents
STARGATE ATLANTIS™
JOE FLANIGAN   RACHEL LUTTRELL   JASON MOMOA   JEWEL STAITE
ROBERT PICARDO and DAVID HEWLETT as Dr. McKay
Executive Producers BRAD WRIGHT & ROBERT C. COOPER
Created by BRAD WRIGHT & ROBERT C. COOPER

MGM

Print ISBN: 978-1-905586-65-3   Ebook ISBN: 978-1-80070-006-2

For Melissa Scott, our partner in crime.

PROLOGUE

THERE WAS nothing. It might have been a few hours. It might have been years. She had no sense of time, no sense of self.

Nothing.

Floating in near-absolute zero space, trapped in a non-functioning replicator body, days might have passed. Or eons. There was nothing.

"Elizabeth."

There was a voice, and in some dim part of her she knew that. She knew *something.* There was a voice, and it said her name.

There was no way she could answer. Frozen synapses and circuits could never respond. She could not even think an answer, not in any conventional way. She knew it was not possible.

She knew. Which should not be possible either. Thought should not be possible. Consciousness should not be possible. She should not hear a voice, or even dream that she heard one.

And at that the part of her that was still Elizabeth Weir leaped, a frail flame trembling in determination. "Who are you?"

There was a net, a golden net that twined around her. For a moment she saw it complete, gold strands formed into knots, each one different, each one tied by hand, "You are safe," the voice said. It sounded like her mother, like a woman's voice, but that couldn't be.

"I am dead," Elizabeth said.

"Not quite," the voice said. "You cannot die and you cannot live, frozen in a replicator's body."

"Who are you?" she asked, and it felt like her voice strengthened with each word, that her mind strengthened with each thought, herself coming back to her as though her whole being was gathered in by the golden net.

"Ran," she said, and Elizabeth saw her, a woman two thirds her height with long, raven black hair and pale skin mottled with all the colors of the sea. She could almost have been human except for her eyes, black and wide with no iris or pupil at all, simply dark lenses.

"This is not possible," she said, for it seemed to her that the woman stood in front of her, and that Elizabeth had a body again, like her own had been when she died, with all its flaws and strengths. It was not possible for her even to imagine this. The circuits necessary to produce such a delusion should be frozen inactive.

"It is," Ran said, her voice timbreless. "Are you ready to leave?"

Elizabeth raised her chin. "To die?" Death would be a mercy, compared to eternal *nothing*. It would be an ending, or perhaps a beginning depending on whose beliefs about the universe were true.

"To live," the woman said, almost tenderly. There was something vaguely familiar about her, about her long four fingered hands that drew the net in gently.

"Do I know you?" she asked.

"Your people worshipped me once," the woman said, drawing in the net from infinite space, each strand glittering in her hands. "She who takes the souls of sailors lost at sea. Ran, the Queen of the Deeps. Are you ready to leave?"

"I can't," Elizabeth said. "If you thaw me, you will reactivate the nanites. We can't afford that. Humanity can't afford that."

"I meant without your body," Ran said gently. "There is one way out, Elizabeth. A way that has always been open to you."

"Ascension." She looked at her, feeling her brows furrow, and surely that was impossible. Surely she had no face, no body, though she felt it around her, felt her face change expressions. "Are you an Ancient?"

Ran did not smile, though her voice seemed amused. Perhaps those lips were never meant for smiling. "Do you think the Ancients are the only ones who ever learned to Ascend?"

"You're not human…" There were pieces of a puzzle here, if she could put it together.

"Nor any other child of the Ancients," Ran said. She held out one long, four fingered hand, and her voice was like the murmur of the sea. "Come, Elizabeth."

She took a deep breath. "What do I need to do?"

"Take my hands," she said. "And let go."

And then there was *something*.

CHAPTER ONE

RODNEY McKay frowned down at his coffee, which had grown ice cold since the beginning of an interminable meeting with Radek Zelenka to plan the science department's schedule. He drank it anyway. There were only a few more hours of lab time left to fill with maintenance and other people's questionably necessary research, and then at least he could get more coffee.

"So we are on systems maintenance for Friday afternoon," Radek prompted.

"Friday, right. We can finish testing the power conduits for damage that might have resulted from flying the city, although given that it's been weeks, any actual significant damage would already have shown itself in the city's power consumption by now, so ultimately that's one more pointless exercise."

Radek pushed his glasses up his nose in obvious frustration. "Tell me, Rodney, is there anything on this week's schedule that you are in favor of our doing? You are the one setting the schedule, so to complain about it at the same time seems more than a little perverse. What do you want us to do?"

"I think we ought to look for Elizabeth."

He hadn't known that was what he wanted to do until he said it, but the words crystallized the sense he'd been having these last few weeks that they were wasting time, letting it pour through their fingers in some way that he hadn't been able to articulate but that he was sure that they'd regret.

There was a lengthy silence before Radek replied, and when he did he seemed to be choosing his words very carefully. "Rodney, Elizabeth Weir is dead."

"I remember what happened to Elizabeth. I'm not an amnesiac. Or crazy."

"Anymore."

"I don't have amnesia anymore, and according to Carson, physically I'm in perfect health and almost 100 percent human again —"

"You still have the white hair."

"I've been thinking of dying it, actually, I've been considering Grecian Formula for Men — and you know what, never mind the hair, that's not the point. My point is, I am feeling much better. And I was never crazy, I was brainwashed and medically transformed into a Wraith."

"You nearly killed me."

"Yes, but I didn't."

"You let the Wraith into Atlantis."

"Yes, and I'm sure that it will really help me to deal with my traumatic guilt about the things that I did while I had amnesia for everyone to keep constantly reminding me."

"All I am saying is that you have been through a great deal."

"I know what I saw," Rodney said doggedly. "When I was in that puddle-jumper headed into the sun, out of reach of anybody's transport beams, Elizabeth saved me. She appeared in the jumper and transported me aboard the *Hammond*. The only way she could have done that was if she weren't dead, but Ascended. And what do we know is the one rule for Ascended beings?" He didn't wait for an answer. "They're not supposed to interfere in the affairs of unascended beings. Or they get kicked out of the higher plane. That's what happened to Dr. Jackson when he was Ascended."

"You think she is out there somewhere, having, what ... unascended?" Radek shook his head slowly. "Rodney, we all understand that you have been having a difficult time —"

"Fine." Rodney slammed down his coffee cup with a thud. "I'm going to go get Woolsey to authorize the gate team to do something about the problem. Since you're not on the gate team anymore, you can finish the maintenance schedule. You don't need me for that."

"Yes, because scheduling is not entertaining and therefore does not require your genius," Radek said. He sounded relieved that they were back to bickering about the schedule.

"I'm going to see Woolsey," Rodney said, and stalked out.

Woolsey steepled his fingers. "Dr. McKay. As much as I would like to believe that Dr. Weir somehow survived being frozen in the vacuum of space —"

"In the body of a Replicator," Rodney said. "So being frozen in space wouldn't actually have killed her, just rendered her completely incapable of any kind of movement or thought."

"Which raises the question of how she could possibly have Ascended while in that state."

"Maybe it doesn't require conscious thought. Maybe it's more of a Zen thing. And, all right, as far as we know it requires certain brainwaves that a frozen Replicator body probably doesn't have, but maybe something happened to unfreeze her, or maybe there's a way around that, I don't know. I suggest we find her and ask her."

"Even granting the possibility," Woolsey said slowly, "do you have any evidence whatsoever to support the idea that this is what actually happened?"

"Someone transported me off that puddle-jumper," Rodney said. "The *Hammond* was out of range, and Sam says that they couldn't and didn't transport me aboard."

"Consider the possibility that the *Hammond*'s transport logs could be in error. The ship was actively engaged in battle and had taken considerable damage at that point."

"They were still out of range."

"Even so, isn't it possible that the transport beam might have worked at an abnormal range as a result of the sun's radiation, or some other unusual circumstance—"

"No," Rodney said flatly. "That's not how it works. Ask Carter. She'll tell you that there's no way that radiation interference could radically alter the capabilities of the Asgard transport beams that way, let alone do it at the perfect moment to save my life." He hesitated, and then added, "And she believes me about Elizabeth."

"I could ask Colonel Carter, if she weren't on her way back to the Milky Way galaxy with the *Hammond*."

"So ask her when she gets there. And in the mean time, we need a plan for how we're going to get out there and ..." He trailed off at Woolsey's expression.

"Dr. McKay," Woolsey said. "I'm absolutely certain that you understand that I can't take Colonel Sheppard and his team off their current list of priorities in order to conduct a search for someone we don't know is actually missing."

"So find out. Let us dial the space gate where we sent Elizabeth and the other Replicators and see if she's still there. If she is, then ... then we know that, and if she isn't, then she has to have gone somewhere."

"All right," Woolsey said after a moment. "I'll send Major Lorne's team to search the area around the gate."

"Even accounting for drift, it's a reasonable area to search. If they're there, Lorne should be able to find them. And if they're not, if she's not—"

"With all due respect, Dr. McKay, suppose we cross that bridge when we come to it." Woolsey considered him from across the desk. "I understand that you feel ready to return to your usual duties, but considering what you've been through—"

"I am fine," Rodney snapped. "Let me know when Lorne doesn't find her."

"I will let you know as soon as I hear anything," Woolsey said, which was unfortunately hard to argue with.

"You do that," Rodney said. "I'm going to go ask Sheppard what he thinks."

"I think you've been under a lot of pressure lately," John said. He was leaning on the balcony looking out over the slate blue sea, the chilly wind whipping the swells into whitecaps and sending them breaking against the pier. Their current planet was colder than either of the previous two, and although it wasn't actually snowing at the moment, the weather still felt wintry.

"Will you stop saying that? I am not crazy."

"I didn't say you were," John said. "I've been in the 'hallucinating dead people' place myself, so I haven't exactly got room to judge. You just need some time to get over this."

"What connection do you see between having been turned into a Wraith and seeing Elizabeth appear out of thin air to save my life?"

"I think you might have been under just a little bit of stress," John said. "Remember the time when you were trapped in a submerged puddle-jumper and you hallucinated Carter in a bathing suit?"

"The life support systems were failing. I was hypoxic."

"And that's nothing like how you were hypoxic when you appeared in the Hammond's medical bay, right?"

"It was Elizabeth," Rodney said. "She was real. We have to go find her."

"Look," John said, his tone growing grim. "No one wanted to save Elizabeth more than I did. If there were any way to get her back, we would have already done it. We don't leave our people behind."

"I know that."

"So you ought to know we did everything we could. You can't let some kind of hallucination—"

"It was not a hallucination. I dreamed about her, when I still thought I was a Wraith. I wasn't hypoxic then."

"And dreaming about dead people is a sure sign that they're alive, right? Listen to yourself, McKay."

"Something transported me aboard the *Hammond*. And don't say it was the *Hammond*'s transport beams having some strange malfunction unless you know more about Asgard engineering than me and Sam put together."

"No one is putting you and Carter together."

"Yes, very funny. My point stands."

"Maybe you figured something out. That's what you do. You come up with these last-ditch solutions to save our asses when things go wrong. So, you came up with some way to transport yourself off the jumper, but then because you were hypoxic, you didn't remember what you'd done."

"I would remember if I'd broken about ten laws of physics."

"If you say so, McKay."

"You don't believe me," Rodney said.

John turned to look at him, no humor at all now in his eyes. "Elizabeth's gone," he said. "I don't know if you blame yourself—"

"Of course I blame myself, I'm the one who reprogrammed the DHD to transport her into space."

"Which she knew. It was the only way."

"I know that."

"I know you know that. And I know that you feel bad about some of the things you did when you were a Wraith, which I don't blame you for, because you had amnesia. But maybe that's, I don't know, bringing up some feelings—"

"Are you trying to psychoanalyze me? Don't make me laugh. You are the last person on the planet who is qualified for that."

"Pretty much," John agreed, sounding a little relieved. "You know, maybe you should talk to Teyla. She's better at dealing with ..."

"Crazy people who hallucinate dead friends rescuing them?"

"That kind of thing," John said.

Rodney ran into Ronon first, clearly on his way back from the gym, with a towel thrown over his shoulder and a stick in hand. He looked cheerful, like he'd been beating up Marines.

"Have you seen Teyla?"

"She went to take Torren to New Athos. He was going to spend the weekend with Kanaan. She should be back by now, though." Ronon looked at him cautiously. "You're not having more Wraith problems, are you?"

And that was still a bit of a sore subject; Ronon had come pretty close to killing Rodney with a weapon that would have destroyed everyone with Wraith genetics, and Rodney had come pretty close to feeding on Ronon while he was still physically a Wraith. As far as he could tell, they were dealing with both of those using the traditional Atlantis method known as "let us never speak of this again."

"All better now," he said, with what he hoped was a reassuring smile. "Except for the hair, which is a problem I can deal with."

"You could dye it."

"I'm thinking about that." Ronon was headed in the same direction as Teyla's quarters, so Rodney hurried his own steps to keep up with him. "I think Elizabeth was the one who saved me from the puddle-jumper," he said, because Ronon already thought he was strange, and at least he wasn't likely to try amateur psychotherapy. "I think she Ascended."

"Could be," Ronon said.

Rodney stopped, and then had to trot to keep up with him. "You don't think I'm crazy?"

Ronon shrugged. "Stranger things have happened."

"So you think she could be out there somewhere?"

"I don't know. I'm not really the person to ask."

"Yes, I know Dr. Jackson is still here, but the two of us haven't exactly worked smoothly together in the past, and I'm not sure I really need his help with this."

"I was thinking more like some kind of priest. Your people have those, right? Or maybe you should talk to Teyla. She knows more about that spiritual stuff. She meditates, and everything."

"I was actually looking for Teyla."

"Good plan," Ronon said.

Teyla poured him a cup of tea. Rodney would have preferred coffee, but it didn't seem like the moment to insist.

"I dreamed about Elizabeth," he said. "When I was a Wraith, when I couldn't even remember that I was human, let alone remember my own name, she helped me. And then she appeared in the puddle-jumper. That wasn't a hallucination. It was the real Elizabeth, and she had Ascended." He spread his hands defensively. "All right, let's get the part where you tell me I'm crazy out of the way."

"Why would I say that?"

"Everyone else thinks so. Except maybe Ronon, but who knows what he really thinks."

"I have dreamed of Elizabeth too," Teyla said seriously.

"You have?"

Teyla nodded. "I dreamed that she spoke to me and showed me things that helped me. I believe that she has become a guardian for her people here in Atlantis, that she watches over us as one of the Ancestors and protects us. Perhaps she Ascended, or perhaps that is part of what happens beyond death. But I believe that she helped you."

"All right, good, someone believes me. Now all we have to do is figure out how to find her," Rodney said.

Teyla put her head to one side. "Find her?"

"Ascended beings aren't supposed to interfere. She even told me that she knew she'd get in trouble for it. If they've sent her back as a human, she's out there somewhere. She wouldn't know Atlantis's current gate address even if she was trying to come home. I've asked Woolsey to authorize a search, but he's dragging his feet about it."

Teyla poured herself another cup of tea before she answered. "I believe Elizabeth is trying to tell you something, but you may need to look deeper to understand her message."

"What do you mean?"

"If you feel the need to look for Elizabeth, perhaps you should try looking within. If you meditate, and open yourself to hearing the voices of your ancestors and guardians, you may find her there."

"I am not talking about a spiritual experience," Rodney said. "I'm talking about contact with someone on another plane of existence." Teyla looked at him as if that didn't make perfect sense. "She was there," Rodney said. "Not as a voice or a guardian spirit or anything mystical. She was right there in the jumper with me, just like we're sitting here right now, and she saved my life."

"I am sure that you saw her there," Teyla said patiently. "And I believe she did save your life, by helping you find a way to save yourself."

"I didn't transport myself off the jumper," Rodney said. "There is no possible way I could have done that."

"You have said yourself that the Ancestors knew far more about their technology than we do," Teyla said. "Elizabeth may have learned things about it that we still have not discovered."

"There is nothing you can do with a puddle-jumper's systems that we haven't figured out by now. And if there is, the *Hammond* would have detected the transport. I wouldn't have just appeared."

"There is another possibility," Teyla said. "You came very close to Ascending yourself once."

"Only because an Ancient device had given me superpowers and I thought was going to die if I didn't," Rodney said.

Teyla nodded encouragingly. "Is it not possible that under great duress, you rediscovered within yourself some of the same abilities —"

"So why this time, and not during any of the other terrifying near-death experiences I have on an all-too-regular basis?"

"Perhaps because this time Elizabeth was there to guide you."

"If you believe that, why don't you believe she's out there for us to find?"

"I believe that people we loved may watch over us and guide us," Teyla said. "But the dead are still dead. They do not simply ... come back."

"Daniel Jackson did."

"Then perhaps you should ask him what he experienced."

"I was afraid you'd say that," Rodney said.

Daniel cleared a chair of books, which made it possible for Rodney to actually sit down. "Sorry about the mess," he said. He waved a hand at his tablet, which was lying on the coffee table still scrolling lines of Ancient text. "I'm reading up on everything we know about early Ancient settlement in the Pegasus Galaxy. I appreciate your team helping me investigate some of the settlement sites."

"Woolsey ordered us to," Rodney said.

Daniel's voice grew dryer. "Yes, I knew that, but I thought we were being polite."

"Let me start over," Rodney said. "What do you know about Ascension?"

Daniel leaned back in his chair and considered him. "More than most people. Why do you ask?"

"I think Dr. Weir may have Ascended," Rodney said. "When I was a Wraith, she appeared to me and spoke to me. And then when I was going to die, she appeared and saved my life. But she seemed to think she was going to be in big trouble for that. Like the kind of trouble where you get kicked out of a higher plane of existence."

"It's possible," Daniel said. "I'm told that while I was Ascended— the first time—I appeared to some of my friends when they were in bad situations. And then when I tried to interfere more directly, I got kicked out. But I don't remember much about what that was actually like."

"You just appeared somewhere, right?"

"Yes, and that's something that you could ask your allies if they've heard anything about. Naked amnesiacs don't show up in the middle of somebody's field every day."

"How serious amnesia are we talking about?"

"I had no idea who I was or where I came from," Daniel said. "I could talk, and I remembered some skills, but most of it was just ... flashes, images. Nothing that made sense. Even after SG-1 found me, it took some time for everything to come back. Of course, it may not have helped that I wasn't entirely sure I wanted everything to come back. In some ways it was restful having a break from remembering everything that had ever happened to me."

"She may not even remember that she's looking for Atlantis. We've got to find her."

"All right. How?"

"I was hoping you'd have some ideas about that," Rodney said, as humbly as possible.

Daniel drummed his fingers on the table for a minute. "When Oma sent me back, I think she wasn't supposed to send me home — I was supposed to start a new life that didn't involve causing any more trouble. But she put me somewhere that SG-1 was going to come sooner or later, because it was a possible site of Atlantis, which we were still looking for at the time."

"She cheated?"

"Never play poker with Oma Desala. Now, we don't know what Dr. Weir's situation is. We don't even know for certain that she was forced to unascend. But it's possible that she, or whoever returned her to human form, wanted her to be found."

"Meaning what?"

"Meaning that your best chance of finding her is probably to continue doing whatever you were planning to do, and to keep your eyes open. I'm assuming that if she'd appeared on New Athos, you'd have heard about it by now."

"They all knew Elizabeth."

Daniel nodded. "I only met her briefly, but she was a remarkable person. I'd like to think you're right."

"As long as you don't think I'm crazy."

"Why does it bother you that people might think you're crazy? I mean, I'm pretty much used to it. Pyramids built by aliens — it was never a popular theory."

"That's you," Rodney said. "I've always —" He was interrupted by his headset radio.

"Dr. McKay, this is Woolsey. Major Lorne has just reported back."

"And?"

"I'm very sorry, Dr. McKay. Dr. Weir's Replicator body was located along with the other Replicators. It appears to still be entirely inert."

"Dead. You mean dead."

"I am sorry."

"Yes, well, so am I," Rodney muttered, and he switched off his headset.

"Bad news?" Daniel said.

"They found Elizabeth," Rodney said. "Still floating frozen in space. So there goes that theory, right? Chalk the whole thing up to an incipient — and well-deserved — psychotic break."

"I don't know," Daniel said slowly. "I don't want to give you too much hope—"

"You know what, excessive optimism has never really been a problem of mine."

"Okay, then. The body that's floating in space isn't Elizabeth's original body. Her consciousness had already been separated from that body, in a state that allowed it to exist in subspace, and then to inhabit a new Replicator body. Yes?"

"As far as we understand, yes."

"So, it's possible that the part of her that makes her Elizabeth could have Ascended, and not taken the Replicator body with her. I think the physical body goes with you in the first place because you're used to thinking of it as part of yourself. But this was a new body for Elizabeth. She may not have identified herself with the body that way."

"And there's no way of knowing if Elizabeth is still in there, because we can't risk thawing her out and asking her," Rodney said.

"I don't expect Woolsey's going to authorize that," Daniel said. "Not to mention that if she is in there, it would be pretty cruel to put her through being woken up when you still don't have a solution for her problem."

"Believe me, we've tried to come up with something," Rodney said. "But if she didn't Ascend, there's nothing we can do that will make it safe to unfreeze her. She's essentially dead, and she's going to stay that way."

"So let's keep our eyes open," Daniel said. "And keep doing what we'd be doing if we weren't looking for Elizabeth, and hope she finds us."

"That's fair enough," Rodney said. "Of course, that means that we're going to be doing exactly what you wanted us to do in the first place."

"As you pointed out, that's what Woolsey already ordered you to do."

"Great. Let's go look for Ancient installations."

"I'm looking forward to it," Daniel said.

INTERLUDE

SHE LAY in the tall grass, feeling it itch along her skin, and opened her eyes. Shadow. She lay face down, her head pillowed on her arm, and turned her head. She lay in a field of flowers. Golden stars surrounded her, deep in the tall grass, while above the largest stalks great pink flowers raised their heads to the sun, their centers black with seeds. They were no flowers she knew, nothing she had a name for. The sun was warm on her back and she lay in a field of flowers.

The sun was warm. Where had she been that it was so cold? Why couldn't she remember? Perhaps it didn't matter much.

There were the sounds of voices, children's voices raised in song, the deeper voices of adults. They sounded happy. That was good. It was good for people to be happy on such a lovely day.

There were the sounds of running feet, and then they stopped. A child's voice sang out very close at hand. "Gran! Gran, come quick! There's a naked lady here!"

More footsteps. A woman's voice. "Kyan, get back. Go to your father."

A hand touched her neck from behind, careful fingers gentle as they felt her throat. Checking for a pulse. She knew that gesture, and she opened her hand against the earth.

"Ah." A woman's voice, then a man further away.

"Kyan, come here."

"She's alive," the woman said.

She wanted to answer, but the words stuck in her throat.

Careful hands lifted her, turning her over, the sun unbearably bright on her face. "Can you hear me?" the woman asked.

A shadow, the man bending over. 'I don't see any blood. Is she hurt?"

Something settled around her shoulders, a cape of soft feathers. She opened her eyes.

An old woman bent over her, concerned brown eyes peering at her face. "Can you speak?"

"I...think so." Her voice was hoarse, as if from disuse.

The cape settled around her, bright green feathers smelling like sunshine and some deeper scent of resin, covering her nearly to the knees.

The man held a little boy by the hand, the boy watching her curiously. Behind were other people and a three wheeled cart pulled by a pair of large dogs. The men's heads were shaved except for the child, each carrying packs or bundles. "Where did you come from?" the man asked.

"Child, can you stand?" the old woman asked.

She took the offered hand, getting slowly to her feet. All around them stretched a plain of wild grass, a prairie filled with wildflowers. "Where am I?"

"Along the route to Iaxila," the man said. "Were you lost from a caravan?" He looked at the old woman worriedly. "There haven't been bandits on this route for a long time, but…"

The old woman held her hand gently. "You've fallen in among honest people. We won't hurt you, I promise. The Ancestors charge us to treat the stranger as our own. What terrible thing happened to you?"

She stood in the bright sun, her hand in the old woman's, looking across the grass from horizon to horizon, and no words came. No thoughts. They ran away like water, any moment before this. "I don't remember," she said.

They camped that night on the open plains, their fire small compared to the fires above. The sky was thick with stars, a wash of them across the eastern sky illuminating almost to twilight. There was a stew of grains and dried meat, some folded dried fruits passed hand to hand. She sat in the clearing where the tall grass had been cut for the fire, her hands around the hollowed gourd that held her stew.

They had found clothes for her, baggy trousers that tied at waist and ankles, a tight fitting top of knitted wool dyed in all the green shades of new growth, as though one skein had been dipped from dark to light and back again. She was warm enough. Everyone was very kind and very careful.

She slept beneath the stars, wrapped in a tanned hide with fur on one side, listening to the quiet sounds of the camp. Waking changed to sleeping and sleeping to dreaming so gradually that it seemed she was still awake.

She lay beside the dying fires, the tents lit from within by their battery powered lights while the adults talked quietly. The radio with its makeshift antenna played, a song about a girl with kaleidoscope eyes. Her parents were talking, nursing cups of strong British tea, while outside the circle of the fires she saw the reflected gleam of green eyes. They watched steadily.

She got to her feet. The green eyes were unblinking. She started toward them, away from the fires.

An arm around her waist, picking her up and carrying her back. "Let me go!" she said. "I want to see the lions!"

"The problem is if the lions see you, little one." He put her down as her mother came hurrying.

"Oh Dr. Birna! Thank you so much. Elizabeth, you must never wander off like that. You have to stay by the fires."

"I want to see the lions!"

"Lions are very dangerous," Dr. Birna said, kneeling down so that she could see his face, dark beneath white hair. "They know better than to attack a camp, but a child who wanders off alone is fair prey. You must do as your mother says and stay by the fires."

"…stay by the fires…" She turned, reaching out.

"You are by the fire. There is nothing to worry about." A man's voice, calming, and she opened her eyes. She lay under alien stars, wrapped in a shearling blanket. The boy's father bent over her. "You're safe," he said. "There are no predators here that will attack a camp as large as this."

"Lions," she said, sitting up. The dream and the present folded together seamlessly. She thought he was Dr. Birna for a moment, but who was Dr. Birna? His face, his name, and then it was gone.

The grandmother had also sat up, turning to face her. "Did you remember something?"

"Kenya," she said. The name was there suddenly. "We were in Kenya."

The man frowned. "I don't know this world, Kenya. Is it your home?"

"No." She shook her head, certain of that. "We were visiting. Traveling. My father..." His face didn't come, but the sense of him did, the shape of his hands with a brush in them, brushing away red earth from bones. "He studied old things. Bones. Looking for clues about how humanity began. We were in Kenya and I was very small."

"Do you have kin there?" the old woman asked gently.

"No. It was a long time ago. And my father is gone." She knew that. He had died a long time ago, an old sadness long healed over.

And that was all — the shape of his hands, the brush moving quickly and carefully over bone, the light of the fires, the eyes in the dark, the radio playing a song about diamonds.

The man put his hand on her shoulder gently. "You don't remember any more?"

The dream was fading. There had been the lions and Dr. Birna and he had handed her to a woman, to her mother...

"My mother called me Elizabeth."

CHAPTER TWO

RONON jogged along the upper catwalks of the city, John following doggedly at his heels. He could still outdistance John easily, maybe even a fraction more easily than he'd been able to four years before, but he preferred the company. He appreciated it, too, as a sign that he hadn't burned too many bridges with John in the last few months.

He'd screwed up, he knew, letting himself be tempted to use Hyperion's weapon, and even worse in keeping it hidden when half the city had been looking for it. He'd gotten people killed in the process, not on purpose, but he still wasn't proud of it. And he had to admit now that while it would have been worth a lot to get rid of all the Wraith, it wouldn't have been worth killing everyone with the Gift. Not worth killing Teyla and Torren, who were as much his family as if she'd been born his sister.

And his duty had been to turn the damned thing over to his commanding officer. If he'd started to doubt some of the decisions his commanding officers made, now that they were making treaties with the Wraith and working with them as allies, disobeying orders still wasn't the way to handle that. He still wasn't sure how he was going to handle that, but he was trying not to think about it very hard.

Apparently that wasn't working. He picked up the pace, grinning fiercely over his shoulder at John. "You got soft while you were in charge of the city."

"A few weeks in a desk job isn't enough to get soft."

"So prove it," Ronon said, and listened for the sound of running footsteps speeding up.

They sprinted to the end of the catwalk, and Ronon slowed his pace to let John catch his breath.

"See? Woolsey's back in charge, and everything's back to normal," John said between gasping breaths.

"Yeah. I'm beating you."

"Like I said, back to normal. Probably to everyone's relief."

"You weren't so bad," Ronon said. "At least having you in charge means having someone who isn't completely stupid."

"Thanks," John said dryly. "You mean unlike Woolsey when he got here."

"He wasn't stupid," Ronon said, considering more carefully. "But he didn't know anything about how things work here."

"He's learned. We've all learned." John looked at him sideways. "I thought you didn't like some of my decisions very much when I was running the city."

Ronon shrugged. "Do you like everything Woolsey decides?"

"I'm not Woolsey."

"Carter, then."

"Not everything. I didn't like everything Elizabeth decided, for that matter. But I liked enough of their decisions that I didn't mind following their orders." John shook out his damp hair, and then added in an apparent effort at scrupulous honesty, "Most days."

"I don't mind following yours."

"Most days?"

Ronon shrugged. "Ready to go again?"

"Bring it on," John said, and Ronon started running again.

The outside seating at the mess hall was deserted in all but the finest weather Atlantis's new home world had to offer. Daniel took advantage of the quiet, making his way to the rail and leaning against it to look up at the city, his hands in his pockets against the chill wind. The spires stretched for the sky, deliberately impractical, the exuberant creation of people who wanted to impress. Or maybe who just liked beautiful views.

After so many failed attempts to arrive in a position where he could see this particular beautiful view, it was hard to believe that he was actually standing in the city of the Ancients without any immediate disaster ensuing. The last time he'd been here, he'd barely managed to scratch the surface of the city's mysteries before exploring the wrong laboratory had resulted in triggering a poorly designed Ancient weapon, leading to a disastrous encounter with the Pegasus galaxy Asgard.

He was sure that he'd have better luck this time. It would be hard to have worse luck, anyway.

Teyla came out onto the balcony and came to join him, turning to look up at the city herself.

"Do you ever get used to it?"

She tilted her head to one side curiously. "To what?"

He shrugged. "Living in the city of the Ancients."

She shook her head, smiling a little. "I do not expect I will ever take living in Atlantis for granted. But after so many years, it has become my home."

"That sounds nice," Daniel said.

"It is for many people. But many others eventually wish to return to their own homes. The city is not for everyone," Teyla said. "I have seen Earth, and it is a beautiful world. And a safer one."

"I think safer depends on who you are."

"If you choose to be on a gate team, you will not have a safe life, certainly," Teyla said, sounding a little amused.

"No. But I wouldn't rather sit around wondering if the Goa'uld or the Ori or whoever shows up next is going to take over Earth and enslave everybody or blow out all life in the galaxy like blowing out birthday candles. They're candles, that—"

"I have seen many birthday celebrations for members of the expedition," Teyla said, now decidedly amused.

"You probably have. Sorry, I tend to over-explain. My point is that I don't think I'd feel better knowing that there were huge threats to Earth and not being able to do anything about them."

"I agree," Teyla said. "I too would rather act than stand by helplessly and wait for whatever comes. But it seems that many on your world are not aware of their dangers and would prefer not to be."

"That's not… ever really been a possibility for me. I keep asking questions until I find out the answers. Even if they're unpleasant answers. Especially if they're unpleasant answers. I'd always rather know the truth."

"Even if it takes you far from home."

"I'm not really sure I have a home. I have an apartment in Colorado Springs. I have friends there, and I like my job – all right, most days I like my job, although not the days when we get tortured by unpleasant people or have to deal with the IOA – but I'm not sure it's really the same as having roots somewhere."

Abydos had been his home, for a brief precious time. He wasn't sure what it would take for him to feel the same sense of belonging anywhere, or the same sense of optimism and purpose. It was possible that he'd just gotten old enough to know better. But if he was going to feel it anywhere, Atlantis might be the place.

"I hope you find what you are looking for," Teyla said.

He nodded. "So do I."

Lorne stretched out his knee for Carson's medical scanner to examine its internal workings. "How does it look, doc?"

"Better than it has any right to, given what you did to it," Carson said.

"Hey, I got hit by a jumper. Being piloted by Dr. McKay, who was out of his mind at the time. I hardly think that counts as my fault."

"All right, maybe not. But try to dodge next time."

"I'll keep that in mind," Lorne said. "Maybe we need those warning beepers for the jumpers that they put on garbage trucks so you can hear them when they're backing up. Except that it wasn't backing up."

"A warning beeper might not be a bad idea," Carson said. "It would also help warn everyone about those of us who aren't the best drivers." Carson was a perfectly competent jumper pilot at this point – good, even – but he'd resisted learning with all his might in the early days of the expedition.

"Hey, it's the hot-shot pilots you have to watch out for. They're the ones trying to set the speed records." Lorne sobered, swinging his leg off the table. "Seriously, though… "

"The fracture healed beautifully. You shouldn't have any long-term problems, although I want you to keep doing the stretches Dr. Keller prescribed."

"That's a relief." He was acutely aware that getting killed and getting promoted weren't the only ways to wind up sent back to Earth. For all its frustrations, he enjoyed his current job far too much to want to wind up stuck behind a desk back home.

"For someone who essentially got hit by a truck, you got off very lightly."

"Don't I know it," Lorne said. "Have you heard anything from

Dr. Keller?"

"She checked in a few weeks ago and sent me some of the results from her first round of tests of the new retrovirus," Carson said. "Frankly she didn't have many results yet to report. I think she just wanted to reassure everyone that she wasn't dead."

"Well, when you're hanging out with the Wraith, people do worry."

"I worry," Carson said. "But not as much as Rodney does."

"Are the two of them… I heard they split up. And also that they were on a break. And also that he asked her to marry him."

"The Atlantis rumor mill never changes," Carson said. "It's like living in a small town full of elderly grannies gossiping over the back fence."

"It's probably none of my business."

Carson shrugged. "It's not as if either of them told me anything about it as their doctor. I don't know what they're doing. I don't think they know what they're doing. But she's going to be gone from Atlantis for some considerable time, and maybe that will give them both time to think about what they want."

"Absence makes the heart grow fonder?"

"Or presents enough distractions that you stop pining after the one you love. One or the other."

"Distractions we've got."

"Truer words were never spoken," Carson said.

John sat in front of his laptop, trying to figure out how to frame the email he was thinking of sending.

Hi Sam, he began mentally. *How's it going? I was just wondering if you think there's any chance that Elizabeth Weir is an Ascended being, rather than being dead in space because we couldn't do anything to save her.*

That sounded crazy. If he got that kind of email from someone, he'd think there was something wrong with them. Like they were having some kind of guilt complex about not being able to save people they cared about. So, screw that.

Hi Sam, he tried mentally composing again. *Hope you're having a good time on the Hammond. I was just wondering if there's any chance that McKay is actually onto something rather than just being a little unhinged by having been turned into a Wraith.*

He could just imagine Sam's bemused expression reading that one. "I'm not a psychiatrist, Sheppard," she would say, with that alarmed look she usually got when she had to deal with problems that involved people's feelings. It was one of the things they understood really well about each other.

He made himself actually start typing this time. *Hi Sam. Hope that you're having as much fun getting shot at in the Milky Way as you did getting shot at here in Pegasus. A weird thing – McKay has started saying he thinks that Elizabeth Weir may have Ascended and showed up to talk to him in his dreams.*

He took a deep breath. *Believe me, I know how that sounds. Still, you've had some experience with this kind of thing, so I thought I'd ask you if that sounded like something that could possibly actually happen. McKay has this idea that she may have gotten in trouble for helping him and wound up getting kicked out of her higher plane. He keeps saying we ought to look for her, and you can imagine how that goes over with Woolsey. Dr. Jackson probably knows the most about it, but he just says "maybe," only in a lot more words than that. And I trust your judgment. It's always been good before. So any advice would be appreciated.*

Say hi to the Milky Way galaxy for me,
John

He clicked to send the email before he could think better of it. He regretted it anyway the moment after it was sent, but by then it was too late; he shut his email and resolved not to think about the question any more until he got a reply.

"So what are we supposed to go look for?" Sheppard asked as Daniel came into the conference room, trying to keep his coffee cup from toppling off the top of his stack of books. Sheppard's team had already staked out one side of the table, with Woolsey at its head. Daniel set down his tablet on the other side of the table, pushing his books to one side, although it made him feel a little like the unpopular new kid in the junior high school classroom.

He cleared his throat. "Well, I'm hoping we can find out more about the early history of Ancient settlement here in the Pegasus galaxy," he said. "We know they came here after a plague wiped out most of the Ancients in the Milky Way galaxy. At that point, there wasn't any intelligent life in the Pegasus galaxy. So, the Ancients started seeding planets with humans."

"And built the Rings," Ronon said. "We know."

"Right, because the Ancients left a lot more traces of their presence here than they did on Earth, where we've just figured out they existed in the last decade. Okay, decade and a half." It never ceased to startle him to be reminded that it had been more than ten years since he'd first walked through the Stargate. "Anyway. Various human civilizations developed over time, eventually there was the war with the Wraith, and the Ancients returned to Earth. We know a little bit about that period, but we know almost nothing about what happened when the Ancients first arrived in this galaxy."

"We know they settled on Lantea," McKay said. "Which we pretty thoroughly explored for any signs of Ancient installations other than Atlantis itself, and found zip."

"I know that," Daniel said.

"I know you know, I'm just reminding everyone."

"Assume we're all up to speed," Sheppard said. "What are we doing?"

"Searching possible sites of very early Ancient settlement in Pegasus," Daniel said. "In the Milky Way, they settled primarily on Earth and Dakara, but they had outposts throughout the galaxy. It seems likely that when they were seeding planets here with life, they actually spent some time on some of those planets, and may have left enough behind that we can get some idea of what they were doing."

"Anything in particular we're looking for?" Sheppard asked. "If they didn't abandon these outposts in any particular hurry, I'm assuming they wouldn't have left all their stuff behind."

"I don't expect we're going to find a new super-weapon or a stash of ZPMs, if that's what you mean. It's very likely that any very early Ancient sites have been at least partially stripped, either by the Ancients themselves or by the local inhabitants. But even the layout of the buildings can tell us something about how the sites were used. And it's possible that they left things behind that they considered unimportant — considered to be trash, even — that will help us understand who they were and how they lived."

He spread his hands in frustration. "That's how actual archaeology works. As opposed to treasure-hunting, which, granted, is what we do around here a lot of the time. At best, I'm hoping we may find some surviving records from that era. We're not likely to find anything you can use to shoot people."

"I was actually just asking if there was anything in particular we were looking for," Sheppard said after a moment.

It took Daniel a moment to shift gears. "Umm. Not really. Anything we find is going to increase our knowledge of Ancient settlement in the Pegasus galaxy from nothing to something."

"I assume, Dr. Jackson, that you have some idea of where to start," Woolsey said. He didn't look particularly enthusiastic, but given his history with SG-1, it was saying something that he'd been willing in the first place to lend him Sheppard's team.

"I actually have a couple of different ideas. First, I've been going through Janus's records. He seems to have taken an interest in abandoned Ancient settlements here in Pegasus, possibly because he wanted to do his unauthorized experiments in places where no one was going to stumble across them by accident."

"I'm getting a little tired of Janus and his experiments," Sheppard said, although McKay brightened a bit.

"Janus doesn't seem to have used any of these sites," Daniel said. "Maybe he put this list together toward the end and then ran out of time before the Ancients went back to Earth, I don't know. But it gives us a set of gate addresses to start checking out."

Woolsey nodded. "You said you had two ideas."

"I'd like to take a look at planets that show evidence of having been occupied by humans for a particularly long time. The original Athos, for example — we know that technological civilization developed there over and over again, with the Wraith knocking them back every time. But even before that, I think it's clear that human settlement on Athos considerably predates the war with the Wraith."

He sketched archaeological strata with his hands. "The problem there is that any kind of Ancient site is probably going to be buried under layer after layer of later cities built on top of it. But I'd still like to take a look around one of the Athosian cities and see if there's any evidence that would support a larger-scale excavation effort. I was hoping that Teyla could get us permission from the Athosians to go take a look around."

"I have spoken about this to Halling and Kanaan," Teyla said. "I see the value myself of finding out more about our own past, as well as about the Ancestors. But my people are still debating whether to agree."

"What's the main issue?" Daniel asked.

"It is complicated. My people did not enter the ruined cities, for fear of attracting the attention of the Wraith. Things may be different now that we have a treaty with the Wraith, but that is very new. Some people are still not comfortable with the idea. And there is the larger issue of what will become of our original world if the treaty holds."

"Do your people want to go back?" Ronon asked.

"Some do," she said, and smiled at him. "Hearing that some Satedans have returned to their homeworld has inspired them. Others are worried that whether or not we return, Athos will be overrun by settlers from some other world interested in mining the old cities for their resources."

"You mean the Genii," Sheppard said.

"It would not be a surprise. And we must attract people to join us, whether or not we return to Athos. We are too few now to be a viable population alone. And we have always taken in refugees and travelers who wished to become Athosian. But they have always come a few at a time, and some of us worry about what will be lost if many people come who have no interest in becoming Athosian. My people do not want to become Genii."

"I do see the problem," Daniel said.

"There are others who are tired of moving from world to world and would prefer to stay where we have made a home, and still others who believe that because the Ancestors sent us to New Athos when they returned, it is where we ought to stay." She shook her head. "It will take time for everyone to talk and come to a decision. In the meantime, I am afraid that any kind of mission to Athos would be perceived as the Lanteans staking a claim."

"We aren't going to jeopardize our relationship with the Athosians," Woolsey said. "Dr. Jackson, I think you had better stick to the sites on Janus's list."

"We'll do that," he said. "I want to concentrate first on the sites that Janus has listed as being on currently uninhabited worlds, on the grounds that those are the sites least likely to have been stripped. First up is M4G-877. According to Janus's notes, both the Ancients and the resident humans abandoned the planet because of hostile wildlife."

McKay looked up with a frown. "How hostile are we talking about here?"

"If the Ancients couldn't deal with it, I'm guessing that it's pretty hostile," Sheppard said. "Come on, Rodney, you know the drill. Planets with Stargates that are uninhabited are uninhabited for a reason."

"Great. I'll be sure to bring my dinosaur repellent."

"It probably won't be dinosaurs," Woolsey said. The glances exchanged around the table suggested that no one else agreed.

INTERLUDE

ON THE third day they came to a town, earth houses with roofs of sod, long grasses growing on the roof, their roots holding everything in place, so that from a distance all one saw was a group of rounded hills, thin streams of smoke rising from chimneys.

"We will ask if anyone knows you," the grandmother said, though she sounded as though she thought that was unlikely. "You must have come from somewhere."

"Maybe the Wraith left her," the boy, Kyan, piped up.

"The Wraith don't leave their prey," his father said.

"The Wraith?" The name meant menace, though she did not know who they were.

The father and grandmother exchanged a glance. "They come through the Ring sometimes," the old woman said. "But our Ring is in orbit. They cull now and again, but we are a lot of work for a very small harvest. Mazatla has no cities."

"This world is Mazatla." Elizabeth frowned. The name ought to mean something. The name of the world she was on ought to be important, but it wasn't.

"Yes." The old woman nodded. "But Wraith or not, something bad has happened to you. Rest and heal, and perhaps it will all come back."

"I shouldn't be on Mazatla," Elizabeth said. "It's not my world." A ring, a ring turning in a flash of blue fire... And then it was gone.

"Rest and try to remember," the man said. "We'll ask at the Gathering if anyone knows you or knows your people. We'll stop here tonight and then go on to the Gathering at the Place of Two Rivers."

"The Place of Two Rivers."

Two rivers wreathed in mist, gray as steel beneath a winter sky, flowing together at a green point... There were bridges over the rivers, struts of iron against the sky woven like baskets of steel. One long span crossed on brick arches, iron rails dark with coal cars... Down the river, smoke rose from high smokestacks...

"Two rivers," she whispered. "A city where two rivers came together."

"Your home?" the grandmother asked.

Summer, and a green park full of people, boats on the river while above the sky lit with flowers of fire, green and gold and purple and blue, while she sat on a blanket.

"A festival," Elizabeth said. "At the end of summer. To celebrate the working man?" The words came back slowly. "There was a boat race on the river between steamboats. We watched from the park where the fort had been. There were people on the bridges watching and cheering. I had a red balloon because it was my favorite color. We ate ice cream when it got dark and waited for the fireworks." Her parents were there. She was older, old enough to go to school. "The City of Three Rivers."

"Do you remember why you were there?" the man asked.

Elizabeth nodded slowly. She remembered, or at least the child she had been did. "My father — he had work there. We had come back after Kenya and we were going to stay. There was a building." The pictures slipped away, and she grabbed at them. "A very tall building with classrooms in it. Very tall. Twenty, thirty, forty stories. A cathedral to learning? I don't know." And then it was gone again, the memories slipping just out of reach, words she had almost found. But she knew one thing. "I am from the City of Three Rivers."

The grandmother looked at the father. "Sateda," she said.

Elizabeth looked up. "Sateda?" The name was familiar, but...

"It sounds like the things they had on Sateda," she said. She put her hand on Elizabeth's shoulder. "Sateda was destroyed by the Wraith years ago. A few people escaped but they wander. They have no homes. Maybe you are Satedan."

Satedan. The word was familiar. "Maybe so."

"If so, you've been wandering a long time," the father said. "I don't know how you got here."

"I have to get back there," Elizabeth said. That was one thing she was certain of. "I need to go home."

"There's nothing left of Sateda," the old woman said gently. "The Wraith destroyed everything. They killed everyone they could find. It's gone."

"I have to get there," Elizabeth said. If the City of Three Rivers was there... "I have to find out what happened." What happened to someone. Who? Who was she worried about?

"We could ask the Travelers," the grandmother said. "Sometimes they come to the Gathering. They might know other Satedans. Sometimes they've had Satedans working on their ships." She looked at Elizabeth. "You know machines?"

Elizabeth nodded. "Machines. Yes. Radios and computers and guns."

"Sateda," the man nodded. "You're Satedan. Well, let's see if the Travelers come and if there are Satedans with them."

"I need to go there."

The old woman patted her hand. "Sateda is gone. But perhaps we can find your people. Or you will find a place with the Travelers as other Satedans have."

The word spread around the Gathering about the woman with no memories, and lots of people came to see her. They camped in the flood plain of two sleepy brown rivers, five thousand people or more, with bright tents in all the colors of the rainbow. The Mazatla did not live in cities, but in the summer there were these gatherings at various traditional locations, part fair, part sports meet, part courtship opportunity. Goods and animals were traded and sold, and there were matches of a game that involved throwing balls back and forth between three teams on an enormous staked out triangular field that went on all day until sunset ended the game. Then the victors paraded by torchlight, beginning a dance that went until dawn.

Elizabeth shared the tent of the family that had found her. When people came to see the woman with no memories she greeted them eagerly. Perhaps they would know where she had come from! But no one did. Each curious person at last went away shaking their heads. The woman with no memories had come from nowhere.

"The Travelers may know you," the grandmother said confidently. "If anyone here does, they will."

The Travelers arrived on the third day. Elizabeth heard shouts and went outside. A spaceship was descending from the blue sky streaked with a few high clouds, its white contrail bright. She raised her hand to shade her eyes, everyone else shouting and pointing too. It was bigger than...

Bigger than what? The comparison she'd meant to make slipped away. Bigger than a small ship meant to carry six to ten people. And smaller than...

Elizabeth frowned. A man in an olive green jumpsuit, bald headed, severe. He had a ship, a ship that was bigger than this one, and yet his name and the name of the ship ran away, lost somewhere among other things forgotten.

'It's the Travelers!" the boy Kyan said. He pulled on her arm. "They'll help you get home."

His father looked worried. "Only one ship this year. Something can't be right."

"Maybe it's because of the Wraith," Kyan said.

"Let's hope not," his father replied, and they walked together to the part of the field where the ship had landed.

Close up, the ship looked battered. It wasn't all the same color, and parts of it looked as though they'd originally belonged to another ship, including a pair of long, organic looking weapons emitters. There was something disturbing about them, something inhuman.

The man coming down the ramp to cheers and greetings was entirely human. He was white haired and burly, wearing a bright red jacket over a jumpsuit. "Hello everybody! We're glad to be here. Give us a few minutes to unload, folks. Then we'll be glad to trade with everybody."

"Lesko!" A man was pushing through the crowd, which parted when they recognized him as Elizabeth did — one of the Mazatla Leading Men, elected to govern this year. "Any news of the Wraith?"

Lesko held up his hands as everyone quieted. "Queen Death is dead."

"I know," Elizabeth murmured, and the grandmother turned to look at her.

No one else had heard, and there were shouted questions.

Lesko held up his hands again. "An alliance of other Wraith and the Lanteans and the Genii killed her."

"The Genii?"

"What did the Lanteans…"

"How could…"

"The Genii have a warship belonging to the Ancestors," Lesko shouted over the din. "It was flown into battle by the Leader Ladon Radim with the assistance of a Lantean pilot, Lorne. It defeated Queen Death's ship and then the Genii boarded it. They killed Queen Death."

Shouts, cheers, people slapping each other on the back…

Elizabeth felt strangely isolated, wrapped in private quiet. Lorne. Ladon Radim. Should she know those names? Why couldn't she find faces to go with those names?

She missed the question, someone shouting how Lesko knew.

"I heard it from the Genii myself," he called back. "They showed me the video of Radim's speech. They showed me the video the Genii took inside the hive ship."

"But there are other Wraith," someone said.

Lesko nodded. "The Genii and the Lanteans are making a treaty with them. Some of the other Wraith attacked Queen Death too."

"A treaty with the Wraith?" the grandmother said incredulously. "You can't make a treaty with the Wraith."

"You can make a treaty with anyone," Elizabeth said. "With the right leverage."

"Don't be ridiculous," someone behind her in the crowd said.

"Don't be ridiculous, Elizabeth." She was sitting at a desk in a room full of people, looking up at a green board covered in words. A man was leaning over her, dark rims to his glasses, dark hair. "You can't negotiate with people bent on global domination."

"I don't see how you can fail to," she responded. Her hands were young and thin and she wore a white sweater with blue floral trim around the wrists. "What other choice do we have? To simply say that we acquiesce? Or that we consider global thermonuclear destruction a viable alternative? Chernenko is a rational man…"

"It is not rational." Mr. Henry's mouth pursed. That was his name, Mr. Henry. He was her teacher. She was fifteen years old. "The Soviet Union does not pursue rational foreign policies, but rather ideological ones. Even when faced with Mutual Assured Destruction…"

"*Surely there are rational voices.*"

"*The rational voices are powerless.*" *Mr. Henry shook his head. "As are those elements in the Eastern Bloc who oppose him. I'm sorry to tell you, Miss Weir, but Solidarity is just as doomed as the Prague Spring or the rebels in Budapest in 1955. The moment tanks roll into Gdansk…*"

Elizabeth blinked. Kyan was shaking her arm. "Are you ok?"

"Yes," she said. The crowd was still yelling questions, though Lesko held up his hands.

"All in good time!" he said. "Come on now. Let my people unload. We'll have plenty of time for news."

"Did you remember something?" Kyan asked cheerfully.

"Yes. I think." Elizabeth shook her head. There was no more of it, just that moment, that frustration, those words that were so freighted with meaning that no one here would know.

Elizabeth put her hands at her side, watching the Travelers. Who am I? she thought. Who am I to feel that I should carry such responsibility?

"This is Atelia Zel," the grandmother said. "Atelia, I'd like you to meet Elizabeth. She is the woman with no memories I told you about."

"I'm pleased to meet you," Elizabeth said.

They stood in the shade of the Travelers' ship, its bulk casting deep cool shadows. A striped awning had been rigged and their wares were laid out on the tops of boxes and shipping crates, bulky things in front and the most valuable things displayed on cloths back near the open hatch where the sellers could keep their eyes on them. Lesko and a number of others haggled with the Mazatla, trading food for cloth, hides for medicines. Some few of them, the most valuable, were kept in a strong box, bottles neatly labeled and swathed in cloth. She only saw them for a moment, but some of them… There was something wrong, something familiar about them. Ramipril 10 mg… Erythromycin…

"Atelia is Satedan," the grandmother said, calling her attention back, and Elizabeth turned to look at her.

Atelia Zel was of average height and young, with lighter skin than the Mazatla but not as pale as Elizabeth's. Her black hair was braided tightly to the scalp, each braid worked with a single strand of gold thread. A little boy perhaps a year old peered curiously over her shoulder from a harness worn on her back over her spacer's coveralls. He looked at Elizabeth curiously, then gave her a four-toothed smile.

She smiled back. "What a beautiful baby!"

At that Atelia smiled too. "Thank you. He's a handful, and I have to watch him every minute so he doesn't get into things." Her eyes searched Elizabeth's face as if looking for something familiar. "They said you might be Satedan?"

"I don't know," Elizabeth said. "I don't remember much before I found myself on this world. Everyone here has been very kind to me, but nobody knows me or where I came from. The few things I do remember — cities, technology — suggest to these people that I'm Satedan." Even as she said it, it felt wrong. And yet this young woman's face was like so many she'd known, her clothes, the casual way she handled the electronics...

"What do you remember?" Atelia asked.

"Cities. Buildings with many stories. Vehicles." Elizabeth shook her head. "Steel bridges over rivers." Her eyes fell on the bottles carefully swaddled in the compartmented box. "Bottles like that. A hospital where sick people went for operations..." *Corridors with nurses in white, a kind dark haired man with an instrument around his neck who stood outside her father's room, talking to her in a low voice...*

"We had hospitals and high rises," Atelia said. "Medicines like these."

"Are those from Sateda?" She didn't quite pick them up. Not quite.

Atelia shook her head. "Not these. All our cites were destroyed and all our industries too. These came from the Genii who traded with the Lanteans for them." She touched the one labeled Erythromycin gently. "These pills are for people who have a sickness in their lungs, a cold that has gone to the chest and their lungs are filling with fluid. When nothing else will save them, these pills will." Her eyes searched Elizabeth's face. "It's a wide spectrum antibiotic for respiratory infections. Do you understand what that means?"

"Yes," Elizabeth said, though she couldn't have said how she knew. "For pneumonia." And it was a good thing, somehow, that these pills were here. A cheap drug, worth almost nothing per dose, rendered nearly priceless to these people, just as she'd seen it in clinics — where? She looked at Atelia. "Are you a doctor?"

Atelia laughed. "I'm a scholar. Or I was going to be. But all that ended a long time ago."

"How did you escape when your world was destroyed?"

"I wasn't there." Atelia looked up at the awning above, put her head back against the baby's cheek. "I was in my last year of studies. I was going to be a scholar who studied other peoples, finding the common threads of culture that help us understand who we are and where we all came from. I was doing field work when Sateda was attacked." Her mouth pursed. "Everyone I knew was killed."

Elizabeth put her hand on her arm. "I am so sorry. And so sorry to have asked."

"It was a long time ago." Atelia forced a smile. "And I've found a place with the Travelers. The technology that everyone understood on Sateda is rare and complicated everywhere else. I have skills that are valuable. I understand what these do." She touched the bottle. "I learned."

"And you have a family," Elizabeth said.

"Oh yes." She nodded, glancing back over her shoulder at the little face behind hers. "I have a son and a husband, though he's not with us now because he's a Hunter."

"What does he hunt?" Elizabeth asked.

Atelia's smile wasn't nice at all. "He hunts Wraith."

CHAPTER THREE

THE IRIS filled with blue as the gate opened, and Daniel leaned back in his seat as John threaded the needle's eye neatly with the jumper. He was used to missions beginning with a hike, and found it an unaccustomed luxury to be able to take the jumper and as much gear as he wanted to haul along without having to be able to carry it all on his back.

They came through the gate into bright sunlight, grassland stretching out around them as far as Daniel could see. The grass was amber rather than green, seed heads swaying in the wind that the jumper kicked up. The distant horizon swam with heat.

"All right, listen up, I'm only going to say this once," Rodney said.

Sheppard spoke up from the pilot's seat. "Promise?"

"No." It was easy banter, comfortable, and it made Daniel wish for a moment that his own team was there. He hadn't been able to justify why he needed SG-1 on this mission – it had been hard enough making a case for him to stay and continue his research rather than going back to work – but he wished Sam were there. Although of course Sam wasn't on SG-1 anymore.

"This planet has a high-oxygen atmosphere," Rodney went on. "Anything that burns here is going to burn fast and hot. Anything that strikes a spark is extremely likely to start a fire. These?" He held up his P90. "Likely to strike sparks."

"We get it," John said. "No weapons fire unless it's absolutely necessary."

"My gun doesn't fire bullets," Ronon said.

"No, it fires directed energy. Did what I just said make that sound like a better idea to you?"

"We will not fire except as a last resort," Teyla said. She glanced at Daniel, as if making certain that he was paying attention, and he nodded.

"Got it."

"Hopefully there won't be anything to shoot at," John said.

"Hostile wildlife," Rodney said, as if John might have forgotten.

"Thousands of years ago. Maybe they've moved on. Dr. Jackson, any idea where we should be looking for your archaeological site?"

"The records mentioned a river near the gate."

"For some definition of 'near,'" Rodney said.

Ronon rolled his eyes at him. "It's not like we're having to walk."

Jinx, Jack would have said. Daniel shook his head, wondering why he was thinking about the early years of his team rather than the actual team he'd left behind. He wasn't nostalgic for those days, he told himself. Nostalgic for the people he'd worked with then, maybe, but not actually for those early days of blundering in the dark, making lethal mistakes more often than they solved problems.

They hadn't even known what questions to ask, then, and there had been no time to look for answers that weren't immediately useful. Now, finally, he had the luxury of doing real archaeology, the kind that didn't involve trying to shoot pictures of artifacts while being chased past them by enemy troops. It was hard to remember how that even felt. He tried to summon up his old enthusiasm for the beginning of a dig, the promise of answers to questions he hadn't even thought of yet, and couldn't quite recapture the feeling. All he could think of was how many questions there were, and how inadequate the answers always seemed.

"All right," John said. "It looks like there's a river about thirty klicks to the northwest of here, so let's go check it out."

Ronon leaned over Rodney's shoulder to look out the front window. "What are we looking for?"

"Hopefully, visible buildings," Daniel said. "Or mounds that have accreted over buildings. I'm hoping we won't end up having to dig too much."

"It would have been nice if they'd built a road," John said.

"They probably did, but we're talking about thousands of years, here. It could be under meters of dirt, and I don't see anything that looks like the track of a road here. You might try the jumper's sensors, though. If the road was paved, you may be able to pick up the building material as distinct from the soil in the local area—"

"Already on it," Rodney said, his hands flying over the console in front of him. "And voilà." The jumper's screen now displayed an enhanced version of the scene outside, clearly showing a three-meter strip of irregular paving stone stretching from the gate to the northwest.

"Nice," Daniel said.

John nodded, one hand moving affectionately over the jumper's controls. "You ought to get yourselves one of these."

"You know, we've asked, but that keeps not happening."

"Oh, please, you have a time traveling jumper to study," Rodney said. "You know we've asked for that back, right?"

"It's like they think we would use it," John said.

"Only as, you know, a last resort," Rodney said. Teyla and Ronon exchanged a skeptical look.

"That's always how it starts," Daniel said. He squinted at the haze of trees now visible to the northwest, and then at the display scrolling across the screen. "It doesn't look like the road goes all the way to the river. Take us a little lower."

John obliged, bringing the jumper down to skim low enough over the grass that it billowed in the wind they kicked up.

"There," he said, pointing to a stand of scrub trees and bushes far short of the meandering green line of the river's course on the horizon.

"That's not near the river," Rodney said.

"It used to be. Look at the contours — there's a depression here just the right shape to be an old ox-bow. The river meanders, a loop gets cut off, it turns into a lake, then eventually the lake dries up. What was an outpost next to the river turns into an outpost sitting in the middle of a field. But those trees suggest there's still some source of water there — try running a more tightly focused scan."

The display on the console shifted as John gave instructions to the jumper, and Rodney's skeptical look changed to one of focused attention. "Oh, that's definitely man made," he said. "There's some kind of rectangular structure down there. And metal piping running down to the water table."

"The Ancients sunk a well. It's probably leaking, and the water source and the slight windbreak caused by the depression in the ground is how you get trees."

John frowned as he brought the jumper lower. "Why would the Ancients put in a well if this used to be right on the river?"

"Ah… I'm not entirely sure. Maybe the river water wasn't drink-able without purification, which makes sense if there was a lot of native wildlife. Or maybe they didn't want their water source to be dependent on the river's present course."

"Taking the really long view?"

"They did that. We're talking about people who seeded entire civilizations. The chance of the river changing its course in a few hundred years might have seemed like next week's problem to them. Try not to put us down right on top of the archaeological site, please."

John set the jumper down well clear of the structure, and Daniel climbed out, pushing his way into the chest-high grass that crunched dryly underfoot as he walked. Teyla fingered a stalk, frowning.

"Problems?" John said, looking sideways at her.

"We call this tindergrass," she said. "It grows in burned-over fields and other places where there has recently been a fire."

"I wouldn't say recently," John said, pushing dry seed-heads aside as he plowed through the tall grass.

"It grows very quickly. And it burns very easily itself."

"So would soaking wet wood, in this atmosphere," Rodney said. "That's why we're all going to be really careful —"

"We get the picture," John said.

Ronon turned abruptly, drawing his pistol, and Rodney slapped his arm. "What did I just say!"

"I thought I saw something."

"Probably some kind of animal," John said.

"I figured that, yes." Ronon pushed his way some distance through the tall grass away from their path, and crouched to brush the grasses aside. "There's a trail here."

"Now we get the tyrannosaurs," Rodney said.

Ronon grinned. "Only if they're two feet tall."

"There were small dinosaurs," Rodney said. "Small but vicious. Probably poisonous."

"Can we put a hold on the extreme pessimism until we actually get to the site?" Sheppard brushed sweat out of his eyes with the back of his hand. "Please?"

"I think they're little grazing animals," Ronon said. "These look like hoofprints."

STARGATE ATLANTIS: UNASCENDED   45

"So, probably not really scary."

"Famous last words," Daniel said.

There was a sudden rustling in the grass, coming rapidly toward them. Daniel drew his own pistol despite Rodney's warnings, although he didn't thumb the safety off. Ronon and Teyla turned toward the sound, backing warily away.

Several small brown forms exploded out of the grass and raced across their path, hooves beating the ground. Everyone stared after them for a moment as they vanished into the sea of tall grass on the other side.

John adjusted his sunglasses, as if they might have been affecting his vision. "Were those horses?"

"Really short horses," Ronon said. "With fangs."

"They did not have fangs," Rodney said.

"You're right, they didn't."

"I think we will all be fine," Teyla said. "Let us see what we can make of Dr. Jackson's archaeological site."

"It doesn't look like much," Rodney said, squinting at the structure. There was definitely a manmade building there, its rectangular lines too regular for anything but a purposeful construction. It was half buried by vegetation, the wind having heaped up the soil against one side of it, leaving the lee side clear enough to distinguish beneath the tangle of scrubby brush. "Under all that dirt, we're looking at, what, a metal box?"

John shrugged. "What do you want, a sign saying 'the Ancients were here'?"

"That would be nice."

"There's nothing here the Ancients could have used to build with," Daniel said. "It would have been easier to use metal than to bring in stone."

"Well, yes, of course, but anybody could have — hello." Rodney was crouching down in front of one wall of the structure, brushing away the weeds.

"It's Ancient, right?" Daniel said without needing to see past him.

"It's built in an Ancient style, and this is Ancient lettering, but technically it's still possible that —"

"McKay," John said.

"All right, yes, it's Ancient. There's something weird about this door, though, it looks like maybe somebody tried to pry it open."

Daniel crouched to see, and Rodney leaned back out of his way somewhat grudgingly. The metal was definitely scored in what he didn't think could be an intentional part of its design. "I think you're right," he said. "Relic hunters?" He glanced up at Teyla for confirmation.

"It is possible," she said. "The devices of the Ancestors are very valuable to those with the ability to use them. There are groups who move from world to world scavenging what they can from Culled civilizations. They would certainly have taken any relics of the Ancestors they could find in hopes of being able to sell them to someone who had a use for them."

"And so much for finding anything useful to us," Rodney said.

"Okay, what part of 'we probably aren't going to find any weapons' was I unclear about? I'm just asking because —"

Daniel broke off at a louder rustling in the grass. Another herd of the miniature horses thundered past, kicking up dust as they went. There was a whirring of wings, and a flock of birds arrowed through the underbrush, past them and gone.

"People," Ronon said. "We have a problem."

"I told you something would turn out to have fangs," Rodney muttered, and then his expression changed as he turned. On the horizon, there was a smear of black and a flickering brightness, and above them the wavering mirage of rising heat. The wind was blowing toward them across the sea of grass, hot and heavy with smoke.

"Let's get back to the jumper," John said.

Ronon shook his head and caught him by the arm. "There's not time."

"Ronon is right," Teyla said, her eyes on the rising smoke. "We would not reach the jumper." Even as she spoke, Daniel could see new patches of flame breaking out ahead of the racing wall of fire, sparks leaping toward them on the wind.

John turned to Rodney. "Can you get that door open?"

"How fast?"

"Fast."

"Then, no."

"Don't open the door," Daniel said quickly. "If we can't get it closed again, the fire could ruin the interior of the site."

"Also us!"

"Move," Ronon said, grabbing Rodney by the arm and pulling him up. Teyla caught Daniel's arm to urge him forward, but he hardly needed the encouragement to run.

Ronon was setting their direction, not directly away from the fire but angling away from it toward the river. The smell of smoke was stronger, but Daniel resisted the urge to turn and look over his shoulder. Ronon was well out ahead of them, clearly having to slow himself down even so, and he did turn back to make sure they were all following. His expression wasn't reassuring. "Pick up the pace."

"Not getting enough of a workout?" John called back from behind him.

"You can do better," Ronon said.

Rodney sounded breathless when he spoke, although he was keeping up as well as Daniel. Clearly his years in Pegasus had given him plenty of practice at running away. "Please do joke about our imminent fiery demise."

"We're not going to – hey!" Ronon went down, sprawling as if he'd tripped over something, but there was something odd about the way he was twisting trying to get up – he was tangled in a net, Daniel realized abruptly, a waist-high, broad woven net stretched between stakes.

"What the hell?" John demanded, slowing his pace to avoid running into the net himself. Ronon was already cutting himself free when Teyla spun, brandishing her sticks. John raised his P90, his arm tensing as if he were struggling with the urge to fire.

The attack came from the side, and for a moment Daniel thought "dinosaur," and then, "really big bird," and then, "I should be getting out of its way." He threw himself to one side at the same time as the creature skidded to a halt, screeching and backing up, ducking its head to inspect them. It was built like an ostrich, but taller and far stockier, with a beak the size of Daniel's head and wickedly sharp claws.

It had a net draped across its body. Entangled in the same net, he thought for a moment, but the edges didn't look torn, the drape of the net too purposeful. As if it were carrying the net, or wearing it.

"Hey, it's okay," he said, putting his hands out, "we're not going to hurt you."

"Teyla, can you take this thing?" Ronon asked. He was up by now, his pistol leveled at the giant bird.

"I believe so," Teyla said. "It would be unwise to shoot."

"It's just a really big bird," John said, backing slowly away from the creature with his hands held up in front of him. "Nice birdie. How about we all just… "

There was the thunder of feet, and another of the enormous birds came into view, this one even bigger, slowing but not stopping as it saw them. It raised its head and made a deep chattering noise, its eyes on the smaller one. Daniel could feel another gust of hot wind from behind them.

As if coming to agreement, both creatures lowered their heads and charged, the larger one heading for Ronon, the smaller for John. "Run!" John yelled.

Teyla swept low with her sticks, trying to knock the feet out from under the one charging John. It screamed and struck at John, its beak coming down like an axe. John swore and threw himself out of the way, and it raised one foot to rake at him.

Daniel threw himself against it with all his weight, and it staggered. It flailed out with its wings, and he saw not entirely to his surprise that the wingtips ended in long, bony fingers. They grabbed for him, trying to entangle them in the net.

Then the creature screeched again and went down as Teyla lashed out again with her sticks, its feet flailing. He could hear fabric tearing as one claw snared his pants leg. Ronon had slashed free a section of the staked net and was wielding it like a gladiator, while the other bird circled him warily.

Then Rodney was tugging him up, somewhat to his surprise. "Go, go!" Daniel needed no more encouragement. He sprinted for the horizon, Teyla and Rodney following.

"Come on, Sheppard!" Rodney yelled.

"We're coming!"

There was an enraged squawk that he interpreted as a large bird being entangled in net. He risked a glance back over his shoulder and saw that both John and Ronon were running after them, already beginning to close the distance between them. His leg was beginning to sting in an insistent way that suggested the claw had connected with more than fabric.

The smaller of the two birds was on its feet, reaching down to bite at the strands of net that still entangled it.

Ahead of them, he could see the green line of brush that sloped down to the river. So could every small animal trying to escape the fire. Anything that wasn't caught in the nets would make for the protection of the water—

"They're going to be waiting at the river," Ronon said, catching up to Daniel. He sounded as though this were no more than an easy jog.

"I know," John called from behind him. "But they don't look like great swimmers, so when we get there, everybody into the water."

"We're going to have to go through these guys," Ronon said.

"We've just met an entirely new intelligent species, and we're about to make first contact by shooting them," Daniel said.

"You got a better idea?"

"Try warning shots," John said. "And, yes, Rodney, I remember why that's a bad idea, but we're heading straight for the river."

"I'm just saying the two things I didn't want in my day were dinosaurs and fire!" Rodney said, unslinging his own P-90 and cradling it as he ran.

"They're not dinosaurs, McKay."

"Birds are essentially dinosaurs, any paleontologist—"

Ronon grabbed the back of Rodney's jacket, thrusting him forward faster. "Shut up and run!"

Daniel could see the bird-creatures as they neared the river, their beaks and feathered heads partially concealed behind bushes and scrubby trees. Unnaturally sharpened sticks protruding from the bushes suggested that some of them had constructed spears to add to their natural weaponry.

The grass ended well short of the greener tangle of brush that led down the bank, with an area of scraped bare ground between them. A firebreak, he realized, and couldn't help wondering if they'd used their claws or some kind of shovel – their wings were too short for a hand-held digging tool to get much leverage—

"Net!" Teyla called, and leapt over it gracefully, landing squarely in the dirt on the other side. Daniel managed to jump it himself, although when he landed, the stinging in his leg increased to an urgent burn. By the time he steadied himself, the others were over, John and Ronon moving out in front.

"Get out of our way!" John yelled.

"I don't think they understand what you're saying," Ronon said. Daniel could see several of them moving closer, and he suspected that meant there were more moving that he couldn't see.

John clearly felt the same, because he fired, a short burst of bullets that spat against the ground between him and the nearest of the creatures.

The nearest bushes went up like a torch. There were cries of alarm from the creatures, several of them backing out into the cleared section of dirt. It looked to Daniel like they had a clear path to the river. Teyla was already moving, and he followed her, shrugging out of his pack on the way and scrambling through the underbrush toward the river bank with its straps hooked over one arm.

The bank dropped off more sharply than he was expecting, and he slid more than scrambled down into the water. There were nets in the shallow part of the river, too, supported by floats, and as he reached them, two of the creatures splashed into the water, paddling toward him. They weren't particularly speedy in the water, but they beat their legs powerfully, churning along with what seemed like determination.

He tossed his pack over and then tugged out a knife and slashed the net, squirming through and then diving, making for the middle of the river where the current was stronger. He stayed under as long as he could, his lungs burning, before he finally broke the surface and rolled over onto his back, lifting his head to make sure the others were following.

They were, and although one of the creatures was pursuing, kicking along like a malevolent paddleboat, they were already outdistancing it. It seemed safe enough to retrieve his pack, now bobbing in the current, and to keep hold of it as he swam. When he looked back again, their pursuer had apparently given them up as not worth the effort, and was clambering out on the opposite bank from the one where a fire was now blazing through the scrubby trees.

He kicked against the current, letting the others catch up to him; Teyla was swimming against the current to get back within earshot. "How far do you want to go downstream?" he called.

John looked back at the milling creatures, several of whom were now hauling nets weighted down with dead or struggling animals across the river, out of reach of the fire. They were still chattering to each other, in what Daniel had to guess was at least a rudimentary language. "A good long way," he said. "Let's give them plenty of room."

The water was probably barely cool, but after the blazing heat of the fire it felt cold on his skin. He swam doggedly downstream, entirely on board with the decision to put as much distance as possible between themselves and the hostile birds.

"What was that?" John said abruptly, rolling over in the water and looking around.

"What was what?" he called.

Ronon kicked abruptly in another direction. "There's something moving in the water. Something big."

"I think we've gone far enough," John said. He started making for the bank, and Daniel followed his lead.

Something broke the water in front of John. Daniel was expecting the smooth slickness of a fish's back, or maybe the scales of something crocodilian. Instead, he had a quick impression of something streamlined but feathered. It surfaced again, and he could see its beady eye, tracking Daniel as it swam, and its six-inch long beak. The beak looked decidedly sharp.

Another one breached behind Daniel, and as he splashed away from it he got a better close range look at the thing than he particularly wanted. It looked like a penguin, he decided a little incredulously, if penguins were mud-colored and as big as Teyla. Another one surfaced, and then another, swimming in swift bobbing motions along the surface of the water between Daniel and the nearest bank.

"I hate to say this, but I think these things are hunting us," John said, as two of them cut off his route toward shallower water.

"We are very big to be prey for these creatures," Teyla said.

"Maybe they're ambitious."

Teyla rolled over with her P90 in her arms and sighted at the nearest of the swimming birds, but held her fire. "If I shoot one, it may drive them off, or spur them to attack."

"I could stun them," Ronon said.

"But can you stun them all before they attack?"

"Sure," Ronon said, rolling over almost lazily and sighting on what Daniel could only think of as a giant penguin. "Couldn't you?"

"Well, do something," Rodney snapped. "Before we wind up penguin food."

"You've seen these things before?" Ronon said.

One of them darted forward and struck at John's pack, which he had been towing along beside him as he swam. The pack jerked out of John's hands and disappeared under the surface of the water. "Hey. Hey!" John called indignantly.

"Better your pack than yourself," Teyla said. Several more of the creatures were now diving toward the submerged pack, and after a moment items that Daniel recognized as Air Force issue began floating to the surface.

"I notice they didn't take your pack," John said.

"Yes, that is fortunate," Teyla said, ignoring his sour tone. Daniel had a clear path now to the bank, and swam hard for it, hauling himself up into the shallow water and slogging through the mud toward the bank. The rest of the team was in shallow water as well, Ronon shaking out his hair and Rodney churning the water in his eagerness to reach the bank.

"We have penguins on Earth," Rodney said. "They're just not terrifying."

"Then these aren't penguins," Ronon said.

"Close enough."

Teyla looked at Daniel in concern as he dragged himself up the bank and well clear of the water, his leg aching with every step. "Are you hurt?"

"That would be a yes," he said, and sat down heavily. In the river, the birds were still fighting over the remains of John's pack. Two of them had found an MRE, and appeared to be trying to consume it packaging and all.

Daniel rolled up the remainder of his pants leg and let her bandage the deep scratch neatly. Ronon had a long scrape down his arm, but didn't seem to consider it worth paying attention to at the moment.

"I'm thinking we get out of sight of the river, and then wait it out for a while," John said. "If you're hanging in there, Dr. Jackson."

"Daniel," he said. "And, yeah, I don't think I'm currently heavily bleeding, so that's probably a good idea."

They stomped some distance away from the river, until they could no longer hear the sounds of splashing or see the water through the bushes.

"We should camp reasonably close to the river in case there's another fire," John said. The grass here wasn't burned, although the wind was carrying the smell of smoke.

"But not close enough for the giant penguins to eat us," Rodney said.

"Yes, not that close, McKay."

"Are we going to make camp?" Ronon said. "We aren't that far down river."

"It's probably not a bad idea," Daniel said. "I'm guessing our friends back there are the ones who originally set the fire—"

"Nice of them," Ronon said.

"They are hunters," Teyla said.

"Burning the grass to drive game into their nets," Daniel agreed. "Only we got in the way. I don't know if we pissed them off, or if they just figured we'd be good eating, but either way, the more time we give them to take their catch and clear out, the better."

"In about ten hours they'll dial the gate to check up on us," John said. "If we haven't made it back to the site by then, I'll tell Lorne to come give us a ride."

They made camp where the bushes thinned out into dry grass. It would have been comfortable if their gear hadn't been soaking wet, and if they had dared to heat up any of their food; as it was, it was tolerable. Daniel ate his cold dinner and leaned back against his backpack, looking up at the darkening sky.

He could almost hear Jack saying *are we having fun yet, kids?*

"You know, archaeology doesn't have to be like this," he said conversationally to the first stars, now hazily visible against the deepening blue.

"Welcome back to Pegasus," John said.

INTERLUDE

THE GRANDMOTHER hugged Elizabeth one last time. "I hope you find your people," she said.

"I hope so too." Elizabeth hugged her back, tears stinging her eyes unexpectedly. Truly she had been taken in by these people, treated as one of their own when she had nothing to offer, a rare and extraordinary kindness.

The grandmother dropped her voice. "Not all of the Travelers are good people, and they're sharp traders. But our Ring is in orbit. If they will take you to a gate in their travels, you can dial Sateda. You remember the address I gave you?"

Elizabeth nodded. "I do. And thank you."

The last people were filing in amid goodbyes, the ship's ramp still extended though everything had been packed away and the Mazatla were moving back to a safe distance. Elizabeth waved once more to Kyan and his father, then hurried aboard.

"This way," Atelia said, leading her through a maze of improvised passages and ductwork. "Just stay out of the way during the lift, and we can talk when we're in hyperspace. Here you go. This one's yours." She stopped in a narrow section of hallway. There were four bunks built into the walls, two on each side, with a thin foam mattress on each and a plastic curtain. One was drawn back to show the niche was empty except for the safety belts that would allow someone to strap in.

"Thank you," Elizabeth said. She only had a small bundle, a change of clothes given her by the Mazatla, and she clipped it to one of the straps within.

"I'd advise you to strap in for lift," Atelia said quickly. "It can be rough. And sometimes the grav generators don't work right."

"I'll be careful," Elizabeth said. She settled back into the bunk as Atelia hurried away, her head pillowed on her bundle as she fastened the seatbelts and drew the curtain. The yellow light fixture blinked, probably warning takeoff, as a slow rumble began somewhere beneath her. The ship's main engines were coming online.

A scratchy voice came over an intercom. "Getting ready for power up. Everybody strap in. Don't unstrap until I give the word."

That was straightforward enough, Elizabeth thought. The roar and vibration grew. Should she be frightened? Wouldn't someone planet-bound usually be? And yet she wasn't, not really. Had she traveled on a space ship before? If so, when? Where those memories should be was nothing but blankness. Elizabeth closed her eyes as the vibration turned to shaking, presumably the actual lift in progress. Why couldn't she remember? What had happened to her? Surely it was there somewhere, like these tantalizing flashes that came at odd moments, scenes of a life interrupted. There must be a way to find it.

She flexed her hands, willing her fingers to relax, stretching them against the leg of her pants. Relax. Deep breaths. Perhaps if she could relax, control her breathing, let the tension flow out, she would find her way. Relax.

The vibration was less now, a soothing sort of motion rather than shaking. Relax. Her eyes closed, her breath coming quietly. Around her, the shipboard noises were comforting rather than distracting, the sounds of machines and people going about their business, distanced by the curtain across her bunk.

Like a dormitory, she thought. Like a dormitory...

The light awakened her, bright through the curtainless window. It was open, and the warmth of an August morning blew in through the leaves of the old tree outside, the voices of students coming up from the walk below, the traffic sounds a distant blur. The breeze smelled of the river and sunshine.

Elizabeth opened her eyes. The other bed was empty, peach comforter pulled up, the clip light on the metal bed frame turned off. Her roommate had already left.

She sat up, pushing back the covers and taking a deep breath. Her blue and white rug covered the scuffed hardwood floor. Her plastic bins were stacked beside the dresser, her boombox plugged in beside the mirror, her suitcase unzipped on the dresser top where she'd gotten her pajamas out the night before. The digital clock said it was seven thirty.

Seven thirty of the first day. Her heart leaped. The first day, her first day of a new life, her first day on her own. Her first day, and these moments alone to savor it in her own place before she went in search of breakfast and the ten o'clock advisor meeting. The first day.

She got up, turning in the light from the window, a small, slow smile beginning. She turned on the boombox radio.

"...big pile up in the northbound lanes of Key Bridge, blocking two lanes at the Rosslyn end. Our advice is to take Memorial this morning, folks. It's going to be a while before they get it cleared. And that's your go-to traffic this morning! We'll be back on the hour with the latest. To get you going, here's John Parr's Man in Motion from the hit movie St. Elmo's Fire!"

The opening chords of one of her favorite songs washed over her, and Elizabeth turned the radio up, buoyed by sheer joy. She was here, and this was the beginning! She was finally here!

A noise, and Elizabeth snapped back to herself. The plastic curtain swayed. "I'm sorry," Atelia said. "I didn't mean to wake you. I didn't realize you'd gone to sleep."

"It's OK," Elizabeth said. The rumble of the engines was distant and constant now. She unstrapped the waist belt and sat up. "I didn't mean to go to sleep."

Atelia was watching her thoughtfully. "You must be used to space travel."

"I must be," Elizabeth said. She had remembered something on purpose, though what it told her was still a mystery. A dormitory, and being a very young woman... It poured away like water through her fingers, whatever happened next, the name of the place, of all those she'd known there.

"You can rest if you like," Atelia said. "It's two full watches before we reach our rendezvous point."

"Where is that? A planet?" Elizabeth got to her feet.

"No." Atelia shook her head. "We're smarter than that! We choose random coordinates in deep space for our meetings, and we never use the same ones twice. That way the Wraith can never guess where we're going to be and wait in ambush for us."

"They would do that?" The Wraith were a mystery still, for all she had supposedly suffered at their hands.

"Some hives are smart enough to. A lot of hives leave us alone as long as we leave them alone, but sometimes they come after us. Who knows why." Atelia shrugged. "They're Wraith. They don't have to make any sense."

"Even your enemies usually make sense," Elizabeth said. "We do evil things because we're evil only works in bad fiction."

Atelia gave her a sharp glance. "Then you don't know the Wraith," she said. "Or you're not Satedan. Because there is no reason and there is no excuse." She turned to go.

"I didn't mean to offend you," Elizabeth said, feeling her eyebrows rise. "I remember very little, so I don't know."

The set of Atelia's shoulders changed a little. "I know," she said. She turned back briskly. "Well, if you're awake I'll show you where to get something to eat. We'll be in hyperspace for a long time. And once we reach the rendezvous you can see if one of the other ships will drop you at a gate if that's what you want."

"I think so," Elizabeth said. She followed Atelia forward down the corridor toward a common room small enough to be crowded with half a dozen people, including an old man holding Atelia's baby on his lap.

A genuine smile crossed Atelia's face. "Hello baby! Hello sweetheart!" She reached down and took him, lifting him onto her shoulder. "How's mama's baby? How's Jordan?"

Elizabeth stopped, halfway to picking up a mug from a hook above the counter. "Jordan?"

"That's his name." Atelia turned with him in her arms. "Jordan, can you smile for Elizabeth?" The baby crowed cheerfully. She frowned at Elizabeth. "Is something wrong?"

"No, not at all," Elizabeth said, taking the mug. "I think I've heard that name before. That's all." Though why it should seem strange eluded her completely. It was just a name.

CHAPTER FOUR

IT WAS a long walk back to the site, made even longer for Daniel by his aching leg and the lack of coffee. Rodney complained about the lack of breakfast until Ronon pointed out that he was the one who'd decided it was too dangerous to use the heaters, at which point he switched to complaining about the length of the walk, until John elbowed him in the ribs and then claimed it was an accident.

Ronon supplemented his breakfast with the roasted remains of some unfortunate small animal that had been trapped in the fire. "Want some?" he said, holding out a charred leg.

"No, thank you, I've had my daily dose of deadly pathogens already from jumping in the river," Rodney said.

"Tastes like chicken," Ronon said, and offered it to Daniel instead.

"No, thanks."

"I thought archaeologists were supposed to eat whatever people offer them," Rodney couldn't help saying.

"First, you're thinking of anthropologists, which I'm actually not, and, second, yes, if I were trying to make cultural contact here, I would eat the... what is that?"

Ronon turned the leg around in his hand. "I have no idea."

"Right. But I'm not, and I don't think this is exactly traditional Satedan food we're talking about here."

"I would not eat that either," Teyla said firmly.

"Your loss," Ronon said. "At least we didn't invent MREs."

"It's military rations," John said. "You must have had military rations."

"Sure, but ours don't taste terrible."

Once they neared the site, they proceeded more cautiously, weapons at the ready. As John pointed out, everything that could burn in a several-kilometer radius had already burned. The ground was still hot, smoke rising from the charred grass, and Rodney appeared to be trying unsuccessfully not to breathe.

"All right, then," John said. "Now let's check out the site."

Every crackle of burned grass underfoot made everyone twitchy as the team made their way through the remains of the underbrush toward the door of the metal structure, but there were no signs of the bird-creatures, and with the grass burned to stubble, it would certainly have been easy enough to see them coming.

"They've probably moved off to butcher their catch," he said. "I wonder if they were already using tools when the Ancients left — it hasn't been very long, although they did refer to them as 'wildlife' rather than a native civilization."

John looked skeptical. "You really think they invented tools since the Ancients were here?"

"Honestly, no," Daniel said. "Wildlife or pre-agricultural tool-users, I don't think the Ancients cared. They were specifically interested in seeding worlds with humans, because they knew humans had the potential to evolve into something like them. Putting humans here would have meant they'd have to compete with our friends back there. I expect that's why they abandoned their outpost here. After all, they had a whole galaxy to choose from. They didn't need to bother with worlds that turned out to be less than ideal. "

Rodney crouched down to examine the door, and Daniel ran his hand down one edge of it; it was warm toward the bottom but not hot, which meant there was a reasonable chance that opening it wouldn't make everything inside burst into flame. He resisted the urge to elbow Rodney out of the way to get a better look, and instead squinted at a rectangular patch of bared connectors and sockets.

"It looks like the original control panel is gone," he pointed out.

"I can see that," Rodney said.

"I'm sorry, I'm just making an observation about my site."

"All right, given that the control panel is gone, how do we get in there?" John said.

"Somebody may have figured out a way to get in there already," Daniel said. "Those pry marks at the bottom of the door."

"You would think that's how they got in," Rodney said. "If you didn't notice that someone's wired their own controls to the original fixture." He finished digging the angular control box out of the dirt, and held it up.

"Please don't actually dig things up before I even get a photograph," Daniel said, snapping a picture.

"I'm sorry, I thought we were trying to get in."

"We are, but… " Daniel clenched his jaw. "All right, you're right, we have limited time, and this isn't the part that matters most. So if that box was wired to the door panel, where's the wire?"

"Wires burn," Rodney said. "Especially in a high-oxygen atmosphere, which, hello. Actually I'm impressed that our scavengers managed to wire this thing up and run current through it without setting themselves on fire. Either they knew what they were doing, or they got awfully lucky."

"Many people who make their living scavenging culled worlds know something about technology," Teyla said. "But few would have the ability to measure the oxygen level in the atmosphere."

"Wraith?" Ronon asked.

Rodney shook his head. "This isn't a Wraith design."

"The Travelers could do it," John said.

"This could be theirs," Rodney said. "I mean, pretty much anything could be theirs. Still, this is… weird." The control box was heavier than seemed reasonable in his hand. "If the Travelers scavenged this, I'd like to know where they got it."

"Weird how?" John asked sharply. "Weird as in it's going to blow up in our faces?"

"No, the interesting kind of weird."

"Like I said."

"It's not going to blow up," Rodney said, reconnecting it to the door panel with a twist of insulated wire. "All it's going to do is… " He pressed one of the two triangular buttons, and was rewarded by seeing the door slide jerkily open. "Open the door."

"That's what you always say," John said. He shone a light inside cautiously, and then stepped inside. On the other side of the door, another of the angular door panels was connected in place of the original Ancient controls.

"They pried the door open first, and then they rigged these controls," Daniel said.

Rodney nodded slowly. "I hate to say it, but he's right."

Daniel gave him a sideways look. "You mean you hate to say it because that suggests that the site was used as a base by scavengers long enough for it to be thoroughly stripped?"

"No, I… never mind."

Daniel was already shining a flashlight around the entry room. Stairs descended from the rear of the room further down; at least part of the installation was underground, then. The stairs were typically Ancient in design, with decorative cutouts in the railings.

Rodney waved a hand at the nearest lighting fixture, but it remained stubbornly dark. "Sheppard, can you turn the lights on?"

"Nope," John said after a minute.

"Or the light switch might work," Daniel said, thumbing a control panel.

Rodney squinted at it in the abruptly bright light. "Okay, yes. Clearly that's a later addition to the site, too."

"Similar design."

"It is, isn't it?"

"What are we thinking?" John said.

"Not Wraith," Teyla said.

"Definitely not," Daniel said. He shone his flashlight around the room and walked a slow circuit of it, stopping once or twice to brush dust away from markings on the wall, all of which proved to be geometric and probably entirely decorative in function. It was mildly interesting as an example of Ancient decorative arts, but they had enough of those. He stopped at the top of the stairs and shone his flashlight down them toward the still dark lower level. "If there was anything in this room but the walls, it's gone now. Let's go see if they left anything downstairs."

The stairs led down into darkness. Rodney took them cautiously, listening for any sound that might have been something large and taloned preparing to launch itself out of the shadows. The only sounds were mechanical, the soft thrum of water running through pipes and the occasional clunk of metal on metal.

He shone his light toward the noise, intrigued, and revealed one end of a long bank of pipes and metal tanks. "What have we got here?"

"You tell me," John said, as the rest of the team came down behind them. Daniel was already investigating the machinery.

"Don't touch that," Rodney said.

"You know, this isn't my first rodeo," Daniel said. "I know not to press buttons."

"Everyone says that, and yet they always press buttons."

"So do you," John said. "Let's focus. What is this thing?"

"I can tell you right now it's not Ancient," Rodney said.

"Janus's records didn't say anything about experimental machinery," Daniel said. "He said this was an observation post for a settlement."

"I told you, it's not Ancient. Believe me, I have seen examples of just about everything they ever built, and they didn't build this. Between this and the lighting controls upstairs, which I'm pretty sure are incorporating high levels of neutronium… " Rodney looked the machinery up and down, and couldn't come to any different conclusion. "I'm pretty sure this was built by the Asgard."

"The fact that it has Asgard writing on it might be a clue," Daniel said.

"I would have noticed that in a moment," Rodney said, craning his neck over Daniel's shoulder to read. "It's, okay, something about the settings —"

"Do not alter settings without authorization," Daniel said. "Basically, 'don't press buttons.'"

"I knew that."

"I thought the Pegasus Asgard didn't leave their own planet," John said.

"Well, they haven't for a long time," Daniel said. "Not since the Wraith went after them and they retreated to a single world."

"A single toxic and unpleasant world," Rodney said.

"Before that, though, they were exploring the Pegasus galaxy just like we are now. I'd guess they found this installation abandoned by the Ancients, and moved in."

"It's a lot cooler down here," Ronon said, leaning back against the metal wall.

Teyla nodded. "We are some distance underground."

"All right," John said. "You two check this thing out. We're going to keep an eye out upstairs in case our friends come back."

Rodney settled down to examining the machinery, while Daniel took pictures of the various inscriptions along its length, most of which seemed to be warnings not to tamper with the device. "Like we're doing right now," Daniel said warily, shining his flashlight into the depths of the machinery but carefully not touching it.

"I'm not tampering. I'm examining. This looks like the original power supply," Rodney said.

"Original?"

"Yeah, it's dead, but this thing is still doing something. Ronon's right that it's cooler down here than it ought to be, and that's not just being underground or the water running through these pipes. Feel the air coming out of these vents."

Daniel held his hand very gingerly six inches from the air vent. "It's blowing cold air."

"Some kind of air conditioning effect."

"Is that possible without electricity?"

"You can build an evaporative cooler, but I think there's a backup power source somewhere in here. Enough to run the air conditioner, but not to activate the other functions."

"What other functions do we think this thing has?"

Rodney sat back on his heels, considering the long bank of machinery. "I think what we're looking at is some kind of climate control device."

Daniel shone his flashlight down the length of the machinery, illuminating its curves and angles. "It's a lot more primitive than most of the Asgard equipment we've seen."

"It's a lot more basic. This isn't their nuclear power plant, it's their camping equipment. It beams down and—" He pointed out the locking seams between pieces of equipment. "—snaps together. Turn it on, plug it into a water source, and you get a comfortable atmosphere. There are probably some kind of controls for adjusting the temperature to suit you."

"'Do not adjust settings.'"

"You don't have to tell me. But… okay, so I've worked in some places where people had fights over the thermostat."

"The SGC, for one."

"At Area 51 they ended up putting a lock on the air conditioning controls. Although you could open it with a paper clip if you really—never mind that. My point is, does it make sense to build an air conditioner and then warn your end users not to adjust the temperature?"

"For the Asgard it might," Daniel said. "They tend to be pretty sure that there are right ways and wrong ways to do things. The device might not need setting if it was already preset to adjust the temperature to whatever its designers felt was ideal for Asgard health and comfort."

"So I wonder what the other settings do?"

"Adjust other aspects of the climate to some ideal? Either on a local level or… this power cell would have been serious overkill for running your basic window air conditioner. And this is the Asgard we're talking about. They could probably affect the entire planet's climate if they wanted to."

"Yep," Daniel said. He took another step back from the machine. "We've seen a device that could control the climate on a planetary scale before, although it wasn't Asgard. The NID grabbed it and brought it back to Earth. That turned out… badly."

"We can deactivate it," Rodney said. "I'm pretty sure this is the auxiliary power pack."

"How sure?"

"Considering the amount of time I've spent studying Asgard power generation systems, actually fairly sure." He pulled the power pack out, and was rewarded by feeling the flow of air through the machine stop.

"So what have we got?" John said, coming halfway down the stairs and looking skeptically at the machine.

"Weather control device," Rodney said.

"You think it might be a weather control device," Daniel said.

"All right, it's a local climate control device that, given it's designed to have enough power run through it to air condition the Sahara Desert, looks to me a lot like a weather control device. I've deactivated it so we can take at least part of it home to study without any chance of making the rotten weather on our new planet any worse."

"The weather's not that bad."

"Are you kidding? The city stays so cold these days that I have to wear three pairs of socks just to feel my feet."

"My quarters aren't cold," John said.

"The city likes you."

"There's a small problem with taking this thing back to Atlantis,"

John said. "If you're sure you've deactivated it—"

"I've seen all that I want to see of attempts to control the weather gone very wrong," Rodney said. "If I say it's deactivated, it's deactivated. Believe me when I say that working in the Pegasus galaxy has given me a lot of practice in how to turn things off."

"It's not going to fit in the jumper. In fact, I'm pretty sure the jumper would fit in that thing."

"We're going to have to take it apart. I'm pretty sure it's designed to come apart in pieces. Maybe not exactly easy pieces to get up the stairs, but that's what we have you and Ronon for, right?"

"Those pieces are the size of refrigerators," John said.

"Hey, it's not my fault that the Asgard probably beamed it down here."

"You're going to help carry it."

"I'd like to finish documenting the find before you take the whole thing apart and start experimenting on it," Daniel said.

"Finish up," John said. "I'll go get the jumper. At least we can park it close enough that we don't have to hike."

Rodney looked at Daniel as Sheppard's footsteps receded upstairs. "Not going to argue that he shouldn't land the jumper on the archaeological site?"

"I think the huge brush fire probably killed any chances of finding something just lying around on the surface," Daniel said. He sat on his heels to investigate another panel covered in Asgard writing.

It grated on Rodney's nerves. "You know, the brush fire wasn't our fault. Blame that on the terrifying bird creatures that tried to set us on fire so they could roast us and eat us."

Daniel looked up at him over the rim of his glasses. "Did I say that the brush fire was your fault?"

"No, of course you didn't say that." He examined the machinery, trying to identify a chunk of it that would be reasonably practical to remove. It was possible that they were going to have to leave the biggest pieces of the machinery in place, but the idea of not being able to study them without returning to a remote site full of homicidal ostriches who set things on fire was unattractive.

"I have to ask. What is your actual problem with me?" Daniel asked conversationally after a while.

"I don't know what you're talking about."

"Yeah. Is it just… see, I don't even actually know. Because being professionally jealous of me —"

"I am not professionally *jealous* of you."

"See, I know you're not, because what I do is so completely unrelated to what you do that it would be like me being jealous of Ronon. It's not like you want to be the world's best archaeologist."

"Please, archaeology isn't even a real science."

"I'm not even touching that one right now. You're not still bitter about the time Sam got you sent to Siberia, are you? Because that was her, you know — well, her and General Hammond — not me."

"I'm not still bitter. I was never bitter, it was a very productive opportunity to learn about naquadah power systems."

"I just thought that since you don't like the cold… "

"And Sam has really come to appreciate me. You know, after her initial desperate crush turned into a more collegial respect."

"Right."

Rodney could hear the skepticism in his voice, and he didn't think it was just for the idea that Sam was pining after Rodney. It stung unreasonably much. He'd put a lot of distance and time between him and the guy he'd been before he went to Atlantis. He understood all too well why people hadn't liked that guy, but he'd also put distance and time between himself and most of the people who'd only ever known that guy.

"Let's just figure out the best way to take this thing apart," he said.

Daniel shook his head. "Fine, let's do that."

INTERLUDE

"COME IN, Ms. Weir."

Elizabeth took a deep breath and pushed open the door of the senator's office in the Dirksen Building. It was very seventies, with orange carpet and bucket chairs, which seemed behind the times in this brave new world. The Cold War was over and even the New York Times had proclaimed the End of History.

But for her it was a beginning, a highly competitive internship on the Hill with the Chairman of the Senate Armed Services Committee. In the first ten weeks she'd done the usual things — answering the phone when irate constituents called, stuffing envelopes, printing name tags for various events. She'd gone to committee hearings, standing among the other young people in their black suits listening to testimony which, for the most part, was unenlightening. She'd eaten in the Senate cafeteria and once she'd seen Senator Kennedy looking just like he did on TV. Oh, and she'd checked in Tipper Gore at a luncheon and had refrained from saying a word about rock music lyrics.

None of these things used her degree, but that wasn't to be expected at this point. And then she'd been asked to write this white paper — an actual white paper to be read by Senator Nunn about the situation in the Former Yugoslav Republic! She'd put fifty hours into it in four days, and Elizabeth could say with all confidence it was her best work. It was the best thing she'd ever done. Now he wanted to talk to her about it. Her palms were sweating as she opened the office door.

"Come on in, Ms. Weir," he said from behind his desk. He was middle aged, affable, looking more like a high school chemistry teacher than a senator. Mild-mannered, her mother would have said, meaning it as a compliment. He had an aww-shucks Georgia drawl and glasses. He gestured to one of the two visitors chairs, a nightmare in orange Naugahyde that must have been the height of fashion about twenty years ago.

"Senator Nunn. It's a pleasure, sir." She stuck out a hand with what she hoped was moxie and firmness.

He shook it, then sat back down. Her paper was open in front of him. "So how's DC treating you?"

"It's great," Elizabeth said. "I like it very much. But since I went to Georgetown, I already know my way around."

"Of course you do." He glanced down at the typewritten pages. "An excellent school."

"Yes," Elizabeth said. The excellence of Georgetown was a nice, safe subject.

"I'd like to talk to you about this white paper," he said slowly, turning one page. "Your analysis of the situation in Bosnia."

"Yes, senator." She caught herself before she added, that's what it is, yes, you've correctly identified this white paper. That was smart ass. She was smart, not smart ass.

He touched his glasses, peering at the page. "You attribute the situation to militarism."

And now was her chance to score, to make a mark. "Senator, disarmament is the only possible..."

He glanced up, his voice mild. "Ms. Weir, no one is a greater champion of disarmament than I am. In fact, if you're familiar with my record, you know that I am one of the primary designers of the Nunn-Lugar Cooperative Threat Reduction Program to dismantle weapons of mass destruction." He closed the white paper. "And this paper is a load of malarkey. If you're attributing what's going on in the Former Yugoslav Republic to militarism, you are missing about the last thousand years of European history. I suggest you dig a little deeper." He tossed the paper back to her across the desk. "Ever been there? Ever met any Croats or Serbs or Bosnians? Ever read any Serbian poetry, any Croatian novels? Do you have any insights deeper than rehashing previous analysis?"

Elizabeth opened her mouth and then shut it again, her face burning.

"You've done just what they trained you to do in college — dig up some sources and cite them. But this is the real world. Anybody can look up some statistics. The point of writing white papers is to inform — to provide new and insightful synthesis of what's going on. It's a big world, Ms. Weir. I rely on my staff to keep me informed of what's going on all over the world independently of the US military and independent of what the State Department chooses to share *with my committee. And that means actually telling me something I don't know. Tell me why."*

"Why?"

"Tell me why, Ms. Weir. I can read what leaders say in the Washington Post. I want to know why. I want to know who's thinking what, and what the cultural background behind it is. I want to know what buttons we're punching, what narratives we're stepping into, what stories we're playing from their point of view. Do you understand?"

"Yes, senator." And she did. She'd never in her life felt embarrassment so acute, but she knew what he meant. No one had ever asked it of her before. "Everyone has a narrative, a story that says what they think is going on, and that's based on their culture and their heritage."

"And we need to know what it is, and what role we're playing in their story. We already know what role they play in ours." He tapped on the edge of her paper. "You've got a fine mind, Ms. Weir. But I expect people have told you that."

"Yes," she said.

"Have you got a fine heart?"

Elizabeth opened her mouth and shut it again.

"The center of diplomacy is understanding, and understanding is built on compassion. You have to want to get the other guy. You have to put yourself in his shoes, no matter how unpleasant those shoes may be. You have to see where he's coming from. We like to treat politics like it's rational, but it's not. Hell, anyone who's ever worked for a campaign knows it's not! People vote based on how they feel about the candidates and the issues. People go to war over how they feel, not over what's rational. Rational self-interest is all very well, but don't count on it to move things your way. Not when pride is involved. Pride, history, belief, prejudice, hope — those are a lot more powerful than rational self-interest." He nodded down at the paper. "You've got some ideas. But you need more than that. You need to understand the data you're looking at. You need to see what it means. What are you planning to do next year?"

Elizabeth blinked at the abrupt change of topic. "I'm planning to apply for graduate work at Yale," she said.

"Don't." Senator Nunn smiled. "Get out in the field. Go to Bosnia. Go to Somalia. You've got all the academic credentials to come back later, but for now get out there. See what it's really like, what refu-

gees are really like, what war is. You can't campaign for disarma-
ment if you don't know what war is. Get out of the box and have some
experiences. See if your heart is as good as your mind." He pushed
his chair back from his desk. *"This town is full of young people who*
think they know things. Be one who actually does."

Elizabeth blinked awake. She had been nodding in a chair in
the common room, but a jolt had shaken the ship and she started.

"It's nothing," Atelia said from where she stood by the window
with her son. "Just docking. Come and see."

Elizabeth got up and came to the window. She had been dreaming again, of an office and a man. The government of some world?
Of her own world, wherever that might be? In her dream all those
names and places had meant something.

"We've come up next to *Durant*," Atelia explained. "They've just
run the walk across. That bump was the latch on."

Through the window Elizabeth could see another ship alongside
them, larger but equally battered, as though parts of various ships
had been welded together haphazardly into a conglomeration that
should be barely spaceworthy. A long plastic tube, segmented like
a child's toy, extended from a hatch on the other ship's side to some
point on this one further forward, presumably to their own airlock.

"Now we can go back and forth," Atelia said. "Trade goods, trade
people back and forth between ships."

"Is your husband coming aboard?" Elizabeth asked.

Her face fell. "I doubt he's back yet. But they may have some word."
Atelia stepped back. "If you're still looking for a ship that can take
you to a Stargate quickly, I expect *Durant* can. And there's a man
there who may be able to help with your memories."

"A doctor?" Elizabeth asked.

"I suppose you'd say so," Atelia said grimly. "I'm not sure we'd
have called him a doctor on Sateda, but he's the best we have."

"Then I'll be glad to talk to him," Elizabeth said. "Anything to
help me remember."

Crossing from one Traveler ship to another was a nerve wracking
experience. Elizabeth did not consider herself especially fearful, but

crossing through the plastic tubes was frightening. It wasn't that it was confining. Yes, the tubes were less than her height in diameter and there was no gravity, meaning she had to swim through, using the ribbing of the walls to propel herself forward. It wasn't that. It was that the plastic was clear.

It was like being in space, in free fall without a space suit.

For some reason that was the most utterly terrifying thing Elizabeth could imagine. She had to halt just outside the airlock for a long moment, her heart pounding. Crossing twenty feet of plastic tube seemed impossible.

Meanwhile, others passed her going in either direction, some of them trundling bulky packs of goods that weighed nothing in zero G.

Why was this so frightening? There was plenty of air. She could see people going to and fro breathing normally. No one even seemed stressed. This was no more extraordinary to the Travelers than… Than what? Than she would find it to cross a room? For a moment something else had presented itself, stepping into a tiny claustrophobic room without windows that took you very quickly between floors. Many people found that mode of transportation unnerving. Many aliens.

On Sateda? That didn't seem right.

The intellectual puzzle was distracting. It had given her a moment to catch her breath. She could do this. She could cross twenty feet of space in a plastic tube. It didn't feel like the worst thing she'd ever done. The key was not to look. Someone had told her that once. Don't look. Just focus on the back of the person ahead of you.

A man brushed past her, an orange cloth duffel bag bulging at the seams as he dragged it behind him on its strap. Look at him. Look at the bag. Don't look at the walls, the floor, the ceiling, the distant stars. She pushed off from the airlock following him. Watch the bag. Watch the man's back.

A woman passed her going the other way. She was in the middle now. Keep watching the bag. The man had reached the far airlock, stopped and pulled it inside with him. He turned and waited for her, a friendly smile on his bearded face. Watch the man.

He reached out a hand and drew her the last few feet inside the dark aperture. "Here you go. Zero gravity takes some getting used to."

"Thanks," Elizabeth said. The airlock was small, the inner doors sealed. They waited until another person going their way came in. Then the man glanced down the tube to see if anyone else was coming. Elizabeth didn't look that way. She studied the door panel.

"All clear," he said cheerfully and reached past her to tap a yellow button.

"Doors closing," a tinny voice announced, and the outer doors slowly slid shut. Elizabeth hoped she didn't sigh with relief when she could no longer see the tube. "Airlock cycling," the voice said.

"It does that just to be careful," the man said. "There's air all the way across but the ship has to equalize pressure as a matter of course." He looked at her carefully. "You new around here?"

"Yes," Elizabeth said firmly, making sure her feet were on the marked floor. "I came aboard at Mazatla."

"Where are you from?"

"Sateda," Elizabeth said. "I was told you have a doctor aboard?"

"That would be Dekaas," the man said. "And I'm Idrim Tollard. Nice to meet you."

"You too," Elizabeth said.

"You can find him aft in the emergency ward, most likely," Idrim said. "Follow the green signs. Green for health. You label that way on Sateda?"

"I don't remember," Elizabeth said.

"Door opening," the tinny voice said, and the inner doors slid open into the corridor of a much larger ship. Two people with packages were waiting on the other side.

Idrim hauled his now-heavy bag inside. "Good luck to you," he said.

"Thank you." The green sign was on the opposite wall amid others, pointing down the hall to her left. She followed it down the long corridor, then right into a cross corridor that was broad enough for someone to pass with a gurney. Ahead there was a bulkhead door labeled with a large green dot, but it opened when she approached, sliding back into the wall jerkily. The owners of this ship had automatic doors, but they didn't entirely work, an interesting thing to note.

The chamber beyond was brightly lit for a Traveler ship, the walls painted white to make it even lighter. There were three beds, all empty. Beside one of them a crewman was talking to an older man, his arm in a sling. The gray haired man put a small bottle into his free hand. "Take one of these every six hours to help with the swelling. It won't do a lot for the pain, but it will bring the inflammation down and help some. The main thing is to not use that arm as much as possible."

"I'll do that," the patient said. "Thanks, doc."

"Come back day after tomorrow if we're still here," the doctor said, and turned to glance at Elizabeth. "What brings you here?" he asked easily. "Have a seat and tell me about it." He gestured to two metal chairs by a table. "I don't believe we've met before."

"My name is Elizabeth," she said, and sat down. There was something about him that was reassuring, though he wore no white coat — whatever that was supposed to mean? He was sixty or so, clean shaven, with salt and pepper hair gone more white than dark, broad shoulders and a face that would have been exceptionally handsome in youth. He wore a brown tunic closed tight at the throat, and his expression was friendly. "I came aboard at Mazatla, and I was hoping you could help me."

The doctor watched the man with his arm in a sling leave. "Tell me about it. My name is Dekaas, by the way."

"It's good to meet you, doctor," she said politely.

He laughed. "Only by experience, not training. But I've had quite a lot of experience in my years."

There was something about him that set her at ease, Elizabeth thought. Experience, yes. And experience of human nature.

"So what's bothering you?"

"I've lost my memory." Said like that it seemed crazy, but he only put his head to the side thoughtfully.

"All at once, or gradually over a period of time?"

"All at once, I think. I don't really know." Elizabeth shook her head. "The Mazatla found me lying in a field. I don't remember anything before that. They thought I might have been attacked by criminals and left for dead, only I didn't seem to have any injuries. I'm not Mazatla. The things that seem familiar — devices, technology — suggested to them that I'm Satedan. But I don't remember Sateda or anything about it."

"So you do remember things." His blue eyes were keen.

"A few things. Scenes." Elizabeth hunted for the words. "Scattered memories. My parents, people I knew a long time ago. Nothing recent. Nothing since I was a young woman."

"And are you old now?" Dekaas asked. "It seems to me that you aren't so old. Mature, maybe. Not a young girl. But certainly not old."

"I don't know how old I am," Elizabeth said. For some reason she thought she must appear younger than her actual age, or at least younger by several years than the span of her actual life. "Can't you tell medically?"

"I could make a good guess if your life span has not been altered," Dekaas said.

Elizabeth frowned. "How could that happen?"

"Any number of things." Dekaas looked away, picking up a small notebook bound at the top of the page from the workbench, and a pen with it. "The Wraith."

"Wouldn't the Wraith have aged me?" She had heard that somewhere, knew it.

"Possibly. It's also possible they would have extended your life." Dekaas frowned thoughtfully. "But I've never heard of that erasing memory. Though I suppose the trauma…"

"How could they do that?" Elizabeth asked. Surely this was a secret, uncommon knowledge.

"It's a gift reserved for favorite worshippers," Dekaas said. "Or extraordinary circumstances. I can see that you might have been restored to life from near death, and that perhaps the trauma caused you to forget."

"But why would I have been left on Mazatla?" she asked. "Why wouldn't the Wraith have killed me or at least kept me prisoner?"

Dekaas took a deep breath. "There have been many upheavals among the Wraith recently. Queen Death — I suppose you've heard of her?"

"A man said she was dead."

He nodded. "She built a grand alliance. And then she was killed by the Genii, or so they say. By the Genii, or some other alliance of hives against her. In any event, there was war between various hives. And sometimes…" He stopped, and for a moment his gaze faltered. "Sometimes when a hive is hard-pressed they will release their worshippers onto a nearby planet."

"Why would they do that?" Elizabeth asked.

He shrugged elaborately, going to fetch another notebook from a different table. "If your house was on fire, would you let the dog out?"

"Of course." A thought came to her, a flash of insight born of his evading eyes, his tunic buttoned up to the throat so that no hint of chest showed. "You were one, weren't you? A worshipper who was released?"

He took a deep breath, turning back to her slowly, though the infirmary was empty except for them, the doors closed. "Yes. But it's not something to speak of. There are those who will kill a former worshipper on sight. Or worse."

"Worse?"

"Hunters want information, and if it is not given freely they will take it." Dekaas shrugged. "Even if that information is decades old and of no use to anyone."

"Hunters."

"There are those who hunt the Wraith, Hunters rather than prey. Some people greatly revere them. Others dread their coming, for fear that they will bring the Wraith in pursuit where they go." Dekaas walked restlessly about the room. "One famous Hunter makes his home aboard the ship that brought you, as much as any Hunter can. It's said that the Wolf and two companions destroyed an entire hive ship once." He shrugged. "I don't know if it's true. Only that it's said."

"Atelia's husband," Elizabeth said.

"Just so."

"And he would harm you?"

"I don't plan to find out," Dekaas said. There was a quirk of humor at the corner of his mouth. "So kindly do not repeat this to Atelia. And certainly do not repeat it if you think that you might have also been a worshipper much more recently."

"I see," she replied.

He looked at her keenly. "You don't seem surprised that the Wraith can heal as well as kill."

"No, I knew a man once…" She stopped.

"A man who…" he prompted.

"It's gone." Elizabeth got to her feet, rubbing her hands on her shoulders impatiently. "A man who was healed, I think. But I don't remember. I don't remember what it was I was going to say."

"Then perhaps you were a worshipper," he said. "Or lived for a time on a hive. That does happen."

"To be a prisoner of the Wraith?"

"More like a pet." Dekaas shook his head, though he was smiling. "I learned much from my time among the Wraith, and medicine not the least of it."

Elizabeth nodded slowly.

"And if that doesn't disturb you, I suspect that means something," Dekaas said.

"There are many different peoples, and they have different experiences," Elizabeth said. "Even when they've encountered the same cultures. There's more than one story. One nation's heroes are another's devils." She took a deep breath. "Maybe I was aboard a hive. I suppose that's possible. Will you tell me what that's like?"

Dekaas sat down heavily. "As different as there are different hives. We tend to think of the Wraith as all one thing, but there are nine lineages and constantly shifting alliances between hives. Each lineage has its own customs and culture, and those have mingled over the years. My experience may be nothing like yours."

"You learned medicine."

"For more than thirty years I was the assistant of a hive's Master of Sciences Biological, something between a pet and a junior scientist as the years went." Dekaas shook his head. "A doctor, I suppose you'd call him. Or a research biologist. He dug deep into genetics, into biotechnology, right to the edge of the forbidden. It was a hive with a queen who stretched the limits of the possible, a hive that had won renown fighting the Asurans long ago." He glanced at her. "You know the Asurans?"

Elizabeth shook her head, fighting a sudden cold dread that gnawed inside. "No," she said quickly.

"I learned many things from him, and he kept me young. Thirty years passed, and I was still a young man." Dekaas glanced down at his hands, old and wrinkled now. "But it's been twenty years since then, since I was cast adrift."

"What happened?"

He shrugged. "What always does. War. The hive was badly damaged, the Queen dead, and the young queen sent away at the last moment for her safety. The Hivemaster was dead, the ship losing atmosphere. The Master of Sciences Physical was bonding with the ship, trying to keep it alive until we could evacuate. The Consort was with the last Darts, trying to keep a corridor open for the young queen's escape. The Master of Sciences Biological shoved me and two others into an escape pod and launched us toward a planet with a Stargate. That was the last I saw of him." Dekaas looked away, swallowing. "If your house was on fire, wouldn't you let the dog out?" he asked softly.

Elizabeth said nothing, and in a moment he resumed. "After a bit we saw the explosion in the sky and we knew the hive was no more. They all died, unless some of the Darts were retrieved by our enemies. I wouldn't like to imagine their fate if that happened." He fell silent.

"And then?" Elizabeth asked at last.

"We dialed a gate address one of the others knew," he said simply. "And I became a wanderer. The Travelers need my skills, and they don't ask too many questions about where I got them." He gathered himself up, smiling with effort. "There are many wanderers in the galaxy. It's not remarkable. So it's very possible you had a similar experience."

"I wish I knew," Elizabeth said. His story touched her, but only in the way a story of hardship does. It wakened nothing buried.

"You're welcome to stay here for a bit," Dekaas said. "I could use an assistant. You could see if anything comes back to you."

"I was hoping to find my way to Sateda," Elizabeth said. "Others have guessed I might be Satedan."

"As you like," he said. "We're trading on Dhalo next. There's a Stargate there. If you come to Dhalo with us, you can dial out to Sateda or wherever you want when we get there."

"That sounds fair," Elizabeth said. "And of course I'll pay for my passage by helping you if I'm able."

"I can always use a pair of agile hands," Dekaas said. "Then let's call it a deal."

CHAPTER FIVE

WHEN JOHN returned with the jumper, he hoped they could make a swift retreat, but Rodney insisted they manhandle part of the climate control device into the jumper. "They" ended up being John and Ronon, wrestling a refrigerator-sized hunk of metal up the stairs while Rodney snapped instructions and Ronon threatened to drop it on Rodney's foot on purpose. It barely fit up the stairs and then barely fit through the door of the jumper, and the jumper protested its weight when they launched, but at least they were finally on their way.

"And then we're going to go back for the rest of it, right?" Rodney said, bracing himself in the limited room left in the cargo compartment with a proprietary hand on his piece of Asgard equipment. Taking it apart was probably his idea of fun. Returning to get the rest of the pieces so that Rodney could take it apart did not sound like John's idea of fun.

"Or something," John said. Ferrying pieces of machinery back and forth sounded like a prime job for someone else.

He ended off passing the job on to Lorne, who didn't look thrilled but duly promised to round up a team to go disassemble the thing. "You're sure this thing is safe?" he asked on his way out.

"McKay says don't press any buttons."

"We know not to press buttons," Lorne said, not sounding comforted.

John shrugged. "As safe as anything else. Watch out for the big ostrich guys with spears and nets. They seemed to think we'd be good with ketchup."

"Will do," Lorne said resignedly.

Woolsey regarded the team across the conference table the next morning, cradling the cup of coffee that was all that made dealing with enthusiastic scientists bearable before noon.

"We need to look for another Asgard installation," Rodney said.

"You have a weather machine to play with," John said.

"Climate control device. Or… actually, it might be something that could very roughly be described as a 'weather machine,' but it's hard to tell when we're missing anything like a set of instructions."

"I thought it said 'don't press any buttons.'"

Rodney rolled his eyes at him. "Useful instructions. Or would you prefer that I start experimenting by pressing the buttons that say 'don't adjust settings if you don't know what you're doing?'"

"Not on the planet where we currently reside, please," Woolsey said.

"Well, right now it's a moot point, because when we tried to power it up—"

"I thought you said you weren't going to experiment."

"We were going to provide just enough power to get some information about its current settings," Rodney said. "Believe me, despite the attractions of doing something about this planet's wretched weather, we aren't that stupid. My point is, when we powered it up, it burnt out half its systems. Maybe our equipment wasn't compatible, maybe the thing was just old, I don't know, but there's no way to fix it without rebuilding large parts of it. Which is hard to do when we don't know how it works."

"You made us haul that thing home," Ronon said.

"It's still useful," Rodney said. "Just not incredibly useful when all we have is one broken device. I think we should try to find another one."

"I actually agree with Dr. McKay," Daniel said, with an expression that made it clear he felt that was a possible sign of the apocalypse. "This is the first early Asgard settlement site – or maybe it's better described as an observation post – that we've seen in the Pegasus Galaxy. Even though it's not nearly as early as the Ancient sites we were originally looking for, I'm tempted to see if we can find out anything else about what the Pegasus Asgard were up to at this point. I realize it may not have immediate practical applications —"

"I agree with you both," Woolsey said.

Rodney looked up in startlement as if he'd been busy preparing his next argument. "You do?"

He put down his coffee cup reluctantly. "How likely is it that the device you found is capable of having more than an extremely localized effect on climate conditions?"

Daniel and Rodney exchanged glances. "Reasonably likely," Rodney said after a moment. "We know that after the Wraith pushed the Pegasus Asgard back to a single planet, they dealt with some fairly horrible atmospheric conditions. And, no, they couldn't fix it, but whatever equipment they came up with while they were trying could have been based on devices like this. We've examined its power supply, and if it's designed to do something on a local level, it's sure not to heat somebody's house."

"We also know that the Asgard have some ability to intervene to prevent natural disasters," Daniel said. "Mainly from situations where they told us that they wouldn't help, but they did strongly imply that they could have."

"Nice guys," Ronon said.

Daniel shrugged. "They had a treaty with the Goa'uld that allowed them to interfere to help other species in certain situations but not other ones. It was a complicated situation. Maybe a little like the one we've ended up in with the Wraith."

Teyla and Ronon both looked uncomfortable at that. Woolsey was aware that the treaty was still a point of contention between them. Teyla was far more optimistic about its consequences than Ronon was, and while Woolsey agreed with her on the whole, he could also see why Ronon was skeptical. Ronon's personal experiences with the Wraith aside, their own previous attempts to work with the Wraith had produced decidedly mixed results.

"Moving on," John said firmly. "Is this really a priority to follow up?"

"Colonel Sheppard, as you may be aware, living in Atlantis can lead to developing a somewhat skewed view of essential priorities," Woolsey said. "From the point of view of the Atlantis expedition, power sources, weapons, and devices that will improve interstellar travel are fundamental needs. But in terms of solving problems for people back on Earth, a functioning device that would allow us to control weather and climate patterns would be even more important."

"And dangerous," Rodney said. "I have to point out that trying anything like that on Earth would also be extremely dangerous."

John looked at him sideways. "You were the one who wanted

to play with it."

"I want to bring it back here to study, but let's have realistic expectations."

"Noted, Dr. McKay," Woolsey said. "But in the realm of realistic expectations, I am fairly confident that the IOA will consider even a possible solution to Earth's climate problems to be a significant find. And in my position it pays to produce at least occasional results that they actually like."

"Understood," Sheppard said.

"I'm glad to hear it. So, you have my official permission to look for more Asgard technology. Where do you propose to find it?"

Daniel and Rodney exchanged glances again, this time as if each of them were hoping the other had a brilliant solution already prepared. "I want to go through the records of previous offworld exploration by the Atlantis expedition to see if there's any evidence that might point us in the direction of Asgard sites," Daniel said.

"I think we would have noticed if there were Asgard bases on the planets we've been to," Rodney said.

"Some have only been briefly explored," Teyla said.

"Usually for good reason," John pointed out.

She smiled and nodded a little, granting the point. "Even so, Dr. Jackson might discover something we missed. We have mainly been interested in contacting local inhabitants and looking for working Ancient devices, not in searching for extremely old settlement sites that may be buried beneath the ground."

"I was also thinking we could ask our allies if they've seen any artifacts that might possibly be Asgard," Daniel said. "Anything with their writing on it, or anything using some of the distinctive features of their architectural style. I can put together a simple briefing on what to look for."

"Please do, Dr. Jackson," Woolsey said. "We're only in irregular contact with the Travelers and the allied Wraith faction, but we can certainly bring the subject up with the Athosians, the Satedans, and the Genii."

"You might also ask them if they've seen Elizabeth," Rodney said, without looking up from his coffee, as if that were a perfectly reasonable thing to say.

It was very quiet at the conference table for a moment. "We'll check in with our allies," Woolsey said finally. "Let's revisit the Asgard question once we hear what they have to say."

John fell in next to Teyla leaving the staff meeting and she looked at him sideways. His brow was furrowed, and there was tension to his walk. "Is something bothering you?" she asked.

"No. Yes." He stopped, waiting for others to pass them in the hall and continue out of earshot. He was looking at the wall somewhere over her head, but at least he answered. "I wish Rodney would get off this thing about finding Elizabeth."

"You think it is a delusion?"

John nodded. "I think Rodney really wants it to be true. And I get why. He went through some really traumatic stuff. But he's got to pull it together."

"I too dreamed of Elizabeth," Teyla said. "And I believe she meant to help us. That much is real."

He did look at her then. "You think she's out there too?"

Teyla shook her head sadly. "No. I do not think the dead return to us that way. A guardian spirit, yes. But a physical person? I do not think so."

"Maybe I should send Rodney to talk to Dr. Robinson," John said. "Even if she can't help, at least that way we'll have dotted our I's and crossed our T's as far as the SGC is concerned. Weird beliefs about the afterlife don't actually get you canned. But going on and on about it in staff meetings is one of those things."

"Perhaps Dr. Robinson can help," Teyla said. "I have great faith in her."

INTERLUDE

DEKAAS, Elizabeth learned, more or less kept office hours in Durant's infirmary during the first watch, though apparently people felt no compunction about waking him up any other time that they needed him. He had his own cabin, but he gave Elizabeth use of a curtained alcove off the main infirmary. There was a cot there which looked much more comfortable than the bunk Elizabeth had used before. For one thing, it had a clean, neatly folded comforter and a pillow.

"Maybe you can triage actual emergencies from people with headaches," he said with a smile, "and keep me from being fetched during the third watch unless I'm really needed."

"Absolutely," Elizabeth said. She was fairly certain she could tell the difference between an emergency and a headache. "I've done this before, sleeping in the aid center to wake the doctor if there's trouble."

"Oh?" Dekaas' voice was studiously casual. "When?"

Elizabeth started, suddenly aware of what she'd said.

"Don't force it," Dekaas said gently, his eyes on hers. "Don't try to know what it means. Just say whatever comes to mind."

"When I was much younger. A place, a tent..." She could see it for a moment, the inside of a large white tent, flap rolled up to show a track turned to mud by the spring rains, gray clouds and a cool day, the bright green of new growth on the mountains.... "There was a doctor." A man who reminded her of Dekaas, though his accent was different. "A white tent, with a red cross on the roof in case of helicopter strikes."

"Helicopter strikes?" Dekaas prompted quietly.

"They had helicopters. They'd already violated the Gorazde Safe Area, but we thought that they wouldn't deliberately hit a Red Cross site."

"Were you a doctor?" he asked in that same, even tone.

"No." Elizabeth was sure of that. "A logistician. To coordinate the food and the refugees. MSF had a full mission on the ground." She said the words even as she wondered what they meant. "There were so many refugees. So many."

She'd never even imagined before what that could mean, children with shrapnel in their bodies, old people walking in the late winter chill with everything they owned on their backs, women clutching their clothes around them and never looking back. Misery upon misery upon misery, until it began to kindle a slow anger in her. She had never understood the desire before, but now she did. Now she understood what she would do with a gun in her hand.

"Rotors," she said. A fear that dropped in her stomach. "The sound of rotors." Pausing at her work, eyes on the ceiling of the tent, looking back down only to realize the girl she'd been talking to, the girl who couldn't have been more than thirteen, had already dived under the metal table. "And then a roar."

"And then?"

"I ran to the door," Elizabeth said. A roar of thunder, a pair of F-16s diving in low, the helicopter gunship aborting its run as the jet wash hit it, the fighters passing one to each side rolling up and away, so low and close that every tent, every bit of loose fabric flapped in their wake. The helicopter pulled up as the F-16s came around again, maintaining a firing lock on the helicopter but not firing, just maintaining lock as it ran flat out. "They were enforcing the no-fly zone," Elizabeth said. "A pair of F-16s from Aviano. I wanted them to fire. I wanted them to fire so badly. Even knowing it was wrong." They hadn't. They dogged the copter, dropping on its tail and then away, until all three were out of sight.

"Darts?" Dekaas asked softly.

"Not Darts. These were human. These were my people. And I'd never until that moment known what that meant. I'd never known that kind of pride. That kind of gratitude." Elizabeth looked for the words. "I wasn't raised rah-rah the flag. We were suspicious of that. It seemed disturbing, frightening, even Fascist. We didn't get teary-eyed about 'our heroes'. That was for people who supported Vietnam. For people who wanted intervention. I'd said we should disband the military. But that moment, that moment in Bosnia, I realized what it was for. Because in a minute, in a few seconds, that helicopter would have opened up just like one had a few days earlier at another site, and I'd have been dead and so would the girl and the doctor and a whole bunch of refugees who had already lost everything they had. And they never fired a single shot. Nobody did."

Elizabeth looked at Dekaas, who was waiting patiently. "Force should be the last resort. But I realized why it existed. I realized why we need to have it, whether we use it or not. And that restraint is far harder than using it."

Dekaas nodded. "I do not know your people, and I have traveled a great deal. I do not know a world where this might have happened."

Elizabeth took a deep breath. The memory was gone, or rather ended. "Neither do I," she said. "But Sateda is where I should begin my search."

Elizabeth slept in the second watch so that she could be awake in the third when Dekaas was off duty. At the beginning of the third watch she got a cup of bitter tea from the ship's galley and settled in to keep office hours. No one came. Apparently the rush of patients had been because of Durant's docking with other Traveler ships which had no doctors, and everyone who had been nursing an illness or injury had already been seen. The entire watch passed without a single person sticking their head into the infirmary. By the time seven hours had passed Elizabeth was more than a little bored. She wondered if she could leave to go back to the galley and seek out a meal, or at least see other people, but decided that the way things worked the moment she did half a dozen patients would show up and wake Dekaas. Instead, she took inventory of the infirmary. She might as well use her time to understand better.

Many of the things seemed familiar, though she couldn't remember where she'd seen each thing. A small refrigerated case held a number of glass vials, each labeled in the same language she'd seen before — insulin, morphine. She touched them carefully. She knew what they were for. She knew exactly. For a moment a man's image floated before her eyes, white coated, dark haired, frowning. But he was dead. She knew that. She'd stood at his memorial service, her hand on the casket that contained his remains...

Elizabeth took a deep breath. There was no more there, just the gaping hole in her memory. She had liked him, called him a friend. She was the one who had recruited him, who had brought him — where? Somewhere dangerous and far from home. And he had been killed. Like so many who had died because of her decisions.

The weight of it bent her head, and Elizabeth closed her eyes over the drawer of tools.

"Wondering what that is?" Dekaas asked. She had not heard him come in.

Elizabeth glanced down at the strange instrument in the drawer. It looked like the handle of something, at first appearing to be made of dark wood, but it hummed faintly with its own power source. The grip had a sliding knob on it, and where a tool or blade might go at the narrow end was a small aperture. "Yes," Elizabeth said.

"It's a Wraith screwdriver." Dekaas smiled as he came over and picked it up. "They use it for mending small tears in the hive's systems, grafting bioelectrical conducts together. I use it," he thumbed the knob, and a blue electric glow began at the aperture, "for mending flesh. It can repair small tears in tendons better than sutures, and it can even repair some severed nerves. It's valuable for those kinds of injuries, ones that aren't life threatening or involve a lot of blood loss, but that can leave someone without the full use of a limb." He turned it off again. "A screwdriver."

Elizabeth nodded approvingly. "That's very clever."

"They have some useful things," Dekaas said.

"I thought humans didn't use Wraith things."

"Most don't." He put it back in the drawer and closed it. "But the Travelers do. The Wraith are the main spacefarers in this galaxy. The Travelers can't afford to scorn Wraith technology when it comes their way."

"The main spacefarers?" Elizabeth asked, a prickle running down her spine.

"There are some others." Dekaas sat down on one of the metal chairs. "The Travelers. The Lanteans. The Ka-Ni. The Asgard."

"The Asgard." Elizabeth frowned. That should be important. It should be. Only no pictures came to accompany the name.

"No one knows where their homeworld is. They show up once in a while on human settled worlds looking for stuff. If you leave them alone, they leave you alone."

"Stuff?" Elizabeth asked. "What kind of stuff?"

"The same stuff everyone wants. Leftovers from the Ancestors."

Dekaas shrugged. "There isn't a lot of that, let me tell you. Anything good that isn't impossible to reach has been plundered a hundred times by humans and Wraith alike. How the Genii got their hands on an Ancient warship I can't imagine."

"The Genii have an Ancient warship?" And that seemed critical, tremendously important for reasons she couldn't name.

"That's what they say," Dekaas said easily. "Me, I haven't seen it myself, so I'm only willing to put so much stock in it. The Genii want to be taken as the leaders of humanity. They'd like everyone to think they have an Ancient warship and defeated Queen Death. Personally, I'm guessing that's exaggerated. But it's certainly true that the Lanteans have some Ancient tech. One of our captains has done some trading with them." He nodded toward the refrigerated case. "That's where we got some of those drugs."

"The insulin," Elizabeth said. "That has to be kept refrigerated. It had to be traded for."

Dekaas got up and opened the case, pulling out one of the vials and handing it to her. "Read me the label."

Mystified, Elizabeth did. "Morphine sulfate injection USP. Preservative free. Warning: may be habit forming. This solution contains no antioxidant, bacteriostat or antimicrobial agent and is intended as a single dose injection to provide analgesia via the intravenous, epidural, or intrathecal routes."

"You read Lantean," Dekaas said.

"What?"

He took the vial back. "This is labeled in Lantean. I can't read it. Nobody on this ship can read it." He paused. "I know what it's used for because it was explained to me. But these letters — this is Lantean."

"Why in the world would I read Lantean?"

Dekaas put the vial back in the cold box. "That is a very good question," he said.

CHAPTER SIX

TEYLA came to see Daniel that afternoon in his makeshift office, where he had installed his books and computer. There was no shortage of space in Atlantis, which was such a change from Cheyenne Mountain that he had installed himself in a spacious corner room with two glass walls that let the sun stream in. He caught himself actually feeling guilty about the profligate use of space, and deliberately spread his books out a bit more.

Teyla had brought him coffee, which was nice of her even if Atlantis coffee managed to be even worse than Cheyenne Mountain coffee, which he wouldn't have thought possible. He took a sip and tried to avoid grimacing. "I suppose a Starbucks franchise is out of the question," he said.

Teyla looked amused. "It is a frequently made request," she said. "Mr. Woolsey says he has suggested it would improve morale, but he doubts the IOA will see it that way."

"I doubt they will, too," Daniel said. "I don't think the IOA believes in morale. I'm surprised that Woolsey does."

"He has been a good leader for Atlantis," Teyla said.

"I know, I know. People change. Maybe here especially. It's just a little hard for me to remember that."

"Was he so unpleasant when you knew him?"

"He was... determined to do things by the book. Let's put it that way. Maybe that's why Atlantis has been good for him. There's not really a book that covers a lot of the things you see here."

"Mr. Woolsey and I have contacted a number of our allies," Teyla said. From her tone he could tell she wasn't here with wonderful news.

"No luck, I take it."

"We have not heard back from the Travelers yet. Of the rest of our allies, most have heard nothing of the Asgard. It is true that on a few worlds, there were very old legends of mysterious beings that appeared and led humans away, only to return them much later or not at all."

"We have those, too," Daniel said. "Probably because aliens kept showing up and messing around with various human cultures. Between the Asgard, the Ancients, and the Goa'uld, it's a wonder anybody has any remaining doubt about whether people really get kidnapped by aliens, or faeries, or the gods, or whatever they were pretending to be at any given time."

"Most people believe those legends speak of the Ancestors, or that they are merely better ways of explaining what had happened to people who were taken by the Wraith. We have nothing as specific as your people's stories of gray aliens."

"I think our Asgard got careless after a while," Daniel said. "Or figured that gray aliens in spaceships was more believable than gods riding in chariots, or more culturally appropriate, or something. It's hard to be sure why they did what they did, now that Thor isn't around to ask. Not that he was the world's best cultural informant anyway. Heimdall was actually better about answering questions without making cryptic pronouncements."

"They were your friends?"

"Our allies. And friends in a weird kind of way. Thor always got along best with Jack, for whatever reason."

"Is that surprising?"

"Well, Jack always says that he's completely average and uninteresting, but since that's almost entirely untrue, no, it isn't. And apparently his genes are an excellent example of human potential to evolve into a higher form, if you look for that kind of thing. Really I think they just liked each other. I know Jack misses having the Asgard around, although he'd never admit it." He shook his head. "Sometimes I miss them too."

"Was there no way for their species to survive?" Teyla asked.

Daniel shook his head. "They didn't think so. They were suffering from genetic damage caused by repeated cloning over hundreds of generations. In the current generation, it was causing a degenerative illness they couldn't cure. As far as I can tell, they really believed their situation was hopeless. All that they ended up able do was choose how their lives ended and what happened to their technology afterwards."

Teyla shook her head. "I am not sure it is a choice that I can imagine making for myself or my people. Any chance of life seems better than none at all. Even if you can see no solution to a problem, there is always some slim hope."

"I think you're right," Daniel said. He shook his head. "But you were telling us about what you'd heard from our allies. It sounds like basically we struck out."

"Not entirely," Teyla said. "None of our human allies appear to have anything more than old legends to share with us, but we were able to make contact with our allies among the Wraith as well. Queen Alabaster says she may have information of interest to us."

"Okay," Daniel said after a momentary pause. "Tell me how bad an idea that is."

"Alabaster was our ally in the war against Queen Death," Teyla said. "She has been faithful to the treaty we agreed to after the end of that war."

"The treaty that the IOA hasn't actually agreed to yet."

"The Wraith have so far been willing to accept our own provisionary agreement to the treaty, as long as none of our warships venture into their territory."

"Have we actually told them that we don't have any authority to promise that, because Earth's battle cruisers don't actually belong to the Atlantis expedition?"

Teyla put her head to one side. "Do you believe that would be a wise negotiating tactic?"

"No, I'm not arguing with everybody acting like we have a treaty, I'm just trying to figure out where we stand. So, we have a treaty, but actually the only ones on our side who've actually agreed to the treaty are the Atlantis expedition. Our battle cruisers report up the chain of the command, which means in practice they report to Jack, who's not going to break the treaty unless he has a good reason to. And the Wraith say they're keeping the treaty, but actually we don't really know what they're doing."

"We have had some reports that the Wraith have offered the retrovirus on several worlds in their territory," Teyla said. "And there have been no recent reports of cullings on the worlds that they have agreed to leave alone."

"So that's something. What's your feeling about Alabaster?"

"I think she will continue to hold to the treaty at least until she has experimented more widely with the retrovirus. She would like to find a way for the Wraith to feed repeatedly on humans without killing them."

"More immediately, do you think she's really willing to meet with us, or do you think it's some kind of trap?"

"We should be cautious," Teyla said. "But Alabaster is a sensible person. I don't believe either she or Guide would betray us without a good reason."

"That's comforting, I guess. Is Dr. Keller still travelling with their hive?"

"So Alabaster says. It would be good to see her, and to make sure that she is all right."

"You don't have to convince me," Daniel said. "I'm up for meeting with Alabaster if Woolsey will go for it."

"Many people hesitate to meet with the Wraith," Teyla said.

Daniel shrugged. "I've been to a meeting of Goa'uld system lords. That was worse. Besides, I figure it'll be interesting."

"I expect it will," Teyla said.

On his way into the dining hall for lunch, Daniel ran into John dumping his tray on the way out. He could see the rest of John's team still eating. Torren was on Teyla's lap, reaching for French fries off Rodney's plate; Rodney scooted the tray back as an evasive maneuver, with a tolerant smile that seemed entirely uncharacteristic. Ronon took the opportunity to steal a French fry from the other side of Rodney's plate, handing it to Torren, and Teyla shook her head at them both.

"Did Teyla tell you we heard from the Wraith?" John said.

"Yep."

"We're trying to set something up. I take it you want to come with us."

"I'm the archaeologist, so, yes."

"I figured you'd say that. In which case, officially I can't recommend that you get Carson to give you the retrovirus before we go, because it's an untested experimental drug. You only get it if you ask for it personally and then sign a stack of waivers saying that it's probably a bad idea and also not guaranteed to work."

"But... "

"But we're going to visit the Wraith, so think about it. Personally anything that makes it less likely that I'm going to die like that makes me feel better."

"Your team has taken the drug?"

"Me and Teyla," John said. "Rodney was thinking about it, but Carson said no, he's not doing anything to mess with Rodney's genes now that he's got him back to normal again. More or less normal."

"I'll talk to Beckett about it," Daniel said. "But I'm basically in favor of not dying, given a choice."

John glanced back at the table, where Torren was now clambering over Ronon's shoulder. "Some people would say it's preferable to the alternative. If you've taken the drug and someone sticks you in a feeding cell, you're going to be there for a long time."

"I'd rather have the chance," Daniel said immediately. "There's always some way out."

John shrugged, unsmiling. "Then talk to Carson," he said.

INTERLUDE

THE TRAVELER ship *Durant* made planetfall on Dhalo at mid-morning local time, though a thick cloud layer covered the landing site until the last moment. Elizabeth assumed they were landing based on instrument readings, since from the windows of the dining room she could see nothing but gray clouds.

Suddenly the clouds thinned, Durant making a wide circle toward their landing point. Beneath was a land of dark green and brown, heavy vegetation along a wide, placid river in the rain. Huge, twisted trees spread massive leaves to the sky, and the ship's course led it over a town partially built out over the river, small boats moored at fragile-looking long docks, while the shore was built up with buildings in white and red, a few on the highest ground of stone with elaborate carvings. It was strange and beautiful and fascinating.

Ahead there was a cleared field marked out in banners like yellow windsocks, and *Durant* settled onto it, sinking heavily into the soggy ground. A rainy season, Elizabeth wondered. Or just a particularly wet day?

The *Durant's* lower hatch opened. Across the field there were figures moving in the heavy rain, a welcome party or a trader party. The comm unit crackled to life. "OK, folks. Going out to get permission to trade. Get your things together if you have independent trades. I'll leave the comm on so you can hear terms."

As they grew closer Elizabeth frowned, trying to get a better look through the rain streaked window. There were twenty or thirty men all wearing bright colors, mostly bright pink and red silks that clung to their bodies in the rain, long black hair pulled back from their faces beneath steel caps. Perhaps that was just a ceremonial uniform, but the bows they carried weren't. They stopped in a semicircle three ranks deep facing the ship.

"This does not look good," Elizabeth said to herself.

The captain came down the ramp smiling. "Hi folks! How's everybody doing? Prince Raiuna! How are you?"

The man at the center of the semicircle took a step forward. His silks were soaked with rain, which also dripped off his neatly trimmed black beard. He was tall, and his bow was still slung at his back. He wore what looked like a sword at his belt. "Begone!" he said. "You're not welcome here."

The captain spread open hands. "Why? What in the world? How have I offended you?"

"It is not you who have offended," the Prince said. "But your people. We will not trade with the Travelers again. Go!" He raised his hand and at the same moment all the men around him nocked arrows to their bows, every tip rising to point at the captain's chest.

The captain took a step back, raising his hands over his head. "I don't understand. We've traded here for years. Will you at least tell me what happened?"

"One of your vessels called here and a party of men asked to stay. We saw no reason to gainsay them. We said they might remain as friends and either leave through the Ring of the Ancestors or wait for another of your ships."

"Did they commit some crime?" the captain asked. "If so, you have my deepest apologies. But they were not even from my ship!"

"It was just before the Time of Tribute, when Queen Death's men came to collect our Tribute, ten men and ten women from all of the Cities of Dhalo," the Prince said. "So it has been for many lives of men. Every six years they come and we pay them Tribute, and they go away again for six years."

Elizabeth took a breath.

"The men of your people had no part in the lottery, as they were strangers. The Tribute was chosen properly and the day awaited. When it came, what do you think happened?" The Prince's voice was harsh with anger.

The captain said nothing.

"One of the men was the one you call Wolf. When Queen Death's men arrived they attacked the envoys. All of them were slain. The Wolf and his men danced on their bodies. And then they went away through the gate. Do you suppose all was well?"

Elizabeth could guess what came next, and she put her hand to the window.

"Queen Death's men returned in force, a full hive ship in orbit above our world. And they put this to us — either we would return the tribute hundredfold, or they would take every human being on this planet and level it to the ground." His voice broke, proud as he was. "And so we paid. A thousand men and a thousand women of Dhalo, chosen by lots. Including both of my sons." His face twisted. "There is weeping in every house. There is no man, woman or child who has not lost someone. And it is the fault of the Hunter Wolf who is of your people. Now go! Go and never return!"

The captain backed slowly up the ramp, his face white.

There was a sound behind her, and Elizabeth turned to see Dekaas watching as well. "Tribute," she said.

He nodded. "That's the way it's done on many worlds. A certain number in tribute from time to time, rather than the uncertainty."

"A devil's bargain," Elizabeth said.

Dekaas shook his head. "A lot of things in life are a devil's bargain."

There was the sound of the ramp rising. A new voice came over the comm. "Prepare for lift. We're leaving Dhalo."

Elizabeth looked sideways at Dekaas. "Do you really think there can be peace between humans and the Wraith?"

His face was sober. "I think there must be, or one of the other of us will be driven to extinction."

CHAPTER SEVEN

RODNEY glared at Dr. Eva Robinson across her desk. "You're going to give me a bunch of stuff about stages of grief and giving up and moving on, right?"

Eva looked at him quizzically. "Am I?"

"Isn't that your job?"

"To be truthful, I'm not completely sure what my job is," Eva said. "I actually don't have any idea whether or not it's possible for someone to unascend. So since I don't have any relevant information, there's not much point in me trying to convince you one way or the other."

Rodney blinked. "You're different."

"What, because I don't offer opinions on things I know nothing about?" Eva shifted in her chair as if searching for a more comfortable position. Her leg was finally out of a cast, but she wore a support strapped on over her pants leg, and a cane propped against the corner of the desk.

"You'd be the only one," Rodney said.

"I don't actually know whether or not Dr. Weir could have ascended or unascended," Eva said. "And I'm a cognitive therapist. So let's just look at it this way — what would you do differently if you knew she was indeed alive? What concrete actions would you take?"

"I'd look for her," Rodney said. "I mean, isn't that obvious?"

"Aren't you looking for her?"

"Well, yes, but…"

Eva put her head to the side. "Are there any concrete actions you would do differently? Given that you don't know where she would be, and that Dr. Jackson has already said that his best guess is that she would be somewhere you might normally go, then what would you actually do differently if everyone believed you?"

"Not much." Rodney frowned. "So that's what this is about, right? That I want people to believe me?"

Eva just smiled in that annoying psychologist way.

"Of course I want people to believe me! I don't want my friends to think I'm nuts!"

"So how do you prevent that?"

"Prove I'm right," Rodney said.

"Suppose you can't. Suppose this is unprovable. Suppose there will never be any way to find out if Elizabeth Weir has unascended."

"That's stupid. There's nothing that's unprovable."

"Really? Lots of people have questions that are unprovable. Did he love me? Did I do the right thing? What would have happened if?" Eva said. "You can't know the answers to those things. All you can do is live with the question."

"There's always an answer. You just don't know it." Rodney heard his own voice rising in anger. "There's always someone who knows only they won't tell you."

"Is there?"

"I mean, a stupid question that I don't even care about the answer, some ridiculous question like whether or not Jennifer loved me, she knows the answer and probably you do too, but you won't tell me because of client privilege or something, but it's not like you don't know. You just won't tell me."

"But I don't know," Eva said. "I actually don't have any idea about that either. Just like whether Elizabeth Weir has unascended, I don't have enough information to have a useful opinion." She leaned forward. "There are things in life we will never know the answers to. And there has to be a way of living with that."

"Not for me," Rodney said.

Settling down in his office, John opened up his laptop and began scrolling through his email. Most of the emails were either reports from the military contingent of the expedition, which he filed to deal with later, or citywide emails that informed him of the regularly scheduled movie night, solicited signatures for a petition to convert part of the northeast pier into a hockey and broomball rink now that the weather permitted, and reminded interested persons that Atlantis's knitting circle was open to all comers.

He shook his head at the last – several of the scientists had broken out in amateurish woolen scarves since they'd arrived at their new home, and recently he'd noticed some of the airmen sporting knitted caps when they weren't in uniform. So far the Marines seemed to be resisting, although he suspected that if they had another outbreak of really cold weather, there would be some Marines knitting away before it was over.

The last email was from Sam Carter. He hesitated for a moment before clicking to open it.

Hi John, it read. *I'm not sure I'd say I'm exactly having fun. Actually, we've been having some trouble with the Lucian Alliance lately, but then there's always something. Otherwise we wouldn't need battlecruisers. I hear it's been a little quieter for you guys lately. You'll have to catch me up on the news if I ever get back out there – right now I'm tied down in the Milky Way for the foreseeable future.*

As for what Rodney has to say—actually, I believe him. At least, I believe it's possible that he could have talked to someone who was Ascended. When Daniel was Ascended, he showed up to talk to Teal'c when Teal'c was really badly wounded. Teal'c was sure that it was really Daniel, and Daniel eventually remembered enough about it to confirm that it really was him.

So, yes, it's definitely possible that if Dr. Weir were Ascended, she would show up to try to help her friends. And that's certainly what got Daniel kicked out of his higher plane of existence. He wasn't supposed to interfere to help anybody he knew, but when people he cared about were in trouble, he had to try to help. I'd probably do the same thing, although I don't think I have the right kind of mindset to Ascend in the first place. I've never been very good at meditation or anything like that myself.

What I bet you're wondering right now is whether it's possible for Dr. Weir to have Ascended in the first place, given that she was frozen with no brain activity. And that's where it gets interesting. I don't think it's possible that she could have Ascended on her own. But whatever it is that Ascends – our consciousness, or neural pattern, or however you want to try to put a scientific name on it – exists outside of normal space and linear time. I think it's theoretically possible that another Ascended being could have communicated with Dr. Weir even though at a particular moment in time, her body was frozen with no ability for her neurons to fire.

I don't know if that's what you wanted to hear. It's all a bunch of maybes, and I get the impression you've heard enough of those from Daniel already. But if you want to know if I think it's possible – yes, I do. And I know if there's any chance of finding her, you and your team will do everything you can. Because that's what we do.

Wave at the Pegasus Galaxy for me, will you? I still miss it sometimes.

—Sam

John sat there looking at the email. He wasn't sure what to do about it, or how to even start thinking about it. It had taken him a long time to give up hope for Elizabeth, but he'd finally managed to do it around the time that she'd walked through that gate into empty space. He'd tried hard to reach a place where it wasn't one of the things that featured in his nightmares.

And now he had Rodney and Sam both saying that there was some chance that she might have found a way out, that she might be out there somewhere waiting for them to find her. They were back to the only answer to whether she was alive being "maybe."

He balled his fists. He hated "maybe" as an answer. Especially when it was still possible that the whole thing was a delusion brought on by hypoxia and the trauma of having been forcibly turned into a Wraith and then mostly turned back.

He thought about talking to Dr. Robinson about it, but he figured she wasn't going to tell him whatever Rodney had told her. Instead, he walked down to the infirmary and found Carson preparing a set of syringes.

"Am I interrupting someone's appointment?"

"Actually, these are for Rodney's cat," Carson said. He looked a little sheepish. "Not that I'm really supposed to be practicing veterinary medicine, but that cat's not much more than a kitten, and he still needs his vaccinations. I had the lot sent to me from Earth, but as I'm allergic to the beasties, I've told Rodney he's going to have to handle giving the injections himself. If he were planning to be squeamish about that kind of thing, he shouldn't have signed up to be a cat owner."

"That should be interesting for everyone concerned," John said.

Carson looked amused. "Maybe he can get Ronon to hold Newton for him."

"Maybe he can get Ronon to stun Newton."

"I can't recommend stunning a cat, medically speaking. You might try wrapping him in a towel, assuming that Rodney ropes you into helping."

"I plan to be busy," John said. "Whenever he's planning to do this." He sobered. "Actually, I wanted to talk to you about Rodney."

"Aye, what about him?"

"Has he told you he thinks he saw Elizabeth?"

"Aye, he has," Carson said more slowly. "He wanted to talk to me as a friend, mind you, not in any professional capacity. Or I wouldn't be able to talk to you about it."

"I understand that," John said. "I was just wondering… "

"Whether I think he's completely mad?"

"As a friend," John said. "Not in a professional capacity."

Carson let out a slow breath. "I know how Rodney felt about Elizabeth. How we all did. I can only imagine how everyone must have felt when she died. When you found me in Michael's lab and I heard that she was gone… it was a tremendous blow, I can tell you."

"You think this is just some kind of delayed grief reaction."

"I didn't say that," Carson said. "I think it isn't like Rodney to say such a thing if it didn't happen."

"There was the time in the submerged puddle-jumper."

"There was," Carson agreed. "But afterwards, Rodney knew perfectly well that Colonel Carter hadn't really been in that jumper with him. And the things she told him were really things he was telling himself. He just needed to hear someone else say them at the time." He shook his head. "Rodney's been through a great deal with this business with the Wraith, but he's back in perfect health. And yet he still maintains that he saw Elizabeth, that she tried to help him, and that she told him she was Ascended."

John shook his head. "I thought we knew for sure what had happened to her. It sucked, and we all hated it, but at least we finally knew."

"Aye, that's the hard part around here, isn't it?" Carson said. "After so many close calls and miraculous reappearances – my own included – it's hard to ever be really sure that anyone's gone for good. If I were Dr. Robinson, I expect I'd have my hands full with people saying 'but how can I get any closure when I'm not sure that the person we just had a sad funeral for this week isn't going to turn up as a clone or a robot or an amnesia victim next week'?"

"And what would you tell them?"

"Thankfully, that's not my job," Carson said lightly. "And from where I'm sitting, I think we're blessed with good fortune to have had so many people who we've given up for lost one way or another turn up safe and sound. Or something of the sort. I can't say that Rodney was exactly safe or sound, for instance, but he's back with us, and that's more than any of us thought was likely for a while. I'll deal with any number of complicated feelings if they come from knowing there are reasons to hope."

"Do you really hope we'll find her?"

It took Carson a long time to answer that question. "I do," he said finally. "It doesn't cost me anything to hope, so, yes, I do."

"I don't know about that," John said. He shook his head abruptly. "If Rodney comes in looking for me to help him wrestle with his cat, I was never here."

"Mum's the word," Carson said with a sympathetic smile that might not have been entirely for John's chances of being mauled by a Siamese cat in the near future.

He found Rodney in his lab, and waited until Rodney finished criticizing the way one of the other scientists had graphed some function that might have represented anything from deep-sea temperatures to the city's power consumption curve, for all John knew. "McKay, can I talk to you?"

"I'm a little busy," Rodney said.

"I'll keep it short."

"Sure," Rodney said after a minute. He followed John out into the hall and stood looking at him with a belligerent expression. "I already talked to Dr. Robinson," he said. "So if you're worried that I'll go round the bend and you'll be held responsible for it, you can stop worrying."

"I think you might be right," John said.

"I know I'm right. I just told you, I talked to—"

"I mean, I think you might be right."

Rodney stopped and looked at him for a moment, his defensiveness draining away. "You mean you think I might be right about Elizabeth."

"I'm not saying you are right," John said. "I think the best that we can say at this point is that we don't know. But if there's a chance – any chance – that Elizabeth might be out there, then we have to do whatever we can to find her. And we will." He swallowed hard. "And that's what I wanted to say."

"Thank you," Rodney said after a moment. "What made you decide you believed me, or do I even want to know?"

John shrugged. "I'm not saying I believe you. I'm saying I think you might be right. Sam did say she thought it was theoretically possible."

"Oh, Sam said! Sam said it, and you believe her? You're going to take her professional opinion over mine? I'll have you know that when it comes to theoretical physics, her grasp of what's possible is nothing compared to mine."

"She's agreeing with you, McKay."

"Yes, but you didn't believe it until she said it."

"She's less personally involved."

Rodney shrugged a little awkwardly, not looking at John. "Well," he said. "Elizabeth is our friend."

"She is," John said. He told himself it didn't cost anything to say "is" rather than "was." It almost didn't hurt. "And if there's anything we can do to find her, we'll figure out what that is and we'll do it."

"Yes, we will," Rodney said, his jaw set, and John was reminded for a moment of the aged hologram version of Rodney from the future he'd been trapped in, the one who had waited and worked his entire life for a chance to save the people he cared about from deaths he couldn't and wouldn't accept. And the craziest thing about it was that he'd done it. It had taken his whole life, but he'd saved them in the end.

"But since we don't have any leads right now, we're going to go talk to the Wraith about the Asgard," John said. "Have you got your head on straight enough to do that?"

Rodney nodded. "We'll keep looking. But right now we know where to look to find out something about the Asgard and our weather machine—"

"You said you weren't sure it was a weather machine."

"It's probably a weather machine. I'd be a lot more certain of that if we could find another one."

"So let's go talk to the Wraith," John said.

CHAPTER EIGHT

DANIEL watched as John brought the jumper down through the orbital gate toward the planet hanging round and blue beneath them. Even after all these years in the SGC, there was still something magical about seeing planets from space, something that walking through a Stargate didn't entirely capture.

The jumper began to dive down through the atmosphere, a map scrolling across the heads-up display and showing coastline and a river. The ground rose up beneath them, resolving into the patchwork of fields and coastline that Daniel was more used to seeing from an airplane, and then into a broad river wending its way toward the sea and branching into meandering tributaries. John followed the course of the river, skimming over an expanse of green marshland.

"Alabaster has agreed to meet us at Pilgrim House," Teyla said.

"Where she used to suck life out of her worshippers," Ronon said.

Teyla appeared unruffled. "In exchange for healing those who were sick and dying."

"We're not going to argue about whether that's a good thing or a bad thing right now," John said firmly. "We're just going to have a little chat and try to find out what she and her people know about the Asgard."

John set the jumper down at the edge of the marsh near what appeared to be a fishing village. A couple of small boats bobbed at anchor, and Daniel could see white sails flashing farther out to sea. Birds wheeled in the air and settled to roost on the ledges of sea cliffs above the waves.

"Not in the marsh again," Rodney muttered as John headed for the back hatch.

"Well, they haven't built us a nice, flat, dry landing pad since last time, so, yes."

"I bet the Wraith used transport beams to get down here."

"You mean culling beams," Ronon said.

John had his hand on the hatch controls, but he turned, his face stone. "We are not doing this here," he said. "Anyone who doesn't want to play nice with the Wraith can stay in the jumper. But we are not arguing about the Wraith in front of the Wraith."

"I hear you," Ronon said after a moment.

"Good." John palmed the controls, and the rear hatchway of the jumper opened, squelching as the end of the ramp sank into marsh grass. "Let's go meet the Wraith."

Daniel would have preferred not to have to be introduced to the Wraith wet to the knees and smelling of marsh, but it didn't seem to be a tactful moment to point that out. He stayed close to Teyla, who seemed to have a better knack than John for sticking to mostly dry ground, and tried to step where she stepped. She was using one of her bantos sticks to sound uncertain footing, and he wished he'd had the foresight to bring a stick himself.

"Is this your first time dealing with the Wraith?" Teyla asked.

"Not exactly my first time, no. A few years back my team and I were accidentally transported to an alternate version of Atlantis – it's kind of a long story. While we were stuck in that universe, I was taken prisoner aboard a Wraith hive."

"And lived to tell about it?" Teyla asked. "You are very fortunate."

"I know I am. I think in retrospect that the Wraith who was my main captor was keeping me as ... something between a pet and a biological specimen. He didn't know what to make of humans who didn't already know about the Wraith. It was an interesting experience."

"I am sure it was."

"That was back in the first year of the Atlantis expedition, so we just filed the report and didn't think about it much. But now that I've looked over your records – and seen the Wraith delegation that came to Atlantis when we were fighting Queen Death – it's interesting, because I think one of the Wraith aboard that ship was the same one that you call Guide. Todd."

"Guide," Teyla said. She looked genuinely interested. "Was he the leader of the hive that captured you?"

"I thought Wraith hives always had queens."

"Usually they do. But it is not unheard of for Wraith to live in hives where the queen has died, or where the survivors of defeated hives have gathered together without a queen. It is a precarious existence, but some prefer it to submitting themselves to a strange queen's authority. Guide was in command of one of those hives for several years."

"This one had a Wraith Queen. Believe me, I met her." He remembered all too vividly being the focus of her cool curiosity, her mind pressing heavily on his own. It wasn't an experience he particularly cared to repeat.

"That universe's version of Alabaster, perhaps."

"That will be a little disturbing. I guess we'll see."

They came out of the marsh onto a path that led toward the village. Several girls who were apparently cutting grasses at the edge of the path stopped to stare at them, and the oldest stepped out a little protectively in front of the others, tucking wayward strands of red hair behind her ear.

"We don't mean you any harm," John said, spreading out his hands in reassurance. "We're looking for Pilgrim House."

The girl relaxed a little, although she still eyed their clothing with some suspicion. "I can show you the way to Pilgrim House. I don't know how much room there is left for you, though. Pilgrims have been coming for days and days. You're come awfully late."

"Is it a special celebration?" Daniel asked.

The girl frowned at him. "The Bride is here again," she said, as if that ought to be obvious.

"Our friend has been sick," Teyla said, putting her hand protectively on Daniel's arm as if she didn't trust him not to wander off.

"Oh," the girl said, nodding in sudden tactful understanding. She spoke to Daniel in the carefully loud tones of someone addressing a senile centenarian. "Come with me."

"She's expecting us," John said. "We're friends of… the Bride."

Ronon's shoulders tensed, but he didn't argue.

"I'm sure that's a great honor," the girl said, although she looked as if she didn't really believe him.

"Let's just do this," Ronon said.

"This way," the girl beckoned. The team followed, and the other girls followed as well, now apparently more interested in the odd strangers than they were shy. The path was little more than a beaten track, although here and there unshaped stones had been set to mark its boundaries, probably to prevent travelers from straying into the marsh. "There's a road, you know," the girl said as if following his thought, looking them up and down with the superiority of a teenager who couldn't imagine being silly enough to go wading in the marsh.

"I'm afraid that we strayed from the road," Teyla said.

"It's hard to miss if you watch where you're going."

"You're being rude, Vannie," one of the other girls said. "They're strangers, like. Anyone could fall in the marsh. My little brother falls in up to his armpits all the time. He does it just to vex my mam, I expect."

"Your little brother is five years old," Vannie said.

"Vannic."

"We are grateful for your help in finding our way. We have only been here once before, and are not used to following the path," Teyla said.

"Then how do you know the Bride?"

"That's kind of complicated," John said. "And I'm not sure you'd believe me if I explained."

"Some people said she went away to the stars," Vannie said, in a highly skeptical tone.

"My mam says she did," one of the younger girls said.

"And how would your mam know?"

"Because the Bride said, before she went away. And her handmaiden that came with her this time, she said, too."

"Some people say all kinds of things," Vannie said, shaking her head.

"Anyway, the important thing is that the Bride came back," a third girl said, in the tones of a peacemaker.

"Of course she came back," Vannie said.

"Of course?" Daniel couldn't help asking.

"She's *our* Bride," Vannie said, as if that were something anyone ought to know.

Pilgrim House was a long, low building that looked more than anything like a barn. Smoke rose from a chimney at one end of the stone building, and the broad doors they faced could have admitted a team of oxen. Behind the building, a tent appeared to have been pitched, maybe to house those who wouldn't fit inside.

The long building might have once been a barn, but inside, it was clearly a cross between an inn and an infirmary. People had spread blankets at one end of a long, low room, making little camps around the hearth. Bundles of their possessions lay on the blankets, and several of them were passing around bowls of some kind of stew that was simmering over the fire.

At the other end of the room, the ill and infirm lay on low beds, most with family members sitting nearby to tend them. A girl who couldn't have been more than ten moaned, and her mother stroked her hair to quiet her. Next to her, an old man with swollen joints shifted as if to ease pain, his expression one of resignation rather than alarm. A woman just as old sat by his bedside with a drop spindle, playing out lengths of undyed wool into a lengthening thread and then winding the thread round the spindle with swift, practiced hands.

A bustling woman with a shawl around her shoulders came up to them and looked them over critically. "You're certainly from far away."

"We are here to see the Bride," Teyla said.

The woman snorted. "So is everyone here, young lady. You'll wait your turn like the rest. I don't see any of you dropping dead on the spot."

"That's Mala," Vannie said. "She'll tell you what to do." She and the other girls hovered around the entrance of Pilgrim House as if hoping that something exciting involving the odd strangers would happen now.

"I see you've shown them the way," Mala said. "Not over well, if they've been bathing in the marsh."

"That was before we found them!" Vannie protested indignantly. "We wouldn't let pilgrims fall in the marsh."

"Not on purpose," one of the other girls said.

"I should hope you were old enough to have that much sense. Now, what's become of those reeds you were cutting?"

There was a general shuffling of feet among the girls, and Mala nodded sharply. "Go and get them, then," she said, and waved the girls off. "Now, as to you, let's find you a place where you can rest while you wait your turn." The last was said in an extremely firm tone.

"I think the Bride will want to talk to us," John said. "We're from Atlantis, and she's expecting us."

The woman's expression changed. "More Lanteans. I should have known from the leather you wear. It's true, the Bride told her handmaiden that she would speak with you when you arrived."

"More Lanteans?" Rodney said quickly. "Is there a Lantean with them?"

"The Bride's new handmaiden," Mala said. "She's outside with the Bride and the other holy ones. I'll go and get her."

She wove her way around pilgrims and bundles of possessions, and ducked outside through a side door. A moment later, Jennifer Keller came in through the same door. She smiled when she saw them, her eyes on Rodney's face, and Rodney lit up at the sight of her. They hurried toward each other, and then checked awkwardly at the last minute, as if not sure whether to hug or not.

Jennifer seemed to settle on an awkward sort of hand-patting gesture. Rodney cleared his throat and turned it into an even more awkward handshake. John and Teyla looked at each other in obvious sympathetic embarrassment.

"Hi, Rodney," Jennifer said.

"Hi, Jennifer. Dr. Keller. Jennifer."

"It's good to see you in one piece, Dr. Keller," John said.

"You mean uneaten?" Jennifer said dryly. "I'm fine. Alabaster and her men are outside in the tent they've set up. Every time she comes in here, people swarm around her, and it was getting to be a bit much."

"Can you fill us in before we go out there?" John said.

Jennifer looked around at the limited privacy available, and then drew them over into the least crowded patch of space she could find. One of the local women offered her a cup of tea, which she took with a nod of thanks.

"We're here testing the retrovirus," Jennifer said, cradling the cup of tea between her hands. "This is our second round of tests on this world. There are three other research sites, and we're making repeat visits to each one. Some of the locals have been keeping an eye on the people who took the retrovirus, checking for any sign of side effects."

"Any problems so far?"

"Nothing unexpected. The same temporary illness when the virus is first administered. Most of the reactions have been mild, but we've had a few cases of seizures. Not the kind of side effect that would be acceptable in a drug being tested on Earth."

"You're still doing it, though," Ronon said.

"We're working on altering the retrovirus to reduce the risk of serious side effects. Alabaster's clevermen are spending a lot of time on that problem in the lab. But Alabaster is determined to go ahead with the testing, and it's either help her or go home."

Ronon shook his head. "You think she'd let you go home if you wanted to?"

"I'm not her prisoner," Jennifer said. "And she's pretty determined to maintain good relations with Atlantis, so she's probably not going to kill me even if I told her I wanted to leave. I don't know how long it would take her to actually get around to dropping me off somewhere with a gate, though."

"We have a jumper right here," Rodney said.

"Thank you," Jennifer said. "But I'm doing okay. I'd rather be here where I can see for myself what the retrovirus is doing." She shrugged. "Besides the initial side effects, we haven't been seeing any long-term problems emerging. Nothing like the Hoffan drug. There have been some people who got sick in the weeks after they took the retrovirus, but no more than in the control group of people who didn't get the injection."

"And the retrovirus works?"

"It works," Jennifer said. "At least, so far it does. All the initial experimental subjects survived being fed on with no apparent long-term side effects. That's one thing we're checking for on this visit. Alabaster and her people are also feeding on some of the same people to see if there are any harmful side effects of repeated feeding."

"Are we sure the people are okay with this?" John asked.

"They say they are."

"They think she's a god," Ronon said. "That's not exactly

'informed consent,' right?" Rodney looked at Ronon sideways, and Ronon met his eyes with a little shrug. "Your people say that a lot."

"I've explained what we're doing and why we're doing it as best as I can," Jennifer said. "Believe me, I know this is all ethically questionable. But so is letting people lose years of their lives or die preventable deaths when we can help them."

"Okay," John said, looking around at his team as if to forestall further discussion. "Dr. Keller is going to go on doing what she's doing. That's not actually up for debate, because it's not actually our mission or our call. We're going to go talk to Alabaster about the Asgard."

"I'll take you to her," Jennifer said.

They followed Jennifer out the side door of the building into a tent, its woolen flaps lowered despite the warmth of the day. It was dim inside, and Daniel blinked to accustom himself to the light.

"I'll let you talk," Jennifer said, and ducked back through the door into Pilgrim House. Daniel turned, and got his first good look at the Wraith they were here to see.

A scarlet-haired Wraith queen was sitting in a woven reed chair across the tent, white-haired males standing by her chair or standing about the tent in attitudes of what Daniel suspected was boredom. One of them he recognized at once, both from photographs and from his sojourn in the alternate universe.

"Hello, Guide," John drawled. "We always love to see you."

"Sheppard." The tall Wraith bared his teeth. Daniel wasn't sure whether to interpret that as a smile or not.

The Wraith queen stood, inclining her head, and both Teyla and Rodney looked up as if she had spoken.

"Hello, Alabaster," John said.

"Welcome," Alabaster said, but addressing Teyla rather than John.

"It is good to see you again," Teyla said, sounding more like she meant it.

The Wraith were a matriarchal society, Daniel remembered from the few cultural notes on the Wraith they'd managed to collect. A few queens ruling over many males, who were themselves divided into castes: warriors, scientists, and the non-sentient drones who served as manual labor and cannon fodder. They had been resistant to attempts to explain that human society wasn't set up the same way; it wasn't clear to Daniel whether they didn't understand, or understood but still couldn't bring themselves to treat human males as equal to females. When they acknowledged that humans were people at all.

"Our test of the retrovirus goes well," Alabaster said. "We have fed on the same humans again, only months after the first experiment. It weakened them, but they will live."

"I'm glad to hear it," John said. Despite the casual words, Daniel wasn't fooled into thinking he was relaxed.

"You'd hate to have to train new pets," Ronon said.

"Ronon," John said firmly.

"I've always thought it was unwise to become too attached to pets," Guide said. "They never live long."

Alabaster looked quellingly at Guide.

"You look very familiar," Daniel said to Guide, because it seemed like they were sliding into a conversational abyss that desperately needed filling. "I wonder if the hive I visited in a parallel universe was a version of yours."

Guide looked at Alabaster. Alabaster put her head to one side and looked at Daniel as if she weren't sure she had understood him correctly. "Tell me about this other universe."

"I'm not sure that's a good idea," John said.

Daniel glanced sideways at him. "How can it hurt anything? We were sent there by accident and we don't know how to get back, so it's not like we're giving away valuable information. And if I understand the theory, there are an infinite number of parallel universes, so basically anything that can possibly happen did happen somewhere. So whatever I say about that universe can't possibly be a surprise."

"You're going to tell them no matter what I say, aren't you?"

Daniel shrugged one shoulder, not feeling the need to answer that question directly. "We accidentally wound up displaced in our quantum state so that we were in an alternate reality," he said. "Do you have any idea what I'm talking about?"

"I have heard of such things," Alabaster said.

"Okay, good. I can't tell you how it worked — well, I wouldn't tell you how it worked if I could, but I also genuinely don't understand how it worked. I'm not that kind of scientist. Anyway, in the other reality, the Atlantis mission wasn't doing so well—"

"How unfortunate," Guide said mildly.

"—and I was taken captive by a Wraith hive. You were one of the ship's officers, I think," he said to Guide. "But the queen wasn't Alabaster. She looked a lot like her, but... older, I think. It wasn't the same person."

"So you have met another Osprey queen," Alabaster said. He wasn't sure what to make of her tone. "There are few of that line left. I suppose she did not favor you with her name?"

"No. I don't think she was used to having long conversations with her human prisoners, frankly. The only Wraith who actually introduced himself to me was called Seeker." He could see both Guide and Alabaster react, although he wasn't certain why. It pricked his curiosity. "You know that name."

"He was one of the lords of my mother's zenana," Alabaster said after a moment. "Her Master of Sciences Biological."

"He kept pets," Guide said. "I always told him that one of them would stab him in his sleep someday." He sounded more nostalgic than annoyed.

"Perhaps one might have, had he lived so long," Alabaster said. "He was killed when my mother's hive was destroyed by her rivals. I escaped, only to be trapped on this planet without a gate for many years." She raised her chin to look at Guide, who bent his head at her expression. "Besides my son, my human 'pets' were my only company."

"There was a younger queen aboard the hive, but I don't think that she was you," Daniel said.

Alabaster shrugged. She circled him as she spoke; it might have been only an unconsciously threatening gesture, but it made him glad he had submitted to the retrovirus injection and endured an uncomfortable afternoon's illness as a result. "Perhaps a sister. Or perhaps in a different universe, my mother had different priorities about what sort of daughter to give to our lineage. We do not leave breeding as much to chance as humans do. "

"How exactly... " Daniel began, and then noticed John's look of impatience. "That's probably not important right now. I'd be very interested in talking to you at some point about Wraith society, though."

"Your new cleverman is curious," Alabaster said to Teyla.

"He is visiting from our home world," Teyla said.

Alabaster looked him up and down. "A pallax of She Who Carries Many Things?"

"Daniel Jackson is a colleague of Colonel Carter," Teyla said. Daniel wasn't sure if that constituted agreement with Alabaster or not.

"Her consort's son," Alabaster said, as if putting pieces together. She nodded slightly more respectfully to Daniel.

It took him a moment to put that one together himself. "Oh, no," he said. "No, no. That's not — Jack is actually a very common name—"

"The Asgard," John said doggedly. "We're here to find out what you know about the Asgard."

"And I wouldn't say that Jack is her—"

"We are very interested in any information you can share," Teyla said smoothly.

Alabaster stopped circling Daniel, to his relief, and settled herself back in her chair. She looked up at them, considering. "My people took little notice of the Vanir — the ones you call the Asgard — when they first appeared in this galaxy. We thought at first they were some misbegotten experiment of the Lanteans. As they did not attack us, we paid them little mind. We had enough trouble with the Lanteans."

"Only then you won the war and the Lanteans abandoned the Pegasus Galaxy," Daniel said.

"And the Vanir began expanding their territory. They began experimenting on humans on worlds that were within our feeding territories. We investigated, and it became clear that we had encountered a new and technologically advanced species."

"More advanced than you," Rodney said.

Alabaster didn't seem to take offense, although Daniel felt that had lacked tact. "In some ways, they were more advanced even than the Lanteans, although their ships proved more fragile than the Lantean vessels. There were clevermen among them who were continuing to improve their technology even as we observed them.

It became clear that we could not risk letting them live."

"Of course not," Ronon said.

Alabaster looked up at him, meeting his eyes calmly. "I might have argued for a different choice, had I lived in those times," she said. "But my people were vulnerable, after our long war with the Lanteans. And the Vanir were not even our distant kin, as the Lanteans were. We did not think of them as people, and they were too dangerous to hunt for food." Alabaster shrugged, as if that led to a foregone conclusion.

"We're looking for any of their early settlement sites," Daniel said. "Places they may have lived before the Wraith pushed them back to the single planet they inhabit now, or where they may have conducted their experiments on humans."

"It was long before my time," Alabaster said, looking up at Guide.

"Not before mine," Guide said. "But Snow's hive never fought the Vanir, or paid them any attention. They did not infest any worlds within our feeding territory."

"You said you knew something about them, though," Daniel said.

"One of my clevermen does," Alabaster says. "He is called Ember, and he was born on a hive that fought against the Vanir long ago. He says he remembers the location of some of their outposts, and may have learned something of their technology from the devices they left behind."

"He's one of Guide's men," John said. "He did some work with Zelenka when we were dealing with Queen Death."

"He is now one of my men," Alabaster said, her tone sharp. "My father does not rule in my hive. Much as I value his counsel."

Daniel couldn't help glancing at Guide to see how he'd taken that; he wasn't sure himself whether it worked out to a compliment or to being put in his place. Guide bared his teeth — was that a smile? — and then sketched an elaborate bow.

"As my queen says."

He was itching to understand the context for that bit of byplay better. Guide was Alabaster's father, which had given him status, and probably the role of supervising her as a child, but as an adult Wraith queen, she was — had to be — in charge. It couldn't be an easy transition, though, under the best of circumstances, and Guide had been in command of his own queenless hive for years.

Alabaster's eyes met Guide's for a moment, and he had the sense of silent communication. He wondered if it amounted to *we are not arguing in front of the humans.*

"Is your cleverman Ember here?" Teyla asked Alabaster. "May we speak to him?"

Alabaster rested her hands on the armrests of the chair, her long claws dark against the woven reeds. "I have not yet heard what you offer in exchange for this information."

"I don't suppose our friendship is enough, here." John said.

Alabaster tilted her head to one side. "Do you threaten that our people will not be friends if we do not share this information with you?"

"We aren't friends now," Ronon said.

"Ronon," John growled.

"What do you want in return for the information?" Teyla asked.

Alabaster leaned back in her chair. "Make me an offer," she said.

"We'd be willing to share the information we learn with you," Daniel said.

"Whoa, wait," John said. "We haven't actually been authorized to do that."

"No one said we couldn't do that."

"We try not to operate on the basis of 'everything that's not expressly forbidden is permitted' around here."

"I don't know, a lot of the time... " Rodney began, and John shot him a sharp look. "Okay, no. We can't just hand over Asgard technology without permission."

"Are you expecting to find examples of their technology?" Alabaster asked with interest.

"Mainly we're hoping to understand more about early Asgard settlement of this galaxy," Daniel said. "Which may or may not include finding any technology they left behind."

"It seems to me that if you will not share your discoveries, we would be making a poor bargain," Alabaster said. "It would be better to send our own men to investigate the sites Ember remembers, if you believe there is useful technology to be found there."

"I am sure we can come to some agreement," Teyla said, looking as if she wished she could hit with a stick the next person on her team who spoke. "We are willing to make the effort to search these sites, with no guarantee that we will find anything of interest. And we will accept any risks involved."

"Like being chased by dinosaurs who set fires," Rodney said.

"They were just big birds," Ronon said.

"The best-preserved sites are likely to be on worlds that are uninhabited by humans," Teyla went on. "We are both aware that those worlds are usually uninhabited for a reason. We are willing to do the work of investigating with all its attendant dangers, and to share any information about the history of the Asgard that we learn with you."

"We are uninterested in the history of these creatures," Alabaster said. "But not entirely uninterested in their technology. We will share our information with you if you are willing to share your discoveries with us."

"We need to talk about this," John said. "Can you give us a few minutes?"

"We are not going anywhere," Alabaster said, leaning back in her chair. She glanced at one of her male attendants, who hurried to bring her a cup of water.

They stepped back into Pilgrim House, where Jennifer was bending over the bed of a man with an injured leg, checking his bandages. She patted his hand reassuringly and spoke quietly to his family before coming over to join them.

"Well?" she said.

"We can't give the Wraith Asgard technology," John said bluntly.

"Oh," Jennifer said. "Yeah, probably not."

"Why not?" Daniel asked. "What we have is a weather machine. Part of a weather machine. And what we're looking for is more climate control technology, right? The Wraith don't live on planets. They need a weather machine like a fish needs a bicycle."

"They could use it to improve their shipboard life support systems."

"Sure, maybe, but under what circumstances is that going to give them a serious tactical advantage, especially if we have the same technology? I'm just saying, this isn't something they're likely to find useful or interesting when they see it."

"And what if we find something else?" Rodney said. He glanced at Jennifer for support, probably unconsciously, and Jennifer nodded.

"Which you might."

Daniel shrugged. "What if they go looking themselves and find something else? I mean, now that we've put the idea in their heads."

"Which was your idea," John pointed out grimly.

"I know. I'm just saying, I think we're all better off if we're the ones who investigate the sites, even if that means sending the Wraith some information about what we find. Because if the Wraith find something interesting on their own, they're not going to come running to share it with us."

John gritted his teeth. "Okay. I see your point. But if we find a cache of Asgard weapons—"

"Doctor Jackson has said that is highly unlikely," Teyla said. She gave them all a pointed look, which Daniel tentatively translated as *let's not plan to double-cross the telepathic aliens in front of the telepathic aliens.*

"It is," Daniel said. "Highly unlikely."

"All right," John said grudgingly. "Let's go make a deal."

Alabaster looked up as they came back into the tent. "Have you consulted with your men to your satisfaction?"

"Indeed I have," Teyla said. "We are willing to share anything we learn from the Asgard sites with you, including information about their technology. That said, as we are the ones investigating the sites, any actual artifacts that we find will of course remain with us."

"You drive a hard bargain," Alabaster said. She glanced up at Guide, who met her eyes for a long moment without speaking aloud. "This is acceptable to us," she said. "I will send Ember with you to show you the location of the worlds he remembers."

"We only need to speak with him," Teyla said.

Alabaster smiled, and he did think that was a smile. She looked like someone enjoying a well-played game of chess. "And yet if none of my men goes with you to the sites, how will I know that you are not holding back information about your best discoveries?"

"Would we do that?" John said.

"We would in your place," Alabaster said. "It would be foolish not to, and surely you do not take me for a fool."

"All right," John said. "He can come back with us to Atlantis. We'll talk to Woolsey about it and see what we can work out."

"And I will instruct Ember that he is not to share information with you unless he is permitted to accompany you to investigate the settlement sites."

"I think we understand each other," John said.

Alabaster looked amused. "So we do." She looked up at Jennifer. "If we are finished with this matter, you may send in the next of the pilgrims."

Jennifer's eyes went to Ronon, who had stiffened visibly at the words. "I don't think you're going to want to see this," she said.

"I don't," Ronon said, and walked out.

"I'm not sure any of us want to see this," John said. "I'll go with Ronon."

"Well, it's my job, so here I am," Jennifer said.

"Actually, I'd like to observe if that's appropriate," Daniel said. "I assume there's some kind of ritual around the process?"

"Perhaps another time," Teyla said, looking at Rodney, whose expression was hard for Daniel to read. "I think it is best if we wait outside."

"As you like," Alabaster said, as the man with the injured leg came in, supported by his wife and a younger man who looked like his son. The two of them began helping him to kneel in front of Alabaster.

"This is Edric," Jennifer said, checking a mark on the younger man's arm circled in black Sharpie. One of the Wraith made notes on a handheld device. "In experimental group two. Retrovirus administered three days ago."

As they went out, the younger man knelt beside his father, and Alabaster stood. Daniel had time to see that her claws were very sharp indeed, and the mouth-like slit on her feeding hand very dark against her pale blue skin, before Teyla drew the door firmly closed between them.

CHAPTER NINE

WHILE THEY waited for Ember to arrive, Rodney took the opportunity to say goodbye to Jennifer. He wasn't sure what there was to say that they hadn't said already when she left Atlantis, but he also couldn't just walk away without a word. The rest of the team were politely pretending to be interested in examining the other end of the long room, with the exception of Ronon, who was still nowhere to be seen.

"You're really all right," Rodney said.

"I'm really all right. Living on a Wraith hive is... interesting."

"I would think disturbing. Maybe bordering on traumatic."

"Well, I've had the retrovirus, so there's that," Jennifer said. "And I stay away from the feeding cells."

The memory was intense and overwhelming: standing in the feeding cells, consumed by hunger, every instinct telling him that the humans hanging there were food. For a moment his feeding hand cramped with hunger, even though when he looked down, his palm was entirely human, the skin unmarked.

"Rodney?" Jennifer said in concern.

"I'm fine."

"I know it's disturbing. Believe me, I'm disturbed. But at least while we're running these trials, every person who's had the retrovirus who gets fed on is one fewer person who gets eaten. And it gives me the opportunity to make a case for having humans aboard under relatively humane conditions."

"Voluntarily, or... "

Jennifer shrugged. "Is Newton in Atlantis voluntarily?"

"Newton is a cat. We couldn't exactly have him sign a consent form."

"The Wraith think we're animals. Because otherwise eating us would be too disturbing for them. The advantage of having worshippers rather than prisoners is that you can train them to do useful things, and if they get out of their cage they won't wreck your house. That's the angle I've got to work with here."

"Some of them know we're not cats."

"And some of us know they're not monsters. But there's an entire galaxy full of Wraith and humans who don't think that way. The thing I can do about it is the thing I'm doing." She shook her head. "Besides, Alabaster really is helping these people."

"Not exactly for altruistic reasons."

"I won't say the Wraith don't get anything out of it. But… " She turned to look at the end of the room where the more seriously ill and injured pilgrims were resting on their beds. "That little girl's leg was caught under an overturned cart. Her ankle is basically crushed. I've given her all the painkillers I can, but even if I tried putting a cast on her ankle, she'd probably never walk normally again. I could take her back to Atlantis, get our best orthopedic surgeons to piece her leg together like a jigsaw puzzle, and hope we're in time to preserve a reasonable amount of function in the joint. Or Alabaster could heal her in five minutes."

"So they need a doctor here."

"They need an entire medical clinic with an electric generator, a stocked pharmacy, and someone to teach surgical techniques. And maybe we can set that up for them eventually. But they don't have it right now. What they have right now is the Bride. Sure, she's not here all the time, but are we?"

She looked over at the elderly man whose wife was still spinning. "That's Garrel. His son was getting ready to take over his fishing boat for him, only then there was a freak storm last year and his son drowned. If I had him back in Atlantis, I could treat his arthritis with painkillers and steroid injections. But that's not going to extend his life by a single minute, or make him able to spend all day working on a fishing boat again. What Alabaster's offering means he can keep working his boat until his grandson's old enough to take over, so that he can feed his family."

She nodded toward a weedy boy in his early teens sitting eating stew. At his side, a middle-aged woman was knitting, her wooden needles flashing as something indeterminate and wooly took shape on her lap. "That's the boy and his mother."

"So which of them… " Rodney couldn't quite finish the sentence.

"The mother," Jennifer said. "I'm trying to keep the trials of the retrovirus limited to adults, even if people here don't entirely understand why I don't consider a thirteen-year-old boy to be a grown man capable of giving informed consent. I'm doing the best I can, here, Rodney. And how hard that makes it to sleep at night is not the important thing right now." Jennifer took a deliberate breath. "So. How is everyone in Atlantis?"

"Fine. You know, the same as usual. I'm sure Carson wishes you were there to help, but he's managing."

"Carson has a lot more patience for being Atlantis's chief medical officer than I ever did," Jennifer said. "I'm sure he'll be fine."

"He is. Fine. We're all fine."

"That's good," Jennifer said. She looked like she was running out of things to say, or at least things that she felt like it was a good idea to say. "How's Newton?"

"He's fine, too," Rodney said. "But he misses you."

"I'm sure Newton will be okay."

Rodney took a deep breath. "Of course he will."

"McKay!" John called from across the room. "Ember's outside. Let's go find Ronon."

Jennifer shook her head. "That should be a fun ride home," she said dryly.

"Tell me about it," Rodney said.

The ride home was tense, but nothing compared to Woolsey's expression when he met them in the jumper bay.

"Would anyone care to explain?" he asked.

Everyone shrugged and looked at John, who squared his shoulders.

"Alabaster's condition for providing us with information was having one of her people accompany us as an observer."

"I see." Woolsey looked as if he were counting to ten, and then tapped his radio on. "Colonel Lorne, please meet me in the gate room with a security team, to escort our Wraith guest to his quarters."

"A security team will not be necessary," Teyla said.

"Yes, it will," Ronon said.

"Colonel Sheppard, I'd like to see you and your team in my office," Woolsey said, and left them standing around the jumper looking like children who'd been called to the principal's office.

"I'll just go and… " Daniel began.

"He means you, too," John said.

Trouble? Ember asked silently. He might have meant the question only for Teyla, but Rodney could hear him, too.

No, Teyla reassured, at the same time that Rodney said, *Maybe.*

Teyla gave Rodney a quelling look, and then spoke aloud. "We'll talk after we have had a chance to debrief."

"Of course," Ember said aloud. *At least you are not throwing me in a cell.*

We would not do that to our guests, Teyla said.

Probably, Rodney said. It was uncomfortably easy to slip back into using Wraith telepathy, and to think of their guest not as "Ember" but as the flavor of banked-fire caution for which any spoken word was an inadequate approximation. He couldn't help wondering if the Wraith still thought of him as the racing, skittering brilliance that had been "Quicksilver."

Ember looked at him with yellow eyes as if he meant to answer, but Rodney deliberately closed his mind; he really didn't want to know.

"Come on, McKay," John said, giving him a push in the direction of the stairs. "Let's go get yelled at."

Woolsey steepled his fingers and looked at them sternly from across his desk. "I would like to know just how you suggest I inform the IOA that we are planning to share Asgard technology with the Wraith."

"Well, that's really a byproduct of the fact that we're cooperating with the Wraith to find Asgard settlement sites," Daniel said. This was an old game, and one that he felt he had mastered. "It's not that we're planning to share the technology, it's just that if we happen to find any technology and we have one of the Wraith with us, of course they'll find out as much as we do about it. Initially. But there's no need to share any further conclusions we come to as we study… whatever it is we find."

"I see no need for that either," Teyla said.

"But we are still cooperating with the Wraith," Woolsey

pointed out. "For a project that, whatever its scientific value, was initially supposed to be an archaeological study of Ancient settlement, and was not supposed to include bringing one of the Wraith to Atlantis."

"It's like you don't want us to do this," John said.

"Right, but the opportunity to cooperate with the Wraith to find Asgard technology — which we've all agreed could be of considerable value to Earth — is really just a byproduct of the strategic reason for bringing one of the Wraith to Atlantis," Daniel said quickly.

"And what would that be?"

"An exchange of hostages. Not that anyone is putting it that way, but they have Dr. Keller aboard one of their ships. We're in a better position to feel confident that she's going to remain unharmed if we have one of their people assisting us in Atlantis."

Woolsey considered him for a long moment. "I always used to hate it when you did this," he said.

Daniel shrugged a little. "I know that."

"All right," Woolsey said finally. "Find out what Ember knows about the Asgard. If you identify a promising site, we will send him along with our team to investigate."

"We should show him the climate control device," Rodney said.

"You mean the weather machine," John said.

"We don't know that it's a weather machine, but, yes."

"I thought you said it was a weather machine."

"I said that our best hypothesis based on our preliminary examination of one piece of broken machinery —"

"Gentlemen," Woolsey broke in. "It's extremely hard for me to justify sharing the one discovery of Asgard technology that we have made entirely on our own with the Wraith."

"You need their help to figure it out?" Ronon asked.

"No, I do not need their help to figure it out," Rodney said indignantly. "I was merely interested in comparing notes with someone who's worked with similar technology in the past. That doesn't mean that I'm dependent on someone else's analysis —"

"I'm glad to hear it," Woolsey said. "Because for now, I'm going to have to say no. Please confine yourselves to finding out what the Wraith know about additional settlement sites."

"Without actually telling Ember what we're looking for," Daniel said.

"I'm sure you can manage that."

Woolsey watched Sheppard's team, plus Dr. Jackson, troop out of his office. Sheppard lagged behind.

"Yes?" Woolsey asked as the door closed.

"I was just wondering," Sheppard said. Worrying, more likely from the expression on his face.

"Wondering what?"

Sheppard sat back down in the visitor chair, leaning back as though he were getting comfortable for a long stay. "There seems to be some tension between you and Jackson. I was wondering why."

Woolsey took a deep breath. "That's a long story." And not one he really wanted to tell, actually. He wasn't proud of his part in it, not anymore. "Let's just say that I had some problems with SG-1 when I worked for the IOA. I don't expect Dr. Jackson has forgotten."

"I wouldn't forget if somebody authorized my execution either," Sheppard said mildly. "That's not how we deal with compromised personnel around here. I'm just having a little trouble squaring that story with how things went down when we got Rodney back."

Woolsey felt his face heat. Of course Sheppard had heard all about it from Carter. Of course. He and Carter were tight, part of the same military fraternity that he was forever excluded from. "The situation was different," he said tightly.

Sheppard crossed his legs, leaning back to see the gateroom floor. The Stargate was dialing, the regularly scheduled communications dump from the SGC most likely, since nobody had called him and clearly an access code had been received. "I'm just wondering what the situation will be if we find Elizabeth. As much of a long shot as that may be."

"Obviously given what happened with McKay…"

"I'm not saying that we shouldn't be careful," Sheppard said. "Hell, given the mess we had with McKay, we've got to be. But I want to know what the parameters are."

"You mean you want to be sure that if we find someone claiming to be Dr. Weir we won't just shoot her," Woolsey said.

"That," Sheppard said.

Woolsey steepled his hands, giving himself time to think. "You think we will find her. After how many years?"

"Jackson was gone a year before SG-1 found him," Sheppard said. "If Elizabeth has ascended, and if the so-called rules are what Jackson says, yes, I think she's out there." His eyes met Woolsey's, clear and absolutely frank. "And if she's out there, we'll find her."

Woolsey took a deep breath. "Then I suppose I'd better start laying the ground work," he said. "We'll need an Alpha Site quarantine. There's no way we can bring her straight back to Atlantis until we've completely ruled out any Replicator involvement. Understood?"

"Understood." Sheppard got to his feet. "Then I'll get Lorne on that. Just in case. He can make that a priority before his next scheduled mission."

"Very good," Woolsey said. He watched Sheppard leave. Two solid years of working together, and he still had no idea what made the man tick.

His laptop chimed softly, letting him know that the email download from the SGC had arrived. One was marked highest priority. He opened that one first and read it with an increasing sense of dread. Then he opened the intercom and called Sheppard back from where he'd been standing in the control room, leaning over Zelenka's shoulder to look at something on his screen. "Colonel Sheppard, can you come back in here a moment?"

Sheppard stuck his head back in. "What's up?"

"Come in and close the door," Woolsey said grimly. He waited until Sheppard had done so and stood with his hands in his pockets. "I've been ordered to report to the SGC tomorrow morning, their time. I'm supposed to leave things 'in good order' with you in charge."

"Not again," Sheppard said.

"I'm afraid so." Woolsey looked away from him, a not entirely unexpected sorrow rising in his chest. "I told you this business with McKay might cost me my job. It looks like it has." He looked up. "I'm not sure I'm coming back this time."

"When they tell you to bring your stuff…"

"Exactly." Woolsey made himself smile, though he suspected it was more of a grimace. "No mention of a review. Just a recall.

That means there's no hearing and no defense. The IOA has made their decision."

"I'm sorry," Sheppard said, and he sounded like he meant it. "I'm really sorry to see you go."

"Well. It's one of those things." Woolsey tried to sound firm and dispassionate, though he didn't at all. "I knew this might happen when we played fast and loose with the Wraith. But that was a risk I was willing to take." He was afraid he was going to say entirely the wrong thing if this conversation continued, something completely unprofessional. "Just wanted to let you know," he said, and stood up. "I'm going to go do some packing now." He pushed past Sheppard and made it into the transport chamber before his expression changed.

Lorne assembled his team in the jumper bay. Sgt. Anthony and PFC Harper were both relatively new to Atlantis, part of the Marine contingent assigned to replace people who'd been transferred out while they were on Earth. They'd spent most of their stay in the Pegasus galaxy so far getting oriented and then immediately facing a Wraith invasion of the city. Pretty much par for the course as far as newcomer orientation went.

The two other Marine privates were even greener, having come out with the latest shipment of supplies on *Daedalus* a couple of weeks ago. They looked like they could barely resist bouncing up and down on their heels at the prospect of actually getting out of the city to explore another world.

"All right," he said. "You've all read the initial survey team's report on M47-533. They say it's suitable for use as an alpha site. I want you to go out there and find out whether that's still true. We all know that there are a million things that a three-hour survey of an entire planet can miss. Let's spend a little more time checking this place out before we set up a lot of tents and equipment there."

"Yes, sir," Anthony said. "How big a base are we talking about? Do we need to be able to evacuate the entire Atlantis expedition there?"

"Not this time. Figure we need room for maybe a dozen people, but they may have to be there for some time. So think about the logistics of that: they'll need food, water, and shelter. As well as not to be eaten by carnivorous beasts, fried by weird radiation, or phased into another plane of existence by glowy rocks. Got it?"

"No glowy rocks," Anthony said. "Yes, sir." He looked like he thought Lorne was joking. Lorne wished he were.

"As you can see from the survey team's report, they found some evidence of previous human activity near the Stargate. Who can tell me what that's likely to look like, based on their report?"

"Some rocks with carvings on them, sir," Harper said promptly.

"That's right," Lorne said. The rest of the team looked relieved. It made him wonder if they'd read the report at all. It was, to be fair, five pages of incredibly dry briefing materials, but the scientists had an alarming way of burying important warnings in the middle of snooze-inducing paragraphs. "So don't put the alpha site down on top of them, or the archaeologists will come yell at us. It doesn't matter if even they think they're boring rocks. They'll still come yell at us, or, more to the point, at me. Which I will not like. Understood?"

"Don't touch glowy rocks," Anthony said. "Don't touch rocks with carvings on them. Got it, sir."

"Then go do it," Lorne said. "And don't be a wiseass."

"Understood, sir," Anthony said.

"So let's talk about Asgard settlement sites," Daniel said. He had volunteered his temporary office as meeting space, and Rodney and Ember were both frowning at a star map display on the screen set into one wall.

He would rather have been talking about the Wraith, he had to admit. They knew so little about the Wraith and their language and social structure, and now he had an opportunity to answer some of the questions no one had apparently even thought to ask. Probably because they were too busy trying not to be turned into breakfast.

But this was the lead he had, and he needed to follow it. Because it would fill in a valuable piece of the story of the exploration of the Pegasus galaxy, and because it might lead them to useful technology. Which ended up driving their exploration every time, no matter how strong a case he made for pure research.

Maybe he should have stuck to looking for evidence of Ancient settlements. It was just hard to ignore the possibility of uncovering an entirely new part of the story. And that was how he'd ended up going down a dozen different avenues in the last few years, the history of the Goa'uld and the Asgard and the Ancients, finding a hundred starting points for a lifetime's worth of work. If only he had a hundred lifetimes.

Ember's hands moved over the computer console, highlighting a series of worlds and displaying their gate addresses.

"All unexplored by us," Rodney said. "And according to the Ancient database... uninteresting. One planet with a small human population, limited by the fact that most of the planet is water."

"Most of our planet is water," Daniel said.

"Most of the planet as in 99% of it," Rodney said. "There's no major land mass, just a lot of small volcanic islands. It hasn't been on our list because we figured the chances of anybody still being alive there were minimal, never mind the chances of their having anything we wanted."

Daniel considered the display. "What about the others?"

"This one was briefly settled and then abandoned because the atmosphere was proving toxic to the crops people were trying to plant, and the native vegetation was toxic to humans. I'm not sure why this one even has a Stargate, since it's covered so deep in ice that the only reason to go there is if you really like skiing."

"What is skiing?" Ember asked, his head to one side.

"It's a winter sport involving wearing curved sticks... " Daniel began.

"It doesn't matter," Rodney interrupted impatiently. "My point is that there's no reason to go there. And the other three don't have Stargates at all."

"Which gives us the best chance of finding unspoiled archaeological sites," Daniel said.

"If you like doing archaeology in a spacesuit. There's no guarantee there's even breathable air there."

"Two of these worlds have human populations," Ember said. "Or did, long ago."

"How do you know?" Rodney asked.

Ember looked at him as if the answer should have been obvious. "They were part of our hive's feeding grounds. We culled both worlds."

"What do you remember about them?"

"What do you expect me to remember?" Ember said, sounding a little frustrated. "It was thousands of years ago, and I never set foot on these worlds. Our clevermen are not part of culling missions. I only remember them at all because some of the blades who went down to the surface brought back interesting artifacts."

"Interesting how?" Rodney asked.

Ember let out a slow breath. "My queen has instructed me not to provide you with information about any technology we possess that you might not."

"And we're not supposed to tell you what we've already found," Daniel said. "Which makes this a lot harder."

"It is understandable if our people do not trust each other," Ember said. "But — a complication, yes." He folded his hands together, considering. Daniel noticed to his interest that there was a chip in the surface of one claw, and that the nail underneath was a far duller color. He wondered if it was some kind of artificial polish, or — "One of our finds was a holographic projector," Ember said abruptly. "Less sophisticated than the devices of the Lanteans, which surely you have had ample opportunity to study."

"So it won't do any harm to tell us about it," Daniel agreed.

"It was a small thing that could be held in the hand. The image it produced was that of one of the creatures you call the Asgard." Ember shrugged. "The device seemed to do nothing else. We assumed it was some kind of... " He sketched with one claw uncertainly in the air, as if trying to find a word for some concept that didn't fit neatly into Wraith. "Decoration," he settled on finally.

And that was interesting, because the Ancient language that the spoken Wraith language had evolved from had certainly had words for "art" and "sculpture" and "portrait." The Wraith had visual decoration — their clothes were heavily ornamented, and at close range showed details that were probably more perceptible to Wraith eyes than human ones. But not representative art. He wondered if that was a cultural taboo, and if so, where it had begun, and when the words had fallen out of their language.

And none of that got them any closer to finding out more about the Asgard. "If there are human populations on worlds the Ancients never settled, it's very likely those are some of the sites where the Asgard were performing experiments on humans," Daniel said.

"Or sites settled by the Travelers," Rodney said.

"Maybe. I don't know how long humans in the Pegasus galaxy have had access to spaceships of their own. The impression I got was that most of the Travelers' technology was scavenged — stuff that the Ancients left behind, or maybe stuff they considered junk. I still think it's our best bet, though."

"Which means we're checking out the worlds about which we know absolutely nothing," Rodney said, frowning.

Daniel shrugged. "What are the odds of it being dinosaurs again?"

"Never say things like that," Rodney said.

INTERLUDE

"IS THIS seat taken?"

Elizabeth looked up from her PDA. Every other table in the airport coffee shop was full, and only a handful of seats remained. A man hovered next to the table, his overcoat over his arm which was burdened with a briefcase, a paper cup of coffee in his other hand.

"No, not at all." Elizabeth rearranged her papers to share half the table, moving her own coffee cup closer, and then bent over her PDA again.

The man sat down and unfolded the Washington Post which he read while he stirred nondairy creamer into his coffee without looking at it. He was thirty-five maybe, good looking in a rugged, dark-haired way, wearing a well-cut conservative suit. Business traveler, she thought. The headline screamed "Will They Impeach?" He was turned at a slight angle, so it was hard to read the article where it dipped below the fold. Something about House sources on the likelihood of a party line vote…

"Here." He handed her the page with a smile. "You can have the first section. I'm done with it."

"Oh." Elizabeth was faintly embarrassed. "I didn't…"

"I'm done with the first page." He picked up the second section. "You shared your table. I'll share my paper." He smiled and unfolded the second section, disappearing behind it.

"Thank you," Elizabeth said. She bent over the first section, reading the article with half her mind. It was unusual to share. It broke the unwritten code. You don't see other people, don't talk to them. Everyone maintains the polite fiction that they aren't in a crowd and that other people aren't tripping over their rolling bags. You don't make eye contact. You certainly don't share your paper as if the person sitting across from you in a Dulles coffee shop was an actual human being. It's impolite.

As if he'd heard her thought, he looked around the edge of the paper and smiled. "Thank you for sharing your table."

"Of course," Elizabeth said.

He disappeared behind the local section again. It was the Virginia edition. He'd probably bought it at the airport.

"You live in NoVa?" she heard herself asking.

He folded the paper down. "Fairfax. You?"

"In the District."

He nodded. Someone stumbled over Elizabeth's roller bag, kicking it and going on without pausing. She pulled it closer under the table. The coffee shop was packed. Through the windows across the concourse she could see the rain-streaked runway. Travelers hurried by with overcoats, not glancing to the left or right. "Messy day," he said.

"Yes." She picked up the first section and disappeared behind it, feeling oddly flustered. The rest of the article about Gingrich, the latest from Ken Starr…

"Have a good trip." He got up, leaving the paper on the table. "Enjoy the paper." He tossed his paper cup in the trashcan and headed off down the concourse.

"Thank you," she said.

Her plane was late boarding, no surprise. She had a window seat on the left side, one seat beside her on the aisle and then the three across of the center section and then the two on the other aisle. Elizabeth had brought the paper with her and read the second section while the rest of the passengers boarded. There was a small commotion in the aisle, and she looked up.

A harried Spanish-speaking woman was remonstrating with the flight attendant. "But I am sure we had two seats together!" She had a little boy about three years old with her. "We have B and C!"

"B is here," the flight attendant said. "C is across the aisle."

"But…"

Elizabeth stood up. "I'll be happy to trade with you," she said in Spanish. "Why don't you take A so that you can sit next to him, and I'll take C?"

"That is so very kind of you!" The woman beamed. "Thank you so much."

"It's no trouble." Elizabeth got up and moved out of her seat, letting the woman help the little boy in and get him settled. She sat down in C. Which didn't have a window, but there probably wouldn't be much to see anyhow.

*"That was kind of you." The passenger in D had come in from
the other side and was in his seat. It was the man from the coffee
shop. "Hello again."*

*"Hello." He seemed almost like an old friend. "So you're going to
Ecuador?"*

*He nodded. He'd taken off his suit jacket and loosened his tie.
"Quito." He'd opened his briefcase and taken out a medical journal.*

"You're a doctor?"

*"A pediatric dentist," he replied, hunting around for the end of his
seat belt. "I'm with Project Toothfairy. Every year I take three weeks'
vacation from my practice and go down to volunteer with a free clinic
in Ecuador." He shrugged. "It's what I can do."*

*"It's an excellent thing to do," Elizabeth said. "Those clinics make
so much difference on a person to person level, changing lives."*

He looked at her keenly. "State department?"

"Amnesty International."

"Ah." He offered his hand. "Simon Wallis."

"Elizabeth Weir."

Elizabeth shook her head, the reverie of memory shredding like
clouds. Out the window of the *Durant's* mess she could see the blue
shifted stars of hyperspace.

Dekaas sat down opposite her. "Thinking?"

"Remembering," Elizabeth said. It was bittersweet.

"Someone you loved?"

"Yes."

Dekaas took a bite of his bowl of warm grains, that same decep-
tively unobtrusive tone in his voice. "What happened to him?"

"I don't remember." She had thought he was dead, but no. That was
a false memory, implanted by... She shivered, her whole body shaking.

"What's wrong?"

"Nothing." There was nothing to be afraid of. Nothing. And
Simon wasn't dead. That memory was false. Though why it being
false was utterly terrifying...

Simon knew she was dead.

That thought came to her suddenly, and though she didn't
know why, tears sprang to her eyes. He would have been told.

Someone — who? Someone would have told him. It would have been someone's job to tell him. To tell him she wasn't coming back.

An older man in a blue suit, colored ribbons on his chest, a man you could scream at in your grief and he would take it, take every hurled accusation and question, a man who knew what it was like to lose someone you loved… "O'Neill," she said.

"That's the name of the one you love?"

"No. O'Neill will have to tell him."

"Tell him what?"

"That I'm dead," Elizabeth said. She looked at Dekaas. "I'm dead. I died nearly three years ago."

Dekaas' voice was calm and kind. "You don't seem to be dead," he said.

"Something happened." Elizabeth put her hands to the opposite shoulders, trying to control her shivering. "My body died." She looked at him, a sudden terror gripping her. "What if I'm not human? What if I'm not really alive?"

Dekaas put his head to the side. "How could that be?"

"What if I'm artificial? A robot? A Replicator?" Her voice shook.

"I can certainly find out if you are or not," Dekaas said. He got to his feet and held out a hand to her deliberately. "Let's go back to the infirmary and run some tests."

"Will that tell you…"

"It will certainly tell me if you're not a biological being. It will certainly tell me if you're a Replicator."

He was humoring her, she thought. Dekaas didn't think for a moment that she was other than human, but he was being kind. Perhaps he was a psychologist as well as doctor, to lay to rest an irrational fear with hard facts. But he was wrong. She wasn't human. It would be better not to know that. It would be better to lie. For her. Not for anyone else.

Elizabeth got to her feet. "Promise me," she said, meeting his eyes firmly. "That if I am a Replicator you will kill me."

Dekaas paused a long moment. Then he took a deep breath. "I promise," he said.

CHAPTER TEN

LORNE strolled out of the Stargate and looked around the barren plateau. "So, this is our potential alpha site. What are we looking at here?"

"Nothing. Nada," Sgt. Anthony said. "The science team's survey report checks out. You got your cactus, your little lizards—"

Lorne squinted at the bushes. "Poisonous lizards?"

"Sir, I have to ask, why does everybody assume they're poisonous lizards? Why is it that when we report that we've seen foot-high cactus, everyone asks 'but does it have poisonous spines that kill you if you touch them'?"

"Actually, those would be venomous lizards," PFC Harper said, tugging at one corner of the tent that she and two of the other Marines were setting up. "Poisonous is when it kills you if you eat them. Venomous is when it kills you if it bites you."

Anthony gave her a suspicious look. "How do you know that?"

"I listened to the briefing when we got here, Sergeant."

"You also probably heard in the briefing when you got here that planets with Stargates that aren't inhabited are usually uninhabited for a reason," Lorne pointed out.

"We're in the middle of a desert," Sgt. Anthony said. "Plus the Stargate is on top of a big shelf of rock, and if you want to go anywhere else, you have to rappel down a cliff and then hike across several more klicks of desert before you get to – wait for it – more desert."

"It can't all be desert," Harper said.

"Actually, it is," Lorne said. "Up near the poles, it's colder desert."

"We took a jumper up and scanned for life signs. We didn't find anything bigger than your shoe. The only sign anyone's ever been here is some carvings in the rocks up here. We took pictures of them for the archaeologists, and we're not going to set up the alpha site on top of them."

"Show me the carvings," Lorne said.

Anthony led him some distance across the rocky tableland to a spot where several large boulders might – or might not – have originally been dragged together into an intentional grouping. Several of them were chiseled with a series of crosses or X's above with what was probably lettering. It wasn't any Pegasus alphabet he recognized, and he'd seen a lot of them by now.

"Anything on the lettering?"

Anthony shrugged. "Not that I've heard. They're going to run it through the computers in case it turns out to be just another phonetic alphabet for writing Ancient."

"All right," Lorne said. He turned around again, looking out at the distant horizon. The only sign of movement from this distance were some large black birds riding the thermals over the desert. "Those birds giving you any trouble?"

"They're just big birds, sir."

"Team Sheppard ran into big birds that set a grass fire and then chased them with nets," Lorne said. "The Pegasus galaxy is like that."

"Noted, sir," Anthony said after a moment. "These birds appear to be… big birds, sir. I think they're hunting some little mouse things. We've seen a couple of those. They were running away. In my professional opinion, not posing an immediate security threat, sir."

"Don't get smart," Lorne said. "Whenever you're sure there aren't any potential security threats on an uninhabited world, it pays to think again." He was beginning to feel like he'd given that same speech so many times he could recite it in his sleep. Each new crop of Marines and airmen thought they knew everything, and some of them would even survive long enough to learn better.

"Sorry, sir. But, seriously, I think this place is deserted because it's too dry to grow crops here, there aren't any animals big enough to be worth hunting, and if there are any valuable natural resources here, they're nowhere within miles of the Stargate. I think this planet is just really boring."

"That's what we like to hear," Lorne said. "All right. Start setting up an alpha site here. Any local water sources?"

"None near enough for us to use. We'll have to bring in water."

"All right, let's get it done. Set up a portable AC unit, too. And keep an eye out for hostile wildlife. Or strange radiation. Or anything that glows. Or anything out of the ordinary at all. Got it?"

"Yes, sir." Anthony slowed down, stopping some distance away from where Harper and the other Marines now had the tent most of the way up. "I hear that Dr. McKay has been telling people that Elizabeth Weir is still alive."

Lorne considered several possible answers to that question, including "None of your business, sergeant," and decided that ducking the question wasn't going to do anything about Atlantis's thriving rumor mill. "That's what I hear," he said.

"So... is he cracking up, or what? I mean, after the Wraith thing... "

"Dr. Beckett and Dr. Keller cleared him to return to duty," Lorne said. "Lots of people around here have been through stuff. I wouldn't go around saying you think one of the senior staff is crazy unless he's talking to the walls or hallucinating Wraith under every rock."

"Understood, sir."

"Besides, maybe he's right."

Anthony looked at him sideways. "You think that's possible?"

Lorne shrugged. "Possible? Sure. Is it likely?" He shook his head slowly. "Dr. Weir was a pretty special lady. She held this expedition together for a whole year when they couldn't get any reinforcements from Earth and had no idea if they were ever going to get home. When she died, that was pretty bad for everybody. When she sort of came back, and then they had to leave her frozen in deep space – that was worse. There are a lot of people on this expedition who still want to believe there's something they can do for her."

"Even if there isn't."

"Probably it's a wild goose chase," Lorne said. "But a few wild goose chases won't kill us. Better than leaving one of our people out there if there's any chance she's alive and we can get her back."

"Copy that, sir."

"Besides, we are in the Pegasus galaxy," Lorne said. "Stranger things have happened."

Ronon stood in the door of Dr. Robinson's office, not sure whether he was supposed to come in without an invitation. "Are you busy?"

"Actually, no," she said, looking surprised but not displeased. "Come in and sit down, please."

He did, settling into her chair and considering how to put his question. He didn't want to insult Eva, who he had decided he liked; for a doctor from Earth, she'd taken surprisingly well to being chased through ice caverns by fanged predators and other risks of living in the Pegasus galaxy. And at least she seemed old enough to be able to give good advice, and had been around military people before. Dr. Heightmeyer had always seemed like she didn't know much about soldiers.

"What exactly is it that you do?" he asked finally. "I mean, what are you supposed to be for? We had doctors on Sateda, but they were just for actual medicine."

Eva looked less offended than he had thought she might be. "You know, a lot of people ask that question," she said. "The way I see it, I'm here to help you understand the way you think and feel, and maybe make some changes to how you think about things so that you can feel better and do your job better."

"Like?"

"Like, sometimes people who've been injured, or who've seen bad things happen in combat spend a lot of time thinking about those things, to the point that it interferes with their daily life. One thing I can do is help people change how they think about those things, and when they think about them, so that they don't cause as many problems for them."

"Everybody here has seen bad things."

"Often that's true," Eva said. "And that can put a strain on a community, but it can also strengthen it when people can help each other to survive and rebuild. I can't fix anybody, but I can help people find ways to help themselves and each other." She looked at him curiously. "Is any of this sounding familiar?"

"Maybe. There were some people in the military — older people who'd seen a lot — who would give you that kind of advice. Told you to ask for leave, or to spend more time doing something that wasn't fighting. That kind of thing."

"And did people listen to them?"

"Sometimes."

"And did it help?"

"Sometimes."

"I'm here if you want to talk," Eva said. "Or if you want advice. I know I can't imagine some of the things you've seen and done. But some of them I can imagine, because I've heard them before. War on Earth isn't always very pretty."

Ronon shrugged. "War isn't. It's just necessary."

"Sometimes it is," Eva agreed. "I wouldn't work for the military if I didn't think that was true." After a minute she added, "So was there something you wanted my advice about?"

"Not today," Ronon said, and Eva shrugged philosophically.

"You know where to find me," she said.

Richard Woolsey worked late on what was probably his last night in Atlantis. After all, they'd said to leave everything in good order. That meant not leaving a bunch of paperwork hanging around for whoever the next person was. For Sheppard, likely. The IOA might spend months arguing over his replacement. In the meantime the work would fall on Sheppard.

The first time he'd stood in this office had been when the Ancients had briefly returned to Atlantis, at least the crew of one ship who had reclaimed their home and turned out the people from Earth like dogs who've overrun a temporarily abandoned building. He'd been one of the dogs. It was a new experience being nothing among people to whom all the accomplishments of his entire civilization were nothing, to whom all the great ideological struggles of Earth's past and present were nothing more than the bickerings of squabbling toddlers. Every consuming problem, every rock-solid identity, whether ethnic, religious or racial, was to them simply foolishness, a bunch of little children arguing over whether it was cooler to wear red sneakers or yellow sneakers.

And yet they'd been killed. The Replicators had exterminated them mercilessly, and they had no idea how to survive that onslaught. Only he and Jack O'Neill had survived. Not that he took any credit for that. O'Neill had saved them both, had held on until Elizabeth Weir had returned with some of her people. Animal smarts had turned out to be the most important thing after all.

Elizabeth Weir. Woolsey shook his head, closing up his laptop carefully. He was not a religious man, and the question of what happened after death was officially not in his job description. All this business of people coming and going from Ascension was — disconcerting. That was the word. Disconcerting. Perhaps Elizabeth Weir was in some sense alive, somewhere, but Dr. McKay's certainty sounded too much like the spiritual epiphanies of so many who have had sudden and life changing trauma. No, the dead were dead, and whatever their fate the dead didn't return to haunt mortals except through their own guilt or love.

But still, there was a point where it was good for people to feel they'd done everything they could. It gave closure. Closure was an important word. It meant an end, a true and final end, the mystery solved and the file sealed. If further fruitless searching, no matter how belatedly, was what his people needed to give them closure, so be it. Eventually they'd come to that conclusion themselves. He'd be long gone by then, one more bureaucrat they used to work for...

Sheppard stuck his head in the door. "Knock, knock."

For a moment Woolsey almost said, "Who's there?" But no. That was inappropriate. "You're working late, Colonel Sheppard," he said instead. It was nearly nine.

"So are you." Sheppard shrugged. "I was wondering if you wanted to go grab a cup of coffee."

For a moment Woolsey started to reflexively refuse, but no. Why not? It was probably his last night in Atlantis. He could have a cup of coffee with Sheppard just like they were friends instead of people who happened to work together. In a little less than ten hours he wouldn't be Sheppard's boss anymore. "Sure," he said.

They made their way down toward the mess hall, the corridors empty of personnel at this time of night. Only the duty crew remained in the gate room. And of course everybody else was off — either enjoying themselves or getting ready to turn in.

"Going to be strange without you around here," Sheppard said.

"You're probably used to it," Woolsey said. "I can't guess how fast they'll send someone out. If you're lucky, they'll give it to Jackson."

Sheppard stopped, looking at him curiously. "Is that an option?"

Woolsey shrugged. "It was last time. But there are IOA members who have doubts about him — serious doubts. They think he's too independent."

"And too much like Carter," Sheppard said shrewdly.

"That too."

The mess hall doors were closed, and Sheppard pushed them open with a sudden grin.

"SURPRISE!"

Woolsey blinked.

The mess hall was full. Almost the whole Atlantis expedition was there and the tables were laid out for a party. On the nearest one was a big sheet cake with giant blue letters on it: We'll Miss You!

Woolsey gulped.

"We wanted to say," Carson Beckett began.

"We wanted to say goodbye," McKay interrupted.

Teyla nudged him in the ribs. "What we wanted to say is thank you. All of us appreciate everything you have done."

"Without you we would not be in Pegasus," Dr. Zelenka said, pushing his glasses back up on his nose. "We would still be on Earth."

"And that would be bad," Ronon said.

"Thank you for giving me a chance," Dr. Robinson said.

"And for not sending me back to Earth when I broke my leg," Major Lorne said.

"We will miss you," Teyla said, and Woolsey was glad that her hug allowed him to hide his face against her shoulder for a moment. Crying would be very inappropriate.

INTERLUDE

ELIZABETH endured all the usual tests, only flinching a little as he put the needle into her arm. She watched the dark blood flow into the syringe, watched as he withdrew it neatly and put the pad of cloth against the tiny hole, the pressure comforting. She held it on as he deftly put a drop of the blood on a slide and bent over a microscope.

Any moment now, he would turn. Any moment now his face would change…

"You're human," Dekaas said, straightening up. "Your blood cells look perfectly normal. The sonic scan of your internal organs looks perfectly normal. Your bones look perfectly normal. I don't see anything that's suggestive of anything else at all."

Elizabeth took a deep, shuddering breath, leaning back against the side of the infirmary bed. Dekaas came and stood beside her, not quite touching, as though he weren't sure whether a comforting arm would be an imposition. "You think I'm crazy," she said.

"I think you've been through a significant trauma," Dekaas said. "Like the Mazatla, I see no sign of recent injury, which does suggest to me that you were healed. Your health is almost too perfect for it to be otherwise."

Elizabeth frowned. "Too perfect?"

"Almost everyone has some minor issues," he replied. "Congestion, bruises, a bad tooth, a sore muscle… To have absolutely nothing wrong with you, not even old bruises or abrasions, is unusual. To me, that suggests Wraith healing." He shrugged. "Or some other kind, but I'm not even sure what that could be. An Ancient device, maybe. I've never seen one that could do that, but I suppose it's possible."

"I suppose." There was some device she'd seen that could do that, but the memory escaped her. Something that was dangerous to use. But it hadn't been used on her. That wasn't what had happened. "O'Neill," she said again. "He would know." He represented something, something powerful in her subconscious. She'd encountered that before, at some time or place she shied away from, some dream that had seemed real.

"O'Neill," Dekaas said experimentally. "I don't know this person you speak of, but perhaps someone does. Is he a relative of yours? A friend?"

"A leader of my people, I think," Elizabeth said slowly. A gate with a turning ring, rather than one that lit. A gate opening in a splash of blue fire... "If I can find O'Neill, I can find my way home."

CHAPTER ELEVEN

GENERAL Jack O'Neill was waiting for Richard Woolsey when he stepped out of the Stargate into the gate room beneath Cheyenne Mountain. He gave him a quick nod through the glass from the control room above as Woolsey made the usual pleasantries to the guards on duty. Even though he'd certainly identified himself before stepping through, there were always precautions.

One young Marine came almost to attention. "Mr. Woolsey, General O'Neill wants to see you immediately, sir."

"Lead the way," Woolsey said. Whatever his neck was on the line about this time, O'Neill would give him the straight scoop. At least he'd know what he needed to prepare a defense for. There did seem to be an unusual number of Marines in the gate room today.

O'Neill was waiting in the conference room above with no sign of General Landry. He was also wearing camouflage instead of his usual pressed blues, a sure sign something was seriously amiss. Woolsey waited until the door shut behind him, then put his laptop case on the table. "We've been attacked?"

"Not here," O'Neill said. "The Lucian Alliance hit one of our outposts a few days ago. But that's not what you're here for."

"I wouldn't think so," Woolsey said. There were a lot of things he might be blamed for, starting with McKay's Wraithification and subsequent de-Wraithification, but a Lucian Alliance attack in the Milky Way was stretching it.

"Roy Martin had a heart attack."

It took Woolsey a moment to change gears. "The US representative to the IOA?" He'd only met Martin a few times, but he'd liked him. "He's dead?"

"Fortunately not," O'Neill said. "But he's had bypass surgery and he's got a long road ahead of him. He's nearly eighty. Anyway, he's tendered his resignation to the President. Says it's time to retire for good."

"That's too bad," Woolsey said. Actually it was worse than bad. Martin had been an unexpected defender of the Atlantis Expedition and of him. If he was out of the picture, things with the IOA were about to get a lot worse. They'd needed him.

O'Neill's brows twitched. "And here I thought you were just one more cutthroat politico."

"He's a good man," Woolsey said. He squared his shoulders. "I take it I'm supposed to explain something or other to the IOA on behalf of Atlantis, and that they've taken advantage of Martin's absence to find fault with something. I don't suppose this can be handled quickly so I can get back to Atlantis."

O'Neill shook his head. "You aren't going back to Atlantis. The President has appointed you to Martin's seat. You're the US representative to the IOA now."

"Damn," said Woolsey, and he meant it.

Rodney piloted the puddle-jumper out of the orbital Stargate, frowning as the sensors began to build a picture of the world that turned beneath. Teyla was in the shotgun seat, with Daniel and Ember behind, Ronon lurking just behind the Wraith. Rodney could feel Ember's wry amusement at that — not an official guard, but more than enough reminder that he was the alien here, the enemy tolerated as temporary ally.

You know, Teyla said mentally so that both he and Ember could hear it, *There are more people who understand mind speech on this mission than those who do not.*

There was a momentary pause, and Rodney felt the Wraith's amusement just as he himself laughed. Right now he was the normal one. And that was different.

"What's funny?" Daniel asked, squinting at the sensor picture.

"Nothing," Rodney said. He turned the jumper slowly onto a search grid.

"So what happens now?" Daniel asked.

"We scan the planet for anything interesting," Rodney said. "Mostly," he glanced at the screen, "It says it's 99% water with a few volcanic islands that rise above sea level. No ice caps. Reasonable atmosphere, but hot."

"How hot?" Teyla asked.

"28 degrees C in the temperate zone below us," he said. Rodney shrugged. "Hot but not horrible."

"So we're scanning for naquadah?" Daniel asked, leaning over the seat.

"Or any other exotic materials. Or buildings. Or humans. No humans so far."

"Those are awfully small landmasses and awfully isolated for humans," Daniel said, his eyes on the map the sensors were building.

Ember also leaned forward. "That is so. But the Ancients liked islands for their experiments."

I know, Teyla said mentally, and then glanced over at him as though she had not meant to speak, a swift, disturbing flash of an island surrounded by icy seas, of a Stargate flaring blue through falling snow — Osprey's memories, her long ago memories of the first Wraith queen who shared her blood. The memory was tinged with fear.

It's OK, Rodney thought. *This isn't that.*

Well I know that, Teyla replied, the warmth of her mental touch like a hand on his arm, appreciation of his friendship and happiness that he had reached out in kindness.

"Ah," Ember said behind, as though he had understood something. "Not so different."

"What?" Daniel asked. "Am I missing something?"

"They're doing that mind thing again," Ronon said. "We're both missing something." He sounded annoyed. "It's rude to have conversations half the team can't hear."

"You're talking telepathically?" Daniel said.

"It's residual Wraith telepathy, OK?" Rodney snapped. "I can hear Teyla and she can hear me. And apparently Ember can hear both of us. I can't help hearing her, so there's no need to be a pill about it."

"I thought you were both just speaking normally," Ember said. "I didn't intend to listen to something private." He sounded abashed as he turned to Teyla. "I apologize. I did not mean to eavesdrop on your conversation with your pallax. Please accept my regret."

"Her what?" Daniel leaned in with an expression that looked like he was taking notes.

"Pallax," Ember said. "One of a queen's chosen companions."

"He is not my pallax," Teyla said. "Rodney is my friend."

"Is that not what I said?" Ember sounded confused.

"We are not physically involved," Teyla said patiently. "To humans there is a distinction in terminology."

"Ah."

Daniel was all over it, of course. "So you're saying that the mental intimacy of the telepathic bond suggested to you that Teyla and Rodney were…"

Ember nodded seriously. "I made the erroneous assumption that he was her pallax from the warmth of their speech. He is, after all, an extremely high status cleverman of distinction, and I presumed that he was also high in her favor."

"That's certainly true," Rodney began.

"It is possible to esteem a male greatly and consider them a close friend without implying physical intimacy," Teyla said to Ember. There was a note of amusement in her voice as she glanced at Rodney. "While it is certainly true that Rodney is brilliant and distinguished, that does not imply that I intend for him to be the father of my future children."

"What? No, I…"

Daniel's glance was going back and forth like a man watching a tennis match. "So you're saying that…"

"His genetic material would be highly desirable," Ember opined.

"I am certain that it would be," Teyla said.

"I wouldn't… I mean," Rodney flailed.

"In order to preserve genetic diversity, and to produce offspring with the most desirable traits, a queen selects carefully among her zenana each time she chooses to bear a child," Ember said to Daniel, who was trying to ask a question. "I am simply stating that McKay's offspring would doubtless possess his high intelligence and good looks."

"Well, of course they would, but…" Rodney said. He was fortunately interrupted by the buzzing of the jumper's scanner. "Ah ha! It looks like we found something."

"What is it?" Ronon asked.

Rodney adjusted the controls. "It looks like a building with an artificial power source. That way. Toward that archipelago." He turned the jumper's course toward it. "Let's go check it out."

"An active power source might be..." Daniel began.

The jumper's alarms shrilled, map replaced by telemetry that identified two streaks of light rising upward.

"...an Ancient installation launching drones," Daniel finished.

"I'm on it!" Rodney said, wrenching the jumper around and heading for space.

"You are not going to outrun them that way," Teyla said. "They are faster than a puddle-jumper."

"I'm getting some room," Rodney said. Behind him, Ember was radiating anxiety in a very distracting way. "Then I'll see if they'll respond to the jumper identifying itself as an Ancient vehicle." He mentally urged the jumper to broadcast, all the while keeping an eye on the vector of the two incoming drones now clearing the upper atmosphere. They were gaining, but not quickly. It actually was possible to run their propulsion plants down, but that would take a long time. It might be a better move to dial the gate, bug out, and then come back in an hour...

"There!" Daniel said, pointing at the heads up display. The drones were indeed powering down and dropping away.

Teyla breathed a sigh of relief. "It seems the installation responded to your message."

"Nice flying, McKay," Ronon rumbled.

Rodney twisted around in his seat. "Thank you," he said.

Ronon shrugged. It was nice to be getting back on good terms with Ronon. The whole Wraith thing had strained their friendship.

Ancient letters flashed across the display. "They're giving you landing coordinates," Daniel said. He looked pleased. "It looks like this installation is still operative."

"Which means it's dangerous," Ronon said.

"Which means it has stuff we want," Rodney said. He frowned at the coordinates and at the screen. "The only problem here is that the coordinates are under water."

Teyla blinked. "The jumper is submersible."

"Well, yes." Rodney didn't like submerged jumpers. No, no, no.

"How are we supposed to get out if it's underwater?" Ember asked.

Rodney turned back toward the coordinates, scanning as they dipped back into the atmosphere. "It looks like the landing coordinates are on a plateau just below sea level on one of the volcanic islands, and that the actual buildings are inside the caldera of the extinct volcano, and are dry. I think we could probably land at the coordinates, extend the shield of the jumper to have a small dry patch around us, and then run for the entrance of the tunnel that leads into the caldera."

"What?" Ronon said.

"And if the shield collapses before we come back out, we swim?" Daniel asked.

"I'm sure it won't," Rodney said. "I can jury rig the shield generator..."

"There may be some Ancient technology in the corridor," Daniel said. "We may be able to hack into that to get more power."

"And then we could use that to extend the shield as far as we needed to in order to keep the water back..."

"Why don't we just land in the caldera?" Teyla asked wearily. "Would not that be much simpler?"

Daniel and Rodney looked at each other.

"Well, yes," Rodney said. "But it wouldn't be as much fun."

Ronon made a noise that sounded like a strangled laugh.

"I don't understand," Ember said.

"We will land in the caldera," Teyla said.

It was difficult finding a flat enough place not to damage the bottom of the jumper, as the floor of the caldera was a mass of jumbled stones that jutted up like spikes. On the third pass Rodney was about to suggest a water landing again when he finally spotted a place.

"That's deliberate construction," Daniel said, pointing toward a pile of rocks off to their right.

"I don't see anything," Rodney said.

"Who's the archaeologist here? Me or you?" Daniel asked.

Teyla took a deep breath and got up from her seat as the jumper settled onto the ground. "We will go and take a look."

Outside, the stone walls of the caldera made a perfect bowl of sky, their black and gray colors livened wherever there was a ledge by long, trailing growths of yellow and pale green plants. The floor of the caldera itself was broken and jumbled, but more of the same plants grew in profusion, some of them waist high, nicely disguising sudden drops and pits.

Rodney found one by falling into it. "Yaaa!" he yelled as his left foot stepped on something that it turned out wasn't there. Ember caught him, feeding hand grabbing the front of Rodney's jacket, and Rodney heard the sudden whine of Ronon's pistol powering up as he scrabbled for a foothold.

Ember pulled him back as Teyla put her hand on Ronon's arm. "It is nothing," she said. "Rodney lost his footing."

"Right." Ronon's voice was grim as Ember released the front of Rodney's jacket. "Be careful." Whether he spoke to Rodney or Ember wasn't clear.

Thanks, Rodney said, hoping he didn't sound shaky.

Of course. Ember looked a little spooked himself, as though he'd caught at Rodney on instinct, not considering how the move looked.

Daniel had already scrambled ahead and was examining the rocks. They might be a section of low walls. "Oh this is interesting!" he called.

The others came over. "What is interesting?" Teyla asked.

"It looks like the structure was made of native materials. That's unusual for an Ancient installation," Daniel replied, running his hands over the stones.

"Where did the drones come from?" Rodney asked.

"Over here." Ronon stood on a little rise. "I've got a metal door here that's been opened recently." The others climbed up. A wide dark metal panel about ten feet by ten feet was set into the stone, scrape marks along it showing where it had slid back into the rock along tracks.

"That's the door," Daniel said. "That's a very standard configuration for a door that covers a drone launcher."

"It's just like the ones in Atlantis," Rodney said, kneeling down. "I can get this puppy open in five minutes."

"And then we'll see what's down there," Ronon said.

Rodney was as good as his word, Teyla thought. It was five minutes before there was a grating sound and Rodney stood up. "Ah ha!" he said as the metal panel began to slide open. Beneath it a dark shaft descended further than they could see.

Ronon looked down. "That's great," he said. "But how do we get down?"

"There is rappelling gear in the jumper's supplies," Teyla said. "We should have a hundred feet of line. Unless you think it is further than that?" She looked at Rodney.

"I wouldn't think so." He shrugged. "Atlantis' drone launchers are only about thirty-five feet."

"The ones in Antarctica on Earth are a lot deeper than that," Daniel pointed out. "We had to cut a shaft more than a hundred feet deep to get to the Ancient installation."

"Yes but that was because the ice had accumulated," Rodney said. "It wasn't that deep originally. It's not supposed to be that deep."

Teyla glanced down the shaft thoughtfully. "I do not see the bottom, but that is because the shaft lies in shadow with the sun beneath the rim of the caldera. It is getting quite late in the day."

Daniel glanced up at the sky as if he had just noticed that the sun was sinking. "This planet has rather short days."

"All the more reason to do this now," Teyla said. "Ronon and Daniel, go and get the rappelling gear from the jumper. You can lower me down first and we will see how deep it is."

Ember frowned. "Surely you will let one of us precede you. We do not know what is down there and if there are hazards…"

"I am the lightest," Teyla said. "And the most accustomed to rappelling." She gave him a smile, as of course he was not used to queens taking the forward position. "We share the hazards based on our skills. And which do you think is easier — that Ronon belay me down or that I belay him down?"

The answer to that was obvious, and Ember inclined his head. For once Daniel hadn't argued. He and Ronon were halfway back to the jumper.

Rodney looked up from where he bent over the door with a smile, though he spoke without words. *Teyla likes being in charge. That's not new, right?*

Certainly not, Ember replied, humor in his mental voice though it did not touch his face.

Teyla felt a sense of satisfaction spread through her, familiar and strange at the same time, the dual mental touches of Rodney and Ember, her dear friend upon whom she relied, and Ember who she was coming to like. It was right to reach for them thus, to feel the sense of them.

And how not? Ember thought. *This is how it is.*

Rodney got to his feet, a thoughtful expression on his face, and she heard his thought before he concealed it — to know what others thought of him, to feel their acceptance and genuine admiration, to have no doubt of friendship or wonder if someone snickered behind his back…

You are my dear friend, Teyla thought to him. *And ever shall be, whether we can speak this way or not.*

The sun dipped behind an outcropping on the caldera rim, casting them into shadow. Rodney turned toward the figures now at the tailgate of the jumper. "Hey Ronon! Bring some lights too!"

Ronon nodded to show his understanding, going aboard to get them from the bench seat storage.

Do you always carry everything with you? Ember asked bemusedly.

We try to, Rodney said. *Never know what you'll need, right?*

The day was ending as Ronon belayed Teyla down the shaft. She descended carefully despite the smooth walls, the flashlight clipped to her belt illuminating the walls beneath her. Ten feet, twenty… "I see the floor," she called up. Another twenty or so feet beneath her was a pitted grid, a round aperture in the midst of it through which protruded the nose of an Ancient drone.

"Great," Ronon called down.

"Now when you get to the grid," Rodney called, "if it's like the ones in Atlantis there will be a panel that swings downward for maintenance. It has a catch on the underside. You'll need to find the catch, reach through and release it."

"I will do that," Teyla promised. Her booted feet were almost at the bottom, and she let herself down the last bit of the way, making certain the grid would take her weight before she stood upon it and unclipped the lines. It gave a little, and she moved her feet off the panel that should open outward. "I have found it," she called out.

The ropes slithered, Ronon hauling them back up. Teyla reached through and unfastened the latch, then let the panel swing down with a rasping, rusty noise. She shone her flashlight through. It was only five feet or so to the floor, the length of the drone that stood on its carousel lifted into the firing position. Teyla sat down on the edge of the grid, then jumped down to the floor. She put her hand to her radio, as it was probably best to use it at this distance. "I am in the firing chamber," she said. "All is well."

A white light jiggled on the wall of the shaft above, and in a few moments she saw Dr. Jackson's feet as he was belayed down.

Teyla touched her radio again. "Rodney? What is next?"

"If you follow the carousel to the empty side you'll come out into a storage room," Rodney replied. "I'll be down in a minute."

And leave Ember and Ronon alone above? That seemed unwise. "No, send Ember down next," Teyla said.

Ronon said something which, via Rodney's radio, sounded like, "It's your funeral."

Teyla shook her head, following the carousel around as Rodney had instructed. She ducked through the opening and was in the storage room. It was empty except for five more drones waiting on the carousel. A very familiar looking door was shut, and though there were intact fixtures there was no light. Well, Rodney would activate them with the ATA gene when he arrived. Teyla tried the door — yes, the manual release was just where it would be in Atlantis. It moved back jerkily on its track.

Dr. Jackson was just behind her. "The lettering on the door says, 'Caution'," he said. "This must be the service corridor for the launching system. There's clearly power. If there's a working ZPM..."

"That will be very useful indeed," Teyla said.

There was a sound behind, and Ember ducked through the opening from the shaft. He did not have a flashlight, but then he did not need one. The dim light suited his vision very well. "Is there a ZPM?" he asked.

"We do not know," Teyla said. "Dr. Jackson is hypothesizing that there may be since it seems that there is power to the systems."

Ember nodded. "That seems likely. I would guess that the control suite is deeper in the installation, closer to what should be the main entrance. Generally the ZPM is not far from the control room."

Teyla flashed her light up and down the corridor. There was some Ancient lettering at eye level to the left. "Dr. Jackson, what does that say?"

"It says Watch Your Step," he replied, his eyes roving over the walls. "Nothing that would give me an idea whether left or right leads us to the control room."

"And that?" Teyla asked, shining her light over lettering on the floor by the carousel.

"Disconnect Power Before Servicing," he said. "The Ancients were pretty prosaic sometimes." He glanced down the corridor. "Let's try right."

As Teyla could see no difference between them, there was no sense in arguing for the sake of arguing. She followed Jackson down the hall to the right, Ember behind her.

"I'm starting down," Rodney said in her earpiece.

The corridor to the right turned and broadened, with several doors along the left hand side before it ended in a downward stair. Flaking paint clung to the ceiling in a shade that might have once been green. Perhaps that meant they were entering less utilitarian parts of the complex? Teyla was forming the question for Dr. Jackson when Ronon's voice sounded loud in her ear.

"We've got a problem," he said.

At that moment there was a rumble, the carousel coming to life and the drone firing systems coming on line.

"We've got a ship incoming," Ronon said.

Rodney heard the faint clicks, the drone in the firing cradle beneath him coming to life, getting ready to launch. Straight up the tube he was dangling in, still ten feet from the bottom of the shaft. "Oh no no no! This is not happening!"

"Rodney! Get out of there!" Teyla yelled on the radio, for all the help that was. Didn't she think he'd get out of there just as fast as he could – if he could?

Now the drone's propulsion systems were coming on. He could feel the wave of heat rising. Wonderful. If the launching drone didn't simply spear through him and carry what was left of him into orbit, it would probably incinerate him.

"I'll pull you up!" Ronon yelled. Like he could do that in the approximately one second left.

This was going to be just like that rogue drone that nearly killed Sheppard and O'Neill in Antarctica…

And Rodney knew exactly what to do. STOP he thought with all his strength. STOP. Power down and stop.

The drone's ignition died. The light that had been building abruptly ceased.

"What happened?" Jackson demanded from below.

"What did you do?" Teyla asked.

Rodney slid down the last ten feet of rope and rested his feet on the grid, hoping his voice was perfectly carefree. "I've got the ATA gene. It's no problem."

"What?" Ember said.

"He told it to turn off," Teyla said. She sounded breathless, and as he looked down through the grid she ducked back into the firing chamber hurriedly. "Rodney, are you all right?"

"I'm great," Rodney said. He unclipped the line and gingerly lowered himself through the hatch.

"We're not," Ronon said grimly. "That ship is still incoming."

"That's not a good sign," Ember said.

From above there was the report of Ronon's energy pistol, and Rodney dodged back away from the shaft, nearly running into Teyla. There was a flash of white light that seared his eyes, and then he knew no more.

There was a hand at his throat, long nails cool against his skin, opening the top of his jacket. Wraith! Some part of Rodney screamed, and he drew a deep, heaving breath, his eyes opening on darkness.

It is I, Ember said as Rodney shoved him away. *We have been stunned.*

No shit, Rodney said. It was absolutely black. He could see nothing. *Where are we? Why're you talking mind to mind ?*

I thought until we knew where we were and what was happening it was best not to speak aloud, Ember said. *As to the rest, I know no more than you. I woke only shortly before you did.* He moved. Rodney could hear the creak of his leather tunic in the darkness. *Jackson lies over there. He is unconscious.*

Teyla? Ronon?

I have not found them yet.

Wraith, Rodney thought.

Ember's mind was cool, considering. *If so, it is another hive,* he said at last. *And I do not know the technology.*

And I should believe you? Rodney asked. *I've seen Wraith mind games, remember?*

He heard the creak of leather again, and Ember's hand found his arm, sliding down to touch palm to palm. *Do I deceive you?*

Open, clear — there was no deceit there. Ember was telling the truth. Which of course didn't mean that there wasn't another hive in this. Ember wouldn't necessarily know.

There was a familiar moan, and Rodney whipped around, eyes searching the darkness fruitlessly. "Teyla?" For once he wished he had his Wraith vision back.

The sound of Ember moving, and then Teyla's voice, mumbling as though she came out from under anesthetic. "Rodney?"

He is here, Ember said mind to mind, *And so am I. We have been stunned and we do not know where we are.*

Where are Ronon and Dr. Jackson?

Rodney put out one hand in the dark. That was Teyla's foot. OK, that was Ember's thigh where he knelt beside her.

Jackson is unconscious over there, Ember said.

Hang on, Rodney said. He pressed the little button for the LEDs that lit the face of his watch. In the absolute darkness the tiny light seemed incredibly bright, but it was just bright enough to make out the general forms of his companions. He turned away, trying to direct the light around. There was another darker lump beyond Teyla. Rodney scrambled over. "Ronon?" He let go of the light, fumbling to find his friend's carotid artery. There was the pulse, slow and steady. *He's alive,* he said to Teyla and Ember. *But he's out cold.*

So is Dr. Jackson, Ember replied.

Teyla sat up, Ember steadying her. Her voice sounded a little stronger. *We have greater resistance to whatever was used than they did.*

I am fully Wraith, Ember said. *And then Rodney. And then you.*

Which does suggest this isn't a Wraith thing, Rodney said. *If it's least effective on Wraith.*

Or that it is, Teyla said darkly. *Like the device we found on the planet that caused half our people to kill each other.*

The one you were immune to, Rodney said. *And Sheppard shot me.*

That one, Teyla said and felt in the pockets of her BDUs, producing a little LED flashlight on a clip. Teyla turned it on, the light seeming unbearably bright after complete darkness.

Ember got to his feet. *I am more interested in finding out where we are.*

I do not know, Teyla said. *But we were not carried here. See?* There were no marks in the dust of the floor around where she lay other than where Rodney and Ember had disturbed it.

Beaming technology, Rodney said. *So if not Wraith, Asgard.*

Vanir, Ember said, his mental tone agreement. *What you call Asgard.*

Rodney got to his feet, trying to illuminate the space around them with his watch, which wasn't much use. It just wasn't bright enough for human vision, but maybe it was enough for Wraith. *Ember, what do you see?*

The Wraith got to his feet. *We are in a small room,* he said. *There is an archway over there with another chamber beyond it. I see no furnishings or equipment of any kind, though there are marks on the walls where there might have been such in the past.*

A typical abandoned Ancient installation, Rodney said with more confidence than he felt.

No locked doors? Rodney could hear the rise in Teyla's mental tone. *That suggests we are not prisoners.* She got to her feet slowly. *I do not see that Ronon and Dr. Jackson are in any imminent danger here. Let us see if we can find a way back to the jumper. Then we can return with the first aid kit and a stretcher if need be.*

With Ember in the lead, since his vision was best, they went through the arch into the room on the other side, Teyla walking right behind Ember with her hand on his back and Rodney behind her with his hand on hers like some kids' game. It was a much larger room with multiple doors like the ones in Atlantis all sitting in the open position, though there was no furniture and equipment remaining. There were also no windows, as presumably they were still underground .

Open. Close. Lights on, Rodney thought. Nothing happened.

There is a lighting fixture over here, Ember said.

Rodney, Teyla began.

I know. On. On. On. Rodney thought at it. Again nothing. He went over and touched it, hands roving over the very familiar fixture.

Will this help? Teyla shone her flashlight so that he could see the fixture a little.

There's no power, Rodney said. *That's the problem.*

There was power to launch drones before, Ember said.

Well, either that was the last power in the ZPM, Rodney began.

Or they have taken the ZPM, Teyla concluded grimly.

Yeah. Rodney blew out a long breath.

Here is a stairwell down, Ember said. *Toward the main levels?*

Worth a try, Rodney said.

They trooped down the flight and through another hall. Nothing stirred. There was no sound. The air was fresh enough, but there was no soft breath of ventilation.

The fans have stopped, Ember said. *The air is good enough for now, but it won't remain so.*

Ah ha! Rodney exclaimed. There was a familiar set of doors ahead, the usual markings for a technical center, and here there were signs of activity. The floor had been wiped clean except in the corners by the passage of large items, and the doors were not quite fully open. Inside, tables stood emptied of their terminals, scrapes and marks showing where they had been recently removed. Even worse, there was the podium to one side, the hexagonal carriage in the upright position and empty.

They took the ZPM, Teyla said. *And who knows what else?*

INTERLUDE

"LORVINE," Elizabeth said. "What world is that?" Dekaas had found her a long sleeved white knit shirt that was warmer for shipboard than the clothes of the Mazatla, and that felt more right to her, more like something she used to wear. With the baggy gray pants she'd acquired, looking in a mirror she recognized herself. Her hair was growing longer than she'd worn it in a while, but she looked like herself. Pale, yes — one would expect that on shipboard. But she looked like herself.

"It's a mining world," Dekaas said. "Or rather, it's a nearly deserted world that has some minor mining operations. The atmosphere itself is toxic, but at some point in the past someone moved their Ring underground. The population is never very large — a few hundred at most — living in the mines themselves in fairly deplorable conditions. But the ores are worth a great deal, and there are always people who find it worth it to work the seams. We trade there from time to time for raw metals."

"What do they get?" Elizabeth asked. She was finding herself fascinated by the shadow economy of Pegasus, by the complex interactions that took place out of sight of all governments. Or perhaps in the absence of all governments was a better term.

"Food mostly," Dekaas said. "We just picked up food on Mazatla, so I expect the captain thinks Lorvine is a logical next stop."

"Aren't they worried about the Wraith?"

Dekaas shrugged. "The mines are too far underground for a hive ship to be a problem, and the Ring is in too enclosed a space for Darts. Sometimes some parties on foot come through the Ring, but not often. It's not a large population, and Wraith biotechnology doesn't depend on metal ores. It's not actually a big problem. The Wraith don't want Lorvine."

Elizabeth nodded. "That's fascinating."

He looked at her sharply. "You have a great deal of interest in how people live."

"I do." Elizabeth considered. "Atelia said that on Sateda she was training to be a scholar who studies other cultures. Perhaps I was a scholar too."

"That could be," Dekaas said. "And a Wraith connection does not preclude Sateda for your origin. Sateda fell ten years ago. You might have been captured then and only recently released."

"That's true," she agreed. It was possible, though nothing about that felt familiar. "Well, if I can dial Sateda from Lorvine, I will go to Sateda."

Elizabeth wondered how the Traveler ship intended to transfer people to the mining colony if it was underground, but she did not have to wonder long. It was no more than a few days before they arrived, the *Durant* settling onto a surface bare and devoid of any visible technology except a landing beacon. Through the windows she could see nothing but a sandy gray surface obscured by great clouds of dust kicked up by the ship's landing. There was the same grinding sound forward she had heard before and the plastic tube snaked out, mating to an airlock door half-obscured on the surface.

"Very clever," she said with a nod. "Also very defensible."

Dekaas had joined her at the mess windows, a medical pack slung over his shoulder. "Very," he said. "A hive ship could blow it up, but what would be the point?"

Elizabeth glanced at the bag. "You're going down?"

"To see if they have any injured who need treating." He shrugged. "It's my trade and my skill. I barter for my work, like anyone."

"I'll help you carry your things," she said.

This time crossing through the transparent tube wasn't difficult at all, not with the planet outside and gravity pulling her firmly down. It wasn't like free fall at all. On the other side of the planet's airlock doors was a wide platform with a metal cage around it that slowly descended into the depths, a few lights here and there not really illuminating the shaft.

"This part always makes me a little uncomfortable," Dekaas said with a smile as they stood among the other traders going down.

"I think I've seen something like this before," Elizabeth said. This wasn't at all alarming.

The caverns below were no more well lit, raw stone walls with openings from one chamber to another. A crowd had gathered around the bottom of the shaft, and Dekaas stiffened. More than one of them was bandaged, mostly with filthy pieces of cloth around their heads or limbs, some with arms in slings. "What happened here?" he asked loudly.

A big woman with cropped gray hair lifted her hand in greeting. "Dekaas! I've got work for you and more."

He stepped out of the cage as soon as it rested, Elizabeth behind him. "Ho, Fenna! Did you have a cave in or an accident with explosives?" he asked concernedly.

"Neither." Fenna spat on the dusty floor. "This was the work of the accursed Genii."

"The Genii?" Elizabeth said.

Fenna nodded. "A day and a half ago they came through the Ring. They took all the prepared ore at gunpoint — told us we were part of their cooperative economic system. Anybody who resisted got it. Mostly people bashed with gunstocks, pistol whipped, things like that, but they did shoot two. One of them's dead." She spat again, apparently at the recitation of the Genii's crimes. "It was the work of a full quarter, and now every bit of it's gone. And a dozen wounded to boot. It was that she-wolf Sora."

"I've heard of her," Dekaas said. "She's bad news. Where are your worst wounded?"

"Right this way," Fenna said. "We've done the best we can for them. But Dekaas, in terms of payment…" She swallowed as if it pained her to say that they didn't have anything left to pay him with.

"Consider it a debt," Dekaas said. "Elizabeth, if you wouldn't mind helping me? I could use another pair of hands."

"Of course," Elizabeth said. "I won't leave when there's work to be done." She followed Fenna and Dekaas to the makeshift aid station.

CHAPTER TWELVE

IT TOOK quite some time for Teyla, Ember and Rodney to find their way out to the jumper, following one passage and then another by process of elimination. By the time they had returned with flashlights and first aid kits, Ronon and Daniel Jackson were awake. Teyla helped Ronon to his feet while Rodney steadied Daniel. Ember watched, his hands at his sides, as if wanting to make sure no one misinterpreted his touch.

"It was the Asgard," Teyla said to Daniel. "That is the logical conclusion. They stunned us and then took the ZPM and whatever else they wanted."

Daniel rubbed his eyes. "But what was it?" he wondered aloud. "And was it sheer coincidence that they turned up here at the same time we did? I mean, they've had thousands of years to loot this planet. They did it today? Coincidentally?"

"That doesn't seem likely," Ember agreed.

"Whatever was here, they took it," Rodney said.

"I need to examine the room," Daniel said. "There may be something left."

"There is not," Teyla said. "There are no instruments left at all."

Daniel shrugged. "Sometimes people drop things. Or there's writing on surfaces. Or they lose some small attached part. There are lots of things you wouldn't have seen in the dark."

"That is true," Teyla said. She took a deep breath. "It will only take a few minutes to search the room, and we are already here. Let us do it. Rodney, you and Ronon go back to the jumper and radio Atlantis and tell John what happened. I will go with Ember and Dr. Jackson."

Together, they descended to the stripped room, which seemed no more promising to Teyla on second glance than on first. She and Ember watched while Daniel examined the floor, crawled under the tables and desks, and inspected the empty mounting brackets on the walls.

"There was some kind of device here," Daniel said at last, pointing to a blank expanse of floor in front of two tables, five empty brackets behind it. "About two meters tall and one meter wide. It took a lot of power. These are multiple heavy duty power couplings."

Ember's brows rose. "And that means that something was connected there. What was it?"

Daniel shrugged. "I don't know. I don't know what it did. But I do know there was something that took a lot of power and that you couldn't go near when it was operating." He pointed to a small line of Ancient symbols on the floor. "Caution Induction Zone. Whatever was being induced, you needed to stand back from it."

Teyla remembered something. "This looks like an installation in Atlantis," she said.

Daniel turned around. "What? Where? I've never seen it."

"Elizabeth insisted that we seal the room," she said. "We found it years ago, and it proved incredibly dangerous. It was a device to help one Ascend. Rodney was nearly killed as a result of it."

"Ah." Daniel looked about, turning in place as though trying to visualize things that were no longer there. "That makes sense. That makes complete sense of these." He pointed to a tiny row of symbols along one of the tables. "This says Reintegration Unit. This isn't for Ascension. It's for a device that causes someone to unascend." He stopped, pushing his glasses up on his nose. "No, that forces them to unascend."

Ember frowned. "Can that happen?"

"You mean can someone unascend? Of course," Daniel said.

"No," Teyla said. "Is it possible to affect someone who is Ascended? I have never heard of any such thing." The very idea was deeply disturbing.

Daniel nodded. "Yes. I mean, we know that it is. Merlin — the Ancient Merlin — projected his consciousness into my brain once so that I would understand how to make a device that would destroy the Ori, and they're Ascended beings. So yes, you can theoretically have a device that could force an Ascended being to return to corporeal form. I have no idea how you would do it, but it could be done."

"And this device," Teyla gestured to the blank space before them, "Might have done that?"

"It's possible," Daniel said.

"And now the Asgard have it and we do not," Teyla said. "That is not a good development."

"The real question," Daniel said, "Is why they want it."

"I don't like stuff we don't know," John said. He looked around the conference table at the familiar faces of his team plus Daniel Jackson. At least he didn't have to have Ember the Wraith in the debriefing. "Why would the Asgard come to that planet at the same time as us? Why did they stun everyone? What did they take and why?"

"They followed us," Rodney said, his fists clenched.

"How?"

"I don't know how!" Rodney sputtered, "But I know they did. Come on. They just happened to show up at the same time? Not likely. They could have visited that planet anytime in the last thousand years. No, they followed us. And that's why they just stunned us."

"We're the stalking horse," Daniel said. "We run the risks, we turn off the Ancient defenses, and then they take the stuff." Which did make sense. It wasn't anything John liked, but it sure made sense.

"But why do they want it?" Teyla was frowning. "To force the Ancestors to unascend is…" She paused as if looking for a bad enough word. "Obscene."

"Maybe they want knowledge one of them has," Daniel said.

"And now they've got the device," Rodney said. "And there's nothing we can do about it."

There was a long moment of gloomy silence as everyone considered this.

"Wait a second," Ronon rumbled, leaning back in his chair. "There's one thing we know about Ancient devices that goes for every single one we've ever found. It doesn't work the way it's supposed to. Just because they've got it doesn't mean they can do what they wanted it for. And they can't use it without the ATA gene anyway, right?"

"That's true," Daniel said more brightly.

"I think we're losing sight of the priority here," Rodney said. "We're looking for Elizabeth."

John folded his hands on the table deliberately. "No," he said. "We're looking for Ancient installations. That's what we found. Too bad the Asgard did too. But nobody was hurt, and we're no worse off than we started."

"I just think this is connected," Rodney said. "If the Asgard are trying to find an Unascension device at the same time that Elizabeth is missing and maybe Unascended…"

"Maybe it is," John said with frustration. "But do you have any bright ideas about how to find the Asgard ship? I thought not. So let's get on with what we're actually doing. Everybody stand down, get some rest, and tomorrow we'll talk about the next site."

Nobody moved.

John got up. "Meeting over. Good night."

"I just…" Rodney began.

"Tomorrow."

"OK."

Daniel got up, opening his laptop and showing it to Rodney. "Can we talk about these three places on the list?" They went out with their heads alarmingly together.

Ronon tilted his chair down. "Want to grab some dinner?" he asked Teyla.

"Perhaps I will be down in a few minutes," Teyla said. She lagged behind as Ronon went out.

John sat down on the edge of the table as the doors slid closed. "What's up?"

Teyla shook her head, a fond smile on her face. "Have you had such trouble leading the team for years? Ronon and Rodney are bad enough, but when there is Dr. Jackson and Ember…" She spread her hands. "I feel that I spend all my time shouting."

John laughed. "That's pretty much it. It's herding cats. Always has been."

She took a step closer, inclining her head to his in Athosian courtesy. "I did not realize the difficulties involved."

"Kind of makes you appreciate me more," John said with a smile.

Richard Woolsey stood in the conference room at Stargate Command, watching the gate turn, a regularly scheduled offworld team returning. It was a little after 06.00 Mountain Time. He'd spent the night in SGC guest quarters, which he had to say were a lot more comfortable than the first time he'd been here. Then, they'd been bunk beds in a concrete room painted olive drab. Now they were a lot like a budget hotel complete with queen beds with pastel quilts and framed prints of scenic beaches on the wall. Possibly this was intended to put guests at ease. Certainly there were no beaches anywhere nearby.

Woolsey took a sip of his scalding coffee. One thing that hadn't changed was the coffee. This was as thick as if it had been sitting on the hotplate all night. Which it probably had.

He paced around the empty conference table, empty and waiting for the next crisis. Everything was very quiet. The bulletproof glass cut out the sounds of the gateroom below entirely. Beyond the head of the conference table the Stargate Command insignia was mounted on the wall, proud encouragement to those who found themselves here for the first time. On the right hand wall was a different kind of plaque — a list of names. Most of them he didn't know: Spec. Robert Riley, Spec. Louise Fernandez, Lt. Aidan Ford. Some he did. Dr. Janet Fraiser. Dr. Elizabeth Weir.

Woolsey took another sip of the terrible coffee. Was it possible that Dr. Weir was alive, as unlikely as that seemed? The answer was probably no. There was no evidence, no reason to think so other than the wishful thinking of a man who had himself been a prisoner of war and then recovered. McKay wanted her to be alive. Everyone wanted her to be alive. Understandably. Death was hard to accept, and doubly so when one felt responsible for the death. But that didn't make her alive. The Atlantis expedition had to face the facts. Elizabeth Weir was not coming back.

Woolsey sighed. Sheppard would come to that. He wouldn't let them spend too much time on a wild goose hunt. It was time to move on.

Just as it was time for him to move on. It was time for him to stop thinking of himself as a member of the Atlantis expedition and to start thinking of himself as a member of the IOA — the US representative to the IOA. His was the position of responsibility, and it was time to take what he'd learned and put it to good use. There was no going back. It was time to go forward. He had the briefing files on this new fiasco, the loss of an experimental base and its personnel, the armed hostilities with the Lucian Alliance that ensued, the loss of several of the *Hammond*'s 302s in the subsequent fight. He needed to get a handle on that. What the gate team in Atlantis did was no longer his job.

Richard Woolsey squared his shoulders. The names looked back at him from the wall. I will do my best, he promised silently. I'll make sure you weren't wasted.

An Airman cleared his throat from the doorway. "Mr. Woolsey? Your car is ready to take you to Peterson, sir."

"I'm coming," Woolsey said. He put the coffee cup down on the conference table and left it there.

INTERLUDE

IT WAS several hours before they had seen all the injured, including a man who had been shot in the leg and lost a lot of blood. He wasn't the worst injured, though. That went to a woman who had been hit in the head with a rifle butt and hadn't regained consciousness since. Dekaas arranged to transport her onto the *Durant* where he had more equipment, shaking his head as he did so. He had no words of comfort for her kin, only that he'd try. Elizabeth watched them go up the elevator to the airlock, the woman wrapped in a blanket on a pallet, Dekaas and her two teenage daughters, their faces pale and pinched with worry.

"She tried to fight back," Fenna said. "Always a mistake."

Elizabeth didn't reply. She took a deep breath, warming her hands against her sleeves.

"So you wanted to use our gate to dial out?" Fenna asked.

"If you'll permit it," Elizabeth said. "But Dekaas asked me to keep an eye on the injured down here while he tends to her, so I'm not leaving just yet."

"Fair enough," Fenna said. "You can trade your help for the use of our gate."

"That's a deal," Elizabeth said, putting out her hand.

After a moment Fenna shook it. "We're going to end this thing deep in the Travelers' debt, but I see no alternative. It's a bad business."

"It seems so," Elizabeth said.

"But now you're welcome to a bite to eat," Fenna said.

"That would be great." Elizabeth walked with her through several corridors and out into the largest cavern she'd yet seen. At the other end of it was a vast ring of dark metal with a pedestal before it. Elizabeth frowned, a shiver running through her. "The Ring," she said. "It's different." There was an inner circle of symbols on a band rather than lights.

"Aye," Fenna said. "It's different from most I've seen. But it works just the same."

"How did it get here?" She had the feeling that there was something wrong about that, something important.

"How did any Ring get anywhere?" Fenna asked. "We found it here when we first came here. These caverns were already hollowed out, but I guess the ore wasn't good enough to be worth the effort, or maybe troubles came and everyone went home. It was all shut down tidily. No bones, no signs of a fight, just abandoned. I reckon somebody pulled out long ago."

"I suppose," Elizabeth said. She frowned. There was something about the gate that was wrong, something she should remember. When had she seen one like it before?

Two figures were silhouetted for a moment against the brightness of the Stargate as they walked through, one with a cap of golden hair, the other tall and muscular. They stepped through, and for a moment the puddle of blue light remained before it faded. The circle of red lit symbols around the gate went dark.

Elizabeth took a deep breath. "Here goes nothing," she said.

The man beside her at the window shoved his hands in his pants pockets. "It's our best shot," he said. "If anybody can do it, Sam and Teal'c can."

"Frankly, I'm less worried about them than us." Elizabeth turned away from the gate room window, pacing around the conference room table. "That modified ship is the most advanced piece of technology Earth has."

The man pushed his glasses up on his nose with one hand. "Think about it this way. That ship exists because of what's in Jack's head. Right now, nobody can access that, including Jack. But if the Asgard can help him, then maybe we can find out how he modified the ship. And everything else he knows but can't tell us."

Elizabeth stopped at the far end of the table. "You have a point," she said.

"I often do." He gave her a boyish smile. "You know, it's not necessary to have an adversarial relationship."

Elizabeth took a deep breath. "Dr. Jackson, I had nothing to do with the President relieving General Hammond. I didn't even know the Stargate program existed! This job was not my idea. But I'm going to see it through, and I'm going to make the best decisions I possibly can."

He perched on the other end of the table, the tension in his body belying his carefully diffident demeanor. "Look, it's not to your advantage or to ours for this to be adversarial. But I can't help wondering exactly who does benefit. Progressive activist given command of an Air Force project, disarmament negotiator given control of Earth's most advanced weapons, DC insider relieving beloved commander — somebody's set up for failure here and I'm not sure if it's you or us."

It was time to trust him, time to take that leap of faith that's always the most deadly in politics. "I know exactly who," Elizabeth said. "And it's both of us set up to fail. This is supposed to discredit both the Stargate program and me. Unless I'm simply a convenient pawn as far as he's concerned."

"Kinsey," Jackson said.

"Got it in one."

"Color me surprised." Jackson smiled again. "Then you know there's one way for both of us to win."

"For us not to fail," Elizabeth said. She came around the table again and offered her hand. "How about it?"

"It's a deal," Jackson said.

CHAPTER THIRTEEN

JOHN bent over Teyla's shoulder at the communications board in the gateroom, shifting from one foot to the other uncomfortably as he looked at the incoming video transmission through the Stargate. "Oh, hi, Larrin," he said.

The woman looked amused. "Hello Sheppard."

"Long time, no see," John said. "Everything OK on your end?"

"Yes." Her smile widened. "The only reason I'm calling is because your friend Mr. Woolsey asked for anyone to let him know if there were any reports of a woman with no memory."

John straightened up as Teyla felt her breath catch in her throat. "A woman with no memory?"

"A couple of our ships were trading recently on a world called Mazatla. One of them just rendezvoused with me and they said that the Mazatla had a woman that they were asking around about. They'd found her wandering around a field and she had no memory. They were asking if anyone knew her."

"What did she look like?" Teyla put in, forestalling John's question.

Larrin shrugged. "Dark haired, pale skinned, average height. Nothing remarkable."

"Mazatla," John said. "Where is that?"

"I'll send you the gate coordinates. It's an underpopulated world with subsistence farming and hunter/gatherers. We trade for food there." She leaned forward to transmit the gate address. "It only has an orbital Stargate."

"Thanks for the heads up," John said. "I appreciate it, Larrin. I'll buy you a drink next time."

"You wish," Larrin said, and cut the transmission.

Teyla looked up at John, one eyebrow rising. "Buy you a drink?"

"Just being friendly," he said. "Friends. As in people who tell you important things you want to know."

"Do you think it is Elizabeth?" Teyla asked.

"I think we need to go find out." John headed briskly to the office, where his jacket lay over the chair.

"You mean we should go find out," Teyla said, following him. "Mr. Woolsey left you in charge in Atlantis."

"It's just a quick fact-finding mission," John said. "Asking friendly people a few questions. Tell Ronon to get up here. We're checking out a jumper." He stopped, that quirky smile at the corner of his mouth, and she knew he'd just been looking for a reason. "It'll take an hour, tops."

"If you say so," Teyla said.

The gate was indeed orbital, high above a planet roughly half water and half land, the land lush with green forests and plains. Massive river systems snaked through low lying areas, and white clouds swirled above.

"I'm taking us down at the coordinates Larrin gave us," John said. "Let's see what they can tell us. Teyla…"

"I know," Teyla said. "I will do the talking."

"You always do," Ronon said from behind her, but there was no heat in it. He was back to his teasing little brother tones, a good sign.

"That's because she's good at it," John said.

"So what are we supposed to do?" Ronon asked.

"Look out for trouble."

"Perhaps it would be best if you discreetly circulate and see if you can find Elizabeth," Teyla suggested.

"That's a thought," John said. "You negotiate. We'll just have a nice, casual look around."

Through the front windscreen Teyla could see golden plains unfolding, grasslands with grazing herds which startled at the jumper's passage. They slowed, a settlement of tents emerging, two characteristic bare spots in the grass where Travelers' ships had landed. At that altitude it was possible to see people, many of them clustered around stalls and cook fires. They looked upward at the jumper curiously, but since it looked nothing like a Wraith ship there was no panic. After all, they traded with the Travelers.

"I'm going to set down there where the Travelers did," John said, bringing the puddle-jumper around in a wide bank.

"They will be less alarmed that way," Teyla said. "Let us keep this as normal as possible. We are Lanteans who also hope to trade."

"That's a plan," John said.

Teyla was pleased by the greeting they received. Though Mazatla had only an orbital gate, clearly the inhabitants had extensive trade with the Travelers, and were not, as so many populations of isolated worlds were, suspicious or frightened of strangers. Indeed, her explanation that they had been told of good trading by the Travelers was accepted with little discussion. That they were Lantean was a matter of some note, but their ship was not so different from those of the Travelers, except that it was smaller.

"Can't carry much in that," one of the headmen said skeptically.

"It passes through the orbital Ring," Teyla explained. "And as we live on a very cold world, we are eager to trade for fresh food."

John shifted behind her, his P90 slung across his chest. It was, after all, a very plausible reason for their presence, and an arrangement they had with various allies across the galaxy.

Consequently she was shown samples of various vegetables, which Teyla spent a great deal of time examining at length, and then spent another hour at least bartering the contents of the jumper's first aid kit for six bushels of grain and two of *kammar*.

John turned one of the green, spiky *kammar* around in his hand. "Like some kind of prickly pear," he said.

"They are very tasty," Teyla said. "And I believe they taste more like your artichokes."

"OK." John picked up one of the bushels and carried it toward the jumper. "We could have some artichokes."

The negotiation had reached the point where their hosts were breaking out the drinks and insisting they stay as spectators for some kind of game, which meant it was time for her question. "Oh, by the way," Teyla began, as though it had just occurred to her. "Our friends said there was a woman here who had lost her memory? We have a friend we are looking for."

"The Forgetting Woman!" the headman said. "She was here. She came with the group from Pina. They've already gone."

"Gone where?"

"Back to their homes, I think." He shrugged. "The Gathering

is nearly over."

"And if we wanted to see if she is our friend, where would we go?" Teyla asked.

A younger man leaned in. "The Forgetting Woman didn't go with them. She went with the Travelers. She went on Lesko's ship."

"Not Larrin's?"

"I don't know Larrin," the headman said. "Lesko was the one who was here. She went with Lesko's people."

"Where did they go?" Teyla asked.

The younger man shrugged. "Who knows? The Travelers go where they want. I think they said she was going to find her home."

Teyla suppressed a sigh of frustration. "Do you know anything else about her? Did she say anything? Did she give a name?"

The younger man nodded. "She said she was from a city. And that her name was Elizabeth."

INTERLUDE

ELIZABETH was changing the dressing on one of the wounded men when Dekaas returned to the aid station. She looked up at him and he shook his head.

"She didn't make it," he said quietly. "Intracranial bleeding."

Elizabeth closed her eyes for a moment. No matter how many dead, no matter if she'd known them or not, it was never easy, never possible to simply dismiss.

There was a sudden rumble, and the inner wheel of the Ring began to turn. Someone screamed, and there were voices shouting out orders, the sounds of people running.

"Evacuate to the back caves!" Fenna yelled. "Get back! It may be the Genii again!"

Of course Elizabeth ran the other way, toward the gate. Why would it be the Genii? They had already taken everything worthwhile. Sora wouldn't return for what was here. Elizabeth didn't even pause a moment to wonder how she knew that. She simply hurried into the large chamber with the Ring.

The last chevron locked and light exploded out. Five or six miners had taken refuge behind boxes, two of them with Genii bolt action rifles and the rest with mining tools. One was Fenna.

"Hold your fire," she said grimly. "Wait until you've got a good shot."

Three figures stepped through the pool of light, dark against the brightness behind. They were not Genii.

"Wraith," Dekaas said at Elizabeth's elbow.

The one in the center wore a long black coat and his hands were empty and held to the sides. He was smooth faced, a tattoo like a sweep of leaves and tendrils up the side of his face, his hair pulled back with a single bronze clasp. The other pair were masked drones holding their stunners at port arms. "People of Lorvine," the middle Wraith said loudly, "I have come to speak with you."

"Obviously," Dekaas muttered, "Or you'd have come through with stunners blazing."

Fenna got up from behind the makeshift barricade. "What do you want?"

"You are their queen?"

"I'm the quartermaster," she said, which seemed to satisfy him.

The gate deactivated behind him. "I have come to tell you that according to treaties recently concluded Lorvine lies within the mandate of my hive."

"You want us to be filthy worshippers?" a man called out.

The young Wraith — for he was young, Elizabeth thought, from the way he hesitated — turned to face the speaker. "You are too few to Cull and we do not need your ore. Fortunately for you, you have fallen inside our mandate instead of some other. We will allow you to live in peace."

"What treaty recently concluded?" Fenna asked with a frown.

"Between the members of the alliance that defeated Queen Death," he replied.

"I thought the Genii defeated Queen Death."

"So they say." He lifted his chin. "But it was my queen who defeated her mind to mind in single combat, not the Genii."

"Who is your queen and what's her lineage?" That was Dekaas, his voice cutting unexpectedly through the hubbub.

The Wraith turned to face him. "Waterlight of the line of Osprey," he said proudly. "And what would you know of such matters?"

Dekaas shrugged.

"What does she want?" Fenna cut in. "What's the price of our lives?"

"She asks that you acknowledge her sovereignty. She asks me to pledge in her name that we will not feed on Lorvine except upon those who have agreed to be part of the trial of a retrovirus, and who have volunteered to do so."

A babble of voices broke out. Dekaas' brows knit. "A retrovirus? Why would we do that?"

"It strengthens the human body so that feeding upon a human doesn't kill them," the Wraith said.

"You mean like that enzyme?" Dekaas demanded. "We've seen the results of that. It's as deadly as the feeding, just slower."

"This is not the same," the Wraith said. "It has been tested on many humans so far with no lasting ill effects. It does indeed allow feeding without death."

"And why would we allow that?" Fenna asked. "That's crazy."

"We will feed in return for providing assistance," the Wraith said. His eyes swept over the crowd. "I see that you have injured among you. We could heal your injured for a price."

"That's impossible," someone said.

"It's not," Dekaas replied. His eyes never left the Wraith. "But life must be taken from one to give to another."

"No longer," the Wraith said. "Our scientists have rendered that unnecessary. A treated human may be fed upon with no ill effects, and thus life may be given to another."

"And what do you get out of it?" Fenna demanded.

"Food, of course." The Wraith looked over them again. "We will return. If any of you have chosen to participate in the trial, you may come with us then." He gestured to one of the drones, who stepped forward to dial the gate.

One of the men with bolt action rifles rose to oppose him, but Fenna gestured him back. "Let them go," she said. "No sense calling trouble down on us."

"A wise choice," the Wraith said.

CHAPTER FOURTEEN

RODNEY glared at John across the desk in what was once again John's office. "So basically you lost Elizabeth. You found people who knew a woman named Elizabeth who had lost her memory, but she went somewhere with somebody and you don't know who or where."

John shifted in the office chair uncomfortably, as though he were more worried than his words admitted. "Rodney, it's not a problem. We know she's on a Traveler ship belonging to a guy named Lesko. The ship's probably in hyperspace or trading somewhere remote right now, but as soon as it rendezvous with Larrin's ship she'll give us a call and then we go get Elizabeth."

"At least you admit Elizabeth is alive," Rodney said.

Teyla thought it was time to put in a word. "It is highly unlikely that there is another woman named Elizabeth who has lost her memory, especially since it is a name from Earth and I have never heard it in this galaxy. So yes, Elizabeth is alive."

"But is she a Replicator?" Ronon asked, and the other three turned to look at him. Ronon spread his hands. "I hate to say it. But I've got to say it."

"We don't know," John said tightly. "We don't have any idea whether she's human or Replicator. And the only way we'll know is to find her."

"She's human," Rodney said.

Teyla closed her eyes for a moment. "Rodney, you cannot know that."

"When Jackson unascended he was human."

"He was human when he ascended," John pointed out.

"Why would she unascend as a Replicator?" Rodney demanded. "That doesn't make sense."

"We don't know!" John was actually shouting, what Teyla thought was clearly a measure of his frustration with the entire situation. "We don't know, Rodney! We have no idea. We're messing with stuff nobody has any idea about! All we can do is find her and then see."

"You don't have to yell about it," Rodney said. "I was just pointing out…"

"Don't you come back the way you went?" Ronon asked.

"We don't know!" John snapped. "So how about everybody refrain from speculating while we look for her? Let's put out another call for Larrin and ask her to let us know when she hears from Lesko's ship." When everyone just sat there he stood up. "Rodney! Go do it!"

"Right." Rodney got up and left, a picture of injured dignity. "Don't bother to say, McKay, you were right."

"McKay, you were maybe kind of right," Ronon said, clapping him on the shoulder as he followed him out.

Teyla waited until the door closed. "Do you think it is Elizabeth?"

"I don't know." John's eyes were worried. "We might be chasing a red herring. Somebody who lost her memory and we supplied the name to the Mazatla. Or it might be a Replicator."

"Or it might be Elizabeth," Teyla said. "But I see your point that we must not rush to conclusions. There are many people in the galaxy who would like to lure us into a trap. Including some we think of as allies."

"The Genii," John said.

"Yes. I do not think they can repudiate their treaty with us at this time, but I am certain there are some who would like to. If we were to make ourselves vulnerable…"

"And there's this business about the Asgard following us. We have no idea how they did that."

"That is indeed disturbing," Teyla said.

"Some kind of subspace… I don't know." John shook his head. "But you were right when you said it was too much of a coincidence. They're following us because they want something and we have no idea what."

"Maybe they found it," Teyla said. "Maybe the device was what they wanted." She paused. "Or maybe it's Elizabeth."

"How would they know about Elizabeth? Even if she were unascended?"

"I do not know," Teyla said. "But it is possible that the Asgard are also hunting for her."

"I know." John looked down at his laptop like he could see some answer there. "I'd like to go charging off on this like McKay."

"But you cannot. You are in charge of Atlantis."

"Until further notice," John said.

Richard Woolsey looked out the window at bumper to bumper traffic moving up Massachusetts Avenue toward Union Station, a cold February rain falling over DC, not quite cold enough to freeze. He supposed it was rush hour though it felt earlier in the day to him, his body still on Mountain Time. Or maybe on Atlantis time. Which he needed to put behind him, because he was here to stay. This was his office. Quickly emptied of former Governor Roy Martin's things, this office in Homeworld Security in downtown DC was his until future notice, until he resigned, the President dismissed him, or he died.

There was a knock on the door and he turned to see the super-efficient Lt. Colonel Davis with a stack of briefing folders. "Come in," Woolsey said. He went around behind his desk and sat down. "If you've got a moment, I'd like to hear from you what the most pressing issues are." And that was a thing he'd learned in Atlantis: the papers could tell you far less about what was really important than an on-the-ball subordinate could.

Davis slid into one of the visitor chairs like he'd expected to be asked. General O'Neill probably employed this technique all the time. "The most critical thing is the logistical support for the expansion of Atlantis personnel."

Woolsey blinked. "What expansion?"

"Atlantis is getting twenty-eight more people leaving on *Daedalus* tomorrow, to be assigned permanently, with another seventeen following on *Daedalus*' next run in eight weeks," Davis replied. "They're all Indian. Sixteen of the current group are civilian scientists and five of the next group. The balance are Indian Air Force personnel who are assigned to support for the *Asoka*." Woolsey must have looked blank because Davis continued. "The *Asoka* is the Indian research vessel that's preparing to launch."

"I thought that was next year," Woolsey said.

"They've moved it up to summer," Davis said. "So they're sending out their support personnel and material beforehand. So that when the *Asoka* arrives in Atlantis there will be any necessary repair and maintenance equipment already there, as well as the people to use it."

"Nobody's told Atlantis anything about it," Woolsey said.

"I don't know why that is, sir," Davis said. "But we've also been working out the logistical support. It's only fair that India is supplying additional rations and supplies, so we're getting a shipment from the Indian Air Force to the SGC."

"Why aren't they just using the Stargate instead of going on *Daedalus*?" Woolsey asked.

"The IAF thought that it would be a good idea for them to become acclimated to spaceflight," Davis said. "Only four of them have been off-world before, and all of those are civilian scientists. So they're riding along on *Daedalus* and seeing it operationally."

And if Caldwell was fine with that, well and good. That was an Air Force problem, not his. His was to make sure that Sheppard knew that they were coming. They'd need quarters and lab space and storage for the spare parts for *Asoka*. If they wanted to be near the landing space on the south platform, there might be room in the tower just north of it to store parts and set up office space overlooking the landing pad...

But that was also not his problem. Sheppard would do that. He had to stop micromanaging Atlantis and think about the big picture.

"This is the first major cooperative operation," Davis said. "The IOA is very invested."

Which was code for 'if it doesn't go well, it's someone's head.'

"It's an exciting opportunity," Woolsey said. "And I'm sure it will go fine. Get me the documentation on who's leaving on *Daedalus* tomorrow so I can brief Atlantis. Let's make sure everything is ready when they arrive." First impressions meant a lot, and arriving to prepared quarters and good food was the first step to a smooth working relationship.

This was the shape of the future, not an isolated expedition on a one-way trip but all nations venturing into the cosmos together, and here, sitting at his desk on Massachusetts Avenue, it was up to him. Richard Woolsey could make it work.

INTERLUDE

HALF the miners started packing up to leave Lorvine. Fenna made no attempt to persuade them to stay. "What can I say?" she asked. "Between the Wraith and the Genii, this has become a real dangerous place." She looked around the well-lit caverns. "Those of us who are staying are staying because we've got no place to go."

"You could come aboard the *Durant*," Dekaas said. "We'll be casting off soon. No point in staying longer."

"Nor risking your ship." Fenna's eyes were suspiciously bright. "And do you speak for your captain then, that you invite us to crew?"

"You've skills we can use," Dekaas said. "And I'd speak to the captain on your behalf. He's a reasonable man."

Fenna glanced around the caverns again, then sighed. "No," she said. "I'll stay. Thank you kindly for the offer, Dekaas." She glanced at Elizabeth. "And you can dial out for Sateda. Just get in line. Lots of people going lots of places."

"Thank you," Elizabeth said, and watched her walk away. She squared her shoulders. "And I will be sorry to say goodbye to you, Dekaas."

The old man smiled. "And I to you, Elizabeth. I hope you find the home you're looking for."

There was one more thing she wondered. "Why did you ask the Wraith about his queen?"

"I thought it might be someone I'd heard of."

"Is she?"

Dekaas shook his head. "I've never heard of Waterlight. Her line — well, I've heard of that." He dropped his voice. "The hive I served on once was an Osprey hive. But that was years ago, and there are many queens. Or were. I'd guess she's young and wasn't very important before this alliance against Queen Death."

"Do you think the Wraith was telling the truth?"

"That she killed Queen Death?" Dekaas shrugged. "It could be. That's how it's supposed to work, mind to mind and hand to hand between queens. Not that it always does. There are plenty who are content to throw men and Darts at each other from a distance. But it could have happened that way. Which would make her much more prominent now, as many of Queen Death's men would be obligated to follow her. She could have staked quite a large claim."

"Including sovereignty over human settled planets?"

"For what it's worth," Dekaas said. "Hives often divide up hunting grounds, and it does make a difference. Some hives Cull recklessly. Others are more occasional hunters. Not that it matters to the prey."

Elizabeth frowned. "What about this retrovirus?"

"That's been tried before," Dekaas said. "And the idea of strengthening humans against the feeding process..." He frowned. "Medically, the way it works is that when a Wraith feeds it injects the prey with an enzyme that temporarily — and I do mean very temporarily — strengthens the human so that it won't die from shock immediately, before the Wraith has finished feeding. There have been many attempts, both by humans and Wraith, to synthesize this enzyme so that humans can survive a feeding. It doesn't work. And the effects of the enzyme on the human system in the long run are deleterious." He drew her aside, away from anyone who might overhear. "Atelia's husband was addicted to the enzyme when he first came aboard the Traveler ships. I helped him get through the withdrawal, and he just barely pulled through. He had continuing problems for months, and there are issues that are never going to go away. Most don't live through the withdrawal. He was lucky and he was a physically fit young man. But messing with the enzyme is a very bad idea."

"But they said this was a retrovirus." Elizabeth frowned again. There was something this should remind her of, some problem, some dilemma she'd seen before. But it wasn't there. Whatever the important memory was, it escaped her.

"And you know what a retrovirus is," Dekaas said. He smiled unexpectedly. "Interesting."

"You don't think I'm Satedan?"

"You may be. But there are other places..." He stopped. "Does Hoff sound familiar?"

"Maybe?" And there was a dark story there too, lost somewhere in the black depths of her mind.

Dekaas put his hand on her shoulder. "I hope for your sake that your home is out there, and that there are people you love who are looking for you."

"But you don't think so?"

"I doubt it," Dekaas said solemnly. "But I understand you need to know. And if you decide you want to come with us, there's good work and a place for you here."

"Thank you," Elizabeth said, unexpectedly touched. "I'll remember that."

Elizabeth stepped through to Sateda at night. Unfamiliar stars shone over the ruined city, dimmed by the lanterns that surrounded the square where the Ring stood. The pavement was cracked but everything was swept clean, and the buildings surrounding the square showed lights here and there in the windows. A series of low fences directed inbound travelers to a kiosk with an awning — some kind of customs booth. Elizabeth looked around in surprise. Somehow she had not expected this. Surely everything should have been rubble? Surely there should be no people?

The façades of the buildings were darkened from fire here and there, upper windows still boarded up, but at street level there were shutters with louvers on them and even a few windows with glass. The bricks had been neatly scrubbed. The streets were clean and well lit. From one building across the square came the sound of music, some kind of stringed instrument and voices raised in song. This city was not deserted. It was alive.

It was cold, and Elizabeth shivered even in the jacket Dekaas had given her. She carried her bundle around the line of fences as a door opened and two men came out. They were unarmed, but their voices sounded official. "Inbound traveler, who are you and what's your business on Sateda?"

"My name is Elizabeth," she replied. "And I have lost my memory. A Satedan who lives with the Travelers thought I was also probably Satedan, so I've come to see if I can find my family or friends."

At that their faces relaxed. "A lot of Satedans have been returning lately."

"I didn't expect it to look like this." Elizabeth gestured around the square. "I thought it was deserted."

"We've been coming back a little at a time," the taller of the men said. "We have a government again. Ushan Cai is our elected leader. You can talk to him in the morning." He pulled out a little note-book and jotted a few lines. "Returning Satedan, name Elzabet. Any skills or profession?"

"I have some experience in medicine."

He nodded quickly, making notes. "That's good. We can always use more medical personnel. Tell you what, go on over to the hotel and tell them you're cleared. You can get a blanket and sleep in the ballroom. Tomorrow you can talk to Cai and figure out where you want to go."

"Thank you," Elizabeth said. She looked around the square again, the buildings of a maddeningly familiar type, and yet not familiar at all. "I can't believe it looks like this. Those are electric lights!"

The second guard agreed proudly. "That they are. We've got a naquadah generator from the Lanteans too!"

"A what?"

"We have electric power again. Limited, but enough for some basic things," the first guard said. "It's the middle of the night here. Go on over to that building there. It's warm and you can get some rest."

"That sounds perfect," Elizabeth said, for all that she wasn't the least bit sleepy since for her it was only mid-afternoon.

Unsurprisingly, lying on a cot with a thin blanket in the hotel ballroom, she couldn't sleep. All around her twenty or so people slept, most on cots or on the floor in bedrolls. The walls of the big room had originally been painted white and gold, though there were places where plaster had fallen exposing lathe and beam beneath. A few holes in the ceiling showed where light fixtures had once hung, but it was dark except for a little lamp on the desk at the door. The broken windows were closed with shutters against the cold. A small space heater cut the chill a little, a white box in a suspiciously familiar design purring softly in the corner.

Was it familiar because it was Satedan? Probably. Surely. Elizabeth rolled over, trying to find a comfortable position.

A night like this, and quiet, the sounds of other people sleeping in a big, empty room in a deserted city...

...she slept in a bedroll in the corner of her office, the room she'd taken for her office. Who could tell what it was supposed to be? Probably it was the office of the person who oversaw the control room just outside the door, but it was impossible to know what the Ancients had intended.

She should sleep. There was a great deal to do tomorrow and the next day and every day after that. But adrenaline wouldn't let her sleep. Nothing would, though it had been nearly forty hours since she had spent her last night at home in one of the guest rooms at the SGC, wondering, hoping, praying, that the gate address would work....

Elizabeth sat bolt upright on the cot. She had remembered something. She had remembered something intentionally. It had been a room just off a big room that echoed, ceiling and windows lofty and strange, patterned with colored glass. There were people there too, sleeping in bedrolls under consoles and around screens, while a few bolder ones had branched out into the conference rooms and suites nearby. Everything was quiet, surrounded by the green light of the sea.

It wasn't her home planet, but it had become home. She remembered it.

Tears filled her eyes. That was home. That was where she belonged. And it wasn't here, not on Sateda. Though she had no idea where it was, what the name of the world was where that city stood, she would find it no matter what.

CHAPTER FIFTEEN

JOHN was in the shower when his radio crackled. "Colonel Sheppard?" Amelia Banks' voice asked.

John turned off the water with a thought — a nice perk of the ATA gene-sensitive controls over in this tower — and jumped out to press the button. "This is Sheppard."

"Larrin's calling in. She says she's rendezvoused with Lesko's ship."

"On my way," John said, already pulling his clothes on.

It was less than ten minutes before he stepped out of the transport chamber in the gate room and hurried over to the console. Larrin smirked at him from the viewscreen. "Busy, Sheppard?"

"Washing. I do that sometimes." He gave her what he hoped was a charming and insouciant grin. "Banks says you've got Lesko's ship."

"Yeah, but I don't have your friend," Larrin replied. "Lesko says she got off when they rendezvoused with another of our ships, the *Durant*."

"What? Why didn't he stop her?" John blurted.

"Why would he? Why does he care where a passenger goes? She was a passenger, not a prisoner." Larrin tilted her chin. "I think it's about time you leveled with me about who your friend is."

Banks looked up at him from her terminal, and John was aware of a sudden hush falling around him.

"She was an important part of our expedition," John said. "And we never leave a man behind. If she's wandering around injured, not even remembering who she is, we have a responsibility."

Larrin's eyebrows rose. "Well," she said, "that makes sense. She went over to the *Durant* because they have one of our best doctors. If she was hurt or hoped he could help with the memory problem, she was smart to transfer over."

Which did reassure John somewhat. That was like Elizabeth, trying to work this problem from the other end, and he let himself feel a tiny glimmer of hope. "OK, thanks," he said. "Any idea where this ship, the *Durant*, is?"

"They're due for planetfall on Manaria day after tomorrow,"

Larrin said.

"Manaria?" John frowned. "Manaria was practically leveled by Queen Death a few months ago."

Larrin nodded. "Yep. That's why they're buying ores from us. They need metal for rebuilding, and we'll bring it in at the right price."

"Which is high," John said.

"We're not philanthropists, Sheppard. Everybody's got problems."

"I know. I appreciate you taking the time to call."

Teyla and Rodney had just come in and were standing back from the camera side by side with expressions on their face that suggested they were having one of their silent Wraithy conversations.

"Just remember that in the future," Larrin said, and cut the communications link.

John turned around. "So," he said.

"Manaria," Teyla said.

"Day after tomorrow," John said. "OK, we're in business."

Which of course meant there wasn't anything he could do about it right that minute. John went down to the mess and got breakfast to bring back to Woolsey's office. No, to his office. Which was not a good thing.

It wasn't that he minded the paperwork necessary for Atlantis' military contingent. It wasn't even that he minded the jobs that kept him in Atlantis rather than in the field. He'd found that he actually liked the training part. There was something really satisfying about helping the new, young airmen and Marines figure out how to deal with a universe they'd never imagined existed a year ago. He didn't even mind dealing with the Air Force brass now that he mostly went directly through General O'Neill rather than General Landry, who hated him ever since the part about stealing a puddle-jumper out of the SGC.

No, what he hated was the IOA. With Woolsey gone about ninety percent of his inbox was IOA stuff — reports and questions and a million nit-picky stupid things which either didn't make any difference or were for reasons that anybody with half a brain could have seen. "Why do you transmit on Tuesdays?" Why not? Tuesday was a perfectly good day to transmit. "Why do you maintain encryption on internal messages?" Because our computer systems have been compromised so many times they look like Swiss cheese, and anything that will slow people down for ten minutes buys us ten minutes.

Overnight there had been another email upload, thirty-seven messages this time, all of them work related. There really wasn't anyone on Earth who sent him personal email messages. And there was one from Woolsey with fat attachments. John opened that one first.

He read it three times, then took a gulp of his coffee and considered. The Indian research vessel, the *Asoka*, was launching earlier than expected. OK — that wasn't actually a surprise. It was a usual Air Force thing to allow more time than you actually needed in case problems came up, and he doubted the Indian Air Force did things differently. If they were anticipating a summer maiden voyage, they must be having smooth trials now, so they were going ahead and sending out research and maintenance personnel. Made sense. That way when the *Asoka* arrived they could look her over after her shakedown cruise. But that was a pretty big contingent. Other than the US contingent, that was the single largest other nationality represented. If the *Asoka's* crew was anything like the size of the *Hammond's*, that meant when they were in port the Indians would be about a quarter of the total population of Atlantis. That would change things. And the *Asoka* wouldn't be going back and forth like *Daedalus* and *Hammond*, nor primarily Milky Way based like the Russian battlecruiser. It would be based in Atlantis and its mission was to explore the Pegasus galaxy. This was going to be really different.

But it was probably a good thing. The more non-US nations that had a stake in Pegasus, the less likely that a political retrenching would close Atlantis down. No, they were here to stay, and the *Asoka* was one part of that. His job was to make it work. So he'd better start talking to whoever the IAF liaison was. It was going to be a brave new world.

Lorne collected his tray in the mess hall and settled down at a table. There was a shipment of trade goods to Sateda scheduled for that morning, but for once he actually had time to sit down and eat breakfast. He had his first bite of scrambled eggs halfway to his mouth when his radio crackled to life.

"Perfect timing," he muttered, and then said more loudly, "Lorne here."

"Sir, we've been working on getting the equipment set up at the alpha site," Sgt. Anthony said. "But we've run into a few problems."

"And those problems would be?" Lorne prompted, watching the eggs on his plate congeal.

"It's the equipment we were issued," Anthony said. "It's junk. The first tent we put up is already falling apart, and one of the ones we just put up ripped as soon as the wind picked up. And two of the water containers that we brought through are leaking."

"So come back and get new ones," Lorne said as patiently as he could.

"Affirmative, sir, I've sent Harper back with the jumper to do that. She could use some flight time in the jumper anyway. But this stuff is out of the shipment that just came out on *Daedalus*. Maybe we just happened to pull some bad equipment, but… "

"But if they sent us defective equipment, we need to know that now," Lorne finished. "I appreciate the heads-up."

"Harper's bringing back the gear that fell apart."

"Great," Lorne said, his mind on his rapidly cooling breakfast. "When she gets back with replacements, get that alpha site set up. We may not need it, but if we need it we're going to need it fast. And we can't park people on a desert planet without water."

"Copy that," Anthony said, and cut the transmission.

Lorne started to go back to his interrupted meal, now complete with an extra helping of nagging worry. He looked up as Radek Zelenka put his tray down. Zelenka was the acting head of the science department – everyone had been a little nervous about handing that responsibility directly back to Dr. McKay, despite all the doctors' assurances that he was fully recovered from having been a Wraith. He ought to know if the scientists were having any similar issues.

"Hey, doc. Have any of the scientists been having any problems with the equipment that came out on *Daedalus*?"

"You mean the most recent shipment?" The Czech scientist frowned. "Not that I have heard. Dr. Elkins in botany complains that the broad-spectrum lights aren't adequate to their needs, but he has made that complaint about every shipment of them we have received. And Dr. Kusinagi reported her new mass spectrometer was damaged in shipment. She expressed herself in fairly strong terms about it."

"Do you think it was defective in some way?"

"No, I think that somebody dropped it. The SGC personnel are not always as careful as they should be with scientific equipment." Radek looked at him over the rim of his glasses. "Why do you ask?"

"One of my teams had some of their gear fall apart. Probably they just had the bad luck to grab the wrong tent and the wrong water containers, but… " But those were two separate items, probably packed in entirely separate shipping containers for the trip from Earth, both of which had turned out to be defective. "But you never know around here," Lorne said, scooping up his scrambled eggs in a piece of toast. "I'm going to go take a look."

"There is the trade mission to Sateda scheduled for this morning."

"I've got time if I eat breakfast and put the fear of God into the supply officer at the same time. I'm in the Air Force, we can multitask."

"I will ask around as well," Radek said. "But I have found that the scientists rarely hesitate to complain. Especially when they know it is me and not Rodney who they will be complaining to." He shook his head. "If they do not put Rodney back in charge soon, I may have to ask him for lessons in appearing less sympathetic."

"He could probably give you some pointers," Lorne said, and headed off, improvised sandwich in hand.

Teyla nodded to the Marine on duty outside the door of Ember's guest quarters and then opened the door. *Ember?* she called silently. *Are you there?*

He was, of course. It was courtesy to ask, as she'd already felt his presence. Ember was sitting before the floor to ceiling window looking out across the city, the only light the bright reflections of the lights of other towers and the distant stars, more than enough light for a Wraith to see by easily. His dark coat blended with the black leather of the bench he sat on, though he rose to his feet immediately. A white ball fell out of his lap and picked itself up indignantly, washing one paw with a superior expression on its little gray face.

The animal was friendly, Ember said sheepishly. *I do not know where it came from. It simply was here.*

That is Newton, Teyla said, shaking her head as the cat looked up at her. *It is Dr. McKay's cat. No matter where he tries to keep it, it gets out and roams where it wishes. I will tell him where it is.*

I did not harm it, Ember said.

So I see. The nearly year old cat was winding its way around Ember's ankles, purring loudly.

Teyla walked over to the window. It was indeed an awe-inspiring view. *You know that you do not have to stay in this room. You are a guest, not a prisoner.*

Ember's reply was the mental picture of the Marine at the door.

That is an escort, not a guard. You are more than welcome to join the rest of us this evening.

In the Mess Hall? Ember's mental voice was amused. *I do not think there are — things — that I would eat.*

*Are you hungry then?"

Not noticeably, Ember said. *I can go several days yet if I do not have to heal myself. If I am still here then…*

If you are still here then, there are many who have had the trial of the retrovirus, Teyla said. *Perhaps a volunteer can be found.*

Ember came and stood beside her. *You would ask one of your men to do this?*

I expect a volunteer can be found, Teyla said, not intending her mental picture of Dr. Zelenka to be seen, but it was.

I gave him great pain before.

But no lasting harm. Teyla put her hand to the glass.

It seems not. There was a shade of embarrassment in his mental voice, and she could find the source of it easily enough — that he had been so far gone in pain as to be without restraint, desperate enough to save his own life that he would have killed the man who had helped him if Radek had not had the retrovirus. *I would have been sorry to kill him,* Ember said quietly.

I know. Teyla took a deep breath. *There are many I have killed for which I am sorry.*

Ember looked at her sideways, as if wary to receive such confidence from one he considered a queen.

But we do what we must to live, or else we die, Teyla said. *And I have never been one who was willing to die.* She shook her head. *And that was the choice of the First Mothers. I cannot say I would have chosen differently.*

His mind was open, and she showed him a shard of memory — *the bright tapestry of a starfield far from any world, beyond heliopause in the silence between systems where the Wraith were safe. Five ships hovered there, small and awkward for hive ships today, but hive ships nevertheless, grown from mollusks found on a distant world a thousand years ago. Five ships and two hundred and seventy four people, four daughters and twenty one sons, two granddaughters and sixty two grandsons, innumerable friends and consorts and men of other lines come to join her — Osprey's family. This was her line, her legacy — these ships, these men, these bright and brilliant daughters — this fleet. They had not simply survived. They had thrived. And they were beautiful. Her heart was filled by a life of such joy. Osprey stretched her mind out over the fleet, feeling her daughters answer, feeling each precious mind. Mother of Queens, First Mother…*

Ember bent his head. To see such a thing from her mind was honor indeed.

I did not know, Teyla said. *I did not know there was beauty. I saw only death. Only hardship. When I first remembered, I felt pity. I pitied Osprey her suffering and for the injustice done to her. That was what I felt at first.*

And now? Ember asked boldly.

I feel pride, Teyla said. She reached down and scooped up Newton where he wound about her ankles. *Come. Let us return Newton to Dr. McKay.*

Atlantis's current supply officer was a young Air Force lieutenant who had been hastily posted to Atlantis as they were leaving Earth. Lorne privately felt they would have been better off trying to get the highly competent Lt. Alberti back, even if it had required twisting multiple arms to do it. What he had, however, was Lt. Winston, who had an unfortunate faith in the reliability of all other links in the supply chain.

"That equipment came out of the shipment we just got a couple of weeks ago when *Daedalus* was here," Winston said.

"That's what I just told you."

"So it should be fine."

"It should be, but it isn't," Lorne said. "Two of the water containers sprung leaks, and one of the tents fell apart as soon as it was set up."

"Maybe it wasn't set up properly."

"That's possible. But that shouldn't make it fall apart like it's been shredded. And are you saying they filled the water cans with water wrong?"

"Maybe they put them down on rocks."

"There's nothing but rocks to put them down on. Come on, now. Let's take a look at the rest of the gear from that shipment and see how much of it is pre-wrecked for our convenience."

"The SGC wouldn't send us defective equipment," Winston said.

"You have got a lot to learn about life," Lorne said. "Or at least about life in the military. Show me the containers."

It took an hour to inventory the contents of the containers that had arrived on *Daedalus*. None of the other gear showed visible signs of damage or manufacturing defects, but then presumably neither had the tent and the water cans before they were used.

"Okay," Lorne said finally. "Did Harper come pick up a new tent and water cans?"

"Right before you got down here," Winston said.

The door to the supply warehouse slid open at that moment, and Harper came in, scowling. "You know those new water cans you issued me? One of them fell apart as soon we took it out of the jumper," she said. "It looks like it melted. The others are still holding water, but I'm telling you there's something wrong with these cans."

"All right," Lorne said. "Get a water trailer out there. We're going to need one anyway if we're going to have people stationed there for any length of time. How's the new tent holding up?"

"They were setting it up when I left," she said.

"Let me know if it stays up. Get the rest of the site set up, and let me know if you have any other equipment failures. I've got to go take Dr. Lynn and Dr. Zelenka to Sateda today, but I'll come out and take a look when I get back." They were dropping off some portable generators to help the Satedans get electric power to areas that crucially needed it, in exchange for letting Lynn explore the Satedan museum more fully, this time hopefully without the threat of Genii soldiers storming in while he was doing it.

He turned to Winston. "Have one of your people set up some of these tents out on the pier, and see if they fall apart. Let's not have a gate team find that out when they're relying on them for shelter in a blizzard. And start testing the water cans, too. Let's find out if any of them actually hold water."

"Yes, sir," Winston said with a martyred expression.

"Because if we do end up with a gate team put in danger because of potentially defective supplies, Colonel Sheppard will start asking questions about whether these potentially defective supplies were tested before they were issued. And I'll have answers for him. Understand?"

"Yes, sir."

"I'm glad to hear it."

Ronon stood in the doorway of Eva's office, not sure whether there was any point in being there or not. "Are you busy?"

"No," she said. "But you can make an appointment if you want."

He shrugged. "I thought I'd come see if you were busy."

"I'm not busy," she said, shifting in her chair to brace her injured leg more comfortably. "Come in and sit down. Tell me what's on your mind."

Ronon sat down. "I think you ought to tell Sheppard and Teyla not to trust the Wraith so much."

"I'm not sure that's exactly my job," Eva said after a momentary pause.

"You said you gave people advice."

"When they ask for it. How about you tell me why you're worried about them trusting the Wraith too much?"

"Because we've got a Wraith in the city again."

Eva nodded. "And you don't like it."

"It's dangerous. So maybe they can help us find some old relics of the Asgard. So what. That's not worth having them here. Having people get used to them, like they're supposed to be here."

"You're afraid that people won't be on their guard if something dangerous happens."

"Sheppard probably will be. I don't know about Teyla."

"Teyla's never struck me as a careless kind of person. Does she strike you that way?"

"Not careless. But she's started sympathizing with the Wraith, even liking some of them. That's… wrong," he finished, unable to come up with a word for it that was as strong as he felt it deserved.

"Which do you think is more important? Whether or not she likes the Wraith, or whether or not she's careful?"

There was an answer on the tip of his tongue, but he bit the words back. "Whether or not she's careful," he said after a moment.

"It won't hurt to remind her to be careful. Vigilance isn't a bad thing when you really are in a dangerous situation. It only starts to be a problem when you can't relax when things get back to normal."

"What if this is normal, now?"

"I don't think anyone's suggested having the Wraith as permanent residents of Atlantis. It may feel like this is lasting forever, but it's really a temporary situation."

"We keep working with the Wraith, though. That isn't a temporary situation."

"And you've certainly got plenty of reasons not to want to work with the Wraith."

He shrugged. "It's not up to me."

"Not whether we have an alliance with the Wraith, no. I'm just wondering if you want me to recommend that you not be assigned to missions that involve working directly with the Wraith."

"You can't do that."

"Well, yes, I actually can recommend that," Eva said. "Now, I can't tell you if Colonel Sheppard would take my advice, but I think he'd at least listen to it. There's plenty of work around here that doesn't involve being an ambassador to the Wraith."

"Yeah, but they're going to keep wanting Teyla to do it."

"That's probably true," Eva agreed. "Teyla has established a good working relationship with Alabaster and her people. No one's going to want to waste that."

"So I'm stuck with it. I have to watch her back."

"Aren't there other people who could do that?"

"Teyla's my family," he said after a moment. "Maybe you don't understand that."

"I understand that," Eva said. "But sometimes what's good for one person in a family isn't good for another person. I know that on a mission like this, you bond with people incredibly tightly. You eat with them and work with them and spend all your free time with them, and it's hard to think of letting go of any of those things."

"But," he prompted when it seemed like there was more she wanted to say.

"But sometimes there are missions that one person on the team would be perfect for and that another person on the team can't do. And sometimes the answer to that is splitting up a team temporarily, and other times it's thinking about whether the way the team is put together still makes sense."

"If I wanted to quit the team, I'd leave Atlantis," Ronon said.

"I'm just saying those aren't your only choices. And maybe that's something for you to think about."

"Maybe," he said. "You won't say anything to Sheppard, right?"

"Not a word," she said.

INTERLUDE

USHAN CAI proved to be an older man in a coat that had known better days, though both it and he were clean, suggesting that they had adequate water for washing. Elizabeth was eating some kind of sweet bread at a long table when he strode up and swung his leg over the opposite bench to sit down with her. "I'm Ushan Cai," he said. "I hear you came in last night."

"That's right." Elizabeth put the bread down quickly. "It's good to meet you."

"The boys said you were a medic." He smiled approvingly. "That's always useful."

"I have some medical skills," Elizabeth clarified. "I'm not a doctor. The truth is, I'm not entirely sure what I am."

"How's that?" He seemed curious rather than skeptical.

"People found me on Mazatla. I had no memory of how I got there or of what happened before that. I remembered things that made them wonder if I were Satedan, so they took me to the Travelers. I met a young Satedan woman there who said she agreed that the things I remembered sounded like Sateda, and that a lot of other Satedans who had been off-world were wandering too. She said some people had started returning home and gave me the gate address. As soon as the Traveler ship I was on came to a world where I could dial out, I did. And so I came here."

He nodded thoughtfully. "What do you remember?"

Elizabeth glanced out the window at the buildings across the square gilded with first light. "Steel bridges across a river. Railroads. A hospital. Doctors, drugs, a university. My parents." She didn't glance at him. "A man who was a doctor. I think he was…" She stopped. "I think Simon was very close to me. I don't know what happened to him. I thought he was dead and then I thought that was just a dream." She looked back at Cai, who was watching her compassionately. But then he must have heard all this before. A doctor's wife, probably. Maybe a nurse or a humanitarian of some kind, traumatized by what had happened, remembering and forgetting his death — it was very plausible.

"Well," Cai said. "You're welcome to stay here and look for your loved ones. Also more people are returning every day. Any time someone might arrive looking for you."

"That's true," Elizabeth said. Someone was looking for her. Not Simon, but someone.

"Everyone here who can needs to work," Cai said. "We don't have a lot, but we share what we have with anyone who returns. But we expect everybody to pitch in as they're able."

"I'm more than happy to pitch in," Elizabeth said. "I've been assisting one of the Traveler's doctors, or I can do other work as you need it." She dusted her hands off on her pants. "I'm no engineer, but I can follow directions. I can even help with the naquadah generator if you need it."

Cai's eyes widened a little. "That's not ours," he said. "Not Satedan. We just got it. How did you know what it is?"

"One of the guards told me last night," Elizabeth said, which was perfectly true. Only...

His face relaxed a little. "Well, let me send you over to the medical salvage team. We've got a team going to all the old clinics and hospitals around the city seeing what equipment and supplies they can salvage. They've found quite a lot, actually." He shrugged. "Not drugs, of course. Most of them would be too old to use or spoiled. But there's some equipment, surgical packs, gurneys, all kinds of useful things. Think you're up for medical salvage?"

"Absolutely," Elizabeth said.

The salvage team was led by a woman named Margin Bri, hard faced and golden skinned, about Elizabeth's age. There were four other people in the party. "Alright folks," she said as they stood in what had once been the lobby of the hotel. "Grab your bedroll and check out two boxes of rations. This is an overnight trip. We're walking up to Paiden and seeing what's left of the Regional Clinic there."

"What's Paiden?" Elizabeth asked.

The man next to her glanced at her. "It used to be one of the suburbs. It's up the rail line."

"That's right," Margin said. "We're going to follow the tracks. No way we can get lost, no matter how different things look! But there used to be a Regional Clinic there. I think since it was out of the city there may be a chance that there's more left of it. We're looking for hand held equipment in working order or large pieces that we can tag and come back for. Particularly if we can find a working x-ray machine, that's a priority. We know the Regional Clinic used to have one. What we don't know is how bad the physical damage was up near Paiden. They were Culled heavily, but hopefully with beams. So let's head out. It's half a day's walk."

The ration boxes proved to be a pair of rectangular containers made out of something like rattan with a hinged lid. Inside were several packets wrapped in oiled cloth, more of the sweetbread from breakfast, dried meat, some dehydrated vegetables. There was also a foil packet in each that looked suspiciously familiar. Elizabeth frowned. "Energy bars," she said.

Margin nodded. "Yep. Two each. One for today, one for tomorrow. Let's get going."

At first they walked through city streets in the early morning chill. Many of the buildings were reduced to piles of rubble and the streets away from the city center were choked with fallen debris. Elizabeth wondered if the all the streets had been like this. If so, Cai and his people had moved an enormous amount with no larger tools than shovels. They had to watch their steps constantly. Shards of broken glass, darkened by sun exposure, protruded from piles of broken bricks everywhere, the remains of windows. This must have been a beautiful city once, Elizabeth thought. It was eerily beautiful even now. Here and there a few small saplings thrust up from gaps in the pavement, spreading pale green leaves in the watery early spring sun.

It took an hour or more for Elizabeth to see the rail line they were following, twisted metal rails down the middle of what had been streets, a streetcar line perhaps? As the morning wore away she got better at seeing where the rails had been. No one spoke much. She supposed this had been their home. What could one say? There was no stench of remains. Ten years or more had passed. Any flesh had long since gone, and if there were bones they lay buried under broken concrete.

They halted when the sun stood directly overhead and ate in the center of what had been a square. A broken statue remained, four sets of legs from the knee down, three men and a woman in what had once been a heroic pose. The letters about the bottom of the statue were still cut clear in the stone, but Elizabeth could not read them. Satedan, she thought.

And yet she could read Lantean. The thought teased around in her head as she ate the dried vegetables in the ration box. Then she got the energy bar out. The silver wrapper had only one line of type on the back but it was perfectly clear. "Not for individual sale."

She handed the energy bar to Margin Bri. "What does this say?" she asked.

The woman shrugged. "I have no idea. That's Lantean."

"Ah," Elizabeth said. Hypothesis tested. She opened the package, nibbling at a corner of the chewy bar. Chocolate. The word came to mind, a flavor she had not tasted anywhere in memory, but she knew it. Chocolate.

"What do you know about the Lanteans?" she asked Margin Bri casually. "Do they ever come here?"

"From time to time." The other woman nodded. "Ushan Cai got them to help broker a deal to keep the Genii out. It's better to trade with the Lanteans than the Genii. They don't want to take over."

"Why is that?" Elizabeth asked.

Margin Bri stood up, dusting off her hands on her pants. "If you had Atlantis, would you want to be here?" She looked around the square. "OK, people. Let's head out."

"Atlantis," Elizabeth said quietly.

The buildings got smaller as they walked on. The rail line now ran through a culvert, concrete walls on each side and a sliver of sky between. Sometimes the way was nearly choked by a fall of concrete on either side, but more often it ran straight and true, the tracks intact.

"This looks like it could be used again," Elizabeth said at last.

One of the men nodded. "Not too much work, actually. Probably the biggest damage is corroded power lines, but that's not nearly as hard to fix as some things." He looked almost cheerful at the prospect.

Ahead, down the straight line of track, a broad curve of concrete rose to one side, spreading out to cover the track like a huge umbrella. "A suburban station?" Elizabeth guessed.

"That's the Paiden station," the man said. "Not far now. We'll leave the tracks there, but the Regional Clinic was only a block from the station."

"It looks pretty much intact," Elizabeth said. The curve of the roof was uninterrupted.

As they drew closer they saw that was true. The glass doors along the front were blown out, and a few pits in the concrete showed where something heavy had hit, but the roof was intact. They walked over the broken glass, past ticket counters and kiosks with faded signs in a language she didn't read, a few scattered bundles here and there. Elizabeth knelt and picked one up, shaking off the dust. It was a dark red jacket with white piping, heavy wool undamaged. Someone had dropped their jacket as they ran. A little further on there was a metal lunch pail and a child's shoe.

She stood up, biting on her lower lip.

"Come on," Margin Bri said. "We're going to lose the light before long."

The Regional Clinic had been ransacked. The building itself was intact, but clearly in the aftermath of the first attack it had been overrun by desperate people. The doors had been forced and the cabinets stood open, empty containers and worthless ones spread on the floor. Even the kitchen had been looted. Of course the kitchen had been looted. Any food was priceless, more valuable to the survivors than the medical supplies.

Margin Bri didn't seem disappointed. She looked around thoughtfully. "Most of the big equipment seems fine," she said. She stopped by a big machine plastered with yellow warning signs. "If we had power we could test it. But it looks good to me."

"I've got some boxes of sterile dressings in here," one of the men called from a room down the hall. "Some gloves, some small equipment. Also some bottled cleaning supplies. That's all worthwhile."

Elizabeth went into an examining room. It looked like the ones from her childhood, with a padded table and a scale in the corner...

Her childhood? Was she Satedan then? Everything about this was more and more confusing.

"You OK?" one of the men asked, and she realized she'd just been standing in the middle of the floor looking.

"Absolutely," Elizabeth said, and began going through cabinets.

Elizabeth dreamed, and in her dream she knew she was dreaming. She walked through a city of high white towers, the sound of the ocean mingling with the voice of the wind around each corner. She walked through each light-splashed corridor, stained glass making patterns of color on the floor. She paused by an open window, and as happens in dreams it opened, the balcony doors off the gate room. She stood in the bright sun looking out at city and sea, and she was content.

"Because you are home," a voice said beside her.

Elizabeth turned. It was none of the people she might have expected, whoever they were. It was a woman a head shorter than she was, long straight black hair falling to her waist. Her eyes were pupil-less and wide, her body slight as a child's. She was alien, and yet strangely familiar. "Do I know you?" Elizabeth asked.

"I am Ran," she said. She looked up at Elizabeth, her expressionless face serene. "I helped you Ascend. And it was I who suggested that you be placed on Mazatla when you were punished."

Elizabeth blinked. "You put me on Mazatla?"

Ran nodded slowly. "I put you in the path of good people who were on their way to the Gathering. I wanted to make sure you would come to no harm, and that you would begin your journey."

"I don't understand."

"You could not go somewhere you were known. Surely you understand that I could not do that. But a world with only an orbital gate, a world where no one had ever heard of Elizabeth Weir — that I could do. And yet I thought you would find your way home."

"Is Sateda my home?" Elizabeth asked.

"Do you think so?"

"No," Elizabeth said. "But I don't know where my home is."

"You will be home soon," Ran said serenely. "It is only a matter of time now. You will remember or you will be recognized now that you are so close. And yet..."

"Then I should thank you," Elizabeth said. "For watching over me. For putting me among good people when I was helpless. That's a big thing."

Ran shook her head, and for a moment she looked immeasurably old. "You broke the rules so that there could be peace. We have always sought peace first, you and I. But now it is I who must ask for your help."

"For my help?" Elizabeth stepped back from the rail. "How can I possibly help you? You're an Ascended being."

"And as an Ascended being, I am forbidden to interfere in the actions of living creatures. Even in self-defense."

Elizabeth frowned. "Self-defense? But what could harm you?" Even as she spoke, she knew there were things. Not devices she'd seen, but something she'd heard of, something in another galaxy…

"There are such things," Ran said. "Though there have been none in this galaxy for a very long time. But the information on how to construct them still exists, and there are those who are seeking that information for their own ends."

"To kill Ascended beings?"

"To force them to unascend." Ran put one long, four fingered hand on Elizabeth's arm. "And you have done so yourself, and so you would be a valuable prize for them. They seek not the secrets of Ascension, but of the Unascended. So I give you both this warning, and ask for your help. They must not gain the knowledge they seek."

Elizabeth squared her shoulders. "OK. Who are they? Where are they?" And yet the dream was already beginning to waver, the sea and sky darkening and blurring to nothing.

"I must go," Ran said. "I will return." For a moment her hand on Elizabeth's arm almost felt warm, almost entirely real. Then the world twisted.

CHAPTER SIXTEEN

ATLANTIS' STARGATE opened in a flare of blue fire, then subsided to a rippling pool of light inside the circle of naquadah. John lifted his P90 and prepared to walk through, Teyla and Ronon behind him.

"Oh, no no no!" Rodney came tearing out of one of the side doors, Dr. Jackson following him much more sedately. "You are not going to chase down this lead without me!"

"Rodney," John began, acutely aware of the entire gate room staff watching. "You and Jackson were going..."

"Jackson is right here," Rodney said. "You are not going to go hunt for Elizabeth on Manaria without me."

"We're checking out a lead," John said. "That's all. A place where this other ship is expected to make a port of call. We don't even know if they're there."

"Which is why you can't go," Rodney said triumphantly. "And I can. If this is going to involve sitting around for hours or days waiting for a ship to turn up, you can't leave Atlantis that long. Who are you going to leave in charge? Zelenka?"

"Zelenka's offworld," John said uncomfortably. It was certainly true that the IOA wouldn't like for him to be gone from Atlantis for an extended period, but what they didn't know wouldn't hurt them.

"Lorne?" Rodney asked.

John had the infuriated feeling that Rodney already knew the answer to that. "Lorne's with Zelenka. They went with Dr. Lynn on a regular trade mission."

"Then who's in charge?" Rodney asked. "Carson? Airman Salawi? Ember? Who do you think is going to pick up the phone if the SGC calls? Who do you think is going to deal with a crisis? And don't tell me that can't happen because it happens all the time."

Jackson looked up at the ceiling as if suddenly noticing something very interesting up there.

Rodney poked Sheppard in the chest with a sharp forefinger. "No, you need to stay here, and I need to go."

Ronon and Teyla were looking at him, and John suppressed a

sigh. Rodney was right that he ought to stay in Atlantis. Something could happen. Something did happen way too often. And even if what happened was a surprise call from General Landry, Landry wouldn't be happy to find out that this was like that *Star Trek* joke where the entire crew of the *Enterprise D* beams down to the planet leaving Wesley in charge. John dropped his voice. "OK, you've made your point. I'll stay and you and Jackson will go. But this is not your mission, understand?"

"But I…"

"Rodney, you're nuts on the subject of Elizabeth. There are not going to be any stupid risks in this picture. Teyla's in charge."

Teyla's eyebrows rose but she said nothing.

"You listen to Teyla. When she says it's time to leave, it's time to leave. Got that?" He looked at Ronon, who was watching with a grin on his face. "And you're backing Teyla up. If you have to carry McKay out kicking and screaming, you will. We are not going to have any unnecessary risks or piss off the Manarians or do any other stupid thing that seems like a good idea at the time. You are going to go, wait for the ship, and talk to the people. If — and this is a really big if — you find someone who resembles or claims to be Elizabeth, you will call in. At that point we'll arrange for Alpha site quarantine."

"We're talking about Elizabeth," Rodney said. "We don't need…"

"Rodney, shut up," John snapped. "We are talking about a key person who was in the hands of the enemy for months and infected with nanites, even if it is Elizabeth. Surely you, of all people, understand why we'd need quarantine? Or if you don't, how about you ask Lorne?"

Rodney turned red, and he did have the good grace to look away. After all, when he'd been compromised by the Wraith he'd led an attack on this very gate room which had cost lives and left Major Lorne seriously injured. Fortunately Lorne had recovered and he didn't seem to hold a grudge against Rodney, but the reasons why they had to be careful ought to be obvious. "OK, I get it," Rodney mumbled.

Enough said. "Teyla, if you get a whiff of trouble or anything that makes you or Ronon think it's a trap, get the hell out."

She nodded sharply. "We will do that. And Rodney will do as I ask." She gave Rodney a sideways glance full of that Wraithy expression that meant business.

"We'll be careful," Ronon said.

John took a step back. "Jackson, listen to Teyla."

"Absolutely," Jackson said.

"Then you've got a go," John said. He watched regretfully as the four of them walked through the Stargate.

Daniel peered out the viewscreen as Rodney landed the jumper next to the much bigger ship that had to be the *Durant*. About the best he could say for the other ship was that it was big; with its mismatched nose and stern, and its odd protrusions at various angles, it looked like something cobbled together in a junkyard. Which it probably had been, he reflected, and it was impressive enough that it actually flew.

"What a piece of junk," Rodney said.

Teyla shook her head at him. "They cannot all be Ancient warships."

"Who cares," Ronon said. There was a general hesitation, as if everyone was thinking that once they crossed the field outside to the other ship, they would have an answer to their question whether it turned out to be an answer they liked or not.

"We have to find out, you know," Daniel said. "If there's any chance that it might be Dr. Weir... "

"Of course we have to find out," Rodney said. He still hesitated.

Ronon was the one who finally stood. "Come on," he said. "Let's get this over with."

They walked across the landing field, which from the close-cropped grass was probably more usually occupied by sheep. A ladder led up to an open hatch, and Teyla stopped beneath it. "Hello?" she called.

A teenage girl wearing coveralls eventually stuck her head out the hatch. "You're never Manarian," she said.

"We are from Atlantis," Teyla said.

"Right, you can come up, we heard about you," she said. "Vyk and Annais have gone to trade with the dirtsiders. Locals, I should say, because I'm supposed to be polite. You want to talk to Dekaas, though, he's the one who talked to the woman with no memory."

"She was here?" Teyla said quickly. "A woman who knew nothing of where she came from?"

"Sure," the girl said without much interest, backing up to make room for them to ascend the rickety metal stairs. "Probably had all her family killed in some Culling. It happens."

"So it does," Teyla said. She didn't look dismayed by the girl's matter-of-fact tone. Probably it was a fact of life here in Pegasus, like natural disasters or fighting in war-torn regions back on Earth.

"She knew something about medicine, so she was helping Dekaas."

Daniel glanced at Teyla, who looked unwilling to commit herself to either hope or disappointment. "Our friend was not a doctor, but she would have known something about medicines, particularly Lantean medicine."

"It's down this way," the girl said. "Follow the green signs, see? And that'll take you to the infirmary."

"Thank you," Teyla said gravely.

"You'd think they'd guard the ship better," Daniel said.

Ronon shook his head. "The girl was wearing an energy pistol," he said. "The Manarians don't have anything like that. She could cut them down without breaking a sweat."

"Besides, the Manarians are hardly likely to anger their trading partners," Teyla said. "Certainly not when they need the metal they have brought to trade."

The infirmary was small, with only three beds, but neat and uncluttered compared to the corridor outside, where coils of wire and crates that smelled of fresh food had been left haphazardly lying. The doctor turned from his workbench where he was sorting pills into smaller bottles, and nodded to them in greeting.

Daniel couldn't help staring. He had assumed the name was a coincidence, a common one in the Pegasus galaxy, but now that he was face to face with the man, he knew he'd seen him before. Or, at least, he'd seen his counterpart in the alternate universe he'd visited using the Ouroboros device. He was a Wraith worshipper, the trusted pet of the same Wraith who'd been so interested in finding out what made Daniel tick, even if he had to take him apart to do it.

This man looked older, though, his hair graying and wrinkles beginning at the corners of his eyes. But then the Wraith could keep their pets artificially youthful, feed them life as well as take it away. "You're the Lanteans?" he said.

"We are," Teyla said. "We are hoping that you can tell us of the woman who has lost her memory."

Dekaas nodded. "Elizabeth."

Teyla's breath caught, and Ronon stiffened. Next to them, Rodney looked suddenly very calm, as if he'd worked out an elegant solution to a problem.

"Elizabeth's alive," he said.

"Is she here?" Teyla asked.

Dekaas shook his head. "We left her on Lorvine. She said she was going on to Sateda."

"If she's on Sateda, we'll find her," Ronon said.

Teyla held up a hand to quiet him, clearly more reluctant to believe yet. "Her name was Elizabeth Weir?"

"She couldn't remember any other name but Elizabeth," Dekaas said. "She was medium height, a little taller than you and I expect a couple of years older. Fair skin, dark hair, blue eyes. She said she couldn't remember her home world. I assumed that she was a survivor of a Culling. Possibly of the Culling on Sateda." His eyes flicked to Ronon.

Teyla frowned in concern. "She remembers nothing?"

"It happens," Daniel said. "When I... went through what we think she went through, I didn't even remember my own name for a while. It took months for most of my memories to come back."

"She remembered a few things," Dekaas said. "She had some medical knowledge. She read Lantean – it shouldn't surprise me that she's one of your people."

"You know that she read Lantean?"

Dekaas reached into one of the metal drawers and held up a packet of sterile bandages, very clearly American military issue. "She could read the writing on this."

"How do they have our supplies?" Daniel asked.

"We gave medical supplies to the Genii," Teyla said. "And to various other worlds."

"And we pay well for them," Dekaas said. "But probably not as much as we'd have to pay if we traded directly with you." He shrugged. "They're being put to good use."

"What else did Elizabeth tell you?" Rodney asked impatiently.

"She had been involved in a war on her homeworld. Some conflict in which she was not a soldier, but was helping refugees. From what she said, the war was fought with technology far beyond any I have seen used except in fighting the Wraith. She spoke of… " He reached for a notebook and flipped back through its pages. "The Red Cross, Vietnam, Bosnia. And a man called O'Neill."

"That's Elizabeth," Rodney said, as if daring anyone to contradict him.

"It certainly sounds like it," Daniel said.

"Come on, it has to be her."

"Or someone with her memories. Last time you saw Elizabeth, she was in a Replicator body."

"Do you have a photograph of her?" Teyla asked.

"That won't tell us whether she's a Replicator," Ronon said.

"Even so."

"I didn't think to take one," Dekaas said.

"The Wraith don't use photographs the way we do," Daniel said, making the connection.

Ronon looked at him sharply. "The Wraith?"

Teyla turned to look at him. "Please explain," she said, and he was reminded abruptly of Jack O'Neill's least friendly moods. He was already regretting speaking the thought aloud, but there seemed nothing to do at this point but answer.

"I know you've spent some time living with the Wraith," Daniel said.

Dekaas's face went very still. "I can't say that I remember you."

"You wouldn't. Dekaas was one of the humans on the hive I visited in the alternate universe," Daniel said, for the benefit of the rest of the team.

"That was in an alternate universe," Teyla said. "We do not know that the same events transpired here."

"No, of course we don't, but… I think I'm right."

Dekaas considered them cautiously. "Alternate universe?"

"It's a long story."

"You are making guesses," Teyla said. "And this is not why we are here."

"No, I'm… well, yes, but it's an educated guess. Alabaster and Guide did say that this universe's version of Seeker also had human worshippers."

"What they said was that he kept pets," Ronon said.

Dekaas seemed to be struggling to decide whether to speak or not. "Alabaster," he said finally. "The Young Queen. She survived?"

"She did," Teyla said. "Guide sent her to safety, and was nearly killed himself."

Dekaas let out a humorless laugh. "Guide. You've seen Guide."

"Oh, we've seen him," Ronon said. "He nearly killed one of our people."

"And has been an ally more recently," Teyla said firmly.

"We're not exactly friends," Dekaas said. "Guide used to tell Seeker that he ought to either eat me or let me go, because I was too dangerous to keep as a pet. I think he inclined toward eating me."

"But Seeker didn't."

"No. He taught me most of what I know about science and medicine. I think at first he wanted to find out how much I could understand. And I think the answer disturbed him as much as it fascinated him."

"You said Guide wasn't your friend. Was Seeker a friend?"

"My captor. My teacher. I… with all due respect, it's really none of your business how I feel about the fact that he's dead."

"I'm sorry. I'd be interested in hearing more about your experiences, though, if you —"

"Why would you want to? And why are we even trusting this person?" Ronon said. "Why do we keep trusting information that came from the Wraith?" His voice was rising, and he took a menacing step toward Dekaas, who returned his gaze calmly. It couldn't be the first time he'd faced down someone who would have liked to kill him.

"I'm not Wraith," Dekaas said.

"No, you're just a Wraith worshipper."

"Okay, let's calm down," Daniel said.

"It doesn't matter," Rodney said. "We need to find out what's happened to Elizabeth."

"That is right," Teyla said. "We are not here to judge anyone for having cooperated with the Wraith in the past."

Ronon scowled. "We're the ones cooperating with the Wraith right now."

"We are here to find Elizabeth," Teyla said. "And we will not discuss the Wraith any further." Her voice cracked like a whip on the last words.

Ronon took a deep breath, looking as though it actually steadied him to be given an order. "Fine," he said. "We'll talk about it later."

Daniel opened his mouth, saw Teyla's expression, and closed it again.

"I was about to say," Dekaas said evenly, "that I ran several tests to determine whether Elizabeth was human. I've done a sonic scan and looked at her blood under a microscope. She appeared to be completely human, in perfect health. Unusually perfect, as if she'd never had any injuries or major illnesses in her life."

"Well, you're obviously woefully under equipped to actually do genetic testing here, but everything you're saying would fit," Rodney said.

"Would it?" Dekaas tilted his head to one side. "I'd very much like to know what you think happened to her."

"What made you suspect she might not be human?" Teyla asked instead of answering.

"She said she was afraid she might be a robot or a Replicator. I assumed it was trauma-related. Sometimes people who have been through traumatic events—"

"Like being attacked by the Wraith," Ronon said.

"—feel detached, like their bodies don't really belong to them." He considered them. "But you are also worried that she might be a Replicator."

"When the Replicators—" Daniel began.

"Our friend was a prisoner of the Replicators before they were destroyed," Teyla interrupted. "It is a long story. But we had long since given up hope that she had survived."

"Every test I could run showed that she was human. As you've pointed out, I don't have the facilities to run a genetic scan, but I saw no evidence of anomalies in her blood. As far as I can tell, she's a human being."

"And she's on her way to Sateda," Rodney said.

"She should have reached Sateda by now. She planned to travel there through the gate from Lorvine, not by ship. I hope you can find her."

"Thank you," Teyla said. "We appreciate your help."

"The captain's gone to trade with the locals. I'm sure he'll want to get the news from Atlantis if you can stay a little longer. All we can pick up here is third-hand news from the Genii, and they don't exactly tell the Manarians everything they know."

"I have matters to discuss with my team first," Teyla said. "If you will excuse us for a few minutes?"

"Of course," Dekaas said. He frowned. "That other one of me," he said to Daniel. "The one in what you call an alternate universe. He's still aboard the hive?"

"As far as I know."

Dekaas nodded. Whether he was glad or sorry, whether he wished he could save his counterpart or would rather have exchanged places with him, Daniel had no idea. "Give Guide my regards," he said, a flicker of amusement crossing his face. "It ought to annoy him to hear that I'm not dead yet."

"I'll do that," Daniel said, and then had to quicken his pace to keep up with the others as they left the room.

They assembled outside the ship. "We need to get to Sateda, not waste time chatting with the Travelers," Rodney said. "We can send them an email or something later."

"We will discuss that in a minute," Teyla said. "First, we are going to discuss how we conduct ourselves in conversations with our allies."

"Some allies," Ronon said.

"I realize that might not have been the tactful moment—" Daniel began.

"Are you even capable of being quiet?"

"I've been asked that before," Daniel said after a moment's pause. "So, all right, shutting up for the moment."

Teyla let out a frustrated breath. "Ronon. We are no longer at war with the Wraith. I know that was not your decision, and I understand how hard that is for you. But at least for now, they are our allies, and we will be dealing with more and more people who have made peace with the Wraith." She looked up into Ronon's face. "You are my friend, and I would trust you with my life. But if you cannot be civil to our allies, I do not want you on my team."

"It's Sheppard's team."

"Not while Colonel Sheppard is in command in Atlantis. Do you question his judgment in placing me in command in his absence?"

There was a pause. "No," Ronon said. "You're in charge. If you order me to be polite to Wraith worshippers —"

"I am asking you to refrain from giving direct insults to our allies, whether they are Wraith worshippers or Wraith," Teyla said. "If you can say nothing civil, at least be silent."

"Asking isn't ordering."

"Then it is an order."

Ronon nodded, not happy, but accepting.

Teyla turned to Daniel. "Dr. Jackson. I have heard a great deal about you from Colonel Carter, and I believe you respect her as much as she respects you. I assume then that you do not respect my authority because I am Athosian, rather than because I am a woman."

"I... no, that's not true."

"I warned you off that line of questioning, and yet you persisted, even when it jeopardized our mission. You held your own idle curiosity to be more important than my authority. Or are you going to tell me that you do not know what I meant?"

"No, I knew you didn't want me to ask him about his time with the Wraith. But it could be important to understanding how the Wraith treat their human worshippers, and how they're likely to interact with humans now that they're administering the retrovirus to them. They need a model for how to deal with humans that's not based on treating them like livestock, and their relationships with their human worshippers are the closest thing they have to equal relationships with humans —"

"That is not our mission."

"You can't just put everything into little boxes and say, we're only going to find out about one tiny thing and not try to fit it into some kind of broader context. If we want to understand the story of the Pegasus galaxy—"

"And you are uniquely suited to doing so, despite the fact that you have only just arrived here?"

"I'm just trying to understand. Like everybody else in Atlantis."

"The members of the Atlantis expedition have shared knowledge of their culture with us as we have shared ours with them," Teyla said. "They have fought the Wraith and the Replicators with us, and many of them have died. They are part of our story, and we are part of theirs. But you are not even part of the Atlantis expedition. You are here at your pleasure, and you are on this team at mine. And I have seen nothing to persuade me that you have any skills at working as part of a team."

"I don't take orders well," Daniel said. "I admit that—"

"Then I will only give you one. Go back to the jumper, and wait there until we have spoken with the captain of the Travelers' ship. That is not a request, and I am not asking you for your opinion about my decision. Is that clear enough?"

"Crystal clear," Daniel said from between gritted teeth.

"I am glad we understand each other," Teyla said.

INTERLUDE

ELIZABETH woke. She lay in a bedroll on the floor of one of the rooms of the Paiden Regional Clinic, the other members of the salvage team sleeping nearby. In the doorway one of the men was keeping watch, looking out over the empty street and the stars paling with the coming dawn.

Already the dream seemed to fade. There had been a woman — an alien woman — and a danger. To her? To Elizabeth? It was hard to remember. But she was certain of one thing the woman had said. She would soon be home.

Their packs were heavy when they left the Regional Clinic. Elizabeth's held three piece of handheld electrical equipment and two manual blood pressure cuffs. They'd left the electric ones behind on the theory that you could take blood pressure just as well with the manual ones, and anything that didn't waste power was good. Her pack also held two dozen metal implements, mostly surgical clamps and scissors, things that were beyond what the Satedans could make today, but which had been commonplace before. She also had two heavy half empty bottles of disinfectant, another thing that used to be dirt cheap but which was now incredibly valuable.

Margin Bri said as much as Elizabeth hoisted her pack onto her back.

"I understand," Elizabeth said absently, adjusting the straps to distribute the load better. "It's the same thing I saw in Bosnia. Everyday things become incredibly valuable when suddenly there's no way to replace them."

Margin put her head to the side. "Where is Bosnia? I haven't heard of that Culling."

"I have no idea," Elizabeth said. The words had just come into her head, but she thought about them as they walked back to the rail station. She was remembering more. There were more pieces to the puzzle she was assembling. "I don't remember a lot of places I've been since I left home."

Margin nodded. "Some don't," she said. "It takes everyone differently. But you're here and that's what matters. You survived."

"I did," Elizabeth said. What she had survived might not be what Margin thought it was, but it was horror enough. Whatever it was, she had completely forgotten it.

The rail station was just as they'd left it and they passed through, turning south to follow the tracks. Suddenly there was a noise behind them, a scattering of stones and the low whine that Elizabeth recognized as the sound of a Satedan energy pistol powering up. They were standing in the middle of the tracks with little cover.

"Get down!" Margin Bri yelled, pulling one of the others off to the side.

There was almost nowhere to go. Elizabeth crouched, dodging back to the edge of the station platform. It only rose a couple of feet at the corner, but at least it was concrete. She reached for her side, for a weapon that wasn't there. She was unarmed. They were all unarmed except for some knives.

"Stand where you are," Margin Bri called out. "Show yourself or we'll return fire."

Nice bluff, Elizabeth thought.

"We've got you in our sights," a man called back. "Identify yourselves!"

Elizabeth didn't hesitate. "If you've got us in your sights, you know we're not Wraith," she said, standing up with her hands well to the sides.

There was a noise at the other end of the platform where a short flight of concrete steps led down to the tracks. An old man with a grizzled beard stood up, holding an energy pistol pointed straight at her. "Who are you then?" he demanded.

"A salvage party from the city," Elizabeth said. "Satedan. Now put the gun away."

"Why should I believe you?" he asked.

"Do we look like Wraith to you?" Elizabeth beckoned to Margin, who stood up, her heavy pack on her back. "We came looking for medical supplies. Which I bet you did too." The old man was wearing a bulky pack, but it looked mostly empty. "Let's talk about this."

"From the city?" the old man said. "That's impossible. They were all killed."

"Some Satedans have returned," Elizabeth said. Her eyes didn't waver. "Put the gun away and let's talk."

"Dad, put the gun away." A young woman stood up from the shelter of the steps, and after a moment a second did too. They were so alike as to be almost twins, but the one who had spoken had hair a shade darker and stood an inch shorter than her sister. "Come on, Dad."

After a moment he wavered, returning the energy pistol to a holster at his belt. "OK." He drew himself up. "I'm Beron Eze. These are my daughters Jana and Vetra."

"This is Margin Bri," Elizabeth said. "And I'm Elizabeth Weir. We're friends."

"How could you have come from the city?" the taller young woman, Vetra, asked. "There was nobody left. The Wraith were using it for their hunting games."

"Not anymore," Margin said.

"There are several hundred people there now," Elizabeth said. "Ushan Cai is their elected leader. The Stargate is open and they are trading with other worlds."

The other woman, Jana, shook her head in wonder. "What happened to the Wraith?"

"There's a treaty," Elizabeth said. "Among hives. They're leaving Sateda alone."

"For now," Margin said. "But that's something. Where did you come from? We haven't found any people from outside the city, though Ushan Cai thinks there must have been survivors."

"Escavera," Beron said. "I have a farm near Escavera, up in mining country. The first Cullings didn't bother with it because we're way out in the country, and then we used the old mine shafts when they came back. They're too deep to detect life signs from a Dart. There are a couple of dozen of us, a few families from remote farms and some miners. Me and my girls here, we're getting by."

"But we needed medical supplies," Jana said. "So I talked Dad into this trip."

"We had no idea there were any people here," Vetra said. "We thought maybe we could salvage some things to take back with us."

"Come to the city with us," Elizabeth said. "It's only another day's walk. We will be there by nightfall. You can talk to Ushan Cai and work out supplies to take back. I know he'll want to talk to you about where survivors are."

Vetra looked at her father. "Dad?"

He nodded slowly. "OK. That seems reasonable."

"I want to see what's happened," Jana said. "We need news. Let's go."

CHAPTER SEVENTEEN

DANIEL tried not to pace around the interior of the jumper. There wasn't really room to take more than a few steps, anyway. Teyla's words still rankled. All right, he'd gone off on a tangent, and one that might not have been tactful, but he'd spent years having to fight to pursue the answers to any questions other than "who's trying to shoot us today and what are we going to do about it?"

He certainly didn't believe he had all the answers. Some days he didn't feel like he had any of the answers. But there had to be some way to fight back against that sense of frustration, to find out enough to be able to piece together the complete story of something. It was all intertwined, the Ancients and the Wraith and the Asgard, and he wasn't sure how to begin understanding the story of Atlantis without knowing more.

It had to fit together, all the pieces that he'd been uncovering over the years. Somehow there had to be a way to assemble them into an actual story, one more satisfying than "a lot of strange and fascinating and tragic things have happened to humanity, but at least we're still here." He just needed more information. Or the right piece of information. Or —

The back hatch of the jumper opened, and he looked up, an apology and justification for his actions forming on his lips. Instead he stared at the two figures standing in the doorway and said, "Who the hell are you, and how did you get in here?"

One of them, a young woman with red-blond hair and a grim expression, pointed a gun at him. "Move away from the controls," she said. Her companion, a tall man with golden skin and close-cropped hair, moved toward the pilot's seat.

"I can't fly this thing anyway," Daniel said. He reached for his sidearm, and she moved fast, jamming the gun against his chest.

"Move and you're dead," she said.

"I thought you wanted me to move away from the controls."

"Don't get smart." She reached for his radio earpiece and divested him of it neatly. She was wearing what looked like a military uniform, dark green and severely cut.

"I don't think you're going to be able to fly the jumper either," he said. "Whatever it is you want, we can talk about it. But how about you put the gun down."

"That's what you think," the woman said. She glanced at the man, who gave her a nervous look from where he sat at the controls.

"I've never seen a control panel like this."

"Figure it out," she said.

"You see, you're not actually going to be able to activate any of the Ancient technology... " Daniel trailed off as the rear door of the jumper closed. "Except apparently you can."

"Thanks to the medical information your people traded to ours," the woman said. "You didn't think that we'd be able to activate the ATA gene successfully. You thought you were cheating us, didn't you?" She smiled, not pleasantly. "Think again."

"I actually have no idea who you are."

"Sora Tyrus," the woman said. "I take it you're new."

"Actually, yes. So whoever it is that you have a problem with in this picture, it isn't me."

"I don't have a problem," Sora said. "I have a new spaceship. My only question is, should I take you with it, or leave you here?"

"I think you should leave me here."

"Take you with us it is," Sora said. "Taka! Come over here and tie him up."

She held her pistol jammed against his chest while the man snapped handcuffs around his wrists and relieved him of his pistol. Sora handed the man a second pair of handcuffs, which he used to cuff Daniel's ankle to his chair.

"These controls aren't much like the pictures you showed me," Taka said, sliding back into the pilot's seat. "It's responding to my commands, but... "

"This ship is a lot simpler than the *Pride of the Genii*," Sora said. "Figure it out!"

"It's a lot more complicated than a train, too!"

"You're Genii," Daniel said. "You're supposed to be our allies."

"She's Genii, I'm not," Taka said.

"Fly the ship," Sora snapped. She turned back to Daniel with a scowl. "Ladon Radim is your ally. I'm not his favorite person any-more, or he wouldn't have sent me out here to watch a bunch of farmers dig in the dirt. He's not my favorite person, either. But now I've got something better than his creaky hulk of a warship that we haven't figured out how to fly yet."

"Our jumper," Daniel prompted. He was getting the impression she was the kind of enemy who craved attention or validation and could therefore be relied upon to brag about her plans to a captive audience. That was always an advantage. The most dangerous ene-mies just kept their mouths shut and shot you.

"Your jumper is the proof that my friends' method for activat-ing the ATA gene works," Sora said. "I was a little worried when it looked like none of the Manarians had even the recessive gene, but checking the Satedans who've settled here paid off. And now I've got a pilot."

"More or less," Taka said.

"Can you fly this thing or not?"

With a shudder, the jumper lifted off the ground.

"Flying a spaceship by trial and error sounds like a really bad idea," Daniel said. "Anyway, your people have the *Pride of the Genii*, right? So you can test your ATA gene activation program with its equipment. You don't need this ship."

"I don't have *Pride of the Genii*," Sora said. "And Radim doesn't know that I've been conducting my own private tests of our gene therapy ahead of his own glacial schedule. He wasn't moving fast enough to suit a lot of people. Some friends of mine were willing to step in and move faster."

"You said this stuff had been tested," Taka said.

"You're fine," Sora said. "Fly the ship." She slid into the seat next to Taka, leaving Daniel trying to work his hands free of the hand-cuffs. He found himself actually wishing Vala were there. She would be out of the cuffs in thirty seconds flat with a shrug of her shoul-ders and an unrepentant smile. Of course, whether she would let him out equally promptly was always a good question.

The jumper lifted the rest of the way off the ground, and began making its way unsteadily toward the gate.

"Dial the gate," Sora said.

"How?"

"The ship has a DHD," Sora snapped. As Taka brought the jumper around, Daniel could see running figures making for the gate.

His radio crackled tinnily in Sora's pocket, and Sora pulled it out and set it on the control panel.

"What is happening?" Teyla demanded over the radio.

"I'm taking your ship," Sora said. "Get out of my way."

"Sora. You do not want to do this."

"I'm tired of being told what I want to do," Sora said. Taka was still struggling to get the ship lined up level with the gate, and Sora reached over to stab at the buttons of the jumper's DHD herself.

"Is Dr. Jackson unharmed?" They had reached the gate, and Rodney had thrown himself full length to the ground in front of the planet's DHD, pulling its maintenance panel open.

"She's dialing the gate," Daniel called, which he felt answered the question as well as providing more important information.

"Shut up!" Sora slapped her hand down on the last of the symbols, and the gate began to hum. It lit, the chevrons brightening, and then immediately dimmed again, its rising hum dropping to an anticlimactic thud. She turned on Taka. "What did you do?"

"We've disabled the gate," Rodney said through the radio. "The jumper's DHD won't do you any good if the gate doesn't have any power."

"Ready weapons!"

"Oh, yes, brilliant idea, fire a drone at the DHD! Only if you'd like to be a permanent resident of Manaria."

"What weapons?" Taka asked.

"Never mind," Sora said. "They're right, we can't fire on them until they move."

"If they move out of the way and then you shoot them, how are you intending to fix the DHD?" Daniel asked conversationally.

"It can't be that hard," Sora said, but she didn't sound entirely convinced.

"Land the jumper now," Teyla said over the radio.

"I don't think so."

Ronon was standing directly between the jumper and the rest of the team. He drew his pistol and fired at the jumper, several bolts of energy that rocked the ship when they hit.

"Shields!" Sora demanded.

Taka looked at her sideways. "We have shields?"

"Get us out of here," she said. "Just get us out of range."

"I can do that," Taka said, and the jumper swerved away from the gate, picking up height and speed as it went. "And I think I've found the shields."

"You think?"

"Trains don't have shields," Taka said. "And they don't talk in your head. You're expecting me to be an expert here?"

"I am warning you, Sora —" Teyla began over the radio. Sora switched it off.

"You're going to have to negotiate if you want to get off this planet," Daniel said into the silence that followed. "Unless you'd like to try to fly the jumper to the nearest solar system at sub-light speeds. That should take, what, a couple of years?"

"I'll negotiate," Sora said. She switched the radio back on. "You have five minutes to repair the damage you've done to the gate. If it's not fixed by then, I'm going to shoot Dr. Jackson in the head."

"This is a very bad idea," Daniel said evenly as Sora snapped the radio off again.

"It's a fair exchange," Sora said. "I don't really want to be saddled with you, and I do want this ship. I'll be happy to throw you out unharmed as soon as your people fix the gate."

"They can't just give you the jumper," Daniel said.

"That's unfortunate for you."

"Even if they did, what are you planning to do with it? If you take it back to the Genii homeworld, we'll know where to find it."

"And Radim will deny having it."

"And we'll tell him that we know you stole it."

"If I leave any of you alive."

Daniel winced inwardly. There was nothing to stop her from making a deal for his return and then firing on the rest of the team as soon as they repaired the gate. Although they were experienced enough to demand his return first. Only Sora seemed experienced enough to insist that they fix the gate first. And he'd rather not be the one sitting there with a gun to his head while they tried to figure out that little tactical problem.

"Do you just want me to circle around?" Taka said.

"No," Sora said. "I don't want to give them the chance to do anything to sabotage this ship. Put some distance between us and the gate."

The jumper turned and began flying over rolling farmland, the bright squares and ribbons of cultivated fields set in between rougher patches of pasture land and copses of trees.

"What do you actually want out of this?" Daniel asked. "Are you trying to get back into Radim's good graces, or trying to show him up, or do you just want the jumper for reasons that have nothing to do with Ladon Radim?"

Sora turned, pressing her lips together tightly. "Why should I tell you?"

"I'm listening. You might say I'm a captive audience."

"Radim wants me dead," Sora said. "And right now he has a parade of successes to keep him in power. Things will look a little different if I have an Ancient ship and the only successful program to activate the ATA gene in our people."

"I thought you said it was Radim's program."

"I've improved on it."

"I thought you weren't a scientist."

"How would you know?"

"You're not interested in how the jumper works. And you didn't try to persuade me that it was your research all along." Daniel tried to spread his hands, only to have them jerked back by the handcuffs. "It was an educated guess."

"I have friends who are scientists," Sora said. Daniel repressed the urge to express surprise that she had friends at all. It really wasn't the time for that. "And we had help."

"Help?"

Sora wanted to talk, he could tell, and keeping her busy was probably the best way to give the team back at the gate time to do something. What they were going to do, he wasn't sure, but at least they had a reputation for being good at improvising.

"What do we do now?" Rodney asked.

Teyla let out a frustrated breath. The jumper was disappearing quickly over the horizon. As impatient as she had been with Daniel, he did not actually deserve to be killed by Sora as part of her continuing grudge against Teyla. "What can you do?"

"I might be able to reprogram the DHD to send her to a different address than the one she dials. It would have to be one that's recently been dialed."

"You mean back to Atlantis."

"And we radio them and tell them to raise the iris," Ronon said.

"No," Teyla said. "I do not want Sora dead. Do what you must to get the gate working again."

Ronon put his head to one side. "She's going to kill Jackson."

"He will be equally dead if he is aboard a jumper that is disintegrated when it hits the iris."

"I'm just saying she's not a great person."

"Even so. I would rather not kill her if there is any other choice."

Rodney turned up his hands. "So, what, we trade her the jumper? We have four minutes to make up our minds."

"We will trade her the jumper," Teyla said. "When the DHD is working again, dial an unpopulated planet. Then call Atlantis and tell them to send two more jumpers to intercept Sora when she arrives there."

"And then reprogram the DHD to send her to that address?" Rodney said. His hands were moving rapidly, his whole body tense with concentration. "We maybe have time to do two of those three things."

"Then we will not call Atlantis. When Sora goes through the gate, we will follow her ourselves."

"We'll be in the same stand-off we're in now," Ronon said.

"Except that she will no longer have a hostage, and therefore we will not have a time limit," Teyla said. "Rodney?"

"I'm working on it," Rodney said. "Why is it never 'take all the time you need, nothing bad will happen if you don't work faster than humanly possible?'"

If he was complaining rather than flatly refusing, it meant that he could accomplish the tasks she had set him in the time they had left. "I have every faith in your abilities," Teyla said.

"I still think we'd be better off smearing her across the iris," Ronon said.

"I went to some considerable trouble to save her life when last we met," Teyla said.

"Funny way of repaying you."

"That is not why I did it," Teyla said, and hoped she wasn't about to regret it.

"I made friends with one of Radim's researchers," Sora said. "He was highly motivated to make friends with me after I showed him what I'd found. A device capable of making certain genetic changes in one person's DNA given a genetic sample from someone else."

"Interesting. I should tell you that we've had some very bad results from using Ancient devices to alter people's DNA," Daniel said. "There was the Ascension device that made people keel over dead if they didn't reach enlightenment fast enough, for one thing. The exploding tumor incident also comes to mind."

"Exploding what?" Taka demanded. The jumper wobbled perceptibly in the air, banking back and forth hard enough to make Sora grab at her chair to stay in it. It would have been the perfect moment to jump her if he hadn't been handcuffed to a chair.

"I'm sure nothing like that will happen," Daniel said.

"How sure?"

"You worry too much," Sora said. "Besides, I'm not even sure it was an Ancient device. It had a setting that made it provide instructions in the language of the Ancestors, but also in some kind of writing nobody could figure out. And it didn't look anything like the devices in *Pride of the Genii*."

"And it wasn't Wraith."

"We've all seen Wraith technology before. Give me some credit. I may not be a scientist, but I'm not an idiot."

"Was the writing – did it look something like this?" He sketched Asgard characters in the air with his fingers, and then shook his head in frustration. "Give me something to write with." Sora shook her head, and he traced the shapes of the same characters more slowly. "Vertical and diagonal strokes, all the same weight." He sketched the letters of the first phrase he thought of, "Thor's hammer," and then after a moment's thought, "genetic pattern," which seemed more relevant.

"That looks like it," Sora said.

"That's Asgard. That's Asgard! And you found a piece of their genetic manipulation equipment? Where did you find it?"

"On Sateda," Sora said. "It was in the city museum. Gathering dust, because no one who knew anything about science had ever taken a good look at it and figured out what they had."

"The city museum that your people agreed not to loot as part of your trade agreement with the new Satedan leaders."

"You looted this from our museum?" Taka said, swiveling around in his chair to face Sora. Daniel wished he wouldn't, as it only made the jumper's course more erratic, but he felt any tensions between the two of them were worth encouraging.

"We made a deal for the artifacts we took off Sateda."

"At gunpoint, the way I heard it," Daniel put in.

"That's not true," Sora said, but Taka was frowning. The jumper's flight became even less stable.

"Maybe you should concentrate on flying the ship," Daniel prompted.

"You said you found the device."

"We did find it," Sora said. "We had a deal with Cai and his people on Sateda to salvage machinery that they were in no position to use. Then the Lanteans got in the middle of it and persuaded them to go back on their bargain." Taka looked like he was at least listening, and Daniel felt it was unfortunate for Sora that she went on, "Besides, what do you care? You're Manarian now."

"You don't understand much." The jumper pitched hard enough that Daniel would have fallen out of the chair if he weren't cuffed to it.

"Watch what you're doing!" Sora snapped.

Taka's eyes were back on the console, but the jumper's nose was down, and they were losing altitude fast. "I am," he said. "But something's wrong! The controls aren't responding."

Sora turned on Daniel, brandishing her pistol. "What did you do?"

"I didn't do anything. I've been sitting here handcuffed, in case you haven't noticed."

"McKay," Sora said. "He must have sabotaged the ship somehow."

"It's not responding to my commands," Taka said. "I can't bring up the displays anymore."

"Fix it!"

"How?"

"I might be able to fix it if you let me get to the controls," Daniel said.

"Not a chance."

"Then we're going to crash," he pointed out. The ground was coming up fast.

"Damn it!" Sora scrambled out of her chair and unfastened the cuff on his leg.

"Handcuffs too."

She bent to unlock them left-handed, holding her pistol on him while she did.

"We're going down!" Taka yelled.

"All right!" Sora said as she freed his hands. "Get this thing working again!"

"I'll do my best," Daniel said, and grabbed for her gun hand.

She brought her knee up hard, and he just barely managed to twist enough for it not to connect in a delicate location. He kicked off from the chair, knocking her down under his weight and rolling as she scrambled to get on top, fighting him for the pistol.

The jumper pitched wildly, and Taka was cursing at the controls. They were going down, and Daniel hoped fervently that Taka could bring the jumper in for a landing that wouldn't kill them all. If he could, he had at least one advantage – he'd probably been in a lot more crashing ships than Sora had.

There was a crash and a sickening series of thuds, the jumper skipping like a stone across the ground. The impact sent them both tumbling toward the back of the compartment, and Sora's grip on the pistol loosened. Daniel kicked it away and drew his own pistol from her belt, jamming the muzzle against the small of her back as the jumper tore its way through the landscape and shuddered to a halt.

"Don't move," he said. "Taka! Throw me the radio!" There was a moment when he wasn't sure if the man was still conscious, and then he turned slowly in his seat, wincing as he stretched his limbs. None of them seemed to be broken from his expression.

"Do what he says," Sora said.

Taka put his head to one side. "I'm beginning to wonder what the point is of doing what you say."

"Because he'll shoot me."

"And then I'll be a lot worse off, right?"

Daniel stretched his left arm and managed to snag one of the pairs of handcuffs. The effort was painful, but while his muscles protested, he didn't feel the unique grinding pain of broken bones. He snapped the handcuffs around Sora's wrists and held onto her by them, although she strained against the cuffs and tried to twist away.

"Toss me the radio," he said again.

Taka picked up the radio and held onto it. "I'm not sure why I should."

"Let me talk to my team, and you can walk away from this."

"I still have work for you," Sora said. "All right, this isn't going the way it was supposed to, but when we get out of this—"

Daniel jerked her hands back harder behind her back. "You're just a bomb-proof optimist, aren't you?"

"If I gave up every time things didn't seem to be going my way, I'd be dead by now," Sora said. It was the first thing she'd said that he felt he could sympathize with.

"Right, fine, you're going to escape any minute now," Daniel said. "But you might not want to bother trying to talk Taka into coming with you if you're relying on him to activate Ancient technology for you. It looks to me like your Asgard genetic manipulation wasn't as permanent as you wanted it to be."

"This doesn't prove that," Sora said. "There's probably something wrong with your ship. I still think your people sabotaged it."

"Try for yourself," Daniel said. He stood with caution, stepping well back from Sora so as not to give her the opportunity to kick his feet out from under him, and pulled down a life signs detector from where it was stowed. He tossed it to Taka. "Turn this on."

"Don't do that, you idiot, it's a trap," Sora said, but Taka was already frowning at the device in his hand.

"Nothing's happening."

"I'm guessing that whatever the Asgard device did to you, it's wearing off."

Sora frowned at him. "What do you know about it?"

"I know that every time we've tried using alien technology that we only sort of understood, it's only sort of worked."

"It doesn't matter. We can do the same procedure again."

"Maybe. If it works more than once on the same person. And if the time that it lasts isn't variable – you really don't want a pilot who's going to suddenly stop being able to fly the ship at some random moment. And if Taka's still interested in working for you, which isn't seeming like such a great gig right now, whatever you promised him."

Taka put down the life signs detector and picked up the radio.

"You give me the radio," Daniel said. "I call my team. We talk this out."

Taka hesitated, and then threw Daniel the radio. He turned it on to hear Teyla's voice on the radio, the words sharp and tight.

"—hear me? We have restored power to the gate. Please respond."

"We're here," Daniel said. "We had some problems with the jumper."

"Dr. Jackson," Teyla said, and he could hear the relief in her voice. "Are you hurt?"

"Only the usual bumps and bruises. Sora's out of commission for the moment—"

"I'm warning you, let me go!" Sora demanded.

"—as you can hear, and I'm having a little talk with her pilot about where we go from here. Actually, he's Satedan, as it turns out, so maybe he'd like to talk to Ronon. Ronon, why don't you tell Taka why getting mixed up in this woman's apparent personal vendetta against Ladon Radim is a fairly lousy idea?"

"Is that Ronon Dex?" Taka asked, his eyebrows going up in startlement. He actually sat up straighter, like someone who'd just been told they were being put on the phone with a celebrity. "*The* Ronon Dex?"

"Who's this?" Ronon asked over the radio.

"Taka. Taka Hendrik."

"This is Ronon Dex. What are you doing with Sora Tyrus? She's bad news."

"She said the Genii would have work for me as a pilot if I could fly the Ancestors' ships," Taka said. "I was a train engineer on Sateda. I make a piss-poor farmer."

"I tried farming once," Ronon said. "On New Athos. They were all pretty grateful when I left."

"That is not true," Teyla protested in the background, but she sounded amused.

"I'm not cut out to be a farmer," Taka said. "Sora said the Genii homeworld has cities. Electric light. Hot baths that don't involve carrying buckets of water after you fight the sheep for it."

"So don't sit on Manaria. Go back to Sateda. They could use people who are good with machinery."

"You stole their ship and kidnapped one of their people," Sora said. "Do you really think they're going to just let you go?"

"We're not the police," Daniel said. "Give us the jumper back, walk away, and we'll chalk this whole thing up to a misunderstanding."

Sora gave him a black look. "Who's supposed to have misunderstood what?"

"To start with, you misunderstood how easy it would be to steal our jumper."

"You're taking this whole thing really calmly," Taka said.

"You don't understand," Daniel said. "This kind of thing happens to me all the time."

Taka nodded in slow appreciation. "Army?"

"I'm a civilian contractor."

"You ought to be in the army."

"I'm a scientist," Daniel said. "It's just that people keep shooting at me."

He pointed the gun at Sora and motioned her to her feet. "I imagine my team is on their way here right now," he said. "Are you going to get out of here, or do you want us to drag you back to Atlantis and hand you over to the Genii?" The radio channel was still open, and he waited to see if Teyla would object, but apparently a side trip to drag a reluctant Sora Tyrus back to Atlantis didn't sound any more attractive to her at this point than it did to him.

"I'm going," Sora said.

"We are on our way," Teyla said.

Sora turned, and then stumbled, apparently still unsteady on her feet. He was reaching out to steady her when she kicked his feet out from under him. She hit the ground herself and rolled with an ease that made it clear she'd shed her handcuffs.

She came up with her pistol in her hand, and Daniel cursed himself for not making sure it was out of her reach. She leveled it at Taka, who spread his hands slowly.

"Some ally you are," he said.

"He won't try to jump me while I have a hostage," she said. "The Lanteans are softhearted that way. I'm not sure I can say the same thing about you."

Daniel kept his own pistol leveled at Sora. "What, you want to find out who can shoot first?"

"I want some leverage when your team gets here."

"I was going to let you go."

"You would have shot me in the back."

"I wouldn't have," Daniel said. "Besides, I thought you said we were softhearted."

"When it comes to your allies you are."

"There's no reason you can't be one of our allies." No reason except the fact that she'd kidnapped him and nearly wrecked the jumper. But compared to some of the people they'd allied themselves with over the years, those were small considerations.

"I don't want to be your ally. I just want to get out of here in one piece."

"I would let you go."

"Let Taka handcuff you to the chair again and I'll go."

"Leave me out of this," Taka said. "And stop pointing that gun at me."

"Sorry," Sora said, although she didn't sound it. "Well?"

"Given what you just said about shooting people in the back, I'm not inclined to do that. I'll wait for the rest of my team to show up, thank you very much."

"Fine," Sora said, and leaned back against the side of the jumper. Daniel shook his head. It was going to be a long wait.

The jumper had dug a deep gouge through a pasture, and several sheep were investigating curiously as the team approached.

"Dr. Jackson, is the jumper secure?" Teyla asked over the radio.

"No, I'm afraid we still have company," Daniel said. "We're at a little bit of an impasse here."

"Let me talk to Sora."

"I don't want to talk to you," Sora said over the radio. "I just want to walk away from this without any tricks."

"Then let Dr. Jackson go."

The rear door of the jumper opened, and Teyla could see that Sora was holding her pistol not on Daniel but on a man she had never seen before, a man who sat in the pilot's seat with an expression of resentment on his face.

"She's holding her own confederate hostage," Daniel said. "She and Taka here have had a little bit of a falling out."

"I told you that you shouldn't have gotten mixed up with the Genii," Ronon said.

The man spread his hands. "You were right."

"I'm going to walk out of here with Taka," Sora said. "And you're not going to stop me."

"So that you can shoot him in the back once you're out of the jumper?" Daniel shook his head. "Not acceptable."

"You see, you are soft-hearted."

"If by that you mean that I don't want perfect strangers to get killed for no good reason, then, yes."

"Put the weapon down and we will let you go," Teyla said.

Sora lifted her chin. "Why should I believe that?"

"Because we do not have the time to return you to Ladon Radim for the punishment you probably deserve. And if I had wanted you dead, I would have let Radim kill you already."

Sora looked at Teyla, her expression wavering, as if she wanted to believe her but wasn't sure that she could. "I'm coming out of the jumper with Taka."

"If you say so," Taka said, and stood. He walked in front of her out of the jumper's hatch.

"Now lower your weapon," Teyla said.

"Ronon has a stun weapon," Sora said. "Tell him to put it down."

"Ronon?"

Ronon slowly set his pistol down on the ground in front of him, although Teyla knew just how fast he could have it back in his hand if necessary.

After a moment Sora lowered her own pistol, although she kept it in her hand. "You'd better not come after me."

"We have better things to do," Ronon said.

"Come show us what you found, and we might be able to help you get the Asgard device working better," Daniel offered as Sora began backing away. "I expect we know a little bit more about the Asgard and their technology than you do."

"I don't need your help," she said.

"Okay. Have fun."

Sora turned on her heels and ran, sprinting for the nearest cover in zig-zag darts that let her look back over her shoulder at them until she was out of what she seemed to consider pistol range. Ronon had his pistol in his hand again, and didn't appear to believe that she was out of range for him.

"Want me to stun her?"

"No," Teyla said. "It is true that we do not have time to deliver her to Radim at the moment." She shook her head regretfully as Sora reached the cover of a line of trees. "Nor to spend more time trying to persuade her that she is making unfortunate decisions." Teyla turned back to Daniel, who was stretching, apparently painfully, as if testing each limb to see if it worked properly.

"Are you injured?"

"Probably nothing broken," he said. "Definitely some interesting bruises."

"Then you got off lightly."

"Good to hear it," Daniel said. He contemplated the damage that the jumper had done to the field. "Think we ought to offer to pay for this?"

"When we return," Teyla said. "I think now it is time for us to go."

INTERLUDE

THE WAY back to the city from the suburbs wasn't quiet. Everyone talked, the salvage team and the Eze family comparing notes on the last ten years. What had happened out in the hinterlands, in the mining valleys a hundred miles from the city? What had happened recently with the returning Satedans? There was so much to catch up on. Elizabeth dropped back, walking last, oddly apart with nothing to contribute to the conversation.

One of the men was talking to Jana. "...so the Genii said the Satedan Band were little flowers, and Caldwell said he'd referee a fight..."

Caldwell. That name meant something. She knew him. That came to her in a breath. She knew Caldwell. He knew her. Was he in the city? Where was Caldwell?

Elizabeth looked up just as Margin Bri dropped back beside her. "That was well done," Margin said.

"What?"

"You've negotiated before."

"Yes."

"Weren't you frightened? You didn't know how many of them there were or if they'd shoot."

"Not really," Elizabeth said. It truly hadn't occurred to her to be frightened. She'd never thought it was a hardened enemy, just a tense misunderstanding that could get out of hand. Those kinds of things needed to be stopped before they started. But no, she'd never been frightened. No one meant to hurt her. She'd done this so many times before that she knew to a fine point where danger was. Why would she be frightened when there wasn't any?

"Who are you?" Margin asked, an incredulous expression on her face.

"I have no idea," Elizabeth said.

They reached the city center just after nightfall. Elizabeth was tired and sore, but their sense of triumph kept her going. Not only had they found some medical supplies, but a tie to survivors of Sateda outside the city. They came down the street leading to the back of the hotel, Beron, Jana and Vetra marveling at the electric lights behind windows, the voices of many people gathering over the end of the day meals.

"Let's go straight to Ushan Cai," Margin said. She held open the back door of the hotel and they went in.

Cai was in his office off the kitchen talking to a man Elizabeth hadn't met before, tall and rangy with dark hair and blue eyes. He was wearing an unfamiliar pants and jacket combination that looked almost like a uniform.

"You're welcome to have a look of course," Cai was saying, "But anything you find is subject to the same terms as before. I won't beggar our people's cultural legacy for boxes of energy bars. Anything Ancient comes straight to me. Then we'll talk about it. Bear in mind our agreement about the light airplane."

"Agreed," the man said. "I'm not from the school of archaeology that's little short of looting."

"I'll take your word on that, Dr. Lynn," Cai said. He looked up as they paused in the door. "Yes, Margin?"

"I've got some amazing news," she said, and ushered in Beron and his daughters, who stood blinking in the electrical light, a wide smile on Jana's face. "We met some survivors from outside the city. There's a settlement of a couple of dozen people up in the old mines near Escavera."

Ushan Cai got to his feet quickly. "Escavra? You've walked all this way? I'm Ushan Cai."

"Jana Eze," the young woman said, putting out her hand. Her father looked a little bewildered, as though he'd thought he'd never see so many strangers in one place again. "It's good to meet you. We didn't know there were people in the city."

"We thought there must be survivors in rural areas," Cai said, clasping her arm wrist to wrist. "We just couldn't get there. That's why we've been making a deal to buy a light plane from the Lanteans. So we can get out there and see."

"You're Lantean?" Elizabeth asked, looking at the man Cai had called Dr. Lynn. Nothing about his face or voice was familiar.

"Er, yes," he said. "I suppose I am. I mean, I'm British. But we're all Lanteans to you."

"How many people? How did you get by?" Cai asked Jana.

Elizabeth drew Dr. Lynn aside. "I have many questions about the Lanteans," she said.

"I'm happy to answer your questions if I can," he said.

"How did you come here?"

"Through the Stargate," Dr. Lynn replied, an answer so obvious as to be useless.

"I assumed that," Elizabeth replied.

Cai was promising Beron and his daughters supplies. "And we've got an electrical generator we can bring out and install. That will give you folks some power to run a radio. We can keep in touch that way."

"That's heavy equipment," Beron said. "And I don't like to say so, but there's rough country between home and here. I don't see how to get something like that back without the trains running."

Dr. Lynn looked over Elizabeth's head. "I can answer that," he said. "We can run the generator over in the puddle-jumper. It shouldn't take more than a few minutes. We can take you home as well, along with whatever you're taking back with you."

Jana blinked. "In an aircraft? A Lantean aircraft?"

"I assure you it's perfectly safe," Dr. Lynn said. "And the puddle-jumper is large enough to carry you and your equipment. It's just outside. That's what we brought the trade goods in. It's much easier to bring the jumper when there are heavy goods."

"A puddle-jumper. Outside." A chill ran down Elizabeth's back. "You have a puddle-jumper outside."

"Yes," Dr. Lynn said, looking mystified.

Elizabeth turned and ran out the door of the office, ran down the hall past what had been the welcome desk, past people coming in with boxes, through the front doors. There, in the middle of the square beside the customs shed, was a stubby metal form. She felt her heart leap. She stopped. It sat not far from the Stargate, the tailgate down. Various Satedans were unloading boxes and crates from the back, no doubt the trade goods Ushan Cai had talked about.

Elizabeth took a step forward, then another.

Two men came around the corner of the shed, a small man with glasses and improbably blue eyes, and a taller one with square shoulders and a weapon slung casually across his chest. They stopped as if they'd hit a glass wall, the small man's mouth open as he muttered something incomprehensible, and pieces suddenly slid into place, final and inexorable as though they had been there all along.

The man with the weapon blinked incredulously. "Dr. Weir?"

She felt herself smile. "Major Lorne, Dr. Zelenka, it's good to see you."

CHAPTER EIGHTEEN

"WELL, that was interesting," Daniel said, collapsing into one of the jumper's seats. He did not appear badly injured, although a bruise was rising on his cheek.

"I am just glad you are all right," Teyla said as Rodney settled into the pilot's seat and began checking the jumper's readouts.

"I'm fine. That could have gone better, though. I'm sorry."

"It could have gone much worse," Teyla said. "You are good at talking to people in volatile situations." She had to admit that Daniel had handled Sora well, keeping her talking and seizing the opportunity to get the upper hand as soon as it presented itself. And he had handled her without hurting her any more than was necessary, even though she was a stranger to him and he had no particular reason to be sympathetic to his kidnapper.

Daniel shrugged. "I've had a lot of practice."

"I still think you are a terrible diplomat."

"I've been told worse things," he said. He shook his head. "I'm sorry. I can be stubborn."

"Really?" Teyla asked sweetly.

"It's not my best quality."

"Still, I admit that you do have some good qualities."

"Well. Good. I think."

"Can we please go find Elizabeth now?" Rodney asked.

Ronon dropped down to straddle one of the jumper seats. "What are we going to do about Sora?"

"Nothing for the moment," Teyla said. "When we return to Atlantis, I expect we should have a talk with Ladon Radim."

"He already doesn't trust her."

"But he may not know that she has allies among the scientists that he is working with. Or that she is close to solving the problem of how to activate the ATA gene."

"Not that close," Daniel said. "What do you think she would do if she figured it out?"

"That depends on how many successes she has," Teyla said.

"Even the recessive ATA gene is rare among the peoples of the Pegasus galaxy. Dr. Beckett tried the process on many Athosians, and none of them acquired the ATA gene as a result."

"Me neither," Ronon said. "But apparently some Satedans have it."

"It's not exactly common on Earth," Daniel said. "SGC personnel who have the gene are more likely to get sent to Atlantis, so that skews the numbers. But, assuming that she could find a number of people who have the right genetic makeup, then what? It would be stupid for them to try to invade Atlantis at this point."

"It would," Teyla said. "But I expect *Pride of the Genii* is less heavily guarded. If I were Ladon Radim, I would remedy that."

"That's all we need," Ronon said. "Sora Tyrus with her own warship."

"That is a problem for another day," Teyla said. "Rodney, can you get the jumper working again?"

"Probably," Rodney said, sliding into the pilot's seat. "It's not like it's exactly a good idea to crash-land these things, but the Ancients built them to be remarkably sturdy. It's like they envisioned that future civilizations were going to come along and fly them very, very badly. They apparently practiced idiot-proofing for the ages."

"Maybe the Ancients also had a lot of really bad pilots," Daniel said. "We tend to assume these things are like fighter planes, but maybe they're more the SUVs of Ancient civilization. Complete with airbags and cameras to help you back up."

"Rodney?" Teyla prompted, in an attempt to head off an incipient discussion of whether Ancient transportation methods were more like one or another transportation method used on Earth. While she was willing to grant that he had handled Sora well, she still felt that Daniel Jackson had an uncanny talent for digressing from whatever the matter at hand might be.

"I can fix it," Rodney said. "Just give me a few minutes to get everything powered back up and make sure we aren't missing anything essential that would make this a very short trip."

The silence as Rodney worked on the jumper was an uncomfortable one. "You really believe it is Elizabeth," Teyla said finally.

Rodney didn't lift his head from the jumper's readouts. "Yes. It's Elizabeth."

"She was frozen in space, unable to think or experience anything," Teyla said. "It is hard to see how she could have ascended while in that state."

"Maybe she had some kind of help," Daniel said. "The Ancient who helped me Ascend the first time, Oma Desala — she used to make a habit of helping members of less evolved species achieve Ascension. I was going to die, and she stepped in and helped me take that last step. Now, doing that didn't work out so well for her in the end, but it's not inconceivable that someone here in the Pegasus Galaxy could be doing the same thing."

"We have never encountered such a being before," Teyla said. "And many of us have died, or been on the point of death." She felt a flicker of anger at the idea that someone who could have helped her friends who had died might have been watching them and judged them unworthy. The ways of the Ancestors were mysterious, and yet...

"I know," Daniel said, his eyes on her face. "I know. Believe me, I've spent a lot of time wondering what it means that I got to Ascend and other people I knew — good people, people who deserved to live, some of them a lot more than I did — died. It's not that I deserved it more. It's probably not even that Oma Desala liked me more, although I wouldn't entirely rule out reasons that random. It's that I'd already gone a long way down that path already. It's like being able to pull someone into a boat if they can grab a rope that you throw them. It's not that you don't care about people who are unconscious in the water. But you can't help them if they can't grab that rope."

"We know Elizabeth tried to Ascend," Rodney said.

"And we know that she repeatedly failed," Teyla said. "Is it not more likely that this is some new trickery of the Replicators?"

Ronon shook his head. "Why would you rather think that?"

"Because I had given up hope," Teyla snapped. "And the last thing I want is to begin hoping that we will find my friend, when what is most likely is that she is dead and this is only some device of our enemies made in her shape."

"I understand that," Rodney said. "Believe me, I'll be the first to say that pessimism is usually a good way to avoid being horribly disappointed."

"And yet you believe."

"She talked to me," Rodney said. "And, before you say it, it was not a spiritual experience, if by 'spiritual experience' you mean 'thing that isn't really happening.' She was there in my head, and she talked to me, and as someone who's had hypoxia-induced hallucinations before, I think I'm in the best position to say that this wasn't one."

"I am not sure that is how I would define a spiritual experience," Teyla said.

"If I had a spiritual experience, it was the spiritual experience of having Ascended Elizabeth talk to me," Rodney said. "That is one hundred percent as spiritual as I get. And it certainly wasn't a hallucination, unless we're willing to accept that it's entirely a coincidence that someone who thinks they're Elizabeth is wandering around with amnesia right now."

"I think you're scared to find out if it's true or not," Ronon said to Teyla.

"Is that so hard for you to understand?"

Ronon shrugged. "No. I don't want it to be some Replicator either. And if Sheppard were here, he'd be going crazy trying not to get his hopes up. But it's better to find out the truth."

Teyla took a deep breath and then let it out. "Sometimes you are very wise, my friend," she said.

"Nice to know I'm not always wrong," Ronon said.

"I did not mean it that way," Teyla protested, but Ronon was smiling.

"All right," Rodney said. "I think we're back in business."

"You think, or you're sure?" Daniel said, looking skeptically at the jumper's controls. "I'd rather not crash in this thing twice."

"I'm never a hundred percent sure," Rodney said. "We're flying around in machines that are thousands of years old. They didn't come with a warranty. But, yes, I am as sure as I ever am that there's no particular reason that the jumper is going to crash again today."

"Well, that's comforting," Daniel said after a moment.

"So can we go?" Rodney said, his hands poised over the jumper's control panel.

"Take us to Sateda," Teyla said.

The open square by the gate on Sateda was as usual full of people making their way between the buildings or sitting outside them to drink tea or talk. Every time they came there, Teyla saw more signs of repairs in progress; windows that had been boarded up a month before now boasted shutters that could be opened to let in light and air, and a few had been mended with scraps of colored glass leaded together so that their patchwork surfaces shone in the sun.

Another jumper was already parked in the square, with a small crowd gathered around it.

"Major Lorne is here with a team to trade," Teyla said, remembering the fact only as she spoke.

"I knew that," Ronon said.

She gave him a sideways look. "We could have radioed and asked them to find out if anyone has seen Elizabeth."

"We were already on our way," Ronon said. "Or are you saying you wouldn't have come just because someone else was here?"

"No, I would have come anyway," Teyla said. It was not the way of the military on Earth, with their belief that one team should be interchangeable with another. She understood their reasoning, and still did not always agree with it. Elizabeth was her friend, and she and Rodney and Ronon could not sit by letting someone else search for her if there was a chance she could be found.

The jumper's subspace radio crackled to life. "Teyla, report," John said. "Where are you?"

"We have just landed on Sateda," Teyla said, as Rodney brought the jumper down to a landing in the square. "Pursuing a lead."

"Lorne just radioed in," John said. She could hear the tightness in his voice, and her own breath caught. "He says they've found Elizabeth."

The jumper was barely on the ground before Ronon was heading out the door, followed at a brisk pace by the rest of the team. Teyla could see the people gathered near the other jumper as she jogged across the square, Major Lorne and Dr. Zelenka standing in the center of the crowd talking to a dark-haired woman who turned toward them in disbelief as they approached.

Teyla found herself face to face with Elizabeth Weir, looking just as Teyla remembered her, though wearing clothes she must have acquired on one of the planets she had visited. "Rodney. Teyla. Ronon?" She spoke their names tentatively, as if not sure whether her memory for them to be trusted.

"Yes," Teyla said, and felt her heart lift, even though she knew that they had not yet proven that this was truly Elizabeth. "You remember us."

"I remember some things," Elizabeth said. "It's coming back slowly. For a while I had no idea where I was from. I couldn't remember Earth, or the Atlantis expedition, or... " Elizabeth's expression grew abruptly troubled. "Where is Colonel Sheppard?"

"Back in Atlantis," Teyla reassured her. Of course she must expect John to be in charge of the team, and guess that something terrible had befallen him if he were not. "He is currently in charge of the city."

Elizabeth's eyebrows went up. "Colonel Sheppard? Not that I'm complaining, but I'm surprised that the IOA went for that." She shook her head. "That was the first thing that came to mind, and now I can't remember what the IOA is."

"It takes some time," Daniel said. Elizabeth turned to look at him, noticing him for the first time, as Zelenka began herding away the curious Satedan onlookers to give them a little more privacy to talk.

"I know you," she said. "But I can't remember your name."

"Daniel Jackson," he said. "I'm with the SGC on Earth. I'm just here in Atlantis temporarily."

"That's what they all say," Elizabeth said. It sounded like her, that dry sense of humor. Could a Replicator, or some other creature inhabiting Elizabeth's shape, seem so much like her? And yet if her blood were filled with nanites, she might be a time bomb completely unawares. "I remember you, though. We dealt with... dangerous parasites?"

"That could be either the Goa'uld or Senator Kinsey," Daniel said. "But, yes. You were briefly in charge of the SGC. It was an interesting experience."

"You'd think it would be memorable," Elizabeth said.

"You're probably going to have partial amnesia for a while," Daniel said. "I did, after I came back from being Ascended."

Elizabeth looked a little skeptical. "Ascended? Is that what happened to me?"

Rodney shook his head at her. "You don't remember?"

"No. I remember waking up in a field, but I don't remember anything about how I got there or where I came from. And before that… " She shook her head. "Something about an attack by the Asurans?"

"That is right," Teyla said. "That was when you… " She hesitated, unsure how best to complete the sentence.

"Died," Rodney said bluntly. "At least, we thought you were dead."

Elizabeth shook her head. "Apparently not."

"I'll go report to Colonel Sheppard," Lorne said, and Teyla nodded as he stepped inside his jumper to do it. They would have to decide what to do about Elizabeth now, and that was not a conversation Lorne would want to have in front of Elizabeth herself.

Elizabeth was frowning at Rodney. "What happened to your hair?"

"There was this thing with the Wraith," he said. At her stricken expression, he hurried on, "They didn't suck years of my life out of me. It was actually a lot more disturbing than that. I'm fine, now, though. I mean, except for some traumatic… anyway, the hair is just one of those quirky things that happens in Pegasus, right?"

"Quirky," Elizabeth said. "That's one way of putting it." She looked up at Ronon. "It's good to see all of you."

Ronon looked at her for a long moment, seeming to have run out of words abruptly, and then threw his arms around her and hugged her, lifting her entirely off the ground in the process. Elizabeth hung onto his hands when he finally released her, as if touching him made him seem more real.

It was as if a glass barrier between them had been broken. Teyla stretched out her hands, and Elizabeth took them, leaning in to touch her forehead to Teyla's. Her hands were warm, and felt as they should in Teyla's own. Her smell seemed wrong for a moment, and then Teyla decided that what was missing was the familiar scent of perfumed toiletries mingled with Air Force issue laundry detergent and the ever-required coffee.

Elizabeth hugged Rodney, who returned the embrace more awkwardly. "I like the hair," she said.

"Really?" he asked, drawing himself up a little bit. "I've been wondering if I should dye it."

"Leave it," Elizabeth said.

Lorne emerged from the jumper. "Sheppard's on his way," he said.

Teyla shook her head. "And who is he leaving in charge in Atlantis?"

"Me, as soon as I can get back there," Lorne said. He shrugged. "You didn't really think he was going to sit this one out, did you?"

"I did not," Teyla admitted.

"Dr. Zelenka, Dr. Lynn, you're coming back to Atlantis with me," Lorne said. "Colonel Sheppard is calling off the trade mission until we get this sorted out."

Lorne dialed the gate and headed through with the two scientists. It was not long before there was the sound of the gate activating again, and then the boiling blue of the wormhole forming. "Colonel Sheppard, I presume," Elizabeth said, and turned to watch as John strode through.

Lorne had barely set foot in the control room when Sgt. Anthony called in from the alpha site. "Sir, we've got problems," Anthony said.

"What now?" Lorne asked, sliding into the seat beside Airman Salawi, who returned her attention to her computer screen. "We need that alpha site."

"The new equipment we brought out is falling apart, too. The tents are just coming apart in pieces. The water cans look like somebody set them on a hot stove."

Lorne waved a hand at Radek, who had been on his way out of the control room. Radek came back up the stairs reluctantly, probably wondering why he was being deprived of ten minutes to grab a cup of coffee before anyone piled new technical problems on his head.

"Just the person we need," he said.

Radek turned and regarded him dubiously over the rim of his glasses. "It is never a good sign when people say that."

"The team out at the alpha site is having equipment problems. Weird ones. What about the water trailer?" he asked over the radio.

"It's fine so far."

There was something about this that was nagging at Lorne. "Stand by, Sergeant," he said. "You too, doc." He called up a view of the pier on the security cameras. Several tents were set up there, anchored with some ingenuity to the available supports. All of them looked structurally sound despite the chill wind that was whipping across the pier.

"Lt. Winston?" he said over the radio.

"This is Winston."

"Have you been having any problems with the tents you set up on the pier?"

"No problems, sir," Winston said. "All of them check out fine. I really think that the damaged equipment must have been mishandled. You'd be amazed how much damage Marines can do to supplies, sir. They're beasts."

"Let's not start an inter-service war over some tents falling apart," Lorne said.

"No, sir," Winston said, sounding at least a little chastened.

Lorne switched the feed over to Anthony at the alpha site. "Sergeant, is any of your personal gear also damaged?"

"Let me take a look at my pack," Anthony said. "Son of a bitch."

"I'm assuming that's a yes."

"The strap tore when I picked it up."

"Sir, my watch band broke," PFC Harper said over the radio.

"Just snapped?"

There was a momentary pause. "Actually, it looks kind of melted," she said.

"Okay. Sit tight. I'm going to get one of the scientists out there to figure out what's going on."

"You think it's some kind of freaky radiation or something?" Anthony asked. He sounded more than a little nervous. "We ran all the standard scans."

"Run them again."

He turned to Radek. "My team out at the alpha site has their gear mysteriously falling apart. Several tents, water cans, a watch band, and the straps on Wilson's pack. No unusual radiation, weird glowing rocks, people aging a hundred years in a day, or anything else out of the ordinary."

"The people appear unaffected?"

"They seem fine. The jumper itself seems to be working fine. So does a water trailer we sent out."

"Let us see what the radiation scan shows. In the meantime — "

"Yes, get coffee, go." He waited while Harper fired up the jumper and used its systems to scan for unusual radiation levels or any other change from the baseline readings. Radek was back, travel mug in hand, by the time Anthony came back on the line.

"Nada," Anthony said. "Nothing. But something weird's happening out here. We're not going to start falling apart, are we?" His voice rose to a perceptibly higher pitch.

"Calm down, Sergeant," Lorne said. "You've already been working out there for hours, and you're fine, right?"

"So far!"

"Just sit tight, and we'll figure this out," he said.

There was the sound of discussion in the background, and then Anthony said, "Harper just took another look at the water trailer."

"Let me guess," Lorne said. "It sprung a leak."

"No, sir. But all its tires are flat."

Radek leaned in to speak into the microphone. "It sounds from what you are telling us that all the gear that is affected is plastic or synthetic materials."

There was brief discussion on the other end of the line. "I think you're right," Anthony said.

"You want to go out there and take a look?" Lorne said.

Radek hesitated, and then switched off his radio.

After a moment, Lorne did the same. "What?"

"I will send someone. But whoever we send will need to stay on the planet until we find an answer. I would prefer to remain in a position to analyze whatever data they can transmit to us here in Atlantis."

"If there's some kind of weird effect, we should get our people out of there."

"If it were some form of radiation, I would agree with you, but the jumper's scans say no. I will send someone to confirm that, but we have no reason to believe the jumper itself is malfunctioning."

"Not at the moment, no."

"So, either this is some effect we do not understand at all – in which case we should quarantine the affected personnel just as a precaution – or there is the possibility that I like the least. That we are dealing with some kind of microorganism that specifically attacks plastic and other synthetic materials."

"That would be bad," Lorne said after a moment.

"Yes. We have hazmat gear, but—"

"But it's made of plastic," Lorne finished. He closed his eyes for a moment. "I've been out to the alpha site. And in the supply depot with the equipment they brought back."

"Have you noticed any effect?"

Lorne examined the soles of his shoes, and pulled out a plastic-coated pen from his pocket. He tried bending it experimentally between his hands, but it didn't give in response to gentle pressure. "Apparently not."

"Maybe I am wrong, then. Or maybe it requires longer exposure."

"All right," he said. "Get somebody out there and let's figure this out. And get the linguistics people to step up trying to translate the inscriptions they found on those rocks. If whoever was there before left us a message, it's starting to sound important to figure out what that is."

Teyla could see the moment John saw Elizabeth, the moment he stopped, swallowing hard, and stood as if frozen in place as Elizabeth began to cross the square toward him. He had lost too many people, Teyla knew, too many friends and teammates dead or gone, never to return except to haunt his dreams. He had the expression of a man unsure whether he was dreaming or waking, and unsure, if it was a dream, whether at any moment it might turn to nightmare.

"Colonel Sheppard," Elizabeth said.

He nodded wary acknowledgment. "Elizabeth?" he asked cautiously.

"It's me," she said, and then embraced him before he could say any more, a long, hard hug. "At least, I think it is," she said, releasing him.

"That would be the problem," he said.

She turned up her hands. "I know. You don't know where I came from or who – or what – I really am. I asked Dekaas – he's one of the Travelers' physicians –"

"We met him," Teyla said, coming up to them with the rest of the team trailing behind her. "He was the one who sent us here."

"He ran tests to try to find out if I was human, and as far as he could tell, I was. But I know our equipment back in Atlantis is a lot more sophisticated."

John nodded. "We'll get Carson to meet us at the alpha site so that he can start checking you out."

Elizabeth's whole body went tense at once, all the openness draining from her expression. "Carson Beckett is dead."

"It is a long story," Teyla said.

"I'm sure it is," Elizabeth said, but she took a step back from them. "I'd like to hear it."

"At the alpha site," John said.

"Before I go anywhere with you."

"We need to go ahead and get you to the alpha site so that you're somewhere we can secure until we're sure that you're really Elizabeth Weir."

"Believe me, I understand that," Elizabeth said, but she had that stubborn set to her jaw that Teyla remembered well.

John's headset radio sounded. "Colonel Sheppard?" Lorne said. "We've got some delays going on in setting up the alpha site."

"What kind of delays?"

"Some thing's breaking down all our plastic gear at the site. Dr. Zelenka is worried that it might be a microorganism of some kind. We've got the site under quarantine while we figure out what's going on."

"Keep it that way. Is Carson stuck there?"

"No, thankfully we hadn't sent him through yet. We're working on an alternative alpha site, but it's going to take us a few minutes to get it checked out."

"Work on it," John said.

John turned back to face Elizabeth — he had to think of her as Elizabeth, and told himself that wasn't committing to any answers to the question of who or what she really was. "All right. So, we're having a few technical difficulties."

"That sounds like the Pegasus Galaxy, all right," Elizabeth said. "I know that you're worried about what might happen if I'm really some kind of tool of the Replicators. I'm worried about that myself. But I've been here nearly twenty-four hours already. Another hour probably isn't going to matter."

"No. Because if you're a Replicator, you could already have infected hundreds of people and machines here on Sateda."

"She's not a Replicator," Rodney said.

John turned on him. "And exactly how do you know that?"

"If she were in an entirely artificial Replicator body, the most basic medical tests would have shown that," Rodney said. "You could stick a needle in her and watch her not bleed."

"There could still be nanites in her bloodstream."

"Why would there be nanites in her bloodstream? The Ancients wouldn't construct her a new body and then booby-trap it by filling it with nanites."

"We are not going to make decisions based on speculation about what the Ancients might or might not do," John said. "We're going to take Elizabeth to the alpha site and let Carson decide whether he thinks she's human."

"Yes, about that," Elizabeth said, steel in her tone.

John ran a hand through his hair. "Ronon, go talk to Cai and ask him if he's got a spare room where we can sit down and talk."

"There is the jumper," Teyla said. John shook his head discouragingly. The last thing he wanted was to give Elizabeth access to the jumper and all its systems when he wasn't sure if she'd been compromised. They could walk through the gate to the alpha site. Once Lorne had finished dealing with their current minor disaster.

"I wouldn't let me in the jumper either," Elizabeth said, looking a little amused.

"I'll talk to Cai," Ronon said.

"Dr. Lynn, please tell me someone's translated the writing on those rocks at the alpha site," Lorne said.

Lynn's voice over the radio was tart with irritation. "You realize I was on Sateda all afternoon? And that I'm not actually a linguist? Why don't you call Dr. Jackson?"

"He's off-world. Tell me somebody down there with a PhD can tell me more than 'somebody made some marks on the rocks.'"

"Let me see if anyone's made any notes," Lynn said, and there was the sound of typing. "All right. You're in luck, someone's actually started working on the translations. Letter frequencies suggest that this is a phonetic alphabet for writing Ancient. We don't have anything with one hundred percent certainty—"

"At this moment, I will take whatever certainty you've got."

"Two of the groups of letters are very likely the words for 'warning' and 'danger.' We see those on a lot of equipment in the city."

"It would have been good to know that several days ago."

"I'm sorry," Lynn said, and sounded like it. "We have a backlog of translations waiting to be done. This wasn't marked as a priority."

Lorne silently counted to ten before he spoke. "Okay. It should have been, and that's my mistake. Can you tell me anything else about the message? Does it say anything about plastic?"

"That's a possible translation of one of the letter groupings," Lynn said.

"Figure out what the message says. Consider it a priority. I'm guessing something like 'warning, something on this planet breaks down plastic, and that's really dangerous.'"

"Ah," Lynn said. "I see that you might have wanted to know that before now."

"You can say that again," Lorne said.

John ended up finding space for the team to get off the street in the lunchroom of an office building that looked out over the gate square. Makeshift shutters had been nailed up over the windows and the floor swept clean, and there were chairs arranged at the long table. The walls were still hung with faded and tattered posters lettered in Satedan, one showing a stylized worker lying crushed under half of an enormous block of stone that had cracked in two.

"I have to ask," John said with a nod toward the poster.

Ronon glanced at the picture, not even trying to make out the faded lettering. "It's supposed to remind people not to make mistakes."

"Maybe we need some motivational posters in Atlantis," Elizabeth said as she sat down.

John shook his head. "Now you're really scaring me." He took his seat at the table along with the rest of his team, and Daniel stopped prowling around the room looking at the posters to come take a seat himself.

It felt like a thousand mornings around the conference table in the early years of the expedition. He reminded himself very firmly that it wasn't.

"Tell me about Carson Beckett," Elizabeth prompted.

"It's not our original Carson Beckett," Rodney said. "Do you remember Michael?"

"The Wraith we attempted to transform into a human," Teyla said.

"That sounds familiar," Elizabeth said, frowning. "An experiment."

"That is right."

"Michael used some of Carson's DNA to create a clone with Carson's memories," Rodney went on. "And before you ask, no, we don't know how he managed that. Our best guess is that he combined some version of the technology that the Wraith use to create drones who already have some degree of imprinted knowledge with his own really disturbing research. He was using that Carson, clone Carson, to help him with his experiments. Eventually we found him locked up in one of Michael's labs and rescued him."

"More or less by accident, since we didn't have any idea he existed," John added.

Elizabeth regarded him from the other side of the table. "You understand this doesn't sound particularly likely."

"You mean unlike the other things that happen to us in the Pegasus galaxy?"

"Even given those."

"It's true, though. Carson spent some time back on Earth dealing with some medical problems — turns out being a clone isn't too great for your health — and now he's back filling in for Dr. Keller while she's on an extended assignment with the Wraith."

Elizabeth's eyebrows went up. "Extended assignment with the Wraith?"

John looked at Teyla for rescue from the task of explaining that one.

"In the last year, one of the Wraith queens claimed authority over all Wraith," Teyla said. "It was not a universally popular claim, and we were able to ally with another faction to defeat her. And there has been another development as well. A retrovirus that makes humans able to survive being fed upon, while still providing nourishment to the Wraith."

Elizabeth nodded slowly. "That must be complicating things."

"It is," Teyla said. "But it offers the possibility of a meaningful peace."

Elizabeth put her head to one side, regarding Teyla curiously. "And that idea is acceptable to you?"

"Yes," Teyla said, at the same time Ronon said, "No." Teyla shot Ronon a sharp look, and went on, "We have discovered that the Wraith are the result of a misguided experiment of the Ancestors. They are descended from our own kin, and they did not ask to be as they are. They have survived as best they can, and created much that is of value that we are only just beginning to understand. I would be glad to see them endure as people who no longer have to kill us to survive."

"Ronon?" Elizabeth asked when it was clear Teyla was finished speaking.

"They're still Wraith," he said. "All this means is that they're going to keep humans as slaves rather than killing them outright. I think we ought to keep fighting them. But it's not up to me right now."

"Right now?"

"Right now. If I come back to Sateda at some point… then we'll see. Cai has this idea that I ought to stand for some kind of election here. I don't know about that. Yet."

Elizabeth nodded, and looked up at John. "And your take on all of this?"

"For the moment, the Wraith aren't attacking Atlantis or killing my people," John said. "I'll take it."

Elizabeth took a slow breath, and then let it out. "All right. I think you're who you say you are."

Rodney looked at her quizzically. "I'm glad to hear it, but what did we actually do to convince you?"

"You haven't tried to persuade me that nothing's changed," she said. "That was what I was most worried about when you told me about Carson. If this were an illusion, something drawn from my own mind, then I would be seeing and hearing the people I remembered. And then after I asked about Colonel Sheppard, he appeared a few minutes later."

"It was not a coincidence," Teyla said. "He wished to accompany the team that was looking for you, and was only prevented from doing so by the knowledge that his place was in Atlantis." She gave him a pointed sidelong look at the last words, and he shrugged.

"I expect someone might have reminded him of that," Elizabeth said. "And I see that. It just made me wonder. But what you're telling me... you sound like yourselves. I can understand why you might have come to these conclusions. But a lot of what you're saying is not exactly what I would have expected you to say. You've changed. People do. And given that I've been gone... " She frowned. "How long have I been gone?"

"Since you died, or since the last time we saw you when we, umm... had to freeze you in space in a Replicator body?" Rodney asked.

Elizabeth raised an eyebrow. "You're saying that was after I died."

"It's complicated," John said. "You've been gone for nearly three years. The last time we saw you — for some value of 'saw' and 'you' — was about eighteen months ago."

"Three years," Elizabeth said. She took a deep breath, and then let it out again, pressing her hands to the tabletop as if to steady herself. "Okay. So what happens now?"

"I go find out why it's taking Lorne so long to get the alpha site set up," John said, and hoped the answer wasn't going to be that their minor problem had turned into another unfolding catastrophe.

Lorne looked up as Radek came into the control room. "We have a problem," Radek said shortly.

"It really is a plastic-eating bug."

"Yes. Yes, it appears to be, according to the data that Dr. Xiao was just able to transmit."

"Before his laptop fell apart?"

"It did do that, but he was able to relay information through the jumper. Thankfully, the materials used to construct the jumper are all metal, crystal, or silicone rather than petroleum-based plastics. Silicone plastics appear to be unaffected."

"That's good, right?"

"Most of the plastic used in our equipment is petroleum-based. The Ancient equipment is safe, but nearly everything made of plastic that we brought from Earth is vulnerable, as well as synthetic fabrics. Polyester is a petroleum product."

"Wonderful."

"Now, we are lucky that many harmful microorganisms do not pass through the Stargate. The gate's own systems are designed to prevent some common forms of contamination from passing through."

"I sense a 'but' coming."

"Some is not all. And as people have been moving back and forth from the alpha site all day long, and we know some of their personal items are affected… "

"It's worse than that," Lorne said, his stomach sinking at a sudden memory. "Harper said she was going to bring the defective gear back to Atlantis. It's probably sitting here somewhere. And if it's infected… "

Radek's expression was grim. "Where did she put it?"

They found the defective tent and water cans piled in a corner of the supply depot. The tent crumbled in Lorne's hand as he tried to pick it up, as if made of something dry and brittle. A plastic storage container was sitting next to them, and he nudged it with his foot. It caved in easily at the slightest pressure.

"Oh, not good," Radek said.

CHAPTER NINETEEN

"I HAVE to say that this is frustrating," Elizabeth said as they waited. "I remember bits and pieces, but not enough to be sure about what happened to me."

"It'll come back," Daniel said. "Most of it." He tried to think back to the first time he had returned from being Ascended, after SG-1 had found him. "Some things I didn't remember until something reminded me. Or until I dreamed about them."

"Dreams," Elizabeth said, and frowned. "I dreamed about a woman… no, that's not right. Not a human woman. She said she had helped me Ascend."

"It's good that you're starting to remember," Daniel said. "Was she one of the Ancients?"

"You would think she would be. But I don't think so. She didn't look human at all. In my dream, she was warning me about… someone who was threatening her. Someone who was looking for a way to… force Ascended beings to unascend?"

She didn't sound sure of that last, but Daniel felt his heart sink. "That's what the Asgard just found," he said. "A device that might be able to force Ascended beings back into physical form."

"The Asgard," Elizabeth said, frowning intently. "Someone show me a picture of one of the Asgard."

Rodney brought out his tablet obligingly and pulled up a picture of one of the Asgard; Daniel thought it was Hermiod, although he had to admit that even he had trouble telling the Asgard apart until they spoke.

"I think the person I dreamed about may have been an Asgard," Elizabeth said, shaking her head slowly. "She had hair, and… " She opened and closed one hand, as if trying to grasp scraps of memory. "More distinct facial features. But the eyes, and the bone structure, and the height, that's all right."

"You think she was one of the Asgard? And that she was Ascended?"

"I think she must have been if she helped me Ascend. And if she was worried about someone having the ability to force her to unascend. She said her name was Ran."

"That's a Norse sea goddess," Daniel said immediately. "Completely unsurprising as an Asgard name, because a lot of the Asgard spent some time on Earth, helping us develop as a species. They were perceived as gods by the local inhabitants, like the Goa'uld, but more benevolently. At least usually."

"Except they weren't Ascended," Rodney pointed out

Daniel nodded, acknowledging that. "We've never heard of any of the Asgard Ascending. As far as we know, they decided that living without physical bodies wasn't an acceptable solution to their problems."

"They decided," Elizabeth said. "But if one person had made another choice, they couldn't actually have stopped her, could they? After all, it's not like humans have gotten together and decided that it's a good idea for all humans to Ascend."

"No, you're right," Daniel said. "But that hasn't stopped a few humans from doing it."

"As far as we know, you're the only one," John said.

"I'm not the only one. There have always been stories of mystics and saints, people who wandered into another world, or were taken bodily into heaven, or whatever your cultural frame of reference might be. The capacity to Ascend is written into our genes. It's just that it's incredibly rare for someone to stumble onto the way to do it."

"It was not even possible for all of the Ancestors to Ascend," Teyla said.

"No. No, that's true. But they were trying, as a people. Most of the Asgard weren't interested. So if one particular Asgard had found a way to Ascend, the same way that a handful of humans have over the centuries, Thor might not have thought it was important enough to even mention to us. If he even knew about it. Maybe from the Asgard point of view, she just disappeared."

Elizabeth shook her head. "If they didn't know that she ascended, they wouldn't be trying to force her to unascend now."

Daniel turned up his hands. "I'm not sure why they would try to force her to unascend. All right, it wasn't something they approved of, but would they really care that much about one person making an unusual choice?"

Ronon shrugged. "Maybe she's causing them problems."

"She can't have been interfering in any meaningful way in their activities, or she would have gotten kicked out by the other Ascended beings." He turned to Elizabeth. "Helping you is right on the line of what an Ascended being can get away with. Trying to push the other Asgard around from the great beyond is definitely over the line."

Elizabeth's eyebrows went up. "The great beyond?"

"Or whatever you want to call it."

"Maybe there's some reason that they want her back," Elizabeth said.

"It can't be sentimental attachment," Rodney said. "All the Asgard who actually knew her are probably long dead by now."

"Or at least recently dead," Daniel said. "No, I feel like there's something we're missing."

Teyla frowned, considering the question. "What have the Asgard in this galaxy wanted in the past?"

"To fix their planet's ecology. To fix their own genetic damage that they caused by cloning themselves over and over again."

Elizabeth put her head to one side. "And to fix their genetic damage, they would need?"

"An undamaged sample of Asgard DNA," Rodney said. From his expression, Daniel thought he followed Elizabeth's line of thought. "One that doesn't come from a clone, or from a computer model that was made after they started frying their own genes."

Daniel nodded. "But all the Asgard who were alive before they started cloning themselves are dead, or —"

"Or Ascended," Elizabeth finished.

"That's what they want," Daniel said at once. "To force an Ascended Asgard back into physical form so that they can use her to restore their species."

Elizabeth shook her head. "She doesn't want to go."

"Then she may be in trouble. We know the Asgard just got their hands on a device that may let them do just that."

"I don't think they know how to use it," Elizabeth said. "Ran said they were still trying to understand how unascension works. And that they… " She looked up, startled, as if at sudden memory.

"That they're looking for people who've done it."

There was a momentary pause. "We may be in trouble," Daniel said.

John gritted his teeth. "We need to get both of you to a more secure location."

"The delay isn't on my end," Elizabeth pointed out.

John thumbed his radio on. "Major Lorne, I need the alpha site set up ten minutes ago."

"Copy that, Colonel, but apparently our equipment damage really is being caused by a microorganism that eats anything based on petroleum. We're trying to get it contained."

"I thought it was contained at the alpha site."

"So did we. But we've got some equipment damage in the supply warehouse that seems to have spread from the damaged supplies from the alpha site. We're hoping we can get a lid on the whole thing, but I've got the city locked down right now as a precaution."

"Not fixing this would be very, very bad," Zelenka said urgently over the radio.

"I get it," John said. He looked around. "What are the chances that I brought this thing here?"

"Hopefully not very much. I'm more worried about the trade goods we just handed over. You should tell the Satedans to keep the supplies we brought in today isolated."

"Until we fix this, right?"

"We're working on it," Lorne said.

"We are, we are. We will contain this," Zelenka said.

"Containing it in the city still lets it destroy the city," Rodney snapped.

"Most of the Ancient equipment does not rely heavily on petroleum-based plastics," Zelenka said. "What is most vulnerable is our equipment that we brought from Earth."

"That's just great," John said. "Do we have a plan for getting rid of this thing?"

"Isolate the microorganism or substance that is causing this and find a way to decontaminate the affected sections," Zelenka said. Daniel had heard Sam put on the spot enough times to understand that what he'd just heard wasn't a solution, but a restatement of the problem in slightly more technical terms. Even so, it seemed to mollify John.

"All right, keep me posted," he said. "And get me the gate address for somewhere we can go that isn't inhabited, isn't uninhabitable, and isn't contaminated by this thing. We may need to proceed there without waiting for the medical team and the security team."

"Working on it," Lorne said.

Ronon turned his head abruptly. "What's that noise?"

"It sounds like an airplane," Elizabeth said.

"We don't have airplanes," Ronon said. "And that doesn't sound like a Dart."

There was the sound of voices raised in consternation from the square outside. "We'll go check it out," John said. He nodded to Teyla and Rodney to follow him. "Ronon, stay with Elizabeth."

Daniel wasn't sure if Ronon was supposed to be guarding Elizabeth from whatever was outside or guarding the rest of them from Elizabeth, but Ronon nodded and moved to stand behind her.

"I'll be fine," Elizabeth said. "Go."

John headed out the door at a run, with Teyla and Rodney close behind him. Daniel went over to the window. The square was emptying fast, people getting under cover as the shadow of a ship passed over the pavement. He craned his neck to look up. It was a small ship, three or four times the size of a puddle-jumper, now hovering over the center of the gate square.

"We've got company," he said as he turned back to Elizabeth and Ronon.

He was in time to see the shimmer of Asgard transport beams as both Elizabeth and Ronon disappeared from sight.

John came running out into the square, Teyla and Rodney at his heels, to see a number of heavily armed Satedans forming up in front of one of the buildings across the square. Apparently Cai had persuaded a few of Sateda's scattered soldiers to return. Not that there was much they could do with rifles and pistols against a spaceship.

The captain in charge didn't seem to agree, shouting an order to fire. Bullets thundered upwards toward the hovering spaceship, but the few that actually reached it spat off its shields to ricochet along with the complete misses in a lethal hail back toward the square.

"Hey!" John shouted, dodging for the cover of the nearest set of brick steps.

The Satedan captain waved him back furiously. "Get under cover! What are you, stupid?"

"We're not the ones shooting at something we can't hit!" Rodney yelled. "They have shields, you—"

"Sheppard!" Daniel yelled abruptly over the radio. "Ronon and Dr. Weir were just grabbed by an Asgard transport beam! They're both gone."

"Damn it!" John dived out from behind the steps, hoping the Satedans would hold their fire for the next few seconds, and started sprinting for the jumper. Teyla and Rodney were right behind him.

He ducked into the lee of the jumper as the Satedan riflemen opened fire again. It would have been good tactics if they'd been shooting at an unshielded Dart, but all they were achieving was spraying stray bullets across the square. The ship was rising, hovering over the building where he hoped Daniel was at that moment taking evasive action.

"You two go cover Jackson," he said. "I'll take the jumper up and see if I can bring this son of a bitch down before it leaves atmosphere."

"I'm taking the other jumper," Rodney said.

"Damn it, McKay—"

Rodney's jaw was set. "They have Elizabeth."

"All right, go," John said after a moment. "Go!"

He scrambled into the jumper and threw himself into the pilot's seat. The Asgard ship was rising faster, skimming over the city. He brought the jumper's systems online with a silent, furious demand, and brought it arrowing up after the Asgard ship.

"You have to adjust the jumper's shield configuration," Rodney said rapidly. "Otherwise they can mimic our shield frequency and transport us aboard. I'm sending instructions now."

"I'm on it," John said, ordering the ship to make the changes as they were transmitted. Below him the other jumper was lifting, and he could see Teyla running across the square for the doorway of the building where they'd been meeting.

"Jackson, you still there?"

"I'm here," Daniel said. He sounded out of breath. "If you keep moving, it's harder for the Asgard transport beams to get a lock on you. Not impossible, though, so anything you can do —"

"They're trying to pull back," John said. "I'm going after them."

He brought the jumper up and over the Asgard ship, forcing them to bank and roll to avoid him, their collision alarms probably screaming. The jumper's computer pointed out helpfully that there were drones available to fire.

"Unidentified ship, respond!" he yelled over the jumper's comm system, hoping that they were listening for transmissions. "You have two of my people! I want them back right now, or I'm opening fire on your vessel!"

He didn't really expect a response, and didn't get one, but he figured it fulfilled any obligation to try to be diplomatic. The computer was still busily suggesting drones.

"I think you're right," he told it. "Preparing to fire. Jumper two, stand clear."

"Copy that," Rodney said. He wouldn't have been John's choice as a jumper pilot in combat — he'd logged plenty hours in the jumpers under normal conditions, but precious few of them under fire — but he had to admit they were better off with two jumpers in the air rather than one.

He readied a single drone, put some vertical distance between himself and the Asgard ship, and fired. He didn't want to tear up the ship with Elizabeth and Ronon aboard, but their shields ought to be able to take a single drone strike. The drone spun toward the Asgard ship and spattered itself against their shields in a blaze of light.

"Teyla! Report!"

"I have found Dr. Jackson, and we are fine," Teyla said over the radio. "He suggests we dial the gate and call for reinforcements from Atlantis."

"Negative," John said immediately. "Whatever that contamination is, we can't risk bringing it here. These people have enough problems."

"Understood."

"Unidentified ship, respond! Come on, talk to me, answer the damn phone."

John kept his own jumper above the Asgard ship as they climbed, hoping that its field of fire didn't extend to directly above its hull. An alarm sounded, and the jumper's sensors registered that the Asgard ship was trying to use its transport beams.

"That's not going to work," John said. "We're way ahead of you. Give me my people back, and I won't have to blow you out of the sky."

The pilot of the Asgard ship seemed to also come to the conclusion that trying to transport John and Rodney aboard wasn't going to work. It banked hard to port, bringing its beam weapons to bear on Rodney's jumper below it.

"McKay —"

"I see it!"

"Evasive maneuvers!"

"I'm taking them!"

The Asgard beam still clipped the jumper's stern, although it didn't look like it had done more than minor damage, the shields absorbing most of its punishment.

"Zelenka's going to make you pay for that jumper if you wreck it," John said.

"He's not the one out here getting shot at! I'd like to see him do better."

The Asgard ship pulled up sharply, its shields bumping the jumper's own ventral shields, making the jumper rattle and kick. He held it on course grimly.

"No, you don't," he said. "You're not going anywhere with our people." He edged the jumper down, their shields shuddering and protesting as they met, and the Asgard ship veered slightly downwards. It was like a game of bumper cars, with the added entertainment of knowing that if he pushed too far and either shield failed, he'd smash the jumper against the Asgard ship's hull.

The Asgard ship rolled to port, and he started to follow its turn, and then had to veer away to avoid colliding with Rodney's jumper.

"Jumper two, adjust your course!"

"I copy, but where do you expect me to go?"

"Follow its turn!"

"Excuse me for not wanting to fly upside down!"

The Asgard pilot had no such reservations, and had rolled his ship entirely over. It edged under John's jumper, which blared a warning that he was fixed in the Asgard ship's ventral sights.

"Crap," John said, and rolled the jumper hard to starboard, but not in time. The Asgard ship's ion cannons battered against his shields, and the jumper's alarms began shrieking. *Shields at 25%. Shields at 10%. Shields at 5%.* "McKay! Get them off me!"

The other jumper veered sharply into the path of the Asgard ship, which pulled up close enough to a collision that Rodney's jumper must have been shrieking its own protest. John had problems of his own.

"I've got damage to main propulsion," he said. The jumper was handling less like a sleek bird of prey and more like the non-aerodynamic brick that it actually was. With an effort he could keep it flying in a straight line, but he was losing altitude. "Jumper two, you're on your own."

"You're kidding me," Rodney said.

"Don't let them get away with Elizabeth."

Rodney's voice over the radio was grim. "Damn right I won't."

Rodney pushed the jumper for more speed. "So now I'm a fighter pilot," he muttered. "That's just great. This is what we have the Air Force for —"

He broke off as the Asgard ship began climbing steeply again. He maneuvered trying to get above it, but couldn't do better than staying on its tail.

"You're letting them gain too much altitude," John warned over the comm system.

"Yes, because what I really need is back-seat driving," he snapped.

"If you let them clear the atmosphere —"

"Then they'll jump to hyperspace and we'll be screwed. I know."

The Asgard ship was still climbing, the overarching sky turning from bright blue to an ominously darker indigo.

"Unknown vessel, respond," John said. "Damn it, respond!"

"I'm firing drones," Rodney said.

"Blowing up their ship would be bad."

"So would letting it get away." Rodney concentrated, and two drones spun away from the jumper, diving toward the Asgard ship. They smashed against its stern shields, and the ship rocked visibly.

Something within it began pouring out smoke.

"Good," John said. "Now get your jumper above it and ride it down."

"I'm working on it," Rodney said tightly. The Asgard ship was losing altitude again, although it was still moving fast. The gate was a long way behind them. But that didn't actually matter, because they couldn't get reinforcements from Atlantis because some incompetent idiot had introduced horrible plastic-eating microorganisms, which he couldn't actually do anything about because he was stuck playing Top Gun.

"Jumper two, what's your status?"

"The Asgard ship is losing altitude," Rodney said. "At least, it was."

"What do you mean, was?"

The ship's course was leveling out, and there was no more smoke streaming from its stern. "I think they're making repairs."

"Stay on them! Don't give them time to make repairs!"

"Again with the backseat driving!" Rodney dived on the Asgard ship in what he hoped was an appropriately menacing fashion. The jumper's proximity alarms screamed warnings, but he ignored them, bringing the jumper low enough that its shields were skipping off the surface of the Asgard ship's shields like a stone off water.

The Asgard ship kicked upward, and he had to veer upward himself to avoid a collision. It began climbing again away from the patchwork of woods and farmland below them, nose up. Whatever damage he'd done wasn't enough to force it down.

"Come on, damn it!" He was falling behind, and the ship's sensors blared an alarm; he was fixed in the Asgard ship's rear sights. "No, no, no… " He forced the jumper into an improbable series of rolling turns, weaving to avoid letting them lock their weapons onto the jumper as a target. "This is not good!"

"Jumper two, report!"

"I can either fly or talk!" Rodney snapped.

"Damn it, McKay!"

The Asgard ship was ascending more sharply, making no more effort to fire on him, but leaving him behind as it climbed high above the rolling hills beneath them. Any minute now it would be out of range of even drones.

He knew now how the rest of his team must have felt as the Dart had swept him up. He'd been taken by the Wraith, and his friends had moved heaven and Earth to get him back, and he wasn't about to let Ronon and Elizabeth slip through his fingers now.

The computer reminded him that drones were ready to fire.

"Yes, yes, fire drones," he said, sending the drones diving toward the Asgard craft. Two of them smashed into the rear shields, and he had the satisfaction of seeing it waver, some of their energy penetrating. The ship was trailing smoke again, whatever repairs its crew had made no longer holding together.

The next two drones struck home at the rear engines, and the starboard engine sputtered and died. The ship's climb halted, and it began to lose altitude again. "See how you like that," he said triumphantly. "Yes!"

In retrospect, he thought the next second, firing a third pair of drones might have been a mistake. They sought out the Asgard ship's engines unerringly, and smashed into the port engine like a pair of bullets crashing into a plate glass window.

"No, no, no," he moaned. The ship's descent went from an easy glide to a precipitous dive. Ahead, rolling hills were turning into the rockier foothills of a looming mountain range. "No!"

"What?" John demanded over the radio. "Jumper two, what's your status!"

"They're going to crash," Rodney said. There was nothing he could do but watch as the Asgard ship plummeted toward an unforgiving mountainside.

Stay in touch...
Follow us on Twitter
@StargateNovels

Find us on Facebook at
facebook.com/StargateNovels

Sign up for our newsletter
at StargateNovels.com

THANKS!

STARGATE SG·1

STARGATE ATLANTIS

Original novels based on the hit
TV shows **STARGATE SG-1** and
STARGATE ATLANTIS

Available as e-books from leading online
retailers

Paperback editions available from
Amazon and IngramSpark

If you liked this book, please tell your
friends and leave a review on a
bookstore website. Thanks!